Dedicated to Linda Dawn Pettigrew, my mother. For believing there is no such thing as an illegitimate child. And for insisting that everybody's crazy in their own way.

TEN GOOD SECONDS OF SILENCE

a novel

ELIZABETH RUTH

THE DUNDURN GROUP
TORONTO · OXFORD

Editor: Barry Jowett
Copyeditor: Cheryl Cohen
Design: Jennfier Scott
Printer: Transcontinental

Canadian Cataloguing in Publication Data

Ruth, Elizabeth
    Ten good seconds of silence

ISBN 0-88924-301-8

I. Title.

PS8585.U847T45 2001   C813'.6   C2001-901609-3   PR9199.4.R88T45 2001

1   2   3   4   5   05   04   03   02   01

THE CANADA COUNCIL | LE CONSEIL DES ARTS
FOR THE ARTS | DU CANADA
SINCE 1957 | DEPUIS 1957

ONTARIO ARTS COUNCIL
CONSEIL DES ARTS DE L'ONTARIO

We acknowledge the support of the *Canada Council for the Arts* and the *Ontario Arts Council* for our publishing program. We also acknowledge the financial support of the *Government of Canada* through the *Book Publishing Industry Development Program* and *The Association for the Export of Canadian Books*, and the *Government of Ontario* through the *Ontario Book Publishers Tax Credit* program.

Excerpts from this book have appeared in the following publications:
    She's Gonna Be: Stories, Poems, Life, edited by Ann Decter. McGilligan Books, Toronto, 1998. Title of excerpt: "Fat and the Fourth Dimension".
    Fireweed Issue 64, Toronto, Winter 1998. Title of excerpt: "Stark Raving Sane".

This story is a work of fiction. Any similarities to actual events or to persons living or dead is purely coincidental.

Front cover (face) photo by Leni Johnston

Printed and bound in Canada.
Printed on recycled paper.

www.dundurn.com

<table>
<tr><td>Dundurn Press
8 Market Street
Suite 200
Toronto, Ontario, Canada
M5E 1M6</td><td>Dundurn Press
73 Lime Walk
Headington, Oxford,
England
OX3 7AD</td><td>Dundurn Press
2250 Military Road
Tonawanda NY
U.S.A. 14150</td></tr>
</table>

TEN GOOD SECONDS
OF SILENCE

"**Quantum Memory** is more than just a memory of facts or images or experiences. Someone could forget all of these, forget his entire history and his quantum memory, his lived dialogue with the past — his personal identity — would still be intact, available to others if not to himself."

Danah Zohar

The Quantum Self

"You don't look back along time but down through it, like water. Sometimes this comes to the surface, sometimes that, sometimes nothing. Nothing goes away."

Margaret Atwood

Cat's Eye

Amazing Grace, how sweet the sound,
That saved a wretch like me.
I once was lost, but now am found.
Was blind, but now I see.

John Newton

Prologue

From Gerrard or Jarvis streets, the Allan Gardens Conservatory with its glass dome ceiling and ornate fence could be mistaken for one of Toronto's many churches. Lilith Boot looks forward all week to visiting, to inhaling the succulent heat. Some might say a greenhouse is a poor excuse for the outdoors, but she insists it's a perfect compromise: halfway between wilderness and civilization. In fact, she's solved some of her hardest cases sitting there. Lilith works best surrounded by all that optimism — even if it is man-made.

In the police station where she also works, she's filled her office with trimmings from spider plants, sat clay pots with hydrangea in all four corners, and stood a three-foot rubber tree beside her desk. Still she has not managed to reproduce the texture and sensuality of the greenhouse, where her fingertips pucker as though she's lingered too long in a bath. She needs to be pliant and surrounded by life in order to receive her visions. Seeing is a porous business. Leaky. Information seeps into the lining of her tissue like aged wine through the cork. Images trickle into her bloodstream. Sensations ooze down her spinal column one vertebra at a time. Before Lilith knows it, she is soaked. And she can't close her eyes; they don't belong to just her any more. So she rolls back in her head and tries to find children. Rolls back like thunder and looks there, where everything spills from the inside out and back again.

What better environment for a clairvoyant to work than in a place filled with liquid promise, where sunshine, water and air exist in their most elemental forms? Chlorophyll. Carbon dioxide. Photosynthesis. The interaction of fundamental particles sweeps Lilith away to a state of mind not explained by science or religion, or even by herself. Only nature. Everything that's already happened reduced to its smallest denominator, and rebuilt in the present. There is nowhere, she is certain, with superior visibility than in a glasshouse.

Lilith works from inside a world only she can taste and smell. She reaches into herself and pulls out something belonging to somebody else: a bootie on the subway, a handful of hair ripped from a kidnapper's scalp a few feet from the scene of the crime. She works in minute particles to solve quantum mysteries — sort of like a witch, a private investigator, a holy reporter, and a Grade 3 detective in the Metro Toronto Police force, simultaneously. When she's getting ready to work, her eager green eyes retreat like a shy schoolgirl running away from a first crush. She doesn't wear lipstick or rouge, but there are small blood vessels creeping under her cheeks like the fetal roots of a maple tree. They expand into two rosy explosions and make a single moving line across her face: her lips. Her forehead is outlined in a thick, silver halo as though she's been struck by lightning and still, somehow, conducting electricity. She attempts to pull her hair back into a tight ponytail, but an army of renegade strands refuses to be held captive and gives the perpetual impression she's been rushing.

Lilith's got a mind like a sieve. Whatever it is — talent, reverse amnesia, a genetic defect — it serves a purpose. And she should know for it is she who works in colour. Blue — electric and powder hues, shades of water because blue is the feeling of sadness that overtakes her when she cannot find who she's looking for. But she keeps this information to herself. Sometimes she feels as if she's said enough already. And no one likes a woman who pontificates.

There are always physical sensations while Lilith works. Her extremities — toes, fingers, nipples, all the leftover bits sticking out in the world — tingle and vibrate like antennae. She's like the Venus flytrap: Everything about her trembles and then waits to catch what she needs. She's used to it. It has been with her all her life. Clairvoyance is no science, nothing to be measured. She'll be the first to admit that. But it's nothing to shake a stick at either.

Information doesn't come to Lilith in flat photographic flashes. No, she holds her breath as if underwater and allows it to pass through her one cell at a time, soaking up the truth until it reaches the surface of her being. Only then can she face the families like a calm pool of water, reflecting back what they need to know. After, she craves chocolate or fruit — it doesn't matter what sort of sugar, it's all fuel for the journey. Without it she becomes light and airy, as though she has no material self, no bulges under her dress, no rolls of flesh anchoring her to the present. She can't prove it, but Lilith knows it's real, so she keeps her purse full of Snickers and Mars bars and her weight close to 250 pounds.

Enough about that, she'd say. Those are merely routine details. It just isn't easy trying to conjure visions with the stress of living in an urban centre full of distracting noise and pollution, and the responsibilities of being a single mother to get in the way. Lilith is grateful to be safe inside the greenhouse where a growing population of cyclists isn't threatening to speed past, accidentally bumping her to the sidewalk with a heavy thud. She moves slowly, punctuating each step with the firm placement of her white sneakers. Her cotton-and-polyester housedress is hiked into the crack of her behind, and she routinely reaches back to dislodge it. Her plastic purse contains file folders and

11

blank paper, and is slung over her shoulder. Immediately upon entering, she removes her straw hat and holds it in one hand, then checks her wrist. Silly habit; she doesn't wear a watch. Lilith knows from experience: Time is unreliable. She mutters inaudible words while she paces.

Some people are easily confused and disoriented there. You can see them on any day, pulling at turtlenecks, and sucking back Ventolin from blue and silver puffers. But Lilith is not one of them. She is more content in the company of flowers than anywhere else she knows. In the greenhouse she is not sitting sweaty in her skin, but settled snugly into the encasement of a large green placenta, warmed by the heat generating off slow-pumping organs — red, orange, yellow. *There is no dandelion abduction in a garden*, she thinks, *only the promise of life.*

Today is Sunday so Lilith is waiting for her bench. Through a white, wood-framed door and down a ramp into the tropical room she sees a man stretched out barefoot, his head propped up with a fishing bag full of crumpled newspaper. He's wearing an old grey suit jacket, with matching pants. His yellow dress shirt is untucked, the four top buttons undone. He has no tie. The pockets of his jacket are hanging limp out the bottom seams, and his beard is a thick underbrush mat, with remnants of food still stuck along the edges of his mouth. A muffin wrapper is on the stone floor along with an empty Styrofoam coffee cup. He sees her coming through squinted eyes. Yeah, yeah. He'll share. They have an unspoken arrangement: The man has mornings, and Lilith has afternoons. The moment she stops beside a small rock pond and a cluster of purple heart, folds her arms across her chest and taps her foot in furious motion, he props himself up, tilts his head to one side and opens an arm, as if to say, "It's all yours, sweetheart." Then he stands and approaches Lilith, who presses a one-dollar bill into the palm of his hand before he wordlessly shuffles from view.

Sitting on the bench Lilith unlaces her sneakers, removes her socks and stuffs them inside her shoes; every pore must be free to breathe. The stench from her feet could probably annihilate even the strongest perfume radiating off the angel's trumpet, but she ignores the frightened and curious strangers who keep their distance. What does it matter? She has a job to do. She closes her eyes and concentrates, using only the top half of her lungs to breathe, skimming like a loon on a northern lake. Again she is going fishing. Not with lines or lures and other tackle, but with her whole being. She faces her vague image in the whitewashed window opposite, bare feet flat on the damp floor, and leans her weight into the wooden slats of the bench. She needs privacy from people in order to work, and being out in public is the fastest way Lilith knows to feel alone.

From where she's sitting she can usually see other Sunday regulars. Two young men in their mid-thirties, one black, one white, linger beside a large chenille plant. The white man sports a bushy brown handlebar moustache and a tight orange and pink tank top with the words "HOMO sapien" stretched across his muscular physique. The other fellow walks with a rainbow-coloured leash connecting his wrist to a white, black and brown Jack Russell terrier. The dog pants and spins figure eights between his owner's legs. They take turns reprimanding. "Down Frances! Good dog." Then Lilith notices the elderly couple from a nearby apartment creep through, dressed to the nines. At this time of year the man usually wears his tan suit and tie, the woman a pinstriped dress. They wander arm in arm as though they might stumble upon an old memory lodged between the petals of a Casablanca lily, or rediscover their first years together languidly wrapped around the stamen of a red anthurium. *It's romantic,* Lilith thinks. *If you go in for that sort of thing.*

She reaches into her purse as though drawing her winning numbers at bingo, and selects a green folder. She reads the first name only. Today it says "Sara." Lilith closes her eyes and imagines four pillars of light, one in each corner of the greenhouse, one for each direction on a compass. A pale blue luminescence fills the room inside her imagination. Once the ritual had been performed and the opening to another dimension prepared, Lilith is usually ready to draw up a contract with her young client. *A true professional always works from a contract.* Once more she reaches into her purse and pulls out a clean sheet of white bonded paper and a purple crayon. She balances the page on her lap and writes: "I hereby promise to do everything within my natural ability to find you — Sara — and return you to your parents." She repeats the promise out loud and adds, "Child, I'm your finder." Then she signs and dates the contract, "October, 1986. Lilith Boot; clairvoyant at large." She folds the page into smaller and smaller squares, and tucks it into her brassiere, for safekeeping. Finally, Lilith bows her head and, in hushed whispers, prays out loud . . . "Blessed be the daisies smiling stupidly above the grass. Bless their naive faces gazing at the sun. Bless the dandelion weeds bending and compromising in the wind. Amen . . ."

After a few seconds the vision begins to leak. Hyacinth, eucalyptus and baby's breath guide her through it, and vibrant colour crawls behind her eyes, spilling back to the here and now. Lilith's breath adopts a mild odour of the child she's trying to locate. Fresh, soapy camomile and mint smells arrive. Then, a talcum powder behind and soiled diapers. A paper cut from her file folder suddenly gives her the feeling of Sara's skin, soft and bruised as a velvetleaf plant, cheek so young it hasn't seen three years. And there are sounds. Lilith can hardly stand them. Sara sounds angry like the raging orange petals of a tiger lily, screaming mad for safety, then her voice folds into itself like the enclosed whimper of a shy tulip, the gurgling defeat of a drowning water lily. It's unnatural. Unforgivable. Still, Lilith concentrates . . .

The sound of lapping water grows until very loud, as though a hard spanking is being administered, and Lilith reaches out with an open hand to stop it. The small voice screams at her from a distance. She stares even harder into the centre of her imagination, through it, beyond the greenhouse windows, beyond the water fountain, a row of townhouses, past Jarvis street, south past Dundas, out onto a crowded city street . . . faster, faster through the maze of downtown sidewalks. She follows her vision until she's led to the lakeshore, turns right until she crosses the city limits. A sign flashes past. "Welcome to Etobicoke." Lilith makes a sharp left turn into a condominium complex, speeds through the parking lot, past the manicured lawns, all the way to Lake Ontario where, out of breath, she finally slows to a complete stop. In front of her, stretched out a quarter of a mile, is a dense rock formation. She looks left and right, then left then right. Finally, the hood of an orange snowsuit poking up between two boulders catches her eye. *Got you,* she thinks. *You poor sweet thing.*

Lilith begins to weep. She fights the impulse to hurry home and touch her daughter, Lemon, just to be reassured that she's safe. Instead, she reaches into her purse once more but finds that the roll of toilet paper she always carries is empty — a hazard of the trade — so she wipes her eyes and nose on the sleeve of her dress, and prepares to complete the necessary paperwork. She retrieves the crayon and a box of wooden matches from her skirt pocket, reaches close to her heart for the contract, unfolds it, and adds a thick check mark beside the child's name. Then Lilith writes: "Girl. Age four. Found on first try. 999 Lakeshore Boulevard. South-west corner of the Marina-Del-Mar complex. Wandered off towards the geese, unattended. Fell and hit her head. Didn't know how to swim."

Lilith strikes a match, touches it to the corner of the page and holds it between her thumb and pointer finger while flames seal the agreement. When fire warms her hand, she leans in over the base of a weeping fig and releases her fingers. "Ashes to ashes," she says under her breath, scattering the contract into fertile soil. Next, she stands to stretch, walks through the greenhouse into the next room twirling loose strands of hair, inhaling in stuttered breaths, exhaling in one slow steady stream. And gradually, regaining her composure. She feels a sad sense of accomplishment; her first job of the day is done but all she can do is stare into a cactus bed as if she's staring into an unmarked grave.

Insight takes work. Not funny business like a set of crystals or a deck of cards. Clairvoyance is a vocation. *It's who I am,* Lilith thinks. *Not just what I do.* It's like motherhood. She is thankful for a fat body that assists her to see children in bed lulling themselves to sleep by rubbing the satin edge between their stubby toes, or to smell the light layer of sweat gleaning off sleeping infants' bodies as they imagine flying, bathing and stuffed television superheroes. She sees the jerk of short limbs tripping off imaginary curbs into dreamland, but more often than not there is only a question left after she opens her eyes, just an unanswered question for many months — no bodies for parents, no addresses for Sergeant Grant. *There are always so many unsolved mysteries looming,* she tells herself. *Too many faceless sunflowers.*

16

Sometimes after she's done searching, Lilith sees her own sadness reflected back in the greenhouse windows or the computer screen on her office desk, a vulgar piece of technology she has no intention of using, and she cannot help but reach into her bag for a chocolate bar. With tears streaming down her face, she often wonders with the weight of the world, "Why do I go on trying to see?" But Lilith doesn't really need to ask. In fact, after all these years, she finally remembers . . .

In 1968, just weeks after my eighteenth birthday, I was standing at the entrance to Mother's kitchen in Vancouver. My muscular legs were spread as wide apart as I could keep them, hands over the material of my dress covering my privates. A wooden bowl full of bananas and crabapples sat in the middle of a pine shaker table with three Windsor-back chairs on either side. Our brand new electric stove was on my right, and a four-tiered spice rack was hanging next to it. Mother was scraping carrots at the counter opposite, scraping their brown outer layer clean with a paring knife, flicking the shavings onto a newspaper in the sink. She had lost herself in the repetition and the satisfying sound — like a new razor on a woman's legs.

"It's time," I said.

Mother looked out the window, the sunlight reddening highlights in her hair, which was pinned into an intimidating six-inch beehive. "It's time," I repeated.

"About time, you mean." She wiped gritty orange hands on her apron. Turned to face me. Mother had been against this from the moment she realized, when she saw me drag that old bassinet up from the basement, and repaint the chipped white wicker. It was just like me to muddle this too, she said. Bad enough getting myself knocked up, refusing to name the father. But dragging the whole ordeal out into the tenth month just seemed like rubbing salt in a wound. And keeping it? Mother had little patience for girls who wore their mistakes so proudly, unapologetically, she said. Like churchwomen donning new Sunday hats.

I ignored her remark.

"Must be my water's broke." I was still holding myself between the legs and standing on the outsides of my feet.

"Well, you think clutching onto it like that will make it any easier?" Mother turned away, ran some water at the enamel sink, and put the kettle on to boil. "You having pain?" she asked.

"Some. Right here."

I pulled my hands away from between my legs to show that the pangs came from higher up. Mother turned only to gasp and step back, digging the edge of the Formica countertop into her kidneys. My hands were coated in a thick, dark red paste. The front of my skirt stuck to the insides of my thighs and now that I'd removed my hands, blood splashed onto the yellow tiles underfoot. Looking at Mother's horrified face, next at the floor, and then at my own hands, I started to scream.

Blood hit the floor in slow motion:

Drip.

Drip.

Drip.

Then my brain sped wildly to reconcile what I expected with what was really happening. I hadn't seen this coming, hadn't imagined tearing the lining of my body, wounds that would take time to heal. It had never for a second occurred to me that I might lose this baby. I scanned the large open room to hold my eyes on something for reassurance. I saw the old icebox Mother used as storage for pots and pans, the glass shelf filled with her collection of salt and pepper shakers, and the yellow eyelet curtains billowing in as the breeze blew through the open window. Nothing helped. My contractions came closer together and lasted longer, and blood trickled in a steady brown rust stream, smattering into small puddles, like clay deposits marking warm earth. I wanted to cover my ears as my own tissue fell away. I wanted to stop time.

I didn't know then that time never really stops, just disguises itself as progress, another chapter closed, old memories. It slips through fingers like dandelion heads in the wind, spiralling up and zigzagging back down; sometimes you can't catch it but it's always there. I was about to learn though: *Memory* is stoppable. Memories can stunt like a malnourished newborn and take on fresh powdery interpretations.

Each contraction spiralled me further into the past. Flashes of my recent life with Randy and Mrs. Moffat mixed with blinding glimpses of the coming child, see-sawing me into the final stages of labour. I reached my arms out on either side of myself for balance. I wasn't sure I'd readied myself well enough for labour. Motherhood yes. But the in-between stage, the passage from single to double, that seemed to be splicing me in two. *A genetic time warp*, I thought. I swear I sensed Lemon enter into the world the moment the *idea* impregnated my mind, but there was unnatural suffering with her physical arrival. It isn't too often that a body opens to the universe. Legs spread wide to mark change: past from future. A red sea parted at my feet as I walked across the yellow squares, birthing a miracle.

I lost more blood and Mother's voice faded to a muffled irritation, an underwater noise to remind me I'd moved on to a deeper place. I stopped focusing on breathing, my lower back pain, and the ringing in my ears: like one hundred wind chimes or the sound of a vacuum cleaner at close range. Instead, I swooned, sucked oxygen inside my lungs until I thought they'd burst, and held it there as long as I could.

When I fell forward my bare knees buckled and I landed on them. Hollow thud! On all fours, I stared at a reflection of the ceiling fan in the pool of blood. The fan sliced through the kitchen air, dividing my life in measured strokes. Round and round. It was reassuring, spiralling Bridgewater and my psychiatrist well back into the past, and my whole miserable childhood further behind where Randy always said it belonged. I was making space for a new life. New priorities. So I stared at the fan which was like a metronome and kept a sane pace propelling me into the future.

It wasn't an easy task, letting go. I felt like I'd snagged on thorny corners of experience, and was being flung against the mossy walls of time. I gagged, becoming dizzy. But I was no longer afraid. *Babygirl*, I thought. *Here you come* . . . I screamed again.

"Bloody hell," Mother muttered under her breath.

Bloody universe.

Then Mother gathered the soggy newspaper from the sink, careful not to leave carrot shreddings to clog in the drain. She lifted the refuse with both hands, opened the cupboard door in front of her and dropped the rubbish down into a bag. You didn't hear her carrying on like a wounded animal at the time of my birth — not even a peep. And she'd lost my twin. Daddy had told me the story so many times. You think anybody came around with flowers or get-well cards for her? Not a chance. Just said be happy for what she'd been left with: me, Lilith. A gift from God. Mother closed the cupboard door with her foot, and wiped her hands over the sink. See? Pain runs in the family.

As my uterus contracted I pushed myself up, balanced on my knees and held my swollen belly with love. Mother watched from behind and I tried harder to focus on the final moment of the task. A sudden torrent of water and blood mixed and gushed from my body at once. Baby pink. I held tightly to consciousness through my vision of a healthy newborn. Sweet and tender. Honeysuckle red. Checkerbloom pink. Fireweed, burning in my belly. *Not long ago I was nothing but a child myself,* I thought. *Now mine is raging to be free.* Baptizing Mother's house. Forcing herself out through every pore. I was covered in sweat, burning up. Temperature well above a safe degree. I felt like I was being torn inside out, my contents turning to liquid and running away from me. Even my nose was dripping, taste buds were overstimulated and I couldn't help the saliva filling my mouth from drooling down my chin. *Stay,* I told myself. *Stay until she gets here.*

I tried my best not to panic. Tried to distract myself even though my uterus *was* bleeding into my cervix, which was ruptured and leaking down onto the linoleum. I thought about snow-capped mountains and the magnificent view of English

Bay from Lions Gate Bridge. I thought about friendship and Randy, and the last time we'd seen each other. How Randy refused to look me in the eye, how she hid under her baseball cap and pretended she was glad for what I'd done, felt fine to be staying behind at the hospital with Mrs. Moffat. "We all do what we have to," she told me. I figured that next to me the baby belonged to Randy. Maybe by recalling her at that precise moment, I let Randy's best qualities soak into my placenta and birth canal, passing Lemon her loyalty and courage.

I felt Randy there like she was my mental midwife, so I closed my eyes and visualized her smile, remembered strong hands and a tidal-wave laugh. A laugh to drown in. I slid onto my back and raised my arm to block the white light from my eyes. I spread my fingers apart and observed a sticky paste connecting the inside of each digit to the next, giving the appearance my hand was webbed. I'm turning into an animal, I thought. *A turtle, who takes home along when it leaves. Or an ostrich able to bury its head.* Ancient creatures. Back to the beginning.

A woman giving birth is as round and resourceful as time.

I remembered the details of Randy's expressions and gestures. Thin brown hair, clinging flat against a pronounced, angry jaw. The way she rolled her own cigarettes like she was making a great scientific discovery with the tobacco machine. How her wrinkled forehead gave away her concentration. And most of all, the special way she'd sacrificed herself for me. *The child must never know what sacrifice smells like,* I thought. *Urine-soaked sheets, stale semen, and salty tears.* This child deserves her own life. But can you ever really be free of your mother's history? I clutched my stomach again. *Why won't the baby come to me?*

I knew this wasn't just any pregnancy — Lemon had chosen me. I reached out behind for Mother who was standing a few feet away, but she stepped back, leaving my hand flailing in the air. Then, almost as soon as the thought crossed my mind about the child needing something more before she would arrive, I had my answer. Lemon wouldn't come until I really had forgotten. Not bits and pieces, but all of it. *Forget everything,* I told myself. *You promised you would. It's better for everyone if you move forward. Only forward, and accept what you were never allowed to. Open to finding. Clairvoyance.*

And so I replaced my memory with the future.

Randy faded feet first, then knees, collarbone and finally, her laugh.

Mother put the receiver down after calling for an ambulance. No need to become frantic. Someone should remain calm. She could see I was bleeding to death; anyone could have seen that. But, what Mother did not envision was that my life would be saved not once, not twice, but three times. And this was only the second time that my Babygirl would rescue me. Blood stopped flowing the instant I made my decision to forget. That was when I started to lose consciousness, and that's when Lemon's head crowned.

When the ambulance arrived the paramedics covered their mouths and noses to filter the odour as they rushed into the kitchen. They found me dripping in my own liquids, so much stale blood that the beige housedress I was wearing seemed black. One of my hands was between my legs, protecting the baby; the other was waving goodbye to Randy before it fell limp at my side. Mother was on her knees next to the table, with an unopened package of sponges in her lap and a pan of clean water and vinegar beside her. Lemon and I had marked the bottom legs of the table and chairs, the counter cupboards and Mother's clothes, and she intended to remove all evidence with both arms fully extended. "You made your bed," she spat. "Now, you'll lie in it."

After I'd delivered and been taken to the hospital, when Mother too was satisfied that the past was well behind us, she scrubbed herself in the bathtub until her skin was furious pink, and raw. When Daddy got home from work he found her there. Later that evening, Mother got out the mop and pail again and then put a load of laundry in the washer.

Years earlier that same kitchen smelt of Mother's fresh-cut cantaloupe and Daddy's coffee beans. If he was smoking his pipe at the breakfast table then Burleigh tobacco added a scandalous comfort. In summer with the downstairs windows cracked and fresh air blowing a predictable but not-too-often warmth over us all, I took liberties — sometimes skipping out on my chores before they were completely done, other times sneaking some baker's chocolate or a Nanaimo bar for a treat. Daddy barbecued out back most evenings and Mother travelled to stay with her own family, helping to can salmon in the Okanagan Valley. She'd been home less than a week when I pulled aside the curtains and peered out our kitchen window, all the way across to the Applebys' front yard.

"Imagine!" Mother said, unloading the dish rack. "A woman that size trying to get to the roof. And you?" She dismissed me with a wave of her hand, moved to put the dry plates away in the cupboards. "How many times have I told you not to run around barefoot."

"But — "

"Always there's a reason with you, Lilith. *Sensing things.* Just last week, Mrs. Massero came by to say you'd been predicting babies in her daughter's future. Angela Massero is only fourteen years old, for Pete's sake! You can't go around spreading nasty rumours about other girls. You'll never make any friends that way."

"I wasn't," I said. "I didn't mean to."

I clasped my hands over my ears. Ooh that sound! I'd tried to warn Mrs. Appleby when she climbed higher and higher, but before I reached her, the ladder collapsed in on itself like a mortal sin had been committed and it was falling to its knees for forgiveness.

Mother shook her head.

"Well, I didn't raise a girl to be so full of imagination."

"But it's true," I insisted. "It's not my imagination. I saw Angela with a baby, and I knew Mrs. Appleby was going to go crashing to the ground. I swear, I saw it all right here." I pointed to my forehead.

"Listen." Mother came towards me wagging a determined finger. "I've ignored your imaginary friends and your silly predictions. I've looked the other way a million times but not any longer, you hear?" I backed up, the smell of her Chanel No. 5 filling my nostrils. "Don't you look at me that way, Lilith Boot. I don't care if your predictions *do* come true. With a strong enough incentive you can change."

Change?

The hair on the back of my neck stood up. How was I going to change who I was?

"I knew before it happened," I whispered. "Why won't you believe me?"

Mother threw her hands up to the ceiling.

"If you know what's good for you, you'll learn to keep your stories to yourself!"

"I don't lie!" I told her, sticking up for myself. "I never lie." Then I started to blubber, wave my hands about my head, and mess my hair wildly. There were so many voices and faces and it was so frustrating to be disbelieved. "I can't stop!" I told her. "I can't! I can't!" Finally my voice weakened and I was out of breath. Mother stared, her arms folded tightly across her chest, so I folded mine. Her face was firm so I turned mine to stone too.

"But you will," she said, calmly. "You have no choice."

That's when I pulled my hair and scratched my arms with my fingernails. I jumped up and down in place, and screamed as loud as I could. It was the only way to make Mother listen. It was the only way to win.

"But I ca — "

"Are you going to make me strike you?" she said. "Is that what you want?"

"No!" I stomped a foot to make my point.

"Lilith, I'm warning you."

"Fine," I spat. "Hit me then, do it! You're going to anyway. Hit me!"

I slammed my forehead into the plaster wall and Mother spun around.

"Stop that!" She backed away calling for Daddy, who was in the living room.

"Jack? Jack you get in here right now, you hear?"

Slam!

"Jaaaaaack!"

Daddy bellowed from the den.

"Jesus. H. Christ, Connie. Control that child, will you? I can't even hear myself think!"

"That's it!" Mother grabbed me by the arm, her nails digging in sharply. "Now you've got your father going." *Smack!* She slapped me hard across the face. "Stop it right this second!"

I resisted, struggled down to the floor and out of her clutches. "You can't make me!" I dared. "You can't make me!"

I really should have thought before I spoke.

"I can and I will," Mother hissed through the wooden slats. "You'll learn eventually; the world does not take kindly to wilful young women and neither do I!"

I pounded on the pantry door with my fists and then with my head.

"Let me out! Let me go! Daaaaadyyyyyyyy!" But nobody came to my rescue. In fact, standing with shelves of blackberry and gooseberry jam jars on either side of me, I heard angry footsteps stomp through the house and then I heard the front door slam shut. "I hate you!" I hollered. "This is not my home! I'd rather be anywhere else!"

Mother's heels tap tap tapped away from me, and her hand flipped the light switch. "Fine!" she said. "If that's how you really feel, I'll see what I can do."

A half-hour later she unlatched the door without a word, and I bolted up and out. I didn't look back to see if she'd followed, just darted out of the kitchen behind our house, stopped, leaned with my hands on my thighs to catch my breath and decided that since Daddy had probably gone down to the pub, I'd sneak into his shed and be safe. Out of sight, out of mind, you know?

On our street Daddy was known to fix things. Lumpy Appleby said my father was a doohickey, thingamajig, gizmo man. It's true he would happily grab whatever was by the side of the road, load it into the back of the station wagon and drive it home. The object would then be born again as something else. Inside the shed I poked around without pulling the string on the overhead bulb. I rooted through a pile of tools under Daddy's work table while my eyes adjusted to the dark, ran my fingers over the top of the serrated blade of his handsaw and eventually, exhausted, settled down into a corner and tried to sleep. *Why did I have to be born a prickly pear,* I thought. *Always rubbing folks the wrong way? Why do I have to be me?*

According to Mother, I wasn't supposed to bang my head or pull my hair or speak about my visions *ever*. Those things were forbidden — sinful — but I did them anyway. Especially when I was by myself. Sometimes I crouched down so low in my bedroom that I couldn't be seen out the window, and thumped myself in the head with my closed fists. (If you hit yourself in the head the bruises don't show.)

After ten minutes in the shed, I calmed down and nodded off. I didn't hear Daddy when he came back and found me curled up like a dog by the side of the road.

"Uh hum?"

I stood up fast before I was fully awake, not sure whether to excuse myself and run or face the consequences. Daddy brought the smell of stale beer with him, and soon it filled my nostrils. He looked me over, saw my red cheek, picked up a lamp sitting on top of his work table and held the long base in his left arm, cradling it across his chest like he was protecting a newborn.

"This one's not been running right for months," he said, offering a diagnosis. "Wiring is screwy."

The base of the lamp was made of burled maple. Its thick dark knots and chunky design were ugly to me but solid, stable, and masculine in the style I knew he admired. I examined the lamp too, looking at both ends, running my fingers along its smooth finish. Daddy scratched his chin, then turned the lamp upside down and made an impatient clucking noise with his tongue. "Might be able to reroute it, but my hand won't fit."

Daddy had worker's hands. Black, greasy and broken-down fingernails attached to callused palms. Each of his digits stuck out like he had no knuckles or joints, just ten miniature sausages. They were the hands that pulled my red wagon through Stanley Park in spring. The hands that lifted me onto broad shoulders on the ferry, so I could see blue whales when we crossed over to the Island in June. The hands that wrapped around Mother's waist and pulled her tight for a kiss. And they were the hands that would seal my fate one day. But I didn't know that yet.

"Think we could fix it, Lil?"

We. My tongue danced wild inside my mouth, side to side. I took a long look at the frayed wire inside the body of the lamp.

"It's broken," I said.

"Hurt," Daddy corrected.

And then I realized my cheek didn't sting so bad any more.

"Lilith? Could you get your arm in there?"

'Course I nodded, even knowing it was going to be tight. *I want you to be proud,* I was thinking. *I want you to love me back.* So I reached inside with my eyes closed, pretending I was smaller and could see through my fingertips. The wooden cylinder suctioned my arm in place like it was being strangled by a boa constrictor. Whenever I tried to move my hand chafed and drew slivers under the skin, but I smiled, not wanting to show discomfort. I was tough. I was worthy.

"Okay, grab the wire," Daddy said. "Got it? That's my girl. Now twist counter-clockwise and pull it out."

"Got it!" I said, freeing my arm in one fell swoop.

He looked inside the base of the lamp.

"You did it. It's fixed."

"Healed," I corrected. Then Daddy chuckled, belched, and threw an old rag at me.

"Wipe yourself off, smartass. And let's not tell your mother you've been tinkering around out here."

Daddy put a shaky finger to his lips to show what he meant.

"Shush," I agreed, mimicking his gesture, and nodding like the trilliums in the Applebys' backyard.

Within weeks of that project, Daddy and I started to work on our first garden together. He said there was no better place in the world for gardening than British Columbia, where spring comes early. One day, he said, we might even go to Butchart Gardens. He brought home pruning and lopping shears and fertilizer, and spoke to me of proper watering techniques. "Once every seven days, Lil," he said. "Remember, *don't* overwater." He hauled a button bush and a chokeberry home in the station wagon, and unloaded thirty or so recycled white bricks which we laid on sand and crushed limestone, to make a path from the back door to the fence. Then we set out a large clay pot filled with castor bean for decoration. Within days we'd started the actual flower beds. We marked off a fifteen-foot by nine-foot area using rope to make a grid, and then dug it up. First we planted delphiniums in the back, filled the left edge with queen of the prairie and tree mallow, and planted scabious on the right side. You can imagine how well they all complemented each other.

Inch by inch, foot by foot, Daddy taught me how to build a lasting show of colour. I wanted something beautiful to last. I wanted to be with our garden all the time, smelling it. Breathing it in. Perfume filling me up like inside bouquets. While I was busy adding even more species, or removing faded blooms or staking the tall flowers if they showed signs of leaning, Daddy spent his free time on Saturdays devoted to planting boxwood around the edge and I helped mulch with a layer of pine bark. I couldn't get enough. I wanted to touch firm stems and delicate petals in my hand, know strong and weak could survive together. I listened up close to their songs rising and falling on the West Coast wind. Flowers make music, you know? Like old-time melodies and classical violins put together. Or an accordion playing a polka, or a harmonica on the high notes. Flowers hum and chant and murmur too. They squeal with delight, and la-ti-da when they don't have a care in the world. But nobody listens much. Being with them, kneeling, crouching and standing there that summer was the happiest time of my young life. I had Daddy for company, and the earth we tended was sure and steady under my feet. So what if I was unusual? So what if my friends were small and fragile and practically invisible just like me? At least I had friends.

Many summers passed with us tending that garden and Mrs. Appleby gossiping across the fence. And during that time Daddy's drinking got worse, Mother turned angrier, and it seemed to me there was shouting all the time. I banged my head when the voices and the noise got too loud. And I got used to being alone or having people stare when they saw me talking to myself. Well, they thought I was just talking to myself. Then in April of 1966, it all changed. Business at Daddy's antique shop, the Tick Tock, took a turn for the worse and he had to start working Saturdays just to make ends meet. Mother wanted me inside then too, where she could keep an eye on me. That's when the music turned ugly. Flowers' songs became only screams to me after that.

It's hard to explain, but without time to put my fingers in the dirt or allow my mind to focus on new life, the visions I'd been trying to control suddenly got the better of me. I couldn't distract myself by planting and pruning and mucking about, so the next thing I knew I was seeing and hearing things before they happened again, and Mother knew it. 'Course I wanted to be just like everybody else back then — finish high school, have a steady to take me to the movies, and please my family. I really did. But it wasn't in me. So instead I slammed my head into the wall again, and hid during inclement weather. I wished I could blow far away on a strong breeze, burn my visions under a hot sun and be released, released, from my lonely circumstance.

One night, while Mother finished doing the books and Daddy read the newspaper, I asked him about us adding a hedge all the way round the garden in the future. "If all goes well, Lil," he said. "I don't see why not."

Mother exploded.

"For crying out loud, Jack Boot! The house is where a young lady belongs, not out there digging in the dirt. At least plant some vegetables. Then we could eat them or better yet, sell them. What on earth am I supposed to do with flowers? They're a waste of time and money."

"No they're not," I defended, my face turning blotchy and red.

"They are when I'm pinching pennies as it is," Mother said. "This family can't afford any more perishables. Anyway," she flicked her wrist, "a cold spell's on its way and that'll be the end of this whole discussion. That'll snap them right in half."

I stopped sweeping. My mouth and throat were dry like parchment paper.

"Snap 'em in half? A cold spell?"

"Never mind," Daddy said, looking at Mother. "We'll talk about it another time."

Later upstairs in my room, I tossed and turned under the sheets. I covered my ears and blocked out my radical ideas. I whispered to myself, *It's okay. Everything's gonna be okay.* But I didn't believe it. Not for me and not for the garden. *It's my fault,* I always thought after my parents argued. *If I was a better daughter everything would improve. Maybe Daddy would stand up for me then. Maybe with enough effort, Mother could soften.* Some days I wasn't convinced there was anyone at fault for the tension in our house, but my parents allotted blame like they were handing out red poppies on Remembrance Day. One for you, and one for you. I was spoilt, Mother said. Because Daddy afforded too much slack. He was under pressure, he argued. Mother was too damned demanding.

That night when the storm picked up outside, I heard my friends wailing for cover, afraid. They pleaded and begged for protection and I felt helpless. "Don't abandon us, Lilith," they cried in their own soft way. "Please don't leave us." The hosta and red phlox, and so many others beckoned me for hours. *Pain is nothing a downpour won't erase,* I told myself as the sound of gurgling and drowning continued. Maybe it was my tears . . . inside . . . locked away. I can't say for sure. But the noise got louder and louder to the point where I knew I wouldn't even be able to step out onto the lawn without hearing each blade of grass under my feet scream in agony. "Sorry, sorry, sorry," I said lying in my bed, imagining myself tiptoeing across to deliver a cup of flour or sugar to Mrs. Appleby. *I'm so sorry.* Even with the door closed, after brushing my teeth and saying my prayers — now I lay me down to sleep, I pray the Lord my soul to keep — *and* with my head under both pillows, I could *still* hear them pleading to be saved. I hit myself harder in the temples — we were in it together after all — boxed my ears to drum out the desperate faces. But it did no good. "Lilith help us! Lilith, don't abandon us!"

I didn't want to . . . I would never willingly hurt . . . But the thing was, I couldn't let them suffer. It was me who had planted them so long ago and encouraged them to grow. I had made them trust me, and then it was me who'd walked away and left them for dead. I should have known better; rejection is a terrible kind of eternity. See, I didn't think about the fact that some would survive into the next season. I did not consider their nature any more than I considered my own. When I heard the tap tap tapping of the storm on my bedroom window that night, it just sounded like someone knocking to wake me up from a recurring nightmare, so I ignored it just like I'd tried to ignore the visions for so many years. And it didn't work. Again I was overwhelmed by sights and sounds and smells. By being implicated in some impending disaster.

Finally, when I couldn't take any more of the voices and visions and the guilt floating around inside my mind, I sat up in bed and crept out of my room and down the hall, past my parents' door. I snuck downstairs and outside into the yard in my nightgown, barefoot. The wind was chilly and a faint frost was starting to settle. All the flowers were trembling, a half-blooming ground cover of fear. What I heard then was the most dreadful and ugly sound yet: a garden of superlatives gone wrong. "It's horrible, Lilith! Living like this is the *worst* pain in the entire world!" I turned to face the garden directly.

"It's okay," I said, calming them with my hands. "I'm here now." Then I walked like I was in a deep sleep, around behind the house where Daddy kept the watering hose, and turned the squeaky tap until a cold stream began to trickle and then pour out. I sloshed back through wet dirt to stretch the hose over to the centre of the garden where I stood with the freesia, and day lilies we had planted last. I bit my bottom lip and looked out at my magnificent garden one final time. Sure it was alive, but it was miserable. There are worse things than death, you know? So I held the hose over the top and started to cry. Before long the yard was a muddy mess, and even the snowdrops, candytuft and forsythia along the edges were waterlogged. Their voices muffled, their brilliant and pastel colours smudged and ran through my tears like a watercolour in the rain. *My only real friends in the world*, I thought as I forced myself to hold the hose still with both trembling hands. Within minutes I had drowned them all. Before they froze to death. Before it all got any worse. After, I looked at what I'd done and thought, *Fine. It's over.*

When I glanced up at the night sky, not a star in sight, cold rain pelted my face. I should have known that a line had been crossed. Each hard drop hit me like a tiny pinprick and my cheeks grew numb, felt like they did after a beating. The rain slapped me and tears rolled down my face and neck, and soaked my nightgown. I was covered in goosebumps and my teeth were chattering. Ten minutes passed, the storm slowed, and the garden was silent except for the sound of water still pouring from the hose. I couldn't feel earth as I walked back to hang up my weapon. Both feet were numb. I couldn't feel my toes or my calves or my legs. I couldn't even feel my heartbeat. But I didn't care. It was finally quiet. No music, no songs — but no screams either. I'd put them out of their misery. I'd put us all out of our misery.

37

Or so I thought.

In the morning I wandered into the kitchen and found Daddy sitting in his chair eating breakfast, reading the paper again as if nothing unusual had happened. He smelt like gin but was showered and shaved and sober. Mother was flipping eggy bread in the skillet. "Morning, Lilith. Sleep okay?"

I nodded even though it wasn't true.

"Breakfast's ready," Daddy said. "Your Mother's made your favourite."

They smiled at each other, obviously having made up. Mother spooned a stack of French toast onto my plate, and set four strips of smoked bacon beside it.

"With real maple syrup from Ontario," she said.

"Thanks."

I poured syrup over everything and for a long time we sat together, eating without a word. I concentrated on how delicious the sugary sweetness was on my tongue, how still and peaceful our little world, until Mother moved to the counter to pour herself a cup of Earl Grey tea.

"We're having a ladies auxiliary meeting at the church this morning," she said. "I'm heading there now to help set up." She rinsed her hands at the sink and looked outside. Next, she ran to the back door, swung it open in one gaping motion and quickly disappeared outside. "My word! Oh, my word!"

Daddy flipped to the sports section and took a swig of black coffee.

"What is it, Constance? Damned coons get into the garbage again?"

I just kept chewing and crunching, my heart racing. How would I explain?

"My God! Jack, come look, what a bizarre thing . . . All your work. All that waste!"

Daddy rolled the newspaper into a cylinder and left it on the table where it immediately unrolled itself. He pushed his empty plate away and stood. The next thing I knew, he was in the doorway belting his robe tightly and running his fingers through his uncombed hair. "Holy Toledo!" he said, stepping outside. "That was some storm."

"Jack!" Mother snapped. "Can't you see what's right in front of you? The entire yard is covered in a thin sheet of ice. There are muddy footprints on the bricks leading up to the house. "It's your daughter who did this!"

Daddy swivelled his head around to check my expression. "Lilith?"

"I told you," Mother said. "I've been warning you for years. The girl is unpredictable. Something like this was bound to happen sooner or later."

"I don't understand," Daddy said. "Why?" Mother started to cry and he put his arm around her shoulder. "There, there, Connie. It'll be all right."

"No it won't," Mother said. "It won't ever be right. Look at this mess Jack. Everything's ruined. Dead! Do you hear me? Don't you see? It's all dead! Dead!"

I started to shake.

Daddy returned to the kitchen and stood a couple of feet away like we'd never really met. His eyes were bloodshot as usual.

"Is that really your doing, Lilith?"

"I dddon't know," I stammered, like I was being held accountable for every bad thing that had ever happened to our family. For Daddy's drinking and my parents' fights, for business at the Tick Tock being so slow. And for my dead twin that started it all. Especially for that. "I dddon't know."

Mother flew through the open door with a sick purple expression on her face, rushed past Daddy to where I was sitting, and shook me by the shoulders.

"Young lady, what on earth's the matter with you?"

"They were hurting," I said, crying myself. "They needed help."

"Liar!" Mother screamed. "Liar!"

"It . . . it . . . it seemed like the only way."

Mother shook me harder.

"The only way? The only way to what?!"

"Thththth . . . the only way *out!*" I spat.

"You are crazy!" Mother shouted, as if until that moment she'd been reserving judgment. She shook me right up off my chair. "Crazy! Crazy! Crazy!"

"Constance!" Daddy said firmly. "Let her go. The damage is already done."

Mother stepped away out of breath, and Daddy knelt down taking my hands in his. "Lil," he started with a gentler voice. "Tell me *exactly* what happened?"

"I dddon't know," I said, scrambling to save myself. "I dddon't remember. I don't know. Maybe I was sleepwalking."

Mother covered her mouth with the palm of her hand.

"First this," she said, gesturing to the backyard. "Next what? Jack we've been over it a dozen times. You know I'm right. Now, before it gets worse. Before she *really* hurts herself. We both know what has to be done."

Daddy dropped his head.

"Lilith this is a terrible thing," he mumbled, releasing my hands but not looking at me. "A terrible, terrible thing."

I scratched my chair across the floor and leapt from my seat, ashamed.

"I'm sorry!" I hollered, running into the pantry and closing the door. "Really, really sorry." I stood inside shaking like a leaf. *Murderer,* I thought about myself. *Bloody murderer!*

And that's why, right before my sixteenth birthday a few weeks later, even though I had no idea what I was getting into, I did agree to drive out to Bridgewater psychiatric hospital for tests. *Maybe I am sick,* I thought. *Maybe Mother's right about me. One thing's for sure: After what I did, I deserve to be locked up!*

Next thing I knew, I was pinned to a hospital bed by a skinny, five-foot-five-inch chrome structure. After lights out it stood over me like some kind of overprotective parent. I guess I panicked at first. Resisted. Got angry — furious even. But when fighting did nothing to free me, I started to laugh and cry and cry and laugh, salt water smearing down my cheeks. Sure, in the beginning I was afraid. That's why I was so emotional. That's just what was killing me: the side-splitting, gut-wrenching fact that I was helpless all over again. Like the garden at home. Passive and dependent and trapped by my circumstances. Or, that's what I thought at the time. That as long as it was just crazy Lilith Boot there with her arms clenched to her sides like a toy soldier, the difference between laughing and crying made no real difference to anyone. Especially not me.

Some nights I woke up afraid of the giant shadow the hospital equipment threw onto the opposite wall. A hook held six feet of translucent rubber tubes that were connected to my arteries. I would've loved to rip them out but things could've been worse. I knew. I'd seen how it was for my roommates, Randy and Mrs. Moffat. I'd been on our ward for over a month, but I was too drugged to know the exact date. *Time flies*, I thought one day, as the nurse replaced the sack of fluid. Time had flown too, and it seemed like an escaped helium balloon that was never going to be returned to me. The nurse smiled and moved on to take Mrs. Moffat's temperature. Nurse Ford wasn't much older than me. Maybe early twenties, fresh from school. She'd been assigned to the hard-to-handles for practice — the ones the doctors didn't know what to do with, the ones like me, who weren't really expected to get better.

Bridgewater was vast and beautiful from the outside. Best view of the Fraser River and Rocky Mountains for miles. The factory building and the greenhouse stood a good distance away, opposite our bedroom window. And we were far enough outside Vancouver that the sky was usually cloudless and the air sometimes fishy. There were suspension bridges on both sides of Bridgewater and I could count on one hand all the different ways people travelled back and forth outside. By water. By land. Or by air. So many methods of transportation right outside our window but we weren't usually going more than up or down a flight of stairs.

Randy called over from across the room whenever she was in the mood. Once she pointed right at Mrs. Moffat. "It's her seventh time. Imagine that, seven admissions?"

"Visits," Mrs. Moffat corrected.

As far as Mrs. Moffat figured, she was just visiting a colony of her homeland. Like she'd been sent from England as an ambassador and the staff were her attendants. "Vacation" or "visitation" was what Mrs. Moffat called any admission. "Rest" was her word for treatment, and "cottage" was a patients' ward. It all sounded better to the staff too, who were uncomfortable saying we were living in the bughouse.

"Right. Excuse me," Randy corrected herself. "Visits."

Randy was good for gossip. She told me all about the other patients and explained that the only thing really wrong with Mrs. Moffat was a) she was afraid of everything b) nobody really, truly loved her, and c) as far as Randy could tell, she pretended to be better than the rest of us. "Admissions are *her* version of divorce," Randy said, bringing her clasped hands up over her head. "Not like mine." I wasn't sure what she meant, but judging by the way Mrs. Moffat slowly backed away, I didn't want to ask either.

Randy disliked Mrs. Moffat's husband as much as she disliked Alice Woodward, the head nurse. She called *her* Alice the Camel, 'cause of the slight rise in her upper back, and she called Mrs. Moffat's husband "The Master," even to his face. Especially when he came sauntering up the hall with a goatee swagger and a wing-tip moustache, and even with a bouquet of flowers in hand. Randy never knew when to let up.

"Hey, Isadora Moffat," she'd holler at the top of her lungs. "That's a real pretty boy you got there. Think he'd get *me* some of them fancy clothes?"

But no matter what, Mrs. Moffat answered in the same old way.

"That's Queen Moffat the First, to you!" Then she'd skirt past Randy and stand in the doorway of our room hopefully, eagerly, like a caged dog at the Humane Society.

"Why can't she stay home," I asked one visiting day. I saw Randy's face flush and right away regretted my question.

She spat into the spider plant on the windowsill and approached my bed.

"Stay away? You mean, like, stay out? Grow up, Boot! This isn't university. I didn't see you filling out no application." But that was different. I'd been placed there to get well. I was crazy; everyone said so.

"I hope she gets help is all," I told Randy, folding my arms across my full chest, turning my head away from her and wishing for walls.

In the beginning I liked it better when Randy stayed in her own area of the room, so I imagined constructing walls in various locations. Sometimes when I wanted to hear Mrs. Moffat's whispers, the walls were made of chipboard. Easy to assemble, but not soundproof. Other times I mixed, poured, and set concrete, piling stone to ceiling and filling in cracks with a caulking gun. I hoped that one day, enough time without privacy and Randy might get the message. So far, it wasn't working.

"Get help like you?" Randy flicked my IV sack with her thumb and pointer finger and continued the conversation. "Or like me?" she said, holding her forearms out and revealing long, deep scars, layer over layer, from wrist to elbow like wind currents in the desert sand. I watched the purple vein swell across her forehead as she shrugged like she didn't have a care in the world. "Aw well, whatcha gonna do?" she said. "Gotta keep your sense of humour, right? Yeah, laugh or cry." Then we watched Mrs. Moffat dump her bouquet in the garbage pail and return to sit on her bed with a get-well card. She started rocking back and forth, staring out the window and whispering to herself.

"Pat-a-cake, pat-a-cake, baker's man. So I do, master, as fast as I can."

I noticed Randy chewing on her thumbnail and thought, *Oh no, here we go again.*

"Never mind," I told her quickly, hoping she'd cool it. But Randy wasn't much of a listener.

"Never mind, Randy. Calm down Randy! SHUT UP, RANDY!" Her voice steadily built like a locomotive coming along the track.

"Shush!" Mrs. Moffat said, rolling over and whispering some more. "Double bubble, get in trouble."

"Knock it off," I blurted through clenched teeth. I was sick of Mrs. Moffat's silly nursery rhymes and Randy's anger. As if anger ever got me where I needed to go! And her laugh always started the same crude way too: a deep-throated "garumph" that grew, infecting her until she couldn't even stop herself. Remember all the laughing you heard when you were a kid? Short, stout guffaw, witch cackle, piggy snort. Remember the asthma wheeze, feline hiss, belly howl? The thief snicker, and the shy tee-hee? Well, it was just like that, only all rolled into one. And I hated it.

Mrs. Moffat pushed discreetly on the emergency button over her bed.

"Servants!" she called out.

"HA HA!" Randy screamed full force. "C'mon be loud! Laugh your heads off!"

Two nurses and an orderly rushed into our room.

Randy's strong arms were swinging high over her head, her grey eyes were wide and her pupils full like harvest moons. "Ho-ho-ho-ho," she sang, her face flushed. By then she was thrashing her arms up and down at the head of Mrs. Moffat's bed like she meant business.

"Oh my!" Mrs. Moffat squealed, clasping her chest. "Someone *do* something!"

Solomon, the orderly, grabbed Randy from behind and pulled her arms back tight, leaving her chest pressed up flat against her thin blue smock. He was there to help the nurses and run errands, and deal with heating and plumbing and electrical needs. He was there to fix things that truly needed fixing. And he thought Randy was a big part of his job. So Solomon squeezed Randy's arms even harder as she continued hollering and kicking her legs, one at a time, as high as she could.

"Look Your Majesty?" she sang, "Isn't this hilarious?!"

The nurses each grabbed one leg, carried Randy to her bed beside mine, and held her down. Poor Nurse Ford stood motionless in the doorway until she was told to attend to other patients. By then, some of them were cheering Randy on.

Mrs. Moffat broke into a quiet song all by herself.

"Hush-a-bye, baby, on the treetop . . ."

Randy continued too, louder than ever.

"Some folks couldn't have a good time if their lives depended on it! Ha-Ha!"

A chorus started chanting in the hallway. "HA! HA! HA! HA!" Randy and the other patients screamed at the top of their lungs, drowning out my tears of frustration and Mrs. Moffat's whispers, and then her demand for silence.

"Her Majesty requests . . ." She pointed at Randy and then at each hyper face peering in through the open door. "Absolute silence!"

Nobody paid her any mind, though.

"*Now*, Miss Ford!" Alice Woodward was really annoyed.

"I'm sick of her," Solomon said under his breath, and I didn't know if he meant Randy, Mrs. Moffat, or Nurse Ford.

Randy continued screaming and laughing, sweat dripping down her rib cage, while Alice injected her with a thick syringe. Diazepam. Then Randy's speech slurred.

"Some fake it though, and then there's . . . the tyyyype thaaat caaaan't . . ."

Solomon wiped his hands like they were covered in crumbs.

"That'll settle Miranda right down," he reassured Mrs. Moffat, guiding everyone else back into the hall. Randy tried to lift her head three inches off the mattress and the ligaments in her neck strained. I could hardly make myself look at her in that condition.

"My name is Randy!" she shouted with all her force. "Randy!" She turned to me still flat on my bed. "And guess what? The joke's on us."

I just turned my head away, started to build walls — that time with bricks. Randy went unconscious and I waited for the whispering, but it didn't start up right away.

"Miss Boot?"

I pretended to be asleep.

"We've soiled the bed again. Miss Boot?"

There was no use pretending.

"Don't worry," I told Mrs. Moffat. "Someone will be along to clean it up."

"Seven's my lucky number," she said, like it was good news.

I closed my eyes so tight it hurt.

"Seven seven go to heaven."

My hands slapped over my ears. *No matter where I am there's noise,* I thought.

"One two buckle my shoe . . . three four shut the door . . ."

I started crying again, silently swearing to do whatever I was told. Bury my visions for good. Get better. Be normal. Empty the last bit of me I had left.

"Be quiet," I said. "Leave me alone."

Still, Mrs. Moffat wouldn't give up.

"I know my lucky number, Miss Boot," she said. "But do you know yours?"

Mrs. Moffat had lucky numbers and favourite colours and was all-round superstitious. And she told me that the red light of an ambulance meant relief. Red was her colour, she said — the colour of war, russet uniforms and broken ruby, garnet and glass engagement rings. Crushed-velvet maternity dresses. She dreamt of being engulfed in red. Sunset. Magenta. Scarlet. I imagined red pouring out her slit wrists, offering comfort. She pined for a warm claret blanket to spread out on the bathroom tiles and tried her best to roll up in it. Red is a peppery cinnamon heart that burns the tongue on Valentine's Day, or a shiny balloon that floats to heaven, if you let it. Red is an apple, the colour of sin, she told me. Red: a woman's colour. An amphibian colour if you feel cold-blooded like she did, for deserting her boy. Her bones practically dissolved into liquid calcium and guilt the last time she had herself admitted.

Mrs. Moffat also told me she felt her husband slide his trembling hands around her waist that day, lift her into a sitting position, lock his arms under hers and hoist her onto her feet. He dragged her downstairs and outside in that position. There were gashes across her wrists so blood dripped onto the carpet. *Drip, drip drip.* The paramedics pushed her stretcher all the way into the cab and her husband just stood there in his pinstriped pyjamas and bare feet, his hair flat on one side from sleeping on it. Pillow creases lined one of his cheeks. They both heard their son crying upstairs in the nursery and Mr. Moffat waved as the ambulance doors shut. "Goodbye," he said, looking a bit relieved.

Mrs. Moffat told me that inside the ambulance she closed her eyes and the vision of that vermilion wave surrounded her again. She let herself be sucked through it, lurched away from her house to flow out into a better place. She wanted to go somewhere she would be loved unconditionally, so she imagined herself travelling in that bloodstained undertow, hoping she'd emerge in a different place and time. I think Mrs. Moffat knew early what most women take a lifetime to figure out. When you can't have the love you need, you end up doing the second best thing. You give it away instead.

She sure was a giver. No doubt about that. And in Bridgewater Mrs. Moffat found herself a way to be erased from her son's day-to-day life. There she could cloak him in her invisibility. Basically, hide out. At least that way, even though she might not be remembered, she sure wouldn't be forgotten either. "Our boy will learn fast," she told me. "Any family is ruled by its sickest member." At least she could give him that. That was everything she had.

Mrs. Moffat also said a hospital was a jungle and she saw all us patients as part of a wild evolutionary condition. Some, like Randy, were rabid with the instinct for self-defence, and others like me would eventually morph and disappear. I laughed at the idea. "Oh, come on," I said. "You're pulling my leg." But I didn't know back then how time can change a person so much that she won't even recognize herself.

Mrs. Moffat just made a sour face and told me how in the ambulance her skinny frame bounced on that stretcher like it was a chariot bumping along tree-lined streets. She wished she had enough energy to sit up and wave as her procession advanced. Children were playing in backyards and she heard their squeals of delight and their rippling laughter. "Ring around the rosy, a pocketful of posies. Husha! Husha! We all fall down . . ." We all fall down . . . we all fall.

Eventually.

And as she was rushed from the tidy residential roads to the highway, the children faded away but her own boy's cry still rang in her ear. Then sun flashed on her eyelids between passing telephone poles and the soothing red of her imagination was interrupted by flashes of hot yellow every three seconds. Yellow slashes cutting into her crimson world. When the ambulance pulled to a stop, Mrs. Moffat tried to sit up and that's when she found out that she was strapped to the stretcher. The paramedics unloaded her and wheeled her into emergency. "But why come here?" I asked about Bridgewater.

Mrs. Moffat didn't answer me for a long time.

"For a title other than Mrs. So-and-so," she finally said.

On the day of her last admittance, it was just like every other time: she was transferred from the emergency of Vancouver General to Bridgewater. And it was Alice Woodward who led her through the halls, to our room inside Ward One, like she was some kind of stubborn migrating bird who refused to keep up with the flock. But Mrs. Moffat didn't mind. She liked the hospital grounds with its cared-for landscape and canopy of clouds hanging overhead, shielding her like a giant white parasol. She needed to feel secure and be surrounded by breathing conifers that healed, and whole forests of bald cypress. I totally understood.

Most of the time she wore clothes too baggy for her frame, like she was a little girl trying on her mumma's wardrobe. Her hospital gowns were extra large even though a small size would have done the trick. Without a belt, her skirts fell to her ankles. The cuffs of her blouses hid her hands, showing long bony fingers. Her paper slippers were too big as well, and sometimes she crumple-crumpled through the halls with only one foot covered. She kept her lustrous black hair long like it was a shaggy curtain covering half of her expression, and she tied important things — her sister's marcasite bobby pins, a love note she'd received from a young suitor once — away in the mass of tangles and curls. I bet it was her safest hiding place. One lucky afternoon at bingo, "B1" was called and Mrs. Moffat won her prized rhinestone tiara. From then on she wore it like a crown. She finally had proof. She really was the queen of Bridgewater.

If you ask me, for a queen she was pretty small. Barely four foot eleven inches. But she was desperate to be bigger than us all and I watched her eating everything in sight just to shrink into her own skin and disappear behind rolls of cellulite. Too bad for her though, her fast metabolism made bingeing pointless. Even if she could convince the cafeteria staff to serve her double portions of mashed potatoes for supper and bread pudding for dessert, she didn't gain. She stayed as exposed as always, and vulnerable — her elbows, knobby knees and hip bones jutting out into the atmosphere, cutting away more space for a gaping open wound.

Her skin was dry and patchy, and sometimes an eczema rash spread from her hands to her eyelids and the bridge of her nose. It made her seem more like a leper than someone with a mental illness. Bags hung under her eyes like caterpillar larvae waiting to hatch. She had a gap between her two front teeth and she walked with a permanent limp not caused by any physical problem as far as I could tell. Just her reluctance to step solidly into the world. Or maybe she just wanted to make a grand entrance. In any case, Bridgewater's one and only monarch moved hesitantly through doors, like she had no right *and* every right to enter a room.

Since that last time Mrs. Moffat was admitted she'd refused to take herself to the washroom any more — I think she liked having staff cleaning up after her. And she drooled — saliva steadily streaming from her bottom lip down to her chin. Her lips were half-numb from the meds which caused her to accidentally bite herself without realizing. More and more her body oozed reminders that what lies festering inside eventually make its way to the surface. But I didn't think of those things then and she didn't seem bothered by any of it. Just continued using her bedpan and speaking through swollen lips that made her words sound like they were coming through cotton batting.

Mrs. Moffat declared signing to be the official language of Ward One, and sometimes refused to communicate unless the rest of us used our hands too. At night she sat on her bed, casting animal shadows on the wall with her fingers. A rabbit. A cat. A giraffe was the hardest. Her animal kingdom came alive there in the shadows where she ruled from an imaginary throne. She whispered to her subjects — whether we wanted to listen or not

— reciting song lyrics from the radio and nursery rhymes her older siblings had read to her when she was young.

This is the way we wash our hands,
wash our hands, wash our hands.
This is the way we wash our hands,
on a cold and frosty morning.

In the hospital Mrs. Moffat was free to admit she was exhausted. Free to yawn and have no one blink. She knew she was less embarrassing when she was tucked away at Bridgewater. We all were. Randy said Mrs. Moffat used to resent her husband being indifferent, but by the time I met her I'm pretty sure she was grateful. Always struggling to keep active, improve, play the good wife, was depressing. It hadn't gotten her anything at home but a stronger prescription for Valium, she said. At least in the hospital she could give up trying to be so damn perfect and go full out for the opposite. To be nothing. Discarded. Left behind. She imagined pain in her lungs and spasms in her muscles, and who's to say it wasn't real? Sometimes I could see she had trouble breathing, sometimes she was deaf. Once in a while she clutched her chest. "Heartache," she'd gasp, between breaths.

"Hurts?" I'd say, trying to be sympathetic.

"Yes," she agreed. "Yes, we do."

There was no question, for either me or Randy, that Mrs. Moffat was suffering. She preferred the angora haze of being drugged to the clear, sober alternative. For her, meds turned our surroundings from dreary to dramatic. The bright overhead lights in the visiting room were blazing torches for her. Signposts for our castle. The red "no entry" sign at the end of our hall blurred if she squinted, and she pronounced it "gentry" instead. Instead of blaring shift changes for staff, the loud-speakers hanging in the halls announced that explorers or entertainers were coming to see us. Under the influence, Ward One wasn't just a ward for schizophrenics, depressives, hysterical women like me, but a palace with moats and a protective drawbridge that doubled as a security rail, and a very strict dress code for its citizens. Citizens. That's what Mrs. Moffat insisted we were. With dignity and pride.

During the early part of the day our doctors made their rounds and divided us into categories of illness. We stuck together like schoolyard girls. The manic-depressives formed a surly gang at the sunny end of the first-floor hall. The feeble-minded, or those just a little bit slower than everybody else, wandered two by two, trailing whatever excitement. If a nurse rushed to help a patient, these were the women who hurried behind. If Randy threw one of her temper tantrums, this crowd gathered to cheer. The schizophrenics were treated like a rare species by almost everyone, and claimed the entire ward as their clubhouse without actually marking territory. They wandered through talking to no one and everyone. Schizophrenics were damned and respected at the same time, and staff kept a watchful eye from a distance. I guess most people can't resist admiring what terrifies them.

If you didn't argue, throw a scene or make trouble, even a queen like Mrs. Moffat could sink into the pale backdrop of the walls, or deep into the vinyl couch in the visitors' area. Her attitude was rewarded by staff. In all her admissions, she hardly ever got restrained like Randy or electroshocked like Jean-Ann. Mostly Mrs. Moffat was prescribed pills and occupational therapy in the factory, like me. She appreciated long days at Bridgewater as long as they were scented with Peak Freans, oatmeal cookies and wooden salad bowls piled high with McIntosh apples, to kill the cravings. Sanity-seeking sweet midnight sugar runs, I called them, because some patients were up late pacing and twitching, itching for something. Anything to help calm the nerves. Sugar-coated sanity was the answer for Mrs. Moffat. Not hard candy. Nurse Ford knew and always turned up on shift with a bag of goodies. "Your Majesty," she'd say. "I've brought sweets."

Mrs. Moffat lumbered about slowly taking in the sights and smells, overseeing the nursing staff and generally making a mental note of anything out of the ordinary. When Alice Woodward secretly stuffed bottles of skin lotion and talcum powder into her purse, Mrs. Moffat just rubbed her chin like she was deciding which form of punishment to assign. If I snooped in Randy's dresser drawers, looking at her photo, Mrs. Moffat watched without a word. If Randy touched herself under the covers at night, Mrs. Moffat rolled over and ignored her.

She felt worthwhile being a monarch travelling slowly back and forth between the cafeteria and our ward, with most of her belongings hanging from pockets or slung over her shoulder in a pillowcase. She was slow but she would get where she needed to, she told me. Because the world would come to her. Maybe she had a point: Time is generous. Time is round. And besides, she saw early on that there were advantages to fitting all the stereotypes, especially when they made you seem useless. "Useless is a kind of freedom," she told me. I don't mean to be rude but I think it confirmed how she felt coming into the hospital and, well, after seven admissions, to be blunt, it fit her like a suit of armour.

At night she wrapped herself up tight in starchy cotton sheets and imagined what it would've been like if her son had entered the world through another woman. I heard her whispering about it under her breath. What if he'd been loved

instantly as he slid from her birth canal? Cherished, as he round-
ed out the encasement of her placenta. What if she'd anticipated
him, as he rotated from side to side with his foot sticking out her
belly? Well, there's no such thing as "if" so she practised reciting
limericks instead. Pretending her boy could hear good wishes
through the echo of her heartbeat. "Rock-a-bye baby, the cradle
is green. Father's a nobleman, mother's a queen . . ." Every night
it was the same. Sentiments for good luck. If she lay down very
very still, stayed in her bed exactly where she was, it wouldn't
matter that her boy didn't know her face from a stranger's, or the
softness of her skin; he would feel her through her absence, she
thought. Eventually, Mrs. Moffat was convinced, he would find
his way back to her. She watched for him. Waited. On more than
one night I bet she saw him swimming outside those hospital
walls, treading water along the shores of her imagination.

When she stayed awake, Mrs. Moffat heard the deeper
voices of the men's ward right next door. Sometimes argu-
ments, sometimes sobs. In Ward One there was also the rolling
tin, tin, tinny noise of an IV sack wheeled from bedside to bathroom, and the faraway *murm, murm, murmur* of night staff with
a television on low volume at the station. Loudest of all was
the babbling trail of comments as we shuffled from room to
room in paper slippers, drugged like zombies. *Crumple-crumple.*
And in summer, just outside our window, none of us could get
away from the raping-mating noise of cats in heat. "They
sound like babies screaming," she told me in the mornings.
"We wish to make them stop."

So, I guess you could say conversation *of a sort* filled Ward One,
and Two, Three, and Ward Four. And maybe our symptoms or our
actions wouldn't exactly be called *real* communication by most
folks. But if you ask me, metaphor is the only mother tongue.

With the help of her dedicated will, Mrs. Moffat did stay awake most nights, and she whispered, "Humpty Dumpty sat on a wall, Humpty Dumpty had a great fall. All the king's horses, all the king's men cannot put Humpty together again." Okay, so she wasn't best at being quiet like I was then, and she wasn't good at standing up for herself like Randy, but Mrs. Moffat knew how to get what she needed and you can't say that about everyone. She was satisfied with her decisions, and proud being the last to close her eyes, the last to look protectively over us — her subjects — all of us trying in our own way to forget about yesterday. And all of us searching for tomorrow's peace.

August 12, 1977.

Dear Mr. _____,

My name is Lemon Boot and today I am nine years and four days old. Mumma says that means I'm in my tenth year which is fine by me because ten's better than nine. It means I'm clear out of the single digits. It really just means I'm done being a kid, I think. I'll be a double-digit for the rest of my life unless I live to be a hundred — which, by the way, I aim to do. I might even zoom ahead in time and come back younger and older all at the once. Anyway, I've decided to start writing you letters even though I don't know your address or your name. I reason if I put them in the mailbox addressed to "My Dad somewhere on Planet Earth," it's a safe bet you'll get them just like when I used to send my Christmas wish list to Santa via the North Pole. I also reason that it's okay to take bubble baths and jump on the bed when you're still stuck in the single digits. But after that, no way. Even Mumma who does some pretty unusual things doesn't do those things any more. She says there's no time, but I think time's just a good excuse for pretending you don't want to. Mostly now, Mumma works at the police station.

I didn't used to mind coming here when school got out early, when I was just a kid. I mean, we needed the money, right? But now not even Jan will wait with me in the precinct. It gets boring. Sergeant Grant almost always gives me a purple popsicle — my favourite flavour — when he and Mumma come out of her office. And he always pretends I don't know what's behind his back, then makes me pick a fist which is so silly, because *I* know before he even opens the door which hand holds my treat. I play along 'cause I don't want to embarrass him, and like I said, Mumma needs the job.

Today's no different. I'm supposed to sit on this chair, amuse myself with this pen and paper, and not move a muscle until I'm told. But I can't help it. After a long time I slide off, walk over to Mumma's door and look at her through the glass slat. She's holding a new file folder on her lap and she runs her fingertips along the edges while she's talking to herself. Then she starts to shake and turn colours — mostly red because Mumma gets really hot when she's working. She's staring off into space, like something more important is happening in front of her, only all that's there is the wall. And me on the other side of it. I know *that* look. It means Mumma's for sure trying to find stupid old Benjamin! That look also means I'm gonna be sitting here a whole lot longer, so I put the pen and paper down, walk across the hall to the washroom, climb on top of the porcelain basin at the far end where I can lean my body against the wall, and look at myself in the mirror.

I wonder if I look like you? My face is very round, and looks even fatter because of the zillion orange curls that spring out of my head. I wear a blue barrette in the front and centre of my scalp to flatten the hair on the top or else when it gets long I can't see through the mess in front of me. The barrette was a good idea, I think, but then the rest of my curls seem more out of place, growing as they do from every direction. Mumma says my cheeks are my trademark, like two shiny lemons sitting high on the bone. She says I was born that way and they're what make me irresistible. My cheeks and the funny birthmark on my thigh are how I got my name: Lemon. That's what I'm called. Sometimes, Lem for short.

Between you and me, I think Mumma can't see *me* at all. Not for all her powers of observation, not if I paid her cash in advance like some of her customers, and not with her sleeves rolled up to her elbows, trying to catch a glimpse of somebody else's kid, another lifetime — even of the future. I've tried to talk to her, well . . . about how much she works, and about you, my Dad. But she says I think too much. I hate that. Mummas think they know best, even when they don't. For example, my Mumma understands nothing about stars or planets or worlds away from this one, or about how the sun is moving closer and closer to earth and one day we might all burn in a heaping ball of flame! She doesn't know I wish we could visit my grandparents instead of only talking to them long-distance after six o'clock or waiting for them to come here to Toronto at Christmas and Easter. She doesn't even know about how I fly in my dreams (Mumma's afraid to fly).

I love Mumma, even more than Jan does, but I don't want to contract a vision like I contracted chicken pox last year. Being psychic's a disease you know — the kids at school told me. And I don't want to be infected. Mostly though, Mumma doesn't understand that while it's true most of my friends' parents *are* divorced, at one time they were actually married and had sex. (I'm not supposed to know what sex is, but Jan told me already. She's two years older and she knows everything.) Jan says she believes in instincts and intuition, so she understands Mumma better than me. She says a lot of things, like she won't wear dresses any more on account of they make her look stupid, and she says she plans to go to university and become a reporter for a national paper. Jan wants to deliver good news and she also wishes she could trade places with me so *her* Dad would disappear instead. Anyway, sex is a scientific fact and what I've noticed is that Mumma seems to overlook it. But I can't because if she really didn't have it, that would make me the weirdest and only miracle bastard among a whole lot of us kids from single-parent families.

Just for the record, I looked into her claims of a virgin birth and I found that actually there is such a thing as an immaculate conception. I mean, it's a bona fide scientific possibility and it's called parthenogenesis! You can bet they don't teach you this kind of thing in school, so last weekend Jan took me down to the Metro Reference Library and we did some research of our own. Jan loves books like her Dad loves rum and Coke, plus she insists she's never getting married; so our discovery might come in handy for her one day too. In parthenogenesis what happens is an outsider like a virus or with any luck, an alien, makes the area inside of a Mumma double up. It's called the chromo zone and that starts her making the beginnings of a baby. Jan says that because there's no Daddy involved, the kid can only turn out to be a girl. Cool, huh?

Then, we found another article that said virgin births (that might be me) occur twice as often as identical twins. Jan says it means I'm rare and priceless 'cause I'm literally one in a million, or one in ten thousand to be more specific. So, when I was an egg, I could have divided on my own inside of Mumma. I don't totally mind the idea, you know, the independence. Except that it would mean I really *don't* have a Daddy. Like you. Jan says it's pretty obvious to her that I don't. And that I'm lucky. Still, you know what I mean. We paid ten cents and xeroxed the article but I haven't shown it to Mumma. She'll just say, "Babygirl, I told you so." For now I slipped it under my pillow. I'm hoping it'll bring me good luck and send the truth in my dreams.

Anyway, like I was saying before, my cheeks are so big that my eyes almost disappear behind them, and I look out over the top like I have faraway mountains in my view. Rocky mountains like the ones they have out west where Grandma Connie and Granddad Jack live. My glasses actually rest on my cheeks, not the bridge of my nose like most people, which is the number one reason why I fold them and put them in my back pocket when Mumma's not around. The number two reason, like now, why I'm not wearing my glasses is because not wearing them gives me a different way to see things. Without my glasses nothing bores me and without my glasses I don't look like Lemon Boot at all. At least, according to the mirror in the bathroom at 52 Division. Here I just look like a giant fuzzy peach or the Boston fern hanging in our kitchen. Or, maybe even a Martian! I don't know because I've never seen one of those, but I hope to one day. I hope to see what you look like too. And sound like. And see Mars and Saturn and whole other universes. Maybe if I start now and practise enough squinting and staring, I'll find a way to outer space. Or at least, a way to fly.

Wanna be pen pals? Let me know.

Your (maybe) daughter,

Lemon.

Fifty-two Division is like a second home to Lilith, with its thick institutional architecture and large cement walkway. She's on a first-name basis with each of the officers, except for the occasional new fellow who mistakes her for an average citizen, someone who accidentally turned left down the hall to Investigations, he thinks, when maybe she meant to turn right and head over to Bail instead. On the rare occasion when she is stopped and questioned, "Excuse me Ma'am, this floor's for staff only, you must be lost," Lilith simply explains who she is: Detective Boot, the first and only staff psychic on the Toronto police force. And then she asks to be escorted to her office — room 107 — so they know for future reference where to find her.

After nearly two decades Lilith has arranged her work environment as comfortably as possible, given that she is, after all, in a professional setting. Whereas at home she'd gain easy access to her kitchen cupboards full of sugar cereal, licorice and frozen waffles at whim, here at the precinct she keeps but a small stash of goodies in the first drawer of her desk and discreetly unwraps the candy when she's alone. In the beginning, proving herself to Sergeant Grant with the rarest of opportunities, Lilith made do in a cubicle no bigger than a closet, with walls that went only halfway up so everyone could watch. Back then she filled her belly *before* coming in and wore a hooded sweatshirt that masked her face. Now, working on a reasonably steady diet of contracts, she hangs her poncho on a hook on the back of her office door, and everybody knows to knock before interrupting.

No one in the precinct has publicly admitted that a psychic solves cases. And it took three years' worth of finds before Sergeant Grant came around — they all do eventually — and offered Lilith a decent rate of pay, handed her a set of keys, swung open the door and said, "Welcome to your new abode, Madame." Lilith's always left the nameplate blank. "Why don't you let me get maintenance up here to fix that?" her boss still asks from time to time. *Naah*, Lilith thinks. *A title like clairvoyant, or psychic, is a bit off-putting for folks. Sort of throws my authority in their faces. I'd prefer new clients get to know me in person before they form any solid opinions.* So, it's a plain grey door with a silver handle for Lilith Boot, just like every other worker on the floor.

Inside she keeps only the bare essentials: a desk made of cheap brown wood, a steel chair that has a tall upholstered back and sturdy armrests and tilts or leans, depending upon how she shifts her weight. The chair sits on wheels so she scuttles across the floor quickly when needs be, using her feet to navigate. The telephone sits on the desk and its cord runs the length of her office. On the rare occasion when Lilith calls her parents from the office, she and Jack gab while she slides back and forth, picking up a file from here and setting it down over there. Sometimes Constance picks up the extension.

The office is a perfect square, just like the living room in Lilith's west-end apartment. The walls are painted regulation grey. *Same shade as old snow on city streets*, Lilith thinks. There is no window for fresh air, which is an impediment to working — a clear mind is imperative, as Lilith knows — and the concrete floor is unyielding, and causes stiffness in her ankles and calves. For this reason Lilith keeps a pair of terry cloth slippers, with extra insoles for cushioning, in the bottom drawer of her desk (along with sanitary napkins, a hairbrush, a couple of covered elastics, a small foam basketball, and an eye mask for when she needs a power nap), and she takes frequent breaks to stretch. For the comfort of her colleagues, Lilith brought in an old throw rug that she had caught her neighbour, Vivian Hines, dragging to the basement garbage bins one afternoon. "Don't you want that any more, Viv? I could sure use it at work." Pink baby elephants aren't really Lilith's taste either, but she's never one to look a gift horse in the mouth.

Now the rug covers an area in front of Lilith's desk where Sergeant Grant or his secretary, Rosemary, or clients' families sit, waiting. There are fluorescent overhead lights in the office that give Lilith a headache, and because the nature of the work itself can often initiate a migraine, she picked up a small desk lamp at Honest Ed's department store to reduce the effect, then got reimbursed for the cost later. As long as Rosemary replaces the forty-watt bulb every now and again, the lamp does the trick, lighting up the whole room in a soothing, amber glow.

The wall directly behind Lilith's desk is covered in maps. Toronto first, followed west to east by each Canadian province, and one smaller map of the United States for tracking cross-border abductions. Lilith uses coloured push-pins to indicate the likely whereabouts of her children. Today green trails from Ontario to Saskatchewan — Emily Chung, missing since last week, apparently reported absent by a daycare worker after a field trip to the Metro Toronto Zoo. Lilith's circled Saskatoon on the map in green Magic Marker. She thinks that one of Emily's parents, in the middle of a messy divorce at the moment, has abducted her. Today Lilith hopes to be more specific, pinpoint the street, house number, the child, and close the case.

On the far wall above her potted rubber tree and beside a miniature basketball hoop, there is another, smaller map of Canada. It's empty of push-pins but the name "Benjamin" and a giant question mark are written across the top. In her downtime, Lilith tosses the foam basketball, and plugs away at this old case trying to jump-start the lingering smells and sounds that have always been a part of her. So far to no avail. She can't give up even if she doesn't realize why. Benjamin is the link between her now and then.

Seeing is vulgar business. Obscene the way a dirty old man's raincoat is obscene. And not knowing a child's whereabouts is even worse. Parents cling to Lilith as if she's a rosary when they first walk into the precinct to file their reports. They hang off her arm, compliment her outfits, anything to win favour. *Their* child is special and can't she see it, the one in a million who's going to be returned? Notice the mole on his backside, they tell her, scattering photographs across her desk. The scar on his knee? Think of it, they urge. *Visualize.* Lilith touches all artefacts offered to her, and breathes deeply; inhaling makes it authentic for them. She never tells clients about the fullness of her visions though. She just writes up her reports, helps out when she can, and collects her paycheque twice each month. As a rule Lilith tries not to think about the fact that most people consider her to be some state-of-the-art form of telecommunication and assume just because they retain her services, she'll see exactly what they want her to see. She knows better.

But Lilith also understands that parents who choose a psychic have already bargained with forces larger than themselves, destroyed marriages blaming each other, taken leaves of absences from jobs. They have nothing left to lose. "Can you see that chipped front tooth?" they ask. "Here, look closer." So she leans in, nodding. Being somebody's last resort is a responsibility Lilith Boot takes as seriously as motherhood. Lemon doesn't always see it that way though. And when she's in the precinct, sometimes she knocks on Lilith's door to interrupt.

"Mumma, when are we going home?"

"A few more minutes, Lemon. I'm just about done!"

Some parents stare as if Lilith's got snakes for hair, hissing poisonous visions that might crumble the hope they hold onto. "As much as I feel for them," she tells her boss, "and I do, between you and me, sometimes it grates on my nerves." After Lilith conducts a search, and Sergeant Grant dispatches the information she's recovered to precincts across the country, the parents might hold her in the highest regard, thank her profusely, grab her hands in theirs and offer any amount of money for future readings. But if she fails to locate their child she might be called a charlatan, her professional reputation stained by malicious gossip. *Okay, so maybe I read whereabouts as if they're written across a body,* she tells herself. *Locations sinking into my skin like emotional tattoos. But you know what? Maybe they expect too much.*

Since Lilith was hired she's always set her own hours. That's not to say she doesn't do her fair share. Everybody at the precinct works long, overtime days and she's no exception. But Sergeant Grant realized a long time ago that her success rate and productivity are much higher if she's allowed to come and go at her own discretion. Eight hours, day after day, inside that angular, bloodless structure and her concentration strays. Lilith usually comes into the office three times a week, and of course on weekends. For this reason, Sergeant Grant never springs a meeting on her without plenty of notice — in the worst cases, calling her at home the night before. He also prioritizes the search strategy, and Lilith is grateful. After all, how could she choose? Once a case is unsolved for three months it's considered rare that the child will be located. After six, Rosemary moves those files to the back of Lilith's cabinet; Lilith certainly can't bring herself to do it.

Today was to be just like every other work day. Lilith focused on one or two specific children, beginning with Emily from yesterday, then met with a set of parents, read files for the week ahead and spent some time on Benjamin. Now as the day drew to a close she was beginning to think about her paperwork.

Her slippered feet were up on her desk, crossed at the ankle, when Sergeant Grant passed by. She leaned back in her chair, red licorice dangling from between her front teeth, and tossed her sponge basketball in the direction of the hoop on the back of her office door. Lemon waited just outside. An hour earlier Lilith had found Billy Wooster, age thirteen, who'd been abducted into a white van on the side of the road in Grosse Pointe, Michigan.

Normally she doesn't handle American cases, but Billy's mother-in-law, Tilly Eaton, was a member of the old Canadian guard before she married into the Ford family, with many powerful connections still in Toronto. Billy — William III as she referred to him — was her first and favoured grandchild, so Lilith had been employed to rule out the need for a Canadian manhunt. From behind her desk she squinted, lifted her hands into the delicate posture of a professional basketball player exactly as Sergeant Grant had shown her, and took a clear shot. She missed by an inch, just as her boss knocked and opened the door. "Free throw's not improving," he said. Then he picked up the ball and tossed it back in Lilith's direction.

Sergeant Grant took note of a trough full of herbs sitting under halogen lights in the corner, and moved to switch off the humidifier on top of the mini-fridge. He approached Lilith's desk as she bit off the end of the chewy red candy and offered him the remainder.

"No thanks. Just came by to tell you we found the Eaton kid fifteen minutes ago, tied up and gagged, but he'll be fine. Got a few cuts and bruises, and his grandmother thinks he's looking malnourished, but he'll survive. I don't think bologna sandwiches are quite what he's used to. Seems our Billy joined a rather rambunctious fraternity, like you said. Apparently they induct their new brothers by scaring the shit out of them."

Lilith rolled her eyes, and tossed the foam basketball once more.

"Jackpot!" It passed through the hoop that time. She sat up, pulled her chair in close to her desk, held her hands together in a steeple formation and rested her chin on her fingertips pensively, as if praying. "Wish I could find Benjamin, though."

"Still no luck?"

Lilith shook her head.

"No. But I've started keeping track."

She lifted the red file folder on her lap so that Sergeant Grant could see it. "This one's just for him." She handed the open file, with all its loose papers, to her boss. "I've charted every encounter as best as I can remember. They go back as far as Lemon's first year." In consecutive order, each of Benjamin's pages listed the date, time, and location of Lilith's most recent search for him, and below had approximately one paragraph citing "Results," most of which simply read "undetermined" but, occasionally, "getting warmer" or "felt his presence." Farther down each page, Lilith had provided space for a brief description of her visceral reactions. "These are very important," she explained, while Sergeant Grant flipped through the stack. "They reveal what's going on inside when I'm looking for him. Helps me find my blind spots."

"Blind spots?"

"You know: mental blocks."

Sergeant Grant read one such description in detail.

"Ears buzzing. Faint blue film covered eyes. Feel like a frog, or a tadpole, some underwater creature. Is there something I forgot?"

"Guess you might as well treat him the same as the others."

Lilith nodded and flipped to the inside flap of the file, and a piece of paper stapled there. "See here? I've done him up a contract too."

Sergeant Grant skimmed the standard crayon format and noticed an irregularity. "I hereby promise to do everything within my natural ability to find you — Benjamin — and return you to your parent."

"How come it doesn't say 'parents'?"

Lilith took back the file, perplexed.

"Huh . . . interesting."

She reached into the top drawer of her desk, into a baggie filled with chocolate-covered raisins, and popped a handful into her mouth. "Yesterday," she began, sounding as though she were speaking through a mouthful of marbles, "I was walking home across the university campus — love seeing all those young folks heady with knowledge — and I was concentrating on his name, *Benjamin. Benjamin.* Suddenly I felt this sharp sway, like I was a magnet and he was pulling me close for a bear hug. I followed it to King's College Circle, walked in and out of the English department, Sigmund Samuel Library, the Medical Sciences Building, and all the while my eyes were tingling. But then, just as fast as my intuition arrived, it was gone again." She looked up at her boss. "I know what you're thinking, but I'm telling you, I'm getting closer day by day."

"Yes." Sergeant Grant placed his hand palm down on two unopened files. "But these aren't even started, Boot. It's hard for me to be enthusiastic about someone who doesn't exist. On paper, at least."

"Now he does," Lilith said. "I just showed you. He was my very first missing child." She tossed the file into her drawer, pulled her dress down at the back, and sniffled. "But that's okay, I'll continue, on my own, unsupported if I have to."

"Aw, don't start that again." Sergeant Grant shifted his weight. "You know I'm not saying you shouldn't keep trying, I'm just saying — "

"He's not a priority."

"He's not my responsibility, is all. You know the drill; I've got no jurisdiction on unauthorized searches."

Lilith picked up the basketball which had landed at her feet. She moved to the door, waved to her pouty daughter through the small window, and stuck the foam basketball to the Velcro patch inside the hoop. Then she turned, opening her arms wide, a guardian angel with invisible wings.

"Lucky for Benjamin, then," Lilith smiled a certain smile. "*Everywhere* is my jurisdiction."

Lilith and Lemon exited the station together, hungry and anxious for home. The streets were busy for 6:30 on a Friday. Rush hour was winding down and a streetcar inched forward in traffic stuttering breaths between Volkswagen bugs and Jaguars, grumbling as it picked up speed, and then slowing and hissing like an old man passing gas. The determined *click-clack* of high heels on sun-baked pavement accompanied chatty voices, and the smell of fried chicken from a nearby fast-food chain caused Lilith's mouth to water.

Lemon skipped and hopped ahead on the sidewalk, a letter to her father stuffed inside the breast pocket of her new overalls. Then she slowed and waited for her mother to catch up before crossing Dundas Street. Hot sun melted tar on the road and mixed with a dark, thick cloud of exhaust. They crossed hand in hand, and on the other side came to an ice-cream vendor who'd parked his bike. Lemon wanted a cone so Lilith bought one: vanilla. After Lemon had licked and swallowed a mouthful, she handed the cone to her mother for safekeeping.

"Mumma, hold this?" She darted off without waiting for an answer.

"Stay close!" Lilith called out.

In the blink of an eye — that's all it takes for your heart to disappear.

Lilith had always worried that her daughter would vanish like so many others, that one day she might find Lemon's bedroom void of music, no pages turning in colouring books, no giggling as she settled down to sleep. And then Lilith's entire life would be empty of meaning. So whenever they were out in public Lilith was alert. In fact, if Lemon hadn't been as old or as stubborn as she was, Lilith would have had her in one of those harnesses children wear at the malls or in downtown parks. Sure they look like they're captive little animals with their freedom curtailed, but why do people take more care with pets than with children?

Lilith had purchased a harness with one of her first paycheques from the department, then kept it in the hall closet until Lemon was old enough to walk. When she was two, Lilith had tried coaxing. She jiggled the harness as though trying to entice a puppy towards its first leash. "Mumma's got a surprise. You wanna see what Mumma's got?" Lemon was seated inches from the TV screen, transfixed by her favourite show. H.R. Puffinstuff danced like a hamburger bun with legs, his arms flailing. Lilith stepped closer, leaned down and jiggled the harness once more. The silver clasps made a distracting sound on the parquet floor. "Look Babygirl, a new toy!" Lemon pushed herself up onto her feet, hands first, while Lilith made encouraging let-me-get-you-to-do-what-I-want noises. "Oooh, look at you. Aren't you Mumma's smartest, sweetest little girl. Yes you ARE!" She clapped her hands together the way she did with Lemon on her lap, playing pat-a-cake.

Lemon stumbled over too quickly, tripped, and landed at Lilith's feet. Then she reached up to grab the material of her mother's housedress and with the help of Lilith's free hand, stood again. She reached for the blue harness dangling in front of her.

"See, see, see?"

Lilith slipped one of her daughter's arms through the strap. By now Lemon was wailing full blood-curdling, bone-chilling screams.

"Noooo! No want, no want, no want!" and squirming away with all her might.

"This is how we play. Hold still, Babygirl."

Lemon resisted, leaned back and craned her neck. The harness was stiff, its strap digging into her young skin and leaving a red welt. The entire cast of "Puffinstuff" gathered to march in a circle and sing the program's theme song. Lemon tried to walk away from her mother in her own circle, but Lilith refused to let go. They pulled and strained. Lemon hurried faster and faster, screaming.

"Noooo! No want!"

Lilith tried to sound cheery.

"Yes! That's good Babygirl!" But, as she whirred around one last time, Lemon stopped dead in her tracks before the television. The image of a cackling woman dressed in a black robe, black hat and with a long, green, warty nose appeared on screen and Lemon pointed directly at Witchy-Poo.

"Mumma bad! Mumma bad!"

Lilith gasped and let go her grip.

Lemon fell forward on the floor and struggled out of the strap. She stood with her back to her mother, recovered quickly and waved as the credits rolled.

"Bye-bye," she said. "Bye-bye."

Lilith stepped out onto the balcony, closing the door tightly behind. She placed her hands on the rail, looked up at the clouds rolling past and took a deep breath. Even though she was special, in some ways her daughter was like everyone else's: always at risk of being lost. And for the first time Lilith realized there were limits to what even she could do about it.

Heading along Dundas after work, she felt the setting sun midway down her back and allowed months' worth of finds to melt away. The Eaton boy. Emily Chung. Even the Baffi case in which young Tommy had been lost in a suburban shopping mall while his mother tried on shoes. Lilith inhaled with gusto, took another lick of Lemon's ice-cream cone and rewarded herself for a job well done.

Lemon thought summer was the best time of year — except for her allergies which flared because of ragweed and pollution. And except that late August, after the wedding season, was when Jan's father always got laid off his job at the catering company. Nevertheless, Lemon enjoyed going barefoot around their apartment, pretending the cement balcony was a beach, sunbathing with Jan, and Jan telling her about the latest book she'd read. Lemon liked it that her best friend practically moved in as soon as school ended. Inside the apartment it was so humid that sweat rolled down her underarms, snaked under her underdeveloped breasts, and made her feel like a sweaty infected piece of fruit left too long on the kitchen counter.

"Gosh darned humidity!" Vivian Hines said, just about every time she came by to collect Jan. "Holy smokes, Lilith. It's sweltering in here. How can you stand it?"

"Oh, Viv, we manage."

"If it wasn't for all these plants I bet you'd run right out and buy a box air conditioner like the rest of us."

Before Lilith had a chance to speak, Jan poked her head out of Lemon's bedroom.

"Lilith likes it this way," she said. "And so do I." Then Jan wiped beads of sweat from her forehead.

Vivian Hines waved, indicating that her daughter was meant to follow.

"All right Janet, you don't want to overstay your welcome. Your father is beginning to wonder if you're ever coming home."

Jan's shoulders sank.

"Please Mrs. Hines," Lemon said. "*Please* can't she stay just one more day?"

"We like having her," Lilith added. "She's no problem at all."

"One more day then," Vivian agreed. "But call me if you change your mind." And that's how it went every few days, until fall rolled around.

Lemon was beginning to have serious doubts about her mother's profession. Not only was Lilith always busy looking for some invisible presence and missing out on Lemon's activities, but Lemon had noticed that other people seemed to find the work dubious. Odd. And most of all, it was hard putting up with Benjamin this and Benjamin that; Lemon was sick of hearing about him. Her mother couldn't even prove he was real; he was just one of her hunches, she said. Something she had to do but didn't know why. Without an official missing persons report, Lilith had only an enduring feeling. She couldn't remember a time when she hadn't been looking for him, Lemon knew. "Missing children are like misplaced heirlooms," Lilith often told both Lemon and Jan. "Watch and see. One day, I'll remember where Benjamin has been put." She refused to give up, so he haunted them all like a ghost who lived in the walls.

Despite her private resentments, Lemon knew better than to hope Benjamin would ever entirely go away. Over the years she'd learned that people who are out of sight are usually always on your mind — like her Grandma Connie and Granddad Jack, all the way across the country. And like her father — wherever. As she grew, Lemon wished instead that Lilith would figure out where Benjamin was as soon as possible, so she could have her mother all to herself for once.

Walking home from 52 Division, Lemon wore a short-sleeved white T-shirt and the purple overalls her Grandma Connie had sent for school. It was the kind with one red button and one orange button, the kind that went well with her complexion.

"How are your new runners?" Lilith called out.

"They run good," Lemon answered, dashing even farther ahead, and chanting.

"Step on a crack."

Hop.

"Break your mother's back."

Skip.

"Step on a line."

Jump.

"Break your mother's spine."

Lemon calculated each step precisely while Lilith sauntered, unaware that with each foot forward her daughter was busy saving her life. Then Lemon stood still, looked down at her new white sneakers with the green shoelaces, and at the sidewalk. *Coast clear,* she thought, before she jumped.

Lilith licked what was left of Lemon's ice cream, and held it out.

"You want this or not?"

Lemon stopped once more, twisting her body around without moving her feet.

"I want it." She headed back towards her mother. There was barely one scoop left, but she didn't say a word. Instead, she licked the outside of the remaining ice cream using her system — from the bottom of the drip up — so it never softened enough to fall off. (Once it happened and once was enough. Spumoni and disappointment splattered across the sidewalk and Lilith hadn't seen her eat anything green since.) Now ice cream melted down the side of the cone, her tiny wrist, and even her bare arm. "Yuk!" Lemon said, trying to catch the drip before it worsened.

Lemon tried to eat her ice cream as fast as possible while she and her mother passed a newspaper box. Psychic's Lucrative Hoax was plastered across the front page. Lilith glanced over Lemon's shoulder. "Clairvoyants are in style," the journalist had written. "Like bellbottoms last year and tie dye in the Sixties." She took Lemon's hand, and pried her away. "Never mind gossip!" But Lemon enjoyed newspapers — all named after elements from outer space. *Star. Sun. Globe.* She read comic books as well, and all the Judy Bloom novels — *Blubber* was her favourite. She even read the same books as Jan, so newspapers were a cinch.

Lilith and Lemon moved on to the corner of Dundas and Bathurst and waited for the traffic light to change. Cars lined up in all four directions. To the south, the classrooms inside the new community centre were vacant and dark; the only movement from the property came from the basketball court where a few teenagers were leaning on their ten-speeds. Looking north, they could see all the way to College Street, the view lined with storefronts and houses, and the streetcar track stretched out like an elastic band, all the way to Bloor Street. *Just one ride,* Lilith thought. *Another short walk over to Christie, and we'll be home.* Lemon tapped her sneaker on the ashen pavement and turned back towards the newspaper box. A chill ran across her bare arms.

On Bathurst the streetcar slowed to a stop and the heavy doors folded open. Lilith and Lemon lined up, and then boarded. Lilith dropped two tickets into the dispenser — one adult's, one child's — and they moved to the back of the car. Lilith squeezed past backpacks and bags of groceries in the aisle while Lemon looked at her slightly pigeon-toed feet and held onto the pole for balance. After descending the streetcar at Bloor Street, mother and daughter approached their apartment building. It stood long and grey and twenty-three stories high, like a giant accordion extended on its side. Each unit was fronted by a steel balcony and windows. A stone path had been laid from the sidewalk to the doors. Grass stretched around the sides and back of the building, like a crescent-shaped area rug. Lemon dawdled and crunched down on her sugar cone, still silently contemplating clairvoyance.

She knew better than to ask, or to push too far with those types of questions. Lilith could become angry very quickly if her skill was challenged. When her mother was irritable Lemon knew because her forehead would wrinkle and tension, even from finding somebody, collected around her eyes. You'd think that when Lilith *had* closed a file for good, had had that final meeting with Sergeant Grant and the family and been validated, that her shoulders would drop in relief, but it wasn't so. Lost or found, solved or unsolved, Lilith's cases came home with her, and Lemon knew it. She smiled widely with a full mouth of vanilla, teasing. Then she stuck out her tongue which was covered in ice cream and brown cone bits. Two women, one in a silk houndstooth pantsuit and the other in a paisley sundress, passed them on the street and glared, registering disapproval with each other and then with Lilith, who burst out laughing. She was proud of what a happy child she'd raised, proud of what she knew in her bones. "Benjamin's a year older than you," she said. "Remember?"

"Uh-huh." Lemon took another bite of her cone and evaluated the sidewalk. She vaulted over a pile of dog droppings, and resumed stretching her tongue as far into the base of the remaining cone as she could reach. She sucked the last dollop of ice cream into her mouth. Then, with her foot across a crack in the sidewalk and cheeks so full they looked as though they might cause her to levitate, she tried on her most serious expression. Suddenly she had gigantic watery eyes, and a creamy river gushed out the sides of her mouth. "Mumma," she whispered. "Would you find me if *I* was missing?"

Lilith stopped smiling. Stopped walking.

"Don't you ever talk like that!" she said, shaking her daughter by the shoulders for the very first time. "'Course I would." She clasped Lemon's free hand tightly and turned down the path to home. "With me holding you this close," she added, swinging open the glass doors of the apartment, "*you* will never be lost."

Not ten seconds later, Lemon remembered the letter she'd folded and put in her pocket. She released her mother's hand just as the elevator door was closing, squeezed through the opening, ran back outside, looked both ways and crossed the busy street. "Babygirl!" Lilith called out, pushing frantically on the elevator button. Outside, alone, Lemon opened the trap door of the mailbox and tossed in her letter. She stood on her tiptoes and peered in to make sure it had been swallowed. Then she smiled, closed the flap and crossed the street again, herself full of hope.

That same night Jan knocked quietly at their door. Lilith had heard something faint and thought maybe Lemon was up late drawing or writing in her diary. But then she heard it again and the second time it was clearer. So she'd looked through the peephole and quickly unlocked the deadbolt and the chain. She was startled by the sight of the little girl's swollen eye and the blood seeping out from beneath a crooked Band-Aid.

"Miss Boot. Could I please stay the night with Lemon?"

"Sure Baby," Lilith said, opening the door and finding words. "'Course you can. C'mon in." The only children she'd seen in this condition had come to her in terrible visions. Now here was Jan, three-dimensional and shuddering. Lilith stepped aside and Jan headed directly to Lemon's bedroom at the end of the hall, where she stood outside fighting back tears. I can't let her see me like this, she thought. I can take care of myself. I can. Jan felt herself melting, as if soon she'd be nothing but a puddle in the middle of the floor. She clenched her fists.

"Let's get you cleaned up," Lilith said, leading her away and into the bathroom.

Jan sat on the toilet seat while Lilith rummaged under the basin for her first-aid kit. Jan tried not to flinch as Lilith slowly peeled off the Band-Aid, and pushed her bangs out of her eyes to inspect the wound. "I bet it's terrible living in your apartment on nights like tonight," Lilith said. Jan looked at her feet. "But pay your Daddy no mind, doll. You're small so it's frightening." Lilith dabbed the exposed cut with witch hazel. "I know." A single tear rolled down her face and Jan, seeing it, felt disgusted with her own diminutive frame, the useless female body that she felt confined her to such a fate.

"I want to grow to be six feet tall," she told Lilith. "I want to have muscles. I hate being a girl!" Lilith kissed the wound after she'd applied a fresh Band-Aid. She placed one hand firmly on top of Jan's head as though sheltering her from nearby grenades.

"Oh, I know," she said. "But being a girl's not the problem. Mark my words, one day you're going to be bigger than him.

Big like me, maybe. And smart — *so* smart — and when that happens the whole world will gather round you with love. Know why?" Jan shook her head but listened as though Lilith were speaking life jackets and she'd been found treading water in the lake for hours. Lilith held Jan by the shoulders. "Because each of us is allotted so much love in a lifetime, and for some reason the universe has been saving all yours up for later."

"I hate him," Jan whispered as she was pulled close for a hug.

"That's okay," Lilith said. "When you get big enough you'll outgrow that too."

Jan felt warm and safe next to Lilith's soft, yielding form and she was relieved, but not because she believed the day would come when her father would change. She smiled because the notion that she could grow up and be like Lilith was indeed something to look forward to. Jan vowed right then to someday repay Lilith's kindness in the best way she could imagine. I don't know how, she thought. But *I'm* going to find Benjamin.

"Thanks, Miss Boot," she said, wiping her eyes on the sleeve of her pyjama top.

"After all these years, Janet Hines, when are you gonna call me Lilith like everybody else?" Jan just shrugged. It didn't seem proper calling Lemon's mother by her first name. Seemed to her that Lilith deserved all the respect she could get.

In the morning when Jan had gone home, Lilith stood in the middle of her one-bedroom apartment between the living and dining spaces, determined to ensure that her own daughter was happy and carefree. On the wall behind her was an unframed poster from the Royal Ontario Museum. Tyrannosaurus rex. Lemon's third-grade field trip from earlier in the year. To the left, on top of a kitchen stool was a large potted jade. Sprawling from there all the way across the living-room wall was a ledge lined with clay pots, filled with violets. A glass fishbowl with two very blanched goldfish sat at the end of the ledge. Below, on the floor, was another shelf fashioned from red bricks that Lilith had gathered at construction sites, and two wooden planks she'd picked from the garbage out behind her building. The planks were now painted royal blue, as was her stool and the wicker laundry hamper overflowing in the well-lit hallway. That shelf too was covered in potted plants. Mostly begonia and cyclamen. There were no curtains covering the windows, nothing maintaining Lilith's privacy when she changed her clothes or slept. "Privacy doesn't exist," she told anyone who commented. "Not for folks like me."

The dining area was smaller than a standard-sized room, but more spacious than the galley kitchen which opened into both the hall and the dining area. The table in the centre was made of steel and yellow Formica. The four chairs were also made of steel and had glittery yellow plastic seat coverings to which, in summer, Lemon's bare legs stuck. A ceiling lamp hung above the centre of the table from a long thick chain. Its shade was made of red crepe paper and had been purchased in Chinatown years before. If the bulb was left on too long, the lampshade overheated and a faint odour of burning paper filtered throughout the apartment. Its red tassels hung from the rim and were faded to a muted version of the original. At night the light bulb shone through it, casting a soft rosy glow upon any face sitting below eating or reading. But now in the afternoon sun, the lampshade merely hung against an eggshell white backdrop like a drop of blood on a clean lab coat. Lilith waved and called out for Lemon's attention. "C'mere, Babygirl." Lemon looked up from where she was curled into the armchair, reluctant to tear herself away from her studies on *Astronomy for Beginners.* Her mother waved once more so she put down the library book and slumped off the chair, eyes bored.

"What, Mumma?" Lilith was excited, her hair extra-curly because of the humidity.

"Turn around. That's it. Now, close 'em."

Lemon squinted. Maybe a letter from her father had finally arrived!

"What is it?"

"No peeking!" Lilith said.

Lemon tapped her foot on the floor. She barely noticed her mother's sneakers step across, but knew Lilith had retreated and returned when she heard the rusty squeal, rattle and choke of something heavy being wheeling across the dining-room floor. Lemon smelt Murphy Oil Soap and Windex. Her heart sank. Oh no, she thought. What now? Lemon wasn't fond of her mother's surprises; she never knew how long they would last or how she'd be expected to react. It was too much pressure.

"But I already had my birthday," Lemon said, disappointed. Obviously there was no mail. "Can I open them now?"

"Not yet. Be patient."

Lemon's eyelids fluttered while she waited. Her mother often surprised her, but not with the sort of offerings she would share with Jan on a sleepover, not like the piñata she'd received from Mrs. Hines on her birthday, or a new pair of black patent leather shoes from Grandma Connie. Now those were the kinds of gestures Lemon held her breath for. Bragged about. What if she didn't like it? What if this proved worse than the matching tartan jumpers Mumma had brought home last year? It was bad enough Lilith wore hers to the precinct, but to make Lemon accompany her in public was, in her daughter's opinion, truly criminal.

Lemon respected Jan's mother. She wore well co-ordinated outfits and kept a sparkling clean household. She said "please" and "thank you," always with a smile, and she never got angry if the superintendent locked the laundry room when she was late. Vivian Hines, unlike Lilith, did her laundry during the designated hours: 11 a.m. to 8 p.m. She understood what was expected. She wore an apron and when she baked cookies, she didn't eat them all before Lemon could get to them. And she said things clearly and with conviction, such as politics was better left for men. Like drinking. And war.

Lemon had observed Mrs. Hines many times, as well as other women from the floor as they dropped garbage bags down the incinerator chute. She fit in. All the wives made reference to their husbands by rolling their eyes in allegiance and understanding. Lilith only rolled her eyes about work or about Lemon. And she never took out the garbage — that was one of Lemon's jobs. So, for reasons of guilt by association, Lemon desperately wanted her mother to try a little bit harder to become like everyone else. Unfortunately, sometimes Mrs. Hines made a point of reminding Lemon that it couldn't be so. "Does Lilith still have that little job with the police?" she'd ask, and Lemon hadn't yet learned to hold her shoulders high. Yes, Mumma still works for Sergeant Grant, she'd think. Yes, she's a bit of a weirdo with poor fashion sense. Yes, I'm the daughter of a clairvoyant and therefore a total social misfit. Yes, yes, yes! Lemon conceded defeat and crumpled into herself like a balled-up piece of paper.

And as time went on, she found many excuses to avoid her mother having contact with the neighbours. On one particular afternoon as she and Lilith prepared to do a grocery shop, Jan finally protested.

"You don't like me any more. Is that it Lem? You never want me around — not even when your Mum invites me herself."

Lemon looked at the floor to find anything with which she might identify — a crack in the parquet, or a spider accidentally crushed by a boot.

"Aw, I just didn't think it would be much fun for you. I guess you can come if you like." Jan brightened immediately and enthusiastically looped her arm through Lemon's.

That day, Lemon spent the next two hours chewing the inside lining of her cheek as she and Jan pushed the grocery cart along each aisle at Safeway in amazement, and Lilith taste-tested almost every product they intended to purchase. Bags were opened and sat in the child's seat of the grocery cart while Lilith chewed on rows of Oreos or Fig Newtons. Transparent bags filled with sunflower seeds and grapes balanced on top of canned goods and were consumed at a rapid rate, subtly, and always with a view to the large round mirror hanging at the end of each aisle. By the time they reached the cashier, half of what had been in their cart was already eaten and the partially emptied containers discarded on a nearby shelf. Lemon was so humiliated that she couldn't speak, but Jan, assuming her best detective-inspector persona, appeared to be having a grand adventure.

"Your Mum's *so* cool," she said afterwards, her stomach aching from too much sugar. "Mine would *kill* me if I stole." Lemon knew better than to object. She'd heard it from Lilith on many occasions. "It's not stealing if you haven't left the store, Babygirl!"

Lilith's voice jolted Lemon back to the present.

"Lemon? Hey? You can open your eyes now."

"Huh?"

"Lemon!" Lilith had repeated herself three times. "Open your eyes."

"Oh." Lemon lifted her eyelids slowly; her cheeks squished together, shoulders hunched up to her ears.

"Well Jesus Lem, you look like you're about to be hit in the face — for Chrissake, take a good look and tell me wacha think?"

Before her stood a floor-length oval mirror set in dark mahogany. Each of its four legs sat on casters.

"Where did you get that?"

Lilith dusted the top with a tea towel.

"It belonged to poor old Mrs. Brant from the second floor."

Lemon placed one hand on her hip, raised one eyebrow.

"Does she know you *borrowed* it?"

"Never mind, smarty-pants." Lilith said, as she tucked a strand of hair behind an ear. "Mrs. Brant's dead now so she knows, I figure. And Mr. Brant said it was in her family for generations but he can't stand to look at it any more. Reminds him too much."

Lemon circled the mirror cautiously, examining the back where the faded indigo ink of the tradesman's stamp was printed. She ran her short fingers along the smooth finish of the wood and felt the faint residue of the soap her mother had used. She leaned in and breathed deeply. *Clean.* Then she walked all the way around until she was staring directly into the sparkling mercury glass. It really was beautiful. Not for sitting or sleeping, not for ironing, not for any reason, it just was. A luxury.

"So, we can keep it?"

Lilith nodded.

"Where are you going to put it?"

"In *your* room."

Lemon gasped. Swallowed hard. Her chest ached. She'd never seen anything so lovely, and it was hers? She would set it in the corner where the sunlight could reflect back, illuminating her entire bed. She would watch herself articulating and practise sitting properly — standing without ever uncrossing her legs like a lady should — like Mrs. Hines. She would study herself and learn to be whoever she wanted. It was perfect.

"*Thank* you, Mumma." Lemon wrapped her arms around Lilith's thick waist. This was the best gift she'd ever received. I want to be just right, she thought, barely able to contain her excitement.

"I want to be perfect when I finally meet my Dad."

"Your who?"

Lemon bit her lip.

"Anyway," Lilith said, changing the subject. "Come stand beside me and take a hard look in there." She gestured towards the glass where Lemon regarded her own image. "See your curls, how they jump out like grasshoppers from a cornfield?" Lemon was growing impatient once more.

"I see them."

"Now look at your eyes."

"Uh-huh?"

"You see mine?"

"Hmm."

"They're the same."

"Oh *Mumma*."

"And your tiny hands . . ." Lilith held Lemon's hand in her own and lifted the chubby arm for them both to see. "Only a few inches shorter than my own." Lemon was annoyed now. Why did her mother make such a big deal out of everything?

"No they're not." She retracted her arm gruffly. "They're very different!"

"Think so, eh?" Lilith gently cupped Lemon's face by the chin, and returned her daughter's gaze to the mirror. "Oh,

Babygirl, when will you learn? Never confuse what you see here." Lilith touched Lemon's temples with her fingertips. "Never confuse what's in here with what other people want you to see."

Our orderly at Bridgewater was a massive man — not six feet tall with shoulders like a linebacker; not an overgrown rutabaga with a hunched back or a protruding jawbone. No, I'd say Solomon was as big as he wanted to be. And the education he got from working at Bridgewater made him feel mightier and younger than his forty-some years. He impressed the nurses with an old-fashioned sense of chivalry. The kind Daddy used on Mother when they weren't busy fighting. Solomon opened doors and pulled out chairs for staff and patients. Some developed crushes, but as a rule, I don't think he believed in chatting up his co-workers. Behaviour like that could ruin a man's career.

Solomon did flirt with me though, if we passed in the hall and no one else was around. If I was carrying heavy bags of topsoil in the greenhouse, or dusting and organizing the books in the patient library, he'd sidle up with his shock of red hair, smooth down his matching moustache, and offer to be of assistance. He'd tell me he was on a coffee break. I learned early on to steer clear of the areas he commonly occupied during shifts. I kept my head bowed, and when he whistled at me, I pretended he was a helium balloon hissing, deflating, a shrivelled piece of rubber. Sometimes it was totally impossible to avoid him because he kept right on ingratiating himself to me no matter what.

"You're too good to be wasting yourself on a convict and a loony-tune. But flagrantly insulting an intelligent young lady such as yourself, pointing out her bad taste in company, just isn't in my nature."

"Good," I said, concentrating on reshelving books in alphabetical order.

"I just don't get what you see in Moffat. Her bones crack when she rises or settles into furniture, and her smile darts across her face like a mouse in and out of a stove-top burner. Nothing like you, with her delusions of grandeur and silly crown of glass."

"No," I said, placing the tallest books on the left side of the shelf. Mrs. Moffat looked bone-weary exhausted and I was pretty robust by comparison.

"Thinks she's upper crust too," Solomon said. "Now take Randy on the other hand. I like *her* attitude. Moving her over here to break apart the mutiny at the women's section of the prison didn't shut her up, no sir. Bridgewater hasn't made *her* any more docile. Shame about her appearance, though. Butt ugly. Looks tough, manly. I think she just needs a good fu —" He stopped mid-thought.

"What?" I asked, finishing shelving the A section and starting on B.

"A good friend," he said. "She needs a really good friend."

"Yes," I agreed. "Everyone does."

"I have to say, your pal is right on a few accounts. Shrinks for one. I keep my distance from them, with their snot-nosed superiority and their airy-fairy words. Tell me Lilith: How in hell are they gonna cure the mind by tinkering with the brain when the mind's a place for ideas like invisible luggage and the brain's an actual organ to see and touch?" I shrugged. "People aren't meant to be cured," Solomon said. "Curing's what you do to dead animals. Or to diseases." I nodded that time. It was the only occasion when I ever agreed with Solomon, but as usual he went too far. "Yeah there have to be defectives same as there have to be men for war and hunting and women for babies and homemaking. We need defectives to show the rest of us what we're moving away from as a species."

"I don't believe in defectives," I told him, realizing it just as I said it.

"I don't mean you, Lilith," he corrected. "Pardon me. I didn't mean you. I'm talking about the others."

He pointed to Jean-Ann who happened to be passing by the library door.

"Then you are talking about me," I said, smiling at her.

Oh sure I knew there were differences between us patients. 'Course I knew that. For most of my time in the hospital I was like a wet blanket when it came to having opinions, whereas Randy was proud with the majestic stature of a five-hundred-year-old forest. Too proud for her own good, sometimes. But we all had more in common than not.

"Lilith, I knew you were special right off," Solomon told me. "I saw it in the way you chose your words so carefully."

"I think people talk too much," I said, hoping he'd take the hint.

"Right. You're going places, a hard worker like you. If there's anything I can do . . . Something to make your stay more pleasant . . . you know, an extra pillow for your bed maybe?" Solomon reached for my hand and I pulled away, pretending nothing had happened. All you could hear then was the sound of hardback books being reshelved — *slip-slide, slip-slide* — until Solomon broke my rhythm. "Just remember, good ol' Solomon's right here rooting for you, cheering you on from the sidelines. I want what is best for you . ." He trailed off like he'd forgotten what he was about to say, then he came back full force and confident. "Like a father wants what's best for his child." I squirmed in my skin. Daddy wouldn't like to find me stuck listening to Solomon. "Don't get me wrong, Lilith," Solomon added. "You can get a little, you know, *odd* sometimes, and I'm not looking to talk myself out of a steady job — especially since there's a bunch of outside do-gooders agitating about unpaid labour here — union bullshit. It's just to say that I never needed a doctor in my whole life, and I doubt you do either."

"Thanks," I said, not sure if it was a compliment. I continued reading each title before I replaced a book on the shelf.

"Didn't even need one when I nearly sliced my hand in half and broke two fingers trying to fix my mother's old wringer washing machine. No Ma'am. Didn't call for help. Tended the injuries myself by breaking my fingers again, resetting them between casts made of popsicle sticks and elastic bands and disinfecting the point of a needle over the gas stove. Goddammit that stung! But then I calmed down, sewed my wound closed, breaking the thread with my teeth, tied it in a knot and wrapped my entire arm in a sling of torn sheets." I must've made a face.

"Don't worry," Solomon explained. "Afterwards I downed a bottle of whisky and obliterated the pain." He chuckled. "My left hand doesn't work as well as it ought to, but it's good enough." He flexed his hand open and closed. "And so are you."

I dropped my eyes, and noticed that up close his hands looked like two gnarly knots in a tree — ugly stumps attached to the ends of his arms. I could see a messy scar cutting across one hand as if he'd reached into a cactus bush.

Solomon pointed to an old book on the shelf right in front of me.

"Here, have a look at this one," he said, still trying to impress. "The author's name is Edwin Hubble."

"You read that?"

"Sure did. Real scientific too. Says time started millions of years ago."

"Time started?"

"Yeah, with a big explosion."

"Time can't start," I said, feeling my heart quicken.

"Well according to that book it did, and it'll end too."

"Really?" I shelved the last of the D section and started to tremble. "Are you sure about that?"

It's not like patients hadn't already figured out that Alice Woodward was impressed by Solomon the moment the penitentiary staff sent him to replace her former orderly. We could tell she liked his stocky build and his deep voice. Once we overheard Nurse Ford gossiping to another nurse that Alice had accidentally forgotten a personal note on her desk when she left for the day. On it was a sketch in blue pen, of Solomon's face, with a small heart underneath. Randy fished it out of the garbage pail when staff weren't around, and stuck it to the glass window of the nurses' station with a wad of Wrigley's spearmint chewing gum. "Alice the camel gets no humps," she sang, and we all had a good laugh.

Alice was relocated to Bridgewater after working for the British Columbia Insane Asylum. I think over there she was steeped in madness and by the time she was unleashed on us, she found it even where it wasn't. I don't want to be too hard on her though — nurses always get a bad rap. She tried to do her job well. Problem was, she seemed to think patients were nothing more than dirty windows who needed to be scrubbed spotless and squeaky clean on a regular basis. So, Alice liked everything about Solomon. Including, I bet, the callused palms on his Mr. Fix-it hands.

Solomon took great pride in his appearance. He was clean, crisp and ironed. He kept up with the latest fashions for men and saved his good clothes for off-duty hours. He polished his shoes and belt buckles and, for special occasions (like an inspection of our ward by the superintendent of the hospital), his set of gold cufflinks. He shaved to prevent his beard or sideburns from growing, but he kept a moustache that wasn't as well manicured as my doctor's or Mr. Moffat's. Solomon brushed his teeth once at the start of shift, once after every meal, and then again before he left to go home. He washed his face and hands a lot too, scrubbing with a strong soap behind the ears and on the back of his neck. He was afraid of all the germs he might contract on the job. Then I noticed that even if he had no plans to be out in public, he splashed his face with Old Spice cologne. You could smell him coming a mile away, and Mrs. Moffat often pinched her nose. Once Randy teased him about it.

"Nice perfume, Romeo."

Solomon stopped to defend himself.

"Personal hygiene is what separates men from the lower life forms."

"No shit?" Randy said, making her eyes wide and innocent. "I didn't know there was a difference."

Even Solomon had to laugh.

Maybe, stretching the imagination, he stood at five foot six inches tall. That's if he wore shoes with thick soles, which he usually did. Army boots to be exact. He bleached the collars of his shirts so they were never yellow. He wore starched shirts and jackets with firmly fastened buttons. The pant legs of his uniform with the perfectly straight seam rubbed together when he moved. We often heard him swishing along the corridor. *Swish, swish,* from behind, like old brooms on hardwood floors. *Swish-swish,* the sound of a thousand whispers in your ear.

His eyes, from across a room, were blue like bachelor's buttons: small, almost turquoise pin-dots against a yellowy-white background. They might have been beautiful to some folks but not to me. Some days they changed to a green hazel with specks of gold microscopically spotting the windows to his soul. His fingers were stubby, with wiry blond hair growing tangled on top of his knuckles. Probably his toes were the same. The nails on his fingers were thick, milky and ridged. Wherever Solomon was short he was also wide. Fingers. Calves. Thighs. Upper arm.

Solomon's slow, deliberate pace made him seem sure of himself. At least when he winked at me or smiled like a stupid old moose. And seeing as Alice Woodward felt safer with his brawn and bulk maintaining order, I didn't think he needed to feel any mightier than he already did, so like I said before, I tried to ignore him. Randy poking fun was a waste of breath, I always thought. We could've been talking about really important things like whether my marigolds would hold their own against the black-eyed Susans, or whether Mrs Moffat had seen her son lately. Instead we all spent too much time on Solomon — especially Jean-Ann Troper.

Jean-Ann insisted she was not a Canadian citizen, but a plantation daughter from the American state of Georgia, with long blonde ringlets and ruffled bloomers under her hospital clothes. It didn't matter at all to us that Jean-Ann was really a tall, broad-shouldered black woman with a Nova Scotia accent, or that her great, great-grandparents had been Canadian slaves. And it didn't matter that she had really bad breath and kept getting caught touching herself in the washroom. Down there. Everybody has problems.

Whenever Solomon made repairs inside Ward One he solicited helpers, and Jean-Ann was his most eager assistant. One rainy Saturday afternoon we were all hanging around the dimly lit hallway waiting like the impatiens we were, when Jean-Ann rummaged through Solomon's red tool box. She tried to pass him a tape measure or a socket wrench or some other tool, and each time he shook his head no and pointed to the screwdriver he wanted instead.

"Why it certainly is comfortin' havin' a man around the house," Jean-Ann sang in her best Southern belle drawl. Randy clutched her stomach and pretended to throw up, which only egged Miss Jean-Ann — as she demanded to be called — further into her feminine delusion. She purred, batting her eyelashes. "Come back tomorrow evenin'," she told Solomon, "and I'll fix somethin' tah eat." He tipped a pretend hat, blew her a kiss, and continued working. Randy scoffed and rolled her eyes. "Well, *you* may have forgotten your manners, Miranda," Jean-Ann added, swishing in her imaginary crinoline, "but I certainly have not forgotten mine. The way to a man's heart is still through his stomach!"

Randy looked at me and I looked at Mrs. Moffat and all three of us pealed into laughter. Solomon stood up and placed his arm around Jean-Ann's shoulder.

"Now don't worry," he said. "These here girls are just jealous, is all." Then he winked at us and Randy shot him the finger.

"I saw that!" Alice Woodward said, barrelling around the corner with her own finger aimed like a torpedo straight for Randy's face. "Now let the man alone to work."

Over time Alice assigned Solomon greater responsibility. Invited him to help out with medication prep and electro-convulsive therapy treatments. We said ECT for short, or just plain shock. Once when I was in the hall, Solomon was asked to restrain Jean-Ann after she refused to co-operate and hit another attendant hard in the face, giving him a nosebleed. There was so much commotion that I just stood there peeking around the doorway.

"That's it, hold her tightly," Alice instructed.

"Oh, no!" Jean-Ann screamed. "Please, please, please!"

But Solomon shackled Jean-Ann to the bed anyway, and pinned her shoulders down with both his hands.

"Nothing personal, Miss." He shoved a rubber mouthguard in Jean-Ann's mouth and then Alice stuck the electrodes over her temples and nodded to the technician to slowly crank the voltage. Jean-Ann's eyes were practically bulging out of her head.

"You won't remember a thing," Alice said, leaning over Jean-Ann's face. "You'll sleep it off and feel much better tomorrow." And then that horrible buzzing noise, like an electric saw, got real loud. Jean-Ann's body leapt up against the restraints and fell back down with each jolt. After two times, Solomon let go and Alice removed Jean-Ann's mouthguard. I saw she was unconscious. The technician wheeled the shock machine into a corner. "Nice job," Alice patted Solomon on the back like he was a farmer shooting a wounded animal. I slunk away unnoticed and shook all night.

Usually though, Solomon was more thoughtful in his treatment of us patients. He'd never wake up a whole room checking on just one person like some staff would. He'd never cause a commotion by checking blood pressure, heart rate and pupil dilation. (Sure nurses had to work, but they didn't have to be so noisy about it!) "Husha, Husha!" Mrs. Moffat used to say. "Keep it down!" But Solomon announced his arrival with the jangling of his heavy key chain, his hard boot heel on a polished floor, and sometimes, I swear, heavy breathing! "No rest for the wicked," he'd say, including himself in the proverb.

Solomon liked helping us out better than he liked working in the men's wards or back at the penitentiary where it was men, men, exclusively men. "Women are cleaner and meaner," he told us. And his preference for us showed in his positive attitude. I have to say, he demonstrated a respectable work ethic and he was never just standing around empty-handed like some staff. No, his arms were either full of laundry, tools and cleaning products or else he was busy lifting, sorting and organizing, keeping track of the humdrum necessities of life. He was the person to count on to hold incontinent patients upright on their mattresses or rub their lower backs, and he'd chuck waste from Mrs. Moffat's bedpan without a word. He was hardy, never flinched, and wasn't bothered if you were in a wheelchair, missing limbs or too doped to speak. He amused us with his stories about rafting up the coast through the Queen Charlotte Islands, and waiting tables at the Sylvia Hotel for extra cash. He treated patients the same as he would treat anyone else — that was the best thing he had going for him.

Still, the question of a mutiny might have entered all our minds at one time or another, and I'm not saying that it didn't. Just that nobody ever started a conversation by asking, "Hey, what do you say we jump this joint?" Well, okay, maybe Randy in her own words. Randy always wanted to overthrow the place in a blaze of gunfire. She wanted to be either Bonnie or Clyde and go out in a glorious stream of consciousness, she said. Bullets flying in all directions. More than anything, she wanted to be on record as the one patient who *never* gave in. So she argued about her diagnosis, haggled with Alice Woodward about the dose of her meds, and pointed out that she preferred yard duties to working in the factory and making those fucking plastic roses for upper-crust socialites from Kitsilano Beach, as she put it. She wasn't getting invited to a wedding any time soon!

Mrs. Moffat, on the other hand, thought resistance was a waste of time and effort, something that was more of a dare than daring, and something bound to stain the reputation of the monarchy. Resistance was entirely beside the point. After all, she'd chosen Bridgewater; it didn't choose her. Mrs. Moffat had a taste for attention from doctors and nurses. Tests and exams. Probing and prodding. It was all better, in her opinion, than no attention at all. Truth is, resistance would have meant living in a world that allowed folks like her to fall apart when they needed to. To fall, but onto soft pillows instead of into padded walls. Mrs. Moffat knew better than any of us. Resistance only comes when we can imagine alternatives.

Occasionally she was rebellious in small ways, and flushing patients' objects down the toilet was one of them. A toothbrush, a comb, a copy of *One Flew Over the Cuckoo's Nest*. Personally, I

think she still sometimes hoped to be swallowed by a tidal wave
— red or any old colour. Swallowed down the pipes. Crushed
and spat out in a cool, solitary, underground place where children didn't cry for impossible comfort, and husbands didn't offer
conditional acceptance. She felt ashamed for leaving her boy, and
in those moments of weakness I know she even wanted to
remove herself from the hospital. Trade her tiara for a crown of
thorns or, in her words, abdicate the throne in the name of love.
So when Mrs. Moffat felt that low she just thought, "We must
get out of this mess." And I've got to hand it to her, a toilet *is*
just another way out.

'Course both Randy and Solomon were more than curious
the morning we found Mrs. Moffat with her urine-soaked hair
spread like a gypsy's shawl on the bathroom floor, and one of the
ward toilets overflowing all around her. She wasn't unconscious,
just pretending.

"I've never seen this before," Solomon said. "Did she try to
go headfirst?"

Mrs. Moffat reached for her tiara.

"Plebe," she said, rising.

"Sewerside!" Randy bellowed.

"Sewerside," Mrs. Moffat whispered with a knowing smile.

Yep, I can safely say that Solomon didn't generally get in our
way or behave disrespectfully. He didn't plug his nose or roll his
eyes. He didn't think he was better than us, and he didn't make
moral judgments. I bet he never wanted to be the subject of one
himself. Sometimes Randy and Mrs. Moffat watched him
hoofin' it across the grounds, and in the sun his red curls glim-
mered from a distance. Randy said it was like the top of a light-
house warning us what was coming, slow and sure through the
fog. I never paid much attention, but then one afternoon some-

thing happened. Mrs. Moffat's hands dug into the window ledge until her fingernails left grooves in the soft wood. Colour drained from her face, making her look even more pasty than usual.

"Behold, a miracle!" she said. "See, see, what shall I see?"

Randy had to look for herself and I followed.

"A miracle?"

"A horse's head where his tail should be."

We peered out the window and found to our amazement that there really was a six-inch glow radiating off Solomon's body. Maybe it was just the dampness and the fog and the way sunlight filters through clouds, concentrating on one small region. Maybe the atmosphere was baffled by him too, and did-n't know what else to do so it gave him what he wanted: the pretence of a God. *It has to be a trick,* I thought. And I couldn't pull myself away from the window or what we all witnessed there: A wolf in sheep's clothing. A madman dressed as a miracle worker.

"Well, don't you know," Randy said, still glued to my side. "God has a funny sense of humour after all." But from then on Mrs. Moffat was certain, even though it wasn't logical or fair. She was certain that Solomon had a higher purpose.

"We are all here for a reason," she whispered. "Every one of us. Even him."

Another lazy afternoon I was sitting on the sofa in the visiting room, one eye on the window watching for my parents' station wagon and the other one on Mr. Moffat across from me with his son. He handed Mrs. Moffat a bouquet of common white daisies which she set on a chair, then held the boy out all jitters and full of advice. "Dori be careful! Here, I'm passing him to you now. Here I go. Careful!" The baby was wrapped so thick in his blankets that even if Mrs. Moffat *had* dropped him, he probably would've bounced! She clutched him to her chest, squeezed, and handed him back to his father just as fast, like even by leaving an imprint on his skin she'd be scarring him for life.

"Lilith!" Mrs. Moffat gestured to me. "Come meet our son."

I stood up and approached, not too sure about handling babies myself.

"Hello again." Mr. Moffat nodded instead of shaking my outstretched hand.

Mrs. Moffat tugged on the sleeve of my day dress.

"Lilith, *this* is my boy."

I looked closely at the tiny alert face and pudgy little hands, his only exposed parts. His eyes were the colour of mission oak, just like his mother's — no hint of red or gold. His hair was pitch black. He stared at me gurgling and cooing like a lovebird.

"Babyboy you're beautiful," I said, reaching out. Mr. Moffat tightened his grip, but just then the child wrapped his whole hand around my thumb and squeezed. "What a strong grip," I added, and Mrs. Moffat beamed. I patted her son's tummy and the pale blue cotton blanket was as soft as his pink skin.

"We should be going now, Dori," Mr. Moffat said, rising.

"Yes, going now," she repeated.

I stepped back and waved with my fingers until the baby shot me a toothless grin. "See you soon." Then I moved off and left them alone again.

It was only one o'clock and my folks usually drove up at the end of the day to avoid other parents. Daddy made it in like clockwork, but didn't stay long, just dropped off Mother's gifts, a can of mixed nuts, and occasionally a paperback romance novel. The nuts amused Randy. "Don't they see the irony?" she once asked, rummaging for cashews.

I didn't think it was funny at all. On visiting days I had no sense of humour. Families brought gifts and light airy outside energy, and made a point of talking in a breathy and uplifting manner, but it felt fake to me. Plus, I knew better than to expect Mother who'd been inside only a few times, not including the morning I was committed. She wrote cards every week and sent me presents, but hadn't come to terms with the fact that nobody listened to her at the hospital; hers wasn't the only opinion that counted about me any more. Just because I had names for it by then didn't mean I was getting special treatment.

Sometimes I thought I heard Mother while I worked beside Randy and Mrs. Moffat in the factory, or by myself, weeding in the greenhouse. Sharp metal-pronged words about my dishevelled appearance or my weak moral character. And I decided that I'd rather not have ever learned about mental illness because it only seemed to give her more ammunition. Daddy was different. He didn't speak about my diagnoses. Never mentioned them as they changed over time, except to say, "We don't know what else to do, Lil. I'd hate to bring you home now, watch you get worse."

Mother did make the drive to the hospital every weekend. She was as concerned as Daddy about my progress but instead of coming in and investigating for herself, she sat in the parked car with her purse on her lap, and her white seed pearl gloves crossed over, waiting. I could see her from the window at the far end of Ward One. I bet she was having the same conversations with God she'd been having all my life, about why he'd taken one child and left her another with defects. It had been years of waiting for signs, to find meaning in the death of my twin. By the time I was sent to Bridgewater, I think even if she never admitted it, Mother wasn't only angry with me — the sole survivor — Daddy for drinking his sorrow down, and even herself for not getting over it; she was furious with creation. That was the year she stopped saying, "God only gives us what he knows we can handle," and in the only way she knew how to cope, handed me back to God. Or my psychiatrist as it turned out.

Mother would have told herself she was right to pray for my improvement. She always said that prayer was the answer to most of life's dilemmas. She said religion was a practice that required nothing but an organized and concrete mind. That's all. Something I needed to learn. Mother had been tried and tested, worked to the bone, but through all my problems she'd remained steadfast and unwavering in her beliefs. That was faith, she said. Something that didn't change no matter what. I have to admit, even though I learned the hard way and Mother didn't mean it *that* way, she was the one who taught me to believe in the unseen. Even then she acted like one of God's messengers, placed here to spread truth. She would do it too, when Lemon was grown. But back then, she just sat in the Bridgewater parking lot like a holy tattle-tale waiting for her time to come. She had faith all right. Unfortunately not enough faith. Not the right kind of faith that she ever believed in me.

Looking back, I think Mother was afraid to think about what it meant to have a daughter who wasn't perfect. I must have inherited my abnormalities from Daddy's line, she said. From the Boots. Like my clairvoyance was a paternal inheritance, instead of a dowry. Maybe the other baby — her stillbirth — gave all his intuition to me and so doubled mine. Twin vision. Or maybe I soaked it up in the womb, emptied the other fetus before he even had a fighting chance! Someone must have done something to bring it on, this curse. It had to be someone's fault, didn't it? Babies who are kicking and turning one day don't just stop breathing. Mother needed someone to blame besides herself.

Minutes after my twin dropped into the world cold and limp, when it was my turn, Mother curled into as small a body as possible. "I can't remember anything except pressing my knees together," I heard her tell Mrs. Appleby on the way home from church one day. "Just thought, let me not go on. Let it be over with." Mrs. Appleby slipped her arm around my shoulder and pulled me close. I smelt her lily-of-the-valley perfume. "I do recall the doctor prying my legs apart," Mother added. "Saying pull yourself together and help me deliver this next child! And Jack was wailing: My son, my boy! He made a real scene from grief, Olivia. Shook his fist at heaven, dropped to the side of my hospital bed. Take me instead! he said. I pushed him off; never could stand to see a grown man cry."

Mrs. Appleby sucked her teeth.

"Terrible thing, losing a child." She knew because one of her boys never came home from the Korean War.

"I tried nursing," Mother continued. "But my heart wasn't in it and Lilith wouldn't take to the breast. Anyhow, I'm no cow, I thought. So after an hour I called the nurse back and had her bind my breasts. Jack went to work, I suppose. Disappeared when a husband . . . when a father was needed."

"Lumpy was the same for both my labours," Mrs. Appleby said. "Pretty much absent. A woman didn't used to be able to get much support in the children department. Sure am glad times have changed."

"Have they?" Mother asked. "I hadn't noticed.

Then Mrs. Appleby picked up her pace.

"Well Jack's found help for Lilith now, Connie. That's a blessing."

"True enough," Mother said. "Someone had to do something. They ask him to sign the paperwork, you know? Never even ask for my opinion. I give it anyway of course."

"Of course," Mrs. Appleby agreed. "A mother knows best."
"Amen."

"Amen," doubled Mrs. Appleby.

I think I understand better now, since I've had my Lemon. Mother just did what any reasonable woman might do after all that pain, after losing what she'd planned for. She prayed to have no more babies — no more — even though I was still inside her waiting to be set free. No more because they break your heart one way or another. Whether they're stolen by death or disease, or by somebody else, once they're gone they're just out of your reach forever. Then there's an invisible tear left in the lining of your soul. That's where the cold blows through.

The first time Randy and I *really* talked was in winter when we were being escorted to the factory to drop her off, and then to the greenhouse to drop me off for work. We were bundled up, scarves and mitts and boots with fleece lining protecting us from a damp wind blowing across the grounds. Nurse Ford and a nurse from another ward, whose name I didn't know, left Ward One with us — one ahead and the other behind. We walked along the skinny road lined with naked, barkless, arbutus trees and then down a small hill towards the main building. The whole Bridgewater property was covered in half an inch of snow which rarely happens there, and every step we took left a fresh, crunchy print. The Fraser River a half-mile in front of us was glassy and peaceful. I could see my breath in the air and Randy's cheeks and ears were bright pink. I hunched my neck into my shoulders and covered my mouth with the collar of the new wool coat Mother had sent with Daddy. "You should've seen me when they brought me in," I said. "What a wreck!" I told Randy about how my parents were sitting together in the corner of my doctor's office discussing what to do about my visions.

"Mr. and Mrs. Boot," the doctor said. "We have some excellent treatments."

I looked around the office for proof that he would be able to help me but his bookshelf was stacked with boring old reference material, his curtains were drawn and brown. His carpet, desk and even his suit and tie were unremarkable. I wasn't convinced.

"Excellent treatments?" Mother repeated.

"Yes we — "

"Bbbbut what's wrong with me?" I stammered, afraid of not having an answer as much as of getting one.

"Yes, what is it?" Daddy added. "I'm paying for this. I want to know."

"It's hysteria!" Mother blurted. "Madness! I knew it."

"Wisteria?" I repeated, confused.

Daddy put his arm around Mother's shoulder, and the doctor ignored me.

"Your daughter exhibits uncharacteristic symptoms," he said. "Non-specific pathology." He lowered his voice. "She's psychotic. I'm afraid I'm going to recommend she remain here for ongoing observation. So she may receive proper treatment and live without the hallucinations. Do you understand what I'm saying?"

"Wait!" I hollered, afraid to have that limb amputated. "I never said I wanted to live *without* them."

Everybody stared at me again, this time like I was the sorriest-looking lost puppy they'd ever laid eyes on. And then the doctor spoke.

"We are confident, Lilith, that with your uppermost cooperation and in good time, we can assist you in accepting your condition — managing it that is — and perhaps reassimilating. You might even get back to your studies."

He winked at my parents.

I looked for their eyes but both pairs avoided mine. All of a sudden my visions had a scientific name that sounded like it had leapt right up from the pages of a medical textbook and slapped me across the face. *Hysteria,* I thought and I looked right at Mother. Her lips were pursed like a schoolyard tease. *Na na na-na-na. Lilith's got Hys-te-ria.* I started to blubber. Mother turned away, pulled a tissue from her purse. Daddy looked at the doctor.

"It'll be okay, right?"

"In time, perhaps," my doctor said.

"Wait . . . um . . . they told me you were going to examine me, but no one mentioned anything about staying behind." Then the doctor handed Daddy an admission form and asked him to sign it, and my heart almost stopped beating. "Daddy?" I said, suddenly real quiet. "I want to go now." He squeezed Mother's hand for strength, looked at his galoshes and then spoke.

"Just for a little while, Lil," he said, signing the paper. "You'll only be away for a while."

So I moved up the chain of command fast.

"Mother, please? I promise to be good. I'll do whatever you want. *Please,* can't I come home?"

Mother looked up to heaven and then to me.

"Yes Lilith," she said firmly. "You may come home when the doctor deems you ready."

I jumped up and yelled right into their faces. "Just give me a hysterectomy, then! Take it out! Fix me if I'm broken!"

"Damaged." Daddy raised a shaky finger to make the point. "Not broken."

No one would answer my direct questions. It seemed like no one really cared. And I couldn't believe my parents were leaving me so I pulled my hair and hit myself in the face with closed fists.

Thump!

"Lilith Boot!" Mother said. "Calm down right this minute!"

"Wrong, wrong, wrong!" I yelled, hitting myself some more.

Daddy squirmed in his seat.

"Maybe this isn't such a good idea."

"Rest assured," my new doctor said. "Bridgewater is the leading research facility in the country on mental illnesses."

I stopped what I was doing. *Mental illness.* I rolled the words around in my brain to see if they fit. 'Course I knew what they meant; they meant I was crazy. A lunatic. No one had shown me what was wrong, even though my parents, my teachers and the women in Mother's church group all agreed there was sure something the matter, a shameful malady they called it. A burden to the family. No one told me directly but I'd seen it in their stares, heard it in the clucking of their tongues against teeth. And finally an expert had confirmed what everybody had been implying for years.

Randy made a fast circular motion with one of her hands to get me to hurry up and finish the story.

"Yeah, yeah, so what did you do next?"

"That's it," I said, hurrying beside her.

"What do you mean that's it? Didn't you try to make a run for it?" I shook my head.

"I didn't want to be stuck away in some ugly hospital, but I didn't know what else to do either."

"Well *I* would've caused some serious damage," Randy said, puffing up like a peacock. "I would have raised the roof!"

"We're both here now," I said. Guess it doesn't matter what we do. Besides, I didn't want to be banging my head on walls forever either." I leaned in while we crossed the grounds, cupped my hand, and whispered, "It's just that nobody listened to me otherwise and physical pain hurts less, you know?"

"Believe you me," Randy said. "I know."

"It's not so bad here," I added. "I'm used to it now. I get to garden more than at home and . . ." I leaned in closer again. "I've done things to be ashamed of."

"Well shit, who hasn't?"

"No, you don't understand," I corrected. "Really, really terrible things. Things that are dangerous . . . even deadly."

"There's dangerous and then there's capital-*D*, dangerous," Randy said, like she knew the difference. "You're nothin' to be afraid of."

"You don't think so?"

Randy sucked her teeth.

"No. You were tricked. They lied to you."

I shrugged.

What did Randy know anyway? She wasn't there for the last few months when I couldn't take a step outdoors without fearing I was trampling on something more vulnerable than me. Or when I flooded the garden. She wasn't there before that when I woke up with visions of danger and warning, so full of dread all the time with nobody to believe me. Nobody to understand.

She wasn't there. I preferred to think my parents were doing what was in my best interest. Even if it was true they made plans behind my back I didn't like to look at it that way.

"They all thought I was loony. How could they all be wrong?"

"Hogwash!" Randy said. "Shitsofrantic hogwash."

I tried to hush Randy's words then. You know? Not speak so loud that the nurses would think of us as trouble. I lowered my own voice.

"But I'm *not* normal. I do see and hear things. I'm not like anybody else."

Randy spat on the ground as we walked the path up to the factory doors.

"So? Special's not the same as abnormal."

"'Course there's something the matter!" I insisted. "I wouldn't be here if there wasn't."

"Suit yourself," Randy said. "It's your life."

"Yes, it's my life," I doubled. "Not yours."

Pause.

"No one ever believes me," I mumbled. "Not even someone like you."

Randy rubbed her hands together in front of her mouth to warm them.

"Someone like me?"

"You know," I said, backtracking. "I mean, I've heard . . ."

"Sure I do. Sure. You'll believe any fool thing you hear. But who's to say what you see isn't real? Is God any more real? Or the Tooth Fairy, or Santa fuckin' Claus?"

Both nurses stared at Randy, and she blew them each a kiss.

"Obviously you don't get it," I said, turning away.

I wasn't used to hearing women swear. I needed to talk so badly you've got no idea (worse than when you have to pee for hours but have to hold it), but I didn't want to participate any more. I'd tried not to believe them, but I *had* heard rumours about Randy from other patients. That she was some kind of evil, a "rabble-rouser," the most dangerous of all the women in the hospital — and definitely not to be trusted. People said she was sleazy and a liar and that she'd murdered her husband. Poisoned him or hacked him to pieces or fed him his own heart for supper. Maybe served it on a bed of greens!

The thing was, whatever she'd done, Randy was too sick to admit she even had a problem. I'd been told: First you had to accept the disease in order to get better and even then, some illnesses could never be cured. Fraternizing with severe cases like Randy would only interfere with *my* progress. So I decided not to tell her any more that day. I did need to talk, but mostly I needed to improve. Just then, we reached the factory doors and the nurse I didn't know led Randy inside by the arm while Nurse Ford continued with me on to the greenhouse. I waved goodbye and Randy called back through closing doors. "Don't believe everything you hear!" she said, bursting out laughing.

How was I supposed to know if she was serious? Did she mean my doctor? My parents? The garden when it called to me? Did she mean what I'd heard about her? All I knew for sure was that controlling the impulse was my main goal. The best to hope for. And even though my visions weren't sudden outbursts like the staff said, but colours and smells and sounds that gradually spilled into my awake brain, taking over, I was sure there must be warning signs if only someone would help me find them. Maybe, I still reasoned, my doctor could do that. As Nurse Ford and I passed the fire hall I just thought how queer, how queer that the whole world could so easily turn upside down. And most of all, I was overcome by smoke billowing out the garbage stacks, and by the lingering smell of all things discarded at Bridgewater.

By my second year I knew that hospital visitors felt safer arriving huddled together like nervous petunias. It took a while longer to figure out the difference between the ones who were new to Bridgewater, and the ones who'd been coming around for years. One afternoon while I waited for Daddy, Randy leaned up against the wall next to me, talking. "The first group I like to call virgins," she said. "Notice how they keep their eyes on the nurses and make a direct beeline from the front door to the visiting area without stopping." We watched as Nurse Ford unlocked the ward door and sure enough, a group of first-timers glanced over their shoulders. Tried to pretend they weren't afraid, but it showed anyhow, as if they weren't a hundred percent convinced they wouldn't be mistaken for patients, then be stuck for all eternity with us mumblers and head bangers and comatose amazons. Randy chuckled. "To a virgin everything looks bigger and more important than it really is."

"What about the others?" I asked.

"The veterans? Oh, they come and go pretty much unfazed."

Randy pointed to a couple of sisters visiting their third sibling. "See that? Watch 'em close. As soon as the doors open, veterans are off, trotting. Act like they own the place. Might stop in rooms to check if their loved one needs clothes, or see whether she has any new roommates, but usually they just smile and wave, calling us by our first names. 'Hi there, Gladys,' they say with a pricey tone only someone free can afford. 'Hello, Laurelai, how you doing today?'" Randy stepped away from the wall. "Veterans don't stick around long enough for questions or answers," she added, as she sauntered off. "They just keep moving till they find what they're after."

I ducked into the visiting room and took a seat. The room was a beautiful rectangle with a long wall of windows all facing south. Each square of glass was outlined in slate and was joined to the next one. The windows went on forever like that, season after season, square after square, and sometimes I thought I'd see a different landscape depending on which small pane I sat in front of. Looking out over the lawns and the fire hall beyond the main administration building, you could follow all the way to the Fraser River. A plant-covered ledge ran along the distance, mostly inch plants — or wandering Jews, as Mother calls them. That day I wished it was me sprouting off in search of more space, but I wasn't ready yet.

Outside, across the walk and down a slope, was the greenhouse where I worked digging roots, pruning and planting bulbs. My doctor called me "high-functioning" and relatively "well behaved" so he felt confident assigning me to the greenhouse because there were staff there too — nurses who doubled as gardeners or gardeners who doubled as nurses, I wasn't sure which. I thanked God or the universe or whatever there is out there that let me have my time back with the plants. A second chance.

Anyway, on Mondays, Wednesdays and Fridays I walked the grounds with an escort, taking in fresh air and enjoying the outdoors on my way to work. Saturdays or Sundays Daddy would take me for a walk and we'd head into the forest behind Ward One where the patient cemetery was, or pass by the car to say "hello" to Mother, or sit on the hill and look out at the water. I did most of the talking and I would tell him all about my new friends and, of course, the gardens. "That's real good," he'd say. "I'm proud of you." On Tuesdays I worked in the factory like everyone else, and on Thursdays when there was nowhere to go, I just sat in the visiting room gawking out the windows. But don't feel sorry for me. I was lucky. I was one of only twenty women chosen for the greenhouse, mostly because it was something Daddy said I could do well. The other fifteen hundred or so patients spent all their days in the factory buildings making plastic roses for civilian weddings and funerals. The roses were bunched and tied into bouquets and then sold to raise money for hospital research.

Ward One's visiting area had six small couches, each in front of the window and each with chairs in a semicircle in front of it. That way, families had some privacy when they came by. Us patients were always practising new ways to find privacy. We found it by reading or staring out windows or fidgeting and wringing hands, or by scribbling with chalk pastels. I had my imaginary walls and sometimes, my gardens. Mrs. Moffat had her queendom, and Randy could entertain herself for hours trying to annoy staff. We knew we needed to be alone and amused, and

125

those who didn't inevitably spiralled out of their minds like balls of coloured yarn rolling down the staircase.

Okay, I'll admit it: At first there *were* times when I wanted a label. A diagnosis to help me understand myself better. But it seemed like my doctor couldn't give me just one. I had two, then three, then he crossed them all out on my medical chart, and started over with the newer, more popular ones. Just when I was sure I'd disproved my most recent diagnosis, it suddenly boomeranged right back at me. *Smack.* Borderline Psychotic. *Smack.* Paranoid and Delusional. *Smack.* Unspecified mental illness. *The labels are punishments,* I used to think. *Serves me right, for being so hard to understand.* Mostly though, it just felt like we were all orphans who'd been given up for adoption and then assigned new names. "Here comes 'Hysteria L. Boot,'" Randy would say whenever I returned from the greenhouse. Or, "Look everyone, it's Schizo Moffat the First." In Ward One we were all a "Mrs. Feeble-minded so-and-so" or a "Miss Somebody, Depressive," so it felt good to laugh about it.

Actually, after all that time it was still impossible for my doctor to say exactly what was wrong. For a long time he was sure I was a victim of something called "latent onset" — which does not (like I first guessed) have anything to do with me not getting my period until I was older than usual. What it actually meant was that I'd been normal for a while, he said, and then suddenly at a later age started to show symptoms of a mental illness. But which one? He didn't know. Maybe, he said, I'd arrived with an altogether new problem. Figures. I've always been an original.

As time went on I got less anxious about it. I wasn't afraid of myself any more. Or stressed out. I just kept on like a jigsaw puzzle my doctor couldn't finish and I didn't mention that I still talked with plants and flowers, or that if I was lucky and it was quiet, I still sometimes saw the world in hazy shades of blue. I knew by then it was best to keep those things to myself. Besides, since I'd been put on meds, I hadn't had one vision escape. My doctor did report, on and off, that I was improving though. "Sure," Randy said when I told her. "'Course you feel better. Now you've got me."

When I was feeling lonely or powerless then, I didn't slap myself in the face or bang my head into walls any more. Instead, I thought about the greenhouse and practised breathing deeply; it was exercise for the soul. *Breathe. Breathe*, I'd think. Azalea. Gardenia. Poppy. But I never totally got away from the nasty label that stuck to Mother's tongue like she'd pressed it up against a frozen pole. *Hysteria*. That's Greek for the rising of the womb. I asked Nurse Ford about it and she explained that the doctors used to think there was too much pressure on a woman's internal organs. They thought our liver and spleen rose up like some kind of insane sun, and banged against our wombs. They used to think that's what made us crazy!

One day after I returned from the greenhouse, Randy pulled a piece of paper out of her dresser drawer and handed it to me.

"What is it?" I asked.

Mrs. Moffat climbed off her bed and came around behind to read over my shoulder. "The Bible," Randy said, poking fun.

I looked at the bold black type and saw the words "Hysterical" and "personality disorder" forced together. I scanned a list of symptoms on the page: "excitability, emotional instability . . . self-dramatization . . . attention-seeking . . . immature . . . self-centred, often vain." I jumped around the page. "Alterations may occur in the patient's state of consciousness . . . amnesia, somnambulism . . . multiple personality . . . *blindness* . . ." I threw down the paper like it had suddenly caught fire in my hand.

"Jesus, Christ!" Randy said, fetching it from the floor. "It's just a bunch of letters. Fine. I'll read it to you myself." She sounded out most of the words like a child just learning to read. The medical language made her feel small, stupid, I could tell because she turned beet red, which I'd never seen her do before, and then she stumbled and stuttered. After about a minute of trying but not making much sense to me, she crumpled up the page and threw it back down on the floor. "Never mind that," she said. "The point is, I know what it means."

Now it was Mrs. Moffat's turn to take up the paper and read.

"Here we go round the mulberry bush. The mulberry bush, the mulberry bush . . ."

"Great," Randy said. "One of us won't look at it, one of us can't read it, and the other one won't speak proper."

"I beg your pardon!" Mrs. Moffat uncrumpled the page. "*We* are speaking the Queen's English."

"Oh for crying out loud," I said. "What does it matter, anyway. My doctor doesn't think I have that. He told me so."

"Well, little Miss I-believe-whatever-I'm-told, I swiped it from *your* shrink's office."

"What?" I snatched the paper out of Mrs. Moffat's hand. "Let me see it again." It was from some doctors' magazine and at the top of the page it said "Hysterical neurosis," followed by "conversion" and "dissociative." I continued reading until I got the basic idea. "Seductive . . . inappropriate lack of concern . . . dependent." It went on and on until the page ran out. "Where's the rest?" I asked, turning it over.

"It's in the magazine, where I left it," Randy said. "What do you want me to do, tear the whole thing out?"

Mrs. Moffat shook her finger the way she did when Randy took things that didn't belong to her.

"But I am not those things!" I blurted. "I'm none of those things!"

Randy held her hands up in front of herself like I had a gun.

"Just thought you should know what these geniuses think up."

I looked for a date on the paper but found none. "Excerpt," it said at the bottom. "*Diagnostic and Statistical Manual of Mental Disorders*, second edition."

"Well it's probably old." I told them both. "Outdated. Things have changed."

Mrs. Moffat and Randy looked at each other in a rare instance that said, *Now who's deluded*, and then Mrs. Moffat returned to her bed, whispering under her breath.

"I do not like thee Doctor Fell, the reason why I cannot tell."

Randy started to laugh and pointed to the words "Book available 1968." I wanted to explode. Blood was smacking up against the insides of my skull, pounding through my veins faster than ever.

What does this mean? I thought. *What in the world does any of it mean?*

"It's not funny!" I hollered. "If these are the kinds of ideas they have . . ." I waved the paper furiously about my head, my voice growing even louder. "If they believe this, what do they really think of me?"

"Careful there Lilith," Randy said, reaching for my hand and pointing to the paragraph where it listed "over-reactivity" as a symptom. "I'm pretty sure that means you're acting the part!"

I dropped the paper, ran over to Mrs. Moffat's bed, reached under it and grabbed her bedpan. I threw it at Randy as hard as I could. It made a horrible, loud and hollow noise that echoed all the way down the hall.

"Woah!" she yelled. "Don't shoot the messenger." Then we all heard heavy boots storming towards our room. Randy stuffed the page down her shirt and folded her arms across her chest just when Solomon rushed in.

"Hey, break it up," Solomon said, like he was going to separate us.

"Hey, you're not at your *other* job," Randy shot back.

"You all right, Lilith? Solomon ignored Randy. "Did she hurt you? You can tell me." *Yes,* I thought. *The truth hurts.* But I shook my head.

"No. Nothing. Just dropped that."

Randy bent down, picked the bedpan up, and tossed it at Solomon.

"Catch," she said.

"What about you, Your Majesty?" he asked, grabbing the pan as it flew through the air. "Everything okay?" Mrs. Moffat dismissed him with one hand. "Well, just in case," Solomon walked towards the door and waved the pan like it was some kid's favourite toy, "I'm taking this with me."

I stood there crying when he left, my shoulders bobbing on either side of me like twin pistons. It wasn't Randy's fault, but I was so angry and it finally felt safe to lash out. From that day on, I knew I didn't have a mental illness. And I was disgusted that nobody before ever bothered to show me what it was the doctors saw when they looked at me. I was disgusted with myself too for not trusting my gut. And I felt like someone had died and all the mirrors in the world were covered in sheets but I didn't know. I was just the last, sad, lonely reminder reflecting back all that was missing. All that was wrong. I was not what most folks wanted to find in themselves. As soon as Solomon was out of earshot, Randy came and put her arm around me.

"Good," she said, while I cried like a baby. "Now, maybe you'll get a life."

You know something? I was crying rage and not just for me, either. For all us patients. It wasn't fair to look down at someone through a microscope or across the pages of a book, and decide they weren't worth listening to any more. Nobody should ever come along, dig up your roots with psychological assessments and leave you to sway like a medicated, free-standing stalk in a harsh wind. And I realized, once you know how to live with madness like we'd all been made to do, in it or surrounded by it, anyone would get intimate with their own demons. Sleep in the same bed with them like some kind of crazed honeymooner. Anyone under hard conditions would crack. Splinter. Split apart. It's nothing to be ashamed of. It's normal and when you know that, you're never the same again.

That afternoon I knew for sure: No matter how hard I tried to get people to like me, no matter how good I was at being believed about the visions or even how good I was at hiding them, I'd never be comforted or comfortable again, sleeping or waking or even standing, next to that other horrible disease, the one Randy always called sanity. And that was fine with me. I saw the trail of blood behind me. I saw marks on the patients of Bridgewater like every woman patient for all time had been made to march naked through the rose bushes. *Hysteria. Crazy.* I gave it up. It wasn't mine. No label was mine. By that name, or any other name, I was still Lilith Boot!

Both my roommates were real influences in helping me to feel better, Randy especially. There was just something about Randy's nerve, her not caring about her own sad situation, that kept me light. Plus, she had something to say about everything. "Love is for other people," she told me. "People who count." Or she'd talk politics, which really got Mrs. Moffat going. "The monarchy should be abolished. Just a bunch of pasty inbred bleeders."

"Excuse me," Mrs. Moffat corrected. "I believe the word you're looking for is hemophiliac!"

I hate to admit it but my favourite times during that second year were when Randy picked on Alice Woodward. Randy had a way of turning things around for us patients. "Now that you know sanity runs in families," she'd tease, "aren't you afraid to have kids?" Randy harassed all the staff into paying attention. I was entertained but I also found myself wondering how could I ever become a whole person? How could I hope for it if I limited myself and stayed closed to exploring and developing my natural capacity for seeing? What about madness? I started to think. What about my visions? I might like it better on that side. Not the right or the wrong side, just the leftover side of my brain.

My meds were reduced to only one pill as time went on, and except for gaining weight and slightly fuzzy eyesight and a ringing in my ears that still comes back, and the feeling that someone had poured concrete over the top of my brain, the side effects were gone. I was left like a hollowed-out maple tree; upright but empty. The pill kept me living more or less like a vegetable, or even like the plants I tended. That's fine if you're born a busy Lizzie, or a sweet william, but I was losing my ability to see, my opinions, and of course, I was losing precious time. Some days, I felt like I was drifting through space with nothing but a single rope tied around my ankle, connecting me back to earth. Other days that rope was attached to a very heavy iron anchor, dragging me all the way down to the sea floor. When I'd complain to Randy about it she just got annoyed. "So? Do something about it. What in hell made you happy before coming here?"

I thought about it hard. When I wasn't in school, I'd cleaned house, done the grocery shopping. I'd accompanied Mother to church group meetings during the week, and to services on Sundays.

"Come on," Randy prodded. "You must have done something for fun."

"Well on Saturdays I helped Daddy at the shop. Or later I worked in our garden." Randy held her pointer finger sideways under her nose like it was a moustache and pretended to be a famous doctor with a European accent.

"Oh, I zinc veer on to some ting."

I laughed.

"Zaturdaze und mine fadder," I said, playing along. "Yah."

But it made me remember how the Tick Tock smelt like furniture varnish and Brasso. And the way Daddy let me polish the silver. I rubbed the tips of my fingers together while I talked to Randy, remembering the soft felt polishing cloth. I enjoyed all the customers at the shop, Lumpy Appleby especially because with his club foot, people treated him like he wasn't quite normal either. Counting change back was easy as pie, and the feeling of the ivory and brass keys on the old cash register, pushing down heavy — *cha-ching* — was divine. "People buy the strangest things," I told Randy. "Broken pocket watches and green glass stumps fished out of lakes and rivers. And dolls with torn cloth faces. Quilts, rocking chairs, lots of mirrors. People buy a lot of mirrors, I remember thinking that. And dishes and tools. I loved the old gardening tools. If Daddy made enough sales, he'd let me take one home. He picked the name himself," I explained. "Tick Tock Antiques. Said his merchandise was timeless."

"What did he say about visions?" Randy asked, dropping the foreign accent.

"Oh," I sighed. "In the beginning, he told Mother I just had a wild imagination. 'She's creative,' he'd say. But that all changed."

"You need to listen to yourself again," Randy said. "No one else will."

"Yeah," I agreed. "You're probably right."

Then Randy wriggled her nose again.

"Mizz Boot. I vood prescribe a doze of retail therapy. Unfortunately shopping iz not permitted at Bridgewasser." We both burst out laughing so hard I had a stitch in my stomach for at least half an hour.

So, I started doing more of what I pleased after that. I massaged my feet, keeping them sensitive to the solid ground below. I hummed and sang songs, getting used to the sound of my own voice again. And more than ever, I let myself live for the varying textures and vibrant colours of the plants and flowers I took care of in the greenhouse. I adored the sensation of moist earth sliding through my fingers and the sound of garden shears, snapping and slicing through a confusion of weeds. That was healing. How wonderful to be able to touch all that life and know that because of me, more life would grow. The greenhouse was my place for penance.

I wanted to help Randy feel better too. Return the favour. But most of the time she was inconsolable. She objected to the flattening of her experience one hundred percent, which meant "no" to meds, "no" to shock, "no" to talking with the doctors. Anything the staff wanted to do Randy said was bad. She refused offers for an escorted walk on the grounds or an extra day of stimulation at the factory. She'd rather sulk in our room for weeks on end if it meant rejecting staff. The factory was boring, she said. "Same shit, different pile." And why should she work for free? There's no question about it: Anything given to

Randy at Bridgewater, no matter how pretty the packaging, was definitely forced on her.

Mrs. Moffat, on the other hand, was still grateful to have relief from the round and slippery planet she was always in danger of sliding off of. She'd agree to just about anything as long as the request started with, "Your Royal Highness." But me, well . . . I didn't fit into either category. I wanted more than what I'd left behind on Quebec Street — by then I had an inkling I deserved better. Problem was, my options were as foggy to me as my surroundings. I still saw where I'd come from clearer than where I was going. I was still waiting around for answers to what the future might hold. Waiting for the days to pass and for me to feel like a regular person again. Waiting for something I never really had. And while I waited and listened and watched, I started to suspect that there probably wasn't enough time left in the universe for any more waiting. If I was ever going to be happy, maybe I was just going to have to imagine the world the way I needed it to be.

Visiting days got harder after that. I was so impatient and grumpy. Visitors only planned ahead to their next visit; that annoyed me. And Daddy skimmed and pasteurized news before sharing. Like my system was too fragile for the truth! "Been out picking night crawlers," he'd say about the worms taking over the garden, or "The aphids are greedy this year." But he'd never tell me if they'd levelled my shrubs.

Randy was convinced that being included in the "reeeeel world," as she pronounced it, waving her hand in a circle at the side of her head, would help us all. Mrs. Moffat was sure it was the real world that had driven her to distraction in the first place, but I couldn't make a fierce distinction since I had always lived inside more than one.

Some of us refused to admit our unfair predicaments. Like Jean-Ann who dressed to the nines and plopped herself down onto a chair, waiting, waiting, and occasionally going back to her room to put white powder on her nose. (Sometimes it seems easier to change yourself than to try and change the whole world.) Or like Randy, refusing help, aggravating the situation like she was picking at a scab that wouldn't heal, but always feeling *she* was making the decisions. We had different ways of getting by and reacting to the hurtful world around us. Jean-Ann developed the habit of following other people's families through the ward, claiming them as her own. And so Mrs. Moffat was trailed whenever her husband and boy visited, and sometimes pinched in the arms, which left giant red welts. Other times, Jean-Ann blew her nose on Mrs. Moffat's shoes. All of this was an insult and Mrs. Moffat scurried faster and faster, making royal decrees as she fled. "Jean-Ann Troper!" she'd yell. "You are forever banish-ed!" Despite her orders, Mrs. Moffat usually ended up nervously holding her sweet boy with Jean-Ann practically breathing down the baby's neck and Mr. Moffat vowing never to return.

Visitors spoke to us through permanent, stapled-on smiles, like retired kindergarten teachers or nurses changing the diapers on an aging widower. "Yes dear, No dear. Very clever!" And when you knew — like Randy — that you wouldn't be greeted at all, I bet it felt worse than being picked last for softball teams, because it meant not being picked ever again. That's why I was so relieved to learn that Randy occasionally got mail from an old friend, Cathy. Cathy with long blonde hair that she rolled neatly into a bun and covered in a snood. Cathy with her slim figure and her pin-dotted dress with the peplum. I'd seen the photograph, Randy's only picture from her early life. In it she was barely eighteen and Randy stood with her arm slipped tight around Cathy's waist. Her back straight. A bright, carefree smile lit up her face. I saw the photo again the morning before Daddy visited me and I sure was struck. There was no forced expression, no evidence of phony laughter. When Randy was in the factory or back at the penitentiary where she used to live — meeting about her appeal — I would sometimes peek at the photo tucked away under pyjamas in the top of her dresser drawer. I couldn't stop myself from wanting to see a different life for my friend.

If Randy had been a man, I wouldn't have thought twice about the photograph, but there was something more that made me curious. Something I've never been able to put my finger on. Randy wore a black and red lumber jacket open at the front, a white undershirt covering her upper body, baggy brown pants decorated by a belt with shiny silver buckle, and men's workboots. Her hair was cut into a duck-tail, short like at Bridgewater, but somehow, she wore it better before, as if in the sunlight of Cathy's kitchen after eating poached eggs and peameal bacon it was a choice, whereas later it turned into a chore. Cathy looked happy but stiff in Randy's arms, like she was the shyer of the two and might have to cover her face from the camera, or run and hide in a closet. "Cathy was my best friend," Randy told me one day. "Before I met you."

On the whole, Randy got no regular mail from Cathy or anyone else and she told me that since word had spread that she was locked up, things had gotten even more distant. And as far as I could figure, no one had ever been to visit Randy with flowers or chocolates, or even new socks and underwear. I waited for two o'clock to roll around and then watched Daddy finally enter through the doors at the end of the hall. That day, I almost felt wanted.

April 1, 1986

Dear Mr _____,

Okay, so I'm in the habit of writing letters now. Maybe one day soon you'll actually get the chance to read them. Things here are not good. Jan's acting weird — quieter than usual — and Ma's working harder than ever. As for me, I've been thinking about reproduction pretty much continuously. Sex. And death. Is that normal? I don't want to die — not really — I just want to step off the planet for a little while. Be weightless. Is that too much to ask? Every day I get fatter and fatter, I swear. One day soon I'm going to explode! If I'm standing on the edge of a subway platform I feel like the opposite ends of a humungous magnet, drawn and repelled at the same time. I think about you then but don't worry. I wouldn't dream of wasting myself on public transit! If it ever gets to that point, I'd jump off the CN Tower. Why not go in style as the tallest free-falling suicide on the planet? I do live in Toronto, after all.

This year I also find myself with my head in the toilet. I just hang there heaving, the spittle plopping into the blue water below. I swear I can smell Saniflush in my dreams! I haven't been able to make myself fully puke yet, but emptying would be a comfort. That release, that exodus, just thinking about it keeps me focused. Recently, the urge has been so strong it's all I can do to find a washroom before I'm on my knees. A little voice nags at me, taunts. Then, it's like an electromagnetic force reaches up from the very centre of my being and grabs me, creating charges that ripple across my abdomen, up my intestines, and almost, if I'm not careful, out my mouth. At least I'm distracted from the ideas bobbing around in my head, seeing things that aren't real, or worse, things that are . . . Ma still believes I've inherited her ability to fuck with destiny. She's so wrong! If I really could affect that kind of change, I'd have located you already.

Sometimes when I can't get away from the whole psychic thing, I think about drawn-out bedside conversations or making lists on a steno pad, leaving my possessions to other people if I suddenly die. I imagine discussions about cemetery plots and caskets and how absurd to spend money on something I'll only use once. I especially imagine you finally turning up when it's already too late. You'll be sorry, then, I think, and wish you'd been easier to track down. Well, I'd better sign off. It's getting late and I have school in the morning. Hope I haven't grossed you out or offended you in any way.

I'll write again soon,

Lemon.

PS. I applied for this great part-time job at the planetarium. Wish me luck!

Lunch for Lemon was a 950-gram bag of rotini, boiled furiously and drowned in a tin of canned tomatoes. The tomatoes were a definite mistake. They're not good in reverse. She wiped her mouth along her sleeve. No more evidence of lunch, she thought. She'd scoured the basin, sprayed air freshener to clear out the bathroom, and would soon change out of her favourite Duran Duran T-shirt, washing it by hand. But first, she caught sight of herself in the bathroom mirror and was horrified. Contact lenses, a gift from Grandma Connie last Christmas, had replaced her glasses but now pale blue and pink streaks of eyeshadow were running down her cheeks, drawing attention to the dark circles under her eyes. Being a redhead highlighted the fact that her skin was a sickly hue, and although she'd patiently grown her hair all one length and recently paid to have it cut, she stared at the fashionable geometric shape — above the ear on one side and below on the other — and thought that now her whole head just looked like a lopsided Brillo pad. Her forehead was damp from sweating so she moved to the towel rack and wiped her face, eyes and forehead.

Lunch had also included three-quarters of a double-layer chocolate cake left over from her eighteenth birthday last Friday, four rows of saltines, and a plastic container of smoked-salmon cream cheese. When she'd asked about the cheese in Kensington Market, the man behind the counter had offered her a taste before she decided to buy it. Lemon accepted the wafer with a glob of cheese twice its size, and allowed it to melt on her tongue religiously. She promised herself *if* she bought a small container and *if* she ate only a bit each day it would be all right. Now here she was, relieved again. Empty of all willpower. Filled with shame. Trying to balance the leaking: those things she'd always known without being told. Things like Jan's Dad, home drunk again last night, loud and breaking glass, or a stranger crossing Bloor Street in rush hour and a minivan above the speed limit stopping him flat. Food took Lemon's mind off things, secrets she kept from herself.

Leaning over the toilet basin Lemon's face had been red, her eyes swollen and watery. Her throat ached and contracted. She'd sat on her knees on the green tile floor, one arm around the back of the toilet as if she were leaning on her oldest friend for support. The glare of the light bulbs shouted rather than spilled into the room, filling it with a white hostility. Lemon found herself unusually familiar with the details of her small bathroom. Paint was chipped off the bottom edges of the cupboard. The white garbage pail always needed emptying. Chrome on the basin and bathtub faucets was speckled with rust. Lemon allowed her head to roll back onto her shoulders and noted her own distorted features in the silver toilet handle. She leaned farther backwards, shrinking her image, but she was sure that she would never be small enough to pass for normal. Real belonging would elude her unless, of course, she did something radical, something dramatic to separate from Lilith and join the rest of the human race. So that's when she'd reached two fingers as far down her throat as was possible and was temporarily transported from one round, multi-dimensional mad world to another. A flatland, where although still afraid, she felt she finally had a blueprint for being just like everybody else. *Thin*, she'd thought. Then I'll fit in.

Lemon had heaved violently, allowing every foreign substance and every reminder of sizes and shapes, dimensions and change, to exit her body. She'd told herself it was only going to happen this one time. And maybe Ma isn't right about everything? I'm not who she says I am, Lemon thought. But if I don't come from the usual places in the usual ways — man, woman, child — from where then? And how? And why? When it was done, she closed her eyes . . . There she was on the bathroom floor of her high-rise, in Toronto . . . Ontario . . . Canada . . . North America . . . planet earth . . . inside this solar system . . . this galaxy . . . this universe. Okay and what does the universe exist inside of? Stop, she told herself. Breathe again. The hair all over her body stood like straw. She ached then burned, as though a blue sirocco was swirling around inside each muscle and landing smack in the pit of her stomach. Stop, breathe again. Open your eyes and stare at the pale green tiles, she thought. Fixate on the mouldy caulking puckering between them. We're all contained by something. There is order. There has to be. There's reason, and yes, the universe must belong to something larger than itself. We all do. Lilith belongs to the children, I belong to . . . Lemon's mind couldn't stretch further without snapping. She'd opened her eyes and flopped her head forward again and stared into the toilet bowl. Fat floats, she'd thought. God, that's really disgusting!

She'd sat there on the bath mat, shivering and defeated with questions running though her mind. Is a father at the centre of a black hole? If he doesn't know he's there does that make his daughter invisible? If time's not linear how do you measure the distance between past and future? It had finally occurred to her that she could be out of control and that despite her best attempt to understand the world as organized, there was chaos too. There were random, inexplicable events that defied reason and order. Like Jan's father when he was belligerent and like missing children. There were also forces — large forces — that existed before the words "time" and "space" and that must go on eternally — and although she wasn't one of them, Lemon was starting to suspect that she could see them if she really concentrated. And hear. And smell. And taste. She'd reached up and pulled the lever.

This morning in class it had started again, this time with fantasies about the cream cheese sitting on the second shelf behind the jug of orange juice, beside the milk. Lemon had tried to push thoughts of it away, to focus instead on her teacher, Mrs. Marsman, who stood no more than four foot five above ground. Mrs. Marsman wore blazers over dress pants that appeared to shorten her stature even further, making it seem she had no legs anywhere. Mrs. Marsman's husband taught Grade 12 chemistry. They smiled passing each other in hallways and at school assemblies, and when it was warm, they ate their lunch together outside. Mmmm, lunch, Lemon thought. Just two hours left.

As Mrs. Marsman moved on to describe how the East Coast waters were overflowing with fish, Lemon could smell the salmon mixed into her cream cheese. She could. The cream cheese didn't just smell wonderful, it seduced her:

Pssst, Lemon, you there?

Go away.

Lemon, you hungry?

Shut up. It's only ten in the morning.

You want me, you know you do.

I don't.

You can't say "no" to me.

"No." There, I said it.

But you don't mean it.

Yes I do.

Who are you kiddin'? We both know what's gonna happen when you get home.

No we don't!

Oh yeah? What happened yesterday?

That was different.

How?

Yesterday was a bad day. It was dark and drizzly, I forgot my homework and had to walk to class, and then Jan wasn't around because she stayed home sick.

Okay Yesterday sucked. But you know what?

What?

Today's gonna suck too.

Lemon set her head on her school desk and closed her eyes to block out the blue light that seemed to have filled the classroom. She drifted off into a daydream and Mrs. Marsman continued her lecture.

It was International Women's Day, well into the twenty-first century. Lilith was sitting in a sound booth at the University of Toronto radio station.

"You've got to be big," she said.

"Could you explain that statement on air, Ms. Boot? It's just the kind of message we want our young listeners to absorb."

"Only if you call me Lilith, baby."

The interviewer shuffled some papers, scribbled notes down the margins, and nodded at the woman on the other side of the glass. A red light turned green, signalling that the show had begun.

"The statistics are alarming! Almost ninety-five percent of anorexics and bulimics are women. And as most women enter the workforce, there is more pressure to conform. The good news is we have strong role models in the studio with us today to discuss the impact body size has had on their self-esteem and jobs. Ms. Boot, we'll begin with you. Have you found yourself treated unjustly, perhaps even discriminated against in employment situations as a result of being a large woman?"

"Oh, I'm not large," Lilith said. "Large is how you might describe a four-by-four or a skyscraper. I'm *fat*."

The interviewer blanched.

"Yes, well, some women choose to identify as ffffat, while others prefer large or, or rubenesque. Nevertheless, many agree that there are too few images of large women succeeding in high-profile professions to be found in magazines and on television."

"You girls are too hung up on money if you ask me. There's more to li — "

"Fffurther evidence of fat oppression can be found in the famous quote, 'A woman can never be too rich or too thin.' " The interviewer shrugged in the direction of the production assistant. "And . . . uh, women receive socio-cultural messages that being thin is equivalent to success. Has that, um, has that *ever* happened to you, Ms. Boot?"

"Never."

"Are you certain?"

"Yep."

"So, are you saying that in a society that worships thinness, you have never been adversely affected by unrealistic beauty ideals?"

Lilith shook her head.

"Not that I remember."

"Perhaps then, you could explain for our listeners, how you have become *immune* to such pressure? Ms. Boot, what's the *cure* for the stigma or sizeism?"

"There's nothin' medical about it. It's just better to be big. Besides, I like to eat, fast food mostly. My daughter says I eat so many preservatives I probably have a shelf life of a hundred years."

The interviewer rolled her eyes at the production assistant.

"Ms. Boot, would you mind telling our listeners just what profession you are in?"

"Sure. I'm a clairvoyant."

The interviewer threw her hands into the air. Papers scattered across the table.

"You mean you're a psychic!"

"I prefer clairvoyant," Lilith winked at the production assistant.

"Fine. And as a *clairvoyant*, fat has worked to your advantage?"

Lilith sat up and smoothed down the front of her dress.

"Now we're gettin' somewhere. See, being a clairvoyant's about time and space. Unfortunately, I wasn't always this size, it didn't come naturally at first. I had to work at it. Now, the bigger I am the wider my reach you might say. It's simple. The more of me there is, the more I can see — like you see things as three-dimensional but I see into the fourth."

The room was silent. Dead air. The green light began to flicker red.

"Our time is just about up for this segment." The interviewer waved a frantic finger at the window. "I would like to thank our first guest for taking the time out of her busy schedule to provide an *alternative* perspective on women and weight preoccupation. Perhaps Ms. Boot will return another time to uh, to continue her discourse on fat and the fourth dimension."

The door opened before they were off the air, and the production assistant ushered Lilith out of the sound booth. She smiled widely . . .

"Lemon Boot!" Mrs. Marsman called. Lemon raised her head. She hadn't heard her teacher's question. "Try to stay with the rest of the class, dear."

"Yes Ma'am." A feeling of dread overtook her. What kind of daydream was that? *That* wasn't normal! Lemon held her stomach. "Um, Mrs. Marsman?"

"Yes, Lemon."

"I'm not feeling well. I think I'd better go home."

As the elevator jerked up, Lemon's stomach turned. Usually she wouldn't dream of taking the stairs: She adored living on the twenty-third floor. Often at night Lemon sat on her balcony, leaning up against the grey cement wall, and offered names to each star: Magnomina, Lucia, Flora — that one especially for her mother. The elevator had rattled as though at any moment the pulleys might give way and she'd be suspended in mid-air until a rescue team of firefighters arrived to pull her out. Or worse, she might plunge straight back down to earth. Lemon crossed her legs as if she were preventing herself from urinating, and bounced up and down. She imagined bile splashing against the sanguine walls of her stomach. The elevator bounced with her. Not a good idea, she'd thought, envisioning the decaying cables holding her somewhere between the seventh, eighth . . . ninth floor as she ascended.

With a stiff rumble, the elevator door opened before it had quite met the selected floor. Lemon squinted down the gap through the lighted shaft, all the way to ground level. Ground control to Major Tom, she thought, and began to hum. She stepped out of the elevator and turned right. Hers was the last apartment down the hall. Her sneakers rubbed along the carpet creating static electricity and she wondered why her building had to have stale yellow carpeting with orange diamonds or brown plaid. Was there some law? The bad-taste regulation? And what about the smell of the incinerator chute, chain-smoking, or ammonia from boxes of cheap hair dye, cat litter, and boiled chicken! And the odour of old, which Lemon was certain could be smelt from her experiences when her grand-parents visited. Yes, old definitely smelt like apartment carpet. Dusty, mothballs, vitamins, and Ben Gay. Just as young had an odour: powder-fresh, spring-water clean. Then Lemon calcu-lated what time she'd ditched class and how long she'd stood waiting before the bus had arrived.

She reached into her knapsack for her house key and unlocked the door. As soon as she stepped inside, all other smells disappeared and were replaced by the powerful scent of euca-lyptus — Lilith's version of house-and-home deodorizer. "Why use commercial brands," her mother often advised. "Nature pro-vides its very own."

"It's her jungle thing," Lemon explained to Jan after discov-ering that Lilith had purchased eucalyptus leaves in bulk. By then her mother's penchant for all things floral was famous in the building so Jan wasn't fazed. Lilith making regular business trips to the Allan Gardens and standing for hours at the corner variety magazine rack researching *Plant Power* or *Canadian Blooms and Baskets* didn't go unnoticed by the neighbours. And eucalyptus helped Lilith to breathe when she was anxious from working on Benjamin's never-ending case. She had also filled the indoor window ledges of her apartment with clay pots and beautifully decorated baskets. Her hanging plants sprouted vines which she then strung along the walls like tentacles and thumb-tacked to the ceiling. And she talked to all of them. "Hey there, fella. How's Mr. Spider doing today? How's Rhoda? How's Ivy? You get lonely don't you?"

Lemon scoffed. She tried to locate a space in the living room not yet touched by plant life and wondered how her mother could seriously believe that the hundred or so trim-mings sharing the apartment (rent free, she wanted to point out) could ever feel abandoned? Abandoned is what a child experi-ences when her mother's otherwise preoccupied.

But Jan once watched with keen interest while Lilith watered her floral menagerie and was impressed in that "far out" way only someone else's mother can be impressive. Mrs. Hines had often sputtered disapprovingly that Lilith's apartment looked as though she'd arranged it *around* her plants, when any good decorator knew it should be the reverse. "Your mom sure has a way with flowers," Jan told Lemon, trying not to sound judgmental.

Lemon wasn't so tactful.

"Yes," she said. "That's because they don't talk back."

Entering the apartment after leaving history class, Lemon dropped her bag and hurried to the small bathroom. The only other annoying thing about living in an apartment building, she thought, aside from the carpet and the smell, was that there were never any windows in the bathroom. While showering, she had to leave the door wide open or else the room filled with steam. After sneaking cigarettes she had to spray artificial air freshener in order to disguise the odour of sulphur and nicotine. And although she'd eliminated eating dairy and red meat — the two foulest food groups — now she knew that anything that had already been digested was going to leave an unpleasant reminder. After a few seconds over the toilet, Lemon lifted her head.

"You okay in there Babygirl?" Her heart leapt into her throat.

"Oh, Ma, hi . . ." Lemon jumped to her feet, pushed the bathroom door shut and looked around frantically, waving her hands at the wrists. Stay calm, she thought. She doesn't know anything. "Be right out."

Lemon found a J-Cloth under the basin and ran some water. She wiped the toilet rim, and quickly down both sides in case she'd missed something. Then she rinsed the J-Cloth under cold water and threw it into the wastebasket. Next, she squeezed twice as much toothpaste as she needed onto a toothbrush.

Lilith called from the other side of the door.

"You sick?"

"No, I'm okay."

Lemon rolled her eyes at herself in the mirror.

"'Cause if you are, we're going to Emergency."

"I'm *fine*." She tried to sound reassuring through a frothy mouth. "Just a stomachache." Lemon brushed furiously, rinsed, spat and wiped her face on a hand towel. When she came around the corner from the hall she found her mother sitting with her feet up. By day, the couch was covered in bright pillows with tassels. By night it was Lilith's bed.

"Let me get a good look. Are you warm?" Lilith put her large hand across Lemon's forehead. "Look down. Your neck stiff?" Lemon did what she was told and shook her head. "Good. No meningitis. What about mono? You look tired, Maybe your allergies are back?"

"I'm fine, *really*. Maybe just something I ate."

Lemon's stomach grumbled loudly.

Very funny. More like everything you ate.

Lemon put her hand over her abdomen to stifle the noise and Lilith pinched her cheeks, and then squeezed her arms, first one and then the other, as though the answer to her malady was hiding somewhere inside the muscle belly.

"Could be food poisoning."

Lemon pulled away. She could see that she needed to provide an action plan before one was thrust upon her.

"Maybe I should go lie down for a while."

"Sleep? No sleeping!" Lilith responded as though she'd just heard the most ridiculous suggestion in the world. "Not until you're past the concussion stage!"

"But I didn't hit my head."

"Right . . . okay . . . Still, I'm checking in every fifteen minutes."

Lemon collected her school bag from where she'd dumped it, and skulked off to her room. She wondered what wild medicinal concoction her mother would now be preparing for supper. Most probably savoury to aid with her digestion and thyme to settle her stomach. Lilith wagged her finger as Lemon passed by the living room once more, on her way to bed. "Lots of liquids, Babygirl. Remember to drink liquids." Lemon smiled meekly. How could she forget?

With the door to her room shut, she breathed a sigh of relief. Whew! She'd made it past the inquisition relatively unscathed.

153

She stood before her full-length oval mirror with a face still flushed from vomiting and shook her head, displeased with who she saw staring back. Through one ear hung a long, dangling earring, and through the other, a matching stud. Her damp T-shirt cut across her neckline, exposing one round shoulder, and she wore a very wide (it was her Madonna look) white plastic belt hanging off her hips, over her short skirt. Her leggings were black. Lemon lifted her shirt. She turned sideways and checked her stomach for flatness.

You look like a fat cow, it told her.

She turned before the mirror and verified this diagnosis from the other side.

Moo!

Unhappy with the result, Lemon threw herself onto her bed and stared at the ceiling, where she saw a faint outline of Cassiopeia and Andromeda floating overhead. They wouldn't come into their full majesty until the sun sank low and allowed them to glow in the dark as they were meant to. Lemon's ceiling, walls, and school desk were covered in press-on galaxies. Castor and Pollux loomed over the north wall, at the foot of her bed. The Big Dipper and Ursa Minor had been stuck directly on the windows; behind them and far in the distance were the real things. She used coloured blinking lights to create an otherworldly atmosphere in the bedroom, as though the aurora borealis shrouded her in mystery and promise, each blinking light a kiss goodnight. Each night as she drifted off, Lemon imagined flying through the atmosphere. From up on high she might locate her father.

The walls in her bedroom were cobalt because, when Lilith announced she was painting the entire apartment forest green a few years ago, Lemon felt she had a right to put her foot down. She wanted something more conservative. Blue, she convinced her mother. Like water. Then she hung nothing except a reproduction of Van Gogh's *Starry Night*, and her own stars and planets. In her galaxy there was simplicity and order. Even furniture in Lemon's bedroom served a functional purpose. There was a plain double box spring and mattress and beside it a floor lamp. There was a desk and chair that Lilith had picked up for her at a neighbourhood garage sale, and a small bookshelf. Under the window sat a trunk full of Lemon's out-of-season apparel. The rest of her clothes were hung neatly inside her closet on wire hangers. The only object in Lemon's small universe that seemed superfluous by comparison was the full-length mirror she adored. However that too, she insisted, served a practical purpose: She needed it to measure her self-worth. Oh, earthlings, she thought. So limited!

Lemon had also recently concluded that her mother was unlikely to ever reveal her father's whereabouts or identity. Indeed, perhaps she didn't know herself. So Lemon had decided to speak about her feelings with a school counsellor. "I wouldn't waste your time." Jan said, when she found out. "It didn't help me."

"You? You're the most private person I know. Why would *you* go to see a counsellor?"

"None of your business," Jan said, picking up a pillow from Lemon's bed and throwing it at her head.

Lemon jumped on top of Jan, pinned her down and tickled her.

"Come on, spill your guts right now!"

"Forget it," Jan said, pushing her off.

"Fess up. Secrets are no fair!"

Despite the fact that Jan was two years older and exercized regularly, she could not successfully free her arms from beneath Lemon's knees.

"Get the hell off me!" Jan screamed. "Leave me alone!"

Lemon rolled to one side. Laughter had turned to monumental silence.

"Sorry, I was just kidding around. I didn't mean to freak you out."

"I know," Jan said, catching her breath. "It's okay. I overreacted. I didn't want anyone to know, but my mom took me to a counsellor once."

Lemon sat up.

"Really? Why?"

Jan lay back and stared at the ceiling.

"Lem?"

"Yeah."

"Do you want a boyfriend?"

Lemon bounced on the edge of her bed.

"No way!"

Jan flopped over, a bit relieved.

"Me either," she confessed.

Then Lemon pointed to her small breasts, bobbing up and down.

"I mean, who would want to touch these?"

"Oh," Jan said, turning and looking straight back up at the ceiling again.

Lemon stopped bouncing and lay down with her head on the pillow next to Jan's.

"Was the counsellor thing last year when you tried to give away all your stuff?"

"Yes," Jan said flatly.

"That was weird."

"Yeah, weird."

Jan had offered Lemon her favourite belongings — her copy of *Pride and Prejudice* and her Rough Trade album. "You keep them," Jan had said. "I don't need them any more."

Lemon's mouth hung open in disbelief.

"But we always listen to that album. Especially, you know . . ." She didn't want to have to spell it out, but for years after Jan's father went off like a twenty-one-gun salute, Mrs. Hines had been sending Jan over to Lilith's apartment with her pyjamas, a toothbrush, and an armful of records. The girls had been hiding out in Lemon's bedroom, listening to records at full volume. Too often for Lemon's taste, *High School Confidential*. Lemon knew that after Jan's hope to be accepted at university, it was the one thing that helped her feel free. "You love Carole Pope," Lemon said.

Jan looked out the window vacuously, across Bloor Street, past the rows of middle-class brick houses, past Dovercourt, Dufferin, practically all the way to High Park. There was a pond there, she knew, and she thought of how Virginia Woolf had sewn rocks into the seams of her skirt and sunk herself in a river, and of how Sappho too had leapt into the sea.

"Well I don't any more."

Lemon observed her with squinted, skeptical eyes.

"Why not?"

Jan shrugged but didn't turn around.

"I don't care about anything."

Silence.

"Oh no!" Lemon said, beginning to understand. "No way, I don't want your stupid stuff. I don't. You're not leaving me here all by myself to deal with Ma. I don't want your stuff, I want you!" She ran to the window and threw her arms around

Jan. "Don't you dare give everything away. You'll need it. In the ffffuture," she stammered. Jan found herself engulfed in desperate and panicked arms that refused to let go. When Lemon did release her grip, she moved directly to her desk, opened a drawer and fumbled through it as though with enough looking she'd find something helpful. "Keep this for me," she insisted, thrusting a small book with the word "diary" across the front into Jan's hand. "You know how nosy *my* mother is. Hide it at your apartment, just for a little while, just until it's safe to bring it back. Okay? Okay Jan?" Lemon was impossible to say "no" to, so Jan sighed, reached out in resignation, and accepted the task. It wasn't until many weeks later, after she'd received her admittance and scholarship to the University of Toronto, that she remembered the diary. Even though Lemon had entrusted her with the book, Jan was too curious to stop herself from opening it. Guiltily she discovered that all its pages were either torn out or blank.

Lying on her bed and still feeling weak, Lemon gazed up at her make-believe universe hoping she could sort her problems out on her own. Maybe when she was ten pounds lighter she could relax. And maybe then she'd share the wonders of the universe with her mother. She was certain it would help with Lilith's work. After all, if missing children — take Benjamin as an example — if Benjamin, gone for almost two decades, were a star, his chances of being located and identified now would be greater than ever before. Science offered hope for the future. Endless possibility. Time travel: Lilith could go back and undo the kidnapping before it ever took place. Lemon could jump backwards and find out who her father really was. What he looked like, sounded like. She could verify whether or not it was possible to love someone without even knowing them. I really need a proper definition, she thought. A father is . . . timeless, she began, and then closed her eyes to thoughts of garnet red, fast speed, and family reunions. Just then, the telephone rang, and a few seconds later the door to her room creaked open and Lilith poked her head in. Lemon rolled onto her side, her back to her mother.

"I'm still here," she said with a sarcastic hint of disappointment.

"I see that," Lilith countered. "That was Jan on the phone. She says to call her back."

A couple of girls from Jan's dorm had invited her to the first diving competition of the school year. The most gorgeous guys at U of T will be there, they said. So Jan packed a copy of her latest read, *Surfacing,* into her knapsack and headed off to the athletic centre with everyone else. The next thing she knew she was watching a beautiful young man on the edge of a diving board. His body was solid, with a V-shaped torso, trim waist, muscular thighs and the washboard stomach of a dedicated swimmer. "James is the captain of the team," someone whispered. Jan observed him standing with his arms outstretched horizontally, his chin pointing high, as he breathed deeply, expanding his chest. Below him was a ten-metre drop, but to Jan he looked confident. Then James glanced down at the surface of the water and out in front, bent his left leg into a forty-five-degree angle, threw his arms above his head and in one powerful and graceful effort, sprang into the air — falling up first and then down. He tucked his head to his chest, his knees close to his body, arms wrapped around them, and allowed his weight and gravity to tumble him in a circular motion — round and round — while he dropped. With a single leap of faith, James became a faded copper coin tossed into turquoise motion, head to tail. Tail to head. And Jan found herself silently rooting for him.

James quickly made one and a half rotations and then jutted his legs out behind, reached for his landing, and split the surface of the water with his fingertips. His body remained firm and tight all the way to the pool floor, where he righted himself, exhaled, pushed off with powerful calves and kicked until he found air once more. As his head emerged, he heard the crowd in the stands cheering and applauding, but he knew the moment he'd lifted from the diving board that he wasn't going to better his previous performances with this attempt. He hadn't kicked out at the right time and so had gone beyond, leaning too far backwards by half an inch. For weeks James's rotations hadn't been clean and his landings produced splash. He was having trouble making dives with low levels of difficulty. The problem was his focus. Lately, his mind was somewhere else.

One of the women seated next to Jan screamed loudly in her ear, "Yeah James!" while a senior from a rival university shook a banner that read, "U of T sucks!" Jan watched the expression on James's face as he took in a mouthful of water, swished it around like mouthwash and let it stream from his lips. Next time, he seemed to be thinking. He'd practise harder and make it exact by the next competition! James swam five easy strokes to the side, where he lifted himself out. This time the woman next to Jan whistled and waved, and when James stood up, he waved back.

One of the organizers handed him a small yellow cloth no bigger than a tea towel. "Always Mr. Popularity, eh?"

Jan couldn't take her eyes off James as he wiped his face, his chest and his arms. He walked beside the pool, passed a bench of excited teammates — one of whom towel-whipped him — and then he sat alongside the others who had already made their last dives of the day. His coach patted him on the shoulder and rose to encourage another athlete. Within seconds all four judges had registered their scores and the announcer read the average over the loudspeaker: "6.3. For James from the home team."

James scanned the crowd of spectators. There were a few familiar faces in the stands: one girl he'd taken to the formal last year, another he'd slept with after a house party in his dorm, two of his professors, and a cluster of first-year students. Oh and there was that hyperactive Beth so-and-so from the women's swim team. Hard to miss her. James waved at her again, but this time noticed the brainy girl sitting beside her, staring right at him. She looked familiar. Yes, he'd seen her walking through the quadrangle outside their residence. She lived in the dorm too and usually had her nose in some book. And he'd seen her in Fung — fungus — the dining hall. James thought she was lovely. Her eyes were warm and oval and deeply intelligent. Eyes that said to him even from a distance, I am wise but I need you. And for the first time in his twenty years, James thought perhaps he was capable of drowning after all.

From the bleachers on the side of the pool, Jan watched this giant seabird watching her, and she became self-conscious. What was he looking at? Her finely featured face? Her thin lips, like a line drawing? Her bony legs that crossed at the ankle? "Lucky," said Beth. "Guess he likes *you*." Jan smiled at James and then nervously looked down at her book as the next diver prepared himself on the edge of the board. James dropped his head between his knees, pulled off his bathing cap and shook the excess water like a dog out of the lake. His lungs swelled like hidden wings.

On Monday morning Jan was sitting in the centre of a large lecture hall with tiered seats and chairs with folding desktops. The course, Major Canadian Writers, was about to begin when she noticed James enter the room, scan the seats, and rest his eyes upon her. He walked up the staircase, shuffled past several students and gestured to the empty seat at Jan's side. She juggled her books, a bagel and her Thermos so that James was able to squeeze past.

"Apparently you're the Johnny Weissmuller of campus," she said, when James was seated.

"Who?"

"Johnny Weissmuller. You know? Tarzan."

James was flattered.

"Right," he said. "Me Tarzan, you Jane."

"That's *Jan*."

"Oh sorry, I was just joking around." James cleared his throat. "I saw you there the other day. At the pool. Do you swim?"

Jan blushed.

"Just for fun," she said. "Nothing serious."

"I can't remember the last time I had fun in the pool," James said. And just then Professor Walker entered the room wearing a brown tweed skirt and a white dress shirt. Dark red lipstick highlighted her full mouth and her brown hair was cut into a neat pageboy. "Have you had her before?"

"No," Jan said. "But I heard she's a tough marker."

James regarded Jan more closely now. Her features were

unassuming and understated but her natural beauty could not be denied. Her hair was an auburn mop suggesting that she'd rolled directly from bed to class without stopping long before a mirror. She unzipped her jacket and revealed two pens — one blue, one red — and one pencil tucked into her sweater pocket. Then she unscrewed the Thermos lid and poured herself a cut of coffee. After a few minutes, Jan pulled off her sweater and James watched as the thin material of her shirt clung to her small breasts. Something grabbed him from below and he was carried away with thoughts of undressing her, caressing her, finding himself reflected back in those large eyes. Get a grip, he told himself.

James was glad for the distraction when a few latecomers rushed in and Professor Walker began her lecture. "I'm going to hand out the required reading list," she said, handing a stack of paper to students sitting on either end of the front row. "Take one and pass it back. And *please* purchase the correct editions. Every year someone spends a fortune on an outdated version of the anthology." James received two pages stapled together and handed the stack to Jan. Without keeping a copy for herself, she passed it directly to the young man sitting on her other side. "Already got mine," she explained. "There's so much reading for this course that I wanted a head start." James looked at his typed list and wondered whether he should pay an extra $150 to take one of those speed-reading classes he'd seen advertised in the refectory.

Jan had gone to the English department and knocked on Professor Walker's door during office hours, the very first week of term. She'd asked questions of all her professors, about upcoming assignments and late penalties. But facing Professor Walker in the crowded little room, discussing her love of literature surrounded by stalagmites of books, Jan had found herself stammering and awkward. She'd felt an intimidating heat spread from the centre of her being to her temples, and *throb . . . throb . . . throb . . .* woman-pulse all the way down to her toes. She'd tried to calm down so the instructor wouldn't notice. There was nothing to be nervous about, she told herself. She's just a lousy teacher! But Jan had been waiting for years to get the chance to go to university, and now that she was there, she wasn't going to blow it.

In the lecture hall, Professor Walker reshuffled her notes on the podium. "Make sure to have read the first two novels by the end of the month. In my class, participation counts for fifteen per-cent of your mark." James ran a finger down his bibliography and then looked to Jan's copy which she'd pulled out of her knapsack. Hers had red marks beside many of the authors' names. "Atwood, Margaret." Check. "Davies, Robertson. Findley, Timothy." Check. Check. James was impressed. Right after practice this afternoon, he was going back to his room to study. He would read both books by the end of the week, maybe run into Jan at the library or in the dorm. They could exchange their thoughts on the use of nature as a literary device, invent possible lewd euphemisms for "wind" in W.O. Mitchell's book, and then decide to go for coffee. Maybe they'd discover that they were both Pisces and he'd say that's why he enjoyed the water so much. Maybe they'd share a resolute dislike for heavy-metal bands, smokers, and girls who chew gum with their mouths open. He'd ask her out to dinner easily. It would be perfect.

Then, without turning his head much or leaning over too obviously, James glanced once more at Jan's list. She was writing herself a reminder. "English assignment due Oct. 18th. Meal card still needs verification. Don't forget to call Lemon. Saturday night CB's." James looked away. Who was "CB" anyway? Collin Brown the rugby senior? Or that dweeby Clive, from the registrar's office? Curtis? Cameron? James rolled his eyes. Of course! What do you expect, he thought. She's beautiful. She's nice. She's smart. She must be unavailable. Figures, he told himself. Figures I'd finally fall for someone who is taken. He sat up straighter in his chair, his competitive nature kicking in. By the end of class he'd get her number anyway. Then James opened his own notebook and wrote in bold capital letters across the inside flap: "English assignment due Oct. 18th. Meal card needs verification. Remember to get your head checked. Loser."

Wanting what he could not have was part of what made James such a good athlete and he knew it. But on dry land, unlike in the water, he usually felt himself to be nothing more than a jealous, withdrawn spectator.

Lemon sat across from Claudia Chester MSW, inside a small private room off the main guidance office. The walls were covered in turquoise paint. The carpet was camel with a floral print. There was no desk, only three upholstered armchairs, a coffee table in the centre of the room with a box of tissues on top, and beside it, an unsolved Rubik's Cube. Claudia wore navy blue wide-leg pants and a rose batik blouse. When she'd greeted Lemon her pants looked like a floor-length skirt. The material was diaphanous and flowed over contours, leaving Lemon with the curious impression that Claudia was not restricted by seams or hemlines, that she could take many forms. A silver pendant of a fat, naked goddess on a long chain hung between Claudia's breasts. Lemon tried not to gag when she noticed. Her stomach churned loudly.

Don't tell me you're asking her for advice?

Once seated, Claudia began by nervously introducing herself.

"Hello. I'm Claudia. It's very nice to meet you."

"Hi," Lemon said.

Silence.

Claudia shifted in her seat.

"So, we've got a limited number of sessions to work with. Why don't we get started."

Silence.

"Okay, maybe *I* should start. Let's see? I'm twenty-seven and — "

"That's young. I mean, sorry, well isn't that kind of young to be a shrink?"

Claudia chewed the inside lining of her cheek.

"I guess I'm not what you expected," she said. "But I think it's positive we're not so far apart in age. And please, don't think of me as your doctor, just a friend with special knowledge. Does that make sense?"

Lemon shrugged.

"Anyway," Claudia continued, "I'm from Halifax and I came here for graduate school to study social work. I especially enjoy young people; that's why I've been placed at your school for my practicum. Do you know what a practicum is, Lemon?"

"Practice?"

"Sort of," Claudia said, clearing her throat. "It means I have to work so many hours for free in order to graduate."

"So . . . I'm an experiment?"

"Oh? Um . . ." Claudia tucked a long strand of her hair behind one ear. "I suppose you might see it that way." She spoke more quickly. "You are my first client. Student. But I want you to know that everything is strictly confidential. Whatever we talk about in here stays in this room; even my notes will be locked up." Claudia tapped lightly on a filing cabinet next to her chair and Lemon noticed that her fingertips were faintly stained with nicotine. "Now. How about telling me something about yourself?"

"What do you want to know?" Lemon said, glancing at the wall clock.

"Well, what brings you in?"

"Oh that's easy. Ma."

Claudia's pen poised on top of her notepad, ready for action. She twirled it between her fingers and then accidentally dropped it.

"Your mother?" She blushed when Lemon bent down under her seat for the pen.

"I have a hard time talking to her."

"Thanks," Claudia said, accepting the pen and trying to appear unfazed. "So, you have a hard time communicating with your mother. Why is that?"

"Well if I knew," Lemon said, "I wouldn't be here."

Claudia's eye began to twitch.

"Why do you *think*?"

"Oh, because Ma insists she knows what's best."

"Sometimes parents act that way." Claudia was writing and talking simultaneously. "Is it the same with your father?"

Lemon picked at her fingernails.

"I don't have a father."

"Oh . . . um . . . sorry. I shouldn't have assumed."

"That's okay, everyone does."

"So then, are your parents divorced?"

"No."

"You just don't see your father often, is that it?"

"I guess you could say that."

Claudia's eyes were wide and sympathetic. Her tone softened. "Because he passed away?"

"No!" Lemon blurted. "He's out there somewhere."

"Um, so . . . your mother spends quality time with you?" Claudia's eye twitch was so pronounced she appeared to be winking at Lemon. "That's what really counts. I mean, do you have *alone* time?"

Lemon played with the silver ring on her thumb, twirling it between her pointer and index fingers.

"I don't know. Sure, why not. I guess so." Ma could make more time for me, Lemon thought. If I'd been kidnapped she would have. But what was Claudia implying? That Lilith was a bad mother? How dare she! "Ma and I are very close." Lemon added, "Very!"

"That's great," Claudia said.

"Yeah, she loves kids. All kids. She really does."

"Your mother spends time with other children too?"

Lemon nodded.

"Sort of."

"Is she a daycare worker?"

"No."

"A nurse?"

"Nope."

Claudia put her pen and paper down and crossed her hands in her lap.

"Okay, Lemon. I'm not going to force you to tell me if you don't want to."

Lemon ran her tongue along her bottom row of teeth. She wondered what Claudia would do if she got any more rattled?

"Fine," Lemon said. "She's a psychic."

Claudia coughed, her eyebrows arched dramatically and she thumped her chest.

"Pardon?"

"A psychic."

"Uh-huh . . . right . . ." Claudia dropped her head, lifted her pen and scribbled furiously on her notepad. "Uh-huh, I see . . . a psychic . . . And how does that feel for you?"

Lemon stared at the counsellor, who obviously hadn't expected such a metaphysical conversation. She had probably expected to hear about a boyfriend, Lemon thought. Or about my exams.

"You don't believe me. You think I'm making it up."

"No. No, I don't think that." Claudia was still writing.

"Then you think I'm nuts?"

"No." Claudia looked up, squinting. "I've just never encountered this . . . this *issue*. It must be very difficult."

"Well it is!" Lemon said. "How many people devote their lives to assisting others? Not many. Ma's a saint. A tried and true old-fashioned martyr."

At least that's how Lemon felt most of the time. Then occasionally there were those other times, the drag-on, don't-want-to-get-out-of-bed days, or the evenings in her room secretly opening canned maraschino cherries and tearing into rolls of prepared cookie dough, eating it all until she thought her stomach would explode. Those were the times when Lemon knew that her mother was drawn to the job for more reasons than simple altruism. A chill swam across Lemon's body. Her stomach grumbled once more.

Lilith is devoted. Her job is a calling, and if she's been called . . .

"I guess I'm resentful," Lemon added quickly. Then she looked out the window beyond Claudia, to a pigeon on the ledge.

"Resentful of what?"

"Of the children." The pigeon began to coo and Lemon thought it sounded like an infant crying in the distance. Lemon thought about Benjamin then and cleared her throat. "Sometimes I'm jealous."

Claudia's voice rose.

"Jealous?"

"Of how concerned Ma is about them." Lemon felt herself growing angry. "They're missing," she added. "Ma finds them."

"Oh, I see," said Claudia. "Now I understand."

"No you don't! You don't even know her so how could you? She talks to plants but not to me. She sees other people's kids but hasn't got a clue what I'm up to half the time, and she thinks she's the Virgin Mary! It drives me bonkers!"

Claudia looked to Lemon as though she might cry at any moment. Instead she tapped her pen on her steno pad.

Tap tap tap.

"It's difficult to remain detached," she said with a quiver in her voice. "In . . . social work."

Lemon exhaled and felt the blood rush back to her fingertips. Maybe Claudia wasn't attacking Lilith after all. Maybe she really would understand. The pigeon suddenly ruffled its feathers, stretched its wings and dropped out of sight.

"It's just that . . . well, sometimes I think Ma notices more about them than she does about me."

"Can you tell me more?"

Lemon clenched her jaw. As soon as the words flew out of her mouth she'd regretted them. Traitor. Baby. Babygirl! Lilith loved her, she knew that. She looked away, wallowing in shame.

"Are you all right?"

"Umm . . ." Lemon stared out the window, filled with self-loathing. " . . . I don't think what I said just now is fair."

Claudia's response was immediate.

"Feelings don't have to be fair, Lemon."

"But what kind of a person is jealous of missing children?"

Claudia leaned forward in her chair and the pendant swung away from her neck.

"Maybe," she said, "someone wanting to be found."

Lemon reached for a tissue from the box on the coffee table, and blew her nose. Then giggled through her tears.

Claudia tried not to appear hurt.

"Did I miss something?"

"It's just that Ma wouldn't believe it if she knew I was here."

"Oh, will you tell her?"

Lemon thought about her mother's visions and size and her own convex belly yet again turning from stop to go.

I'm in charge, her abdomen said. *Better stick with me.*

She thought about the vomiting, and her father whose presence was gradually taking up more and more space in her imagination.

Don't do it, Lemon. Don't be a tattle-tale!

And her unanswered letters, and the ongoing definition. A father is . . . gentle? Sturdy? Absent. She hadn't got very far yet. The girls' washroom was on the other side of the guidance office and a good twenty feet down the hall.

"Probably not," she answered. "I probably won't tell her."

Later that evening Lilith sat at the kitchen table drinking coffee and shelling fresh peas. The television was turned on in the next room, and Lemon emerged clean from a long, lingering bath. She was in her pyjamas, smelling of cocoa-butter body lotion and green apple shampoo, when she pulled out a chair and decided she would, after all, try and speak with her mother about counselling. And as she recounted parts of the session, Lilith scrunched her face tightly until her eyes disappeared.

"Quality time? What are you talking about? When it comes to children, *all* the time is quality time."

"I give up," Lemon said, sorry for even trying. "It's impossible to reason with you."

"Well what's this blabbing about shrinks all of a sudden?"

"How many times do I have to say it?" Lemon rolled her eyes. "Claudia's not a shrink. She's a psycho-thera-pist." Lemon pronounced the word in slow, loud morsels, hoping it would be easier for her mother to digest.

"I'm not deaf, Babygirl. You don't have to say it like it's about to go out of style. Teenagers! Think they've discovered it first — whatever it is!" Lilith plucked a firm strand from the side of the pea pod and it slid open. She held the split pod over a bowl and thumbed out the round, green balls one at a time. She sighed heavily, weary of the discussion already. "I know exactly what you mean, Lemon Boot. I know." Lemon crossed her fingers under the table and waited while Lilith cleared her throat. "'Psycho' comes from Greek or Latin and means, 'mental.' And 'therapist' comes from old English and means just what it says — 'the rapist.' Put it all together and you get a really bad idea." Lilith took another gulp of coffee.

Lemon dropped her head on the table in resignation.

"Ma, *please!* You haven't got a clue what you're talking about."

"I might not know fancy words but I know what I see. You. Letting some stranger in with fool ideas about your own flesh and blood. Now that tells me some things, doesn't it? And what it tells me is your head's shrinking already." Lilith resumed shelling and as each hard pea fell into the stainless-steel mixing bowl it made a musical sound. D sharp.

C flat. Depended what part of the bowl it landed on and from how high.

"Ma, you're not listening. I have *issues*. I think someone with specialized training — with the right tools — could help." She grabbed her own pile of pods from the bag on the table. "I know it's not your thing," she added for sway. But Lilith was insulted.

"Got plenty of my own tools, Babygirl." She grabbed a handful of hair and held it away from the side of her head. "For example, this is *mood* hair," she said forcefully. "It predicts change — like a weather vein. Curly for happy. Frizzy for confused. Flat for sad."

Lemon could stand it no longer.

"You are trying to tell me that hair — HAIR — is an accurate therapy technique?"

"Right. Why not," Lilith said. "See?" She indicated the limp hair clinging lifeless to the sides of her face. Lemon covered her own face with her hands. *I hate you*, she thought. *And this crappy apartment and my balloon body. I hate my whole stinking life!*

"Fine!" Lemon shouted. "Don't listen to me." Then she began to sob.

"Christ Almighty." Lilith set the pea pods down and wiped her hands on her shirt waist. "You don't have to blubber. I was just having fun." She held her arms outstretched. "C'mere a minute." Lemon lifted her face from her hands to see if her mother could be trusted. "If it'll make you stop running around here like there's a firecracker up your ass," Lilith said, embracing her daughter, "I'll try to mind my own business." She held onto Lemon tenderly, stroking her forehead from front to back, as if she could remove all impure thoughts. *No use getting angry*, Lilith reasoned. *Lemon will learn for herself soon enough. She doesn't need a shrink, she just doesn't know who she is yet.* Lilith patted Lemon's back and rocked her gently. Lemon's nose ran onto her mother's chest, leaving a damp spot on Lilith's blouse. *Growing stains*, she thought. "It's gonna be okay, Babygirl. Time will tell. Everything in good time. Just promise me one thing?"

"What?" Lemon contorted away, still angry.

"You'll ditch the psychobabble. It gives me the creeps."

"Fine."

"Fine." Lilith doubled, imagining Claudia in a blazer and comfortable shoes, and thinking she'd be happy to tell this busy-body a thing or two about mind control.

Despite her mother's feelings about counselling, Lemon was back in the school guidance office the very next week. The clattering, clamouring noise from the busy street faded, a streetcar passed outside and she was sitting in her usual chair with her arms hugging her knees. Each attempt she made to describe her dreams fell away from consciousness. As soon as she began to speak out loud the images faded and this void that she escaped into nightly, disappeared. Had she invented this mysterious zone or was it part of her from the beginning, like a hideaway attic storing treasures and secrets?

Claudia fidgeted with a plastic button on her jacket.

"Take your time," she said. "There's no hurry."

Lemon closed her eyes and tried to remember. She felt her legs tingle and her arms grow lighter. She explained that in the dream her father was trapped on the other side of a wall but in order to reach him she had to choose from several doors. When she couldn't find her way out of the room, she'd become desperate and even wished for wings. Then she'd smelt the antiseptic odour of vinegar and water, seen the floor polished to a shine and observed her own distorted reflection gleaming up from a toilet bowl. Sewerside, she'd found herself thinking. It's the only way out. The room spun and a deep voice boomed from a loudspeaker.

"Lemon Boot, come on down! You're our next contestant on "The Price is Sight." Lemon looked up. A metronome counted the seconds.

Tick.

Tock.

Perspiration ran down her rib cage.

"Do you select door number one, door number two or . . . which door will it be, contestant?"

Tick.

Tock.

"Contestant?"

Tick.

Tock.

I don't know how to choose, Lemon thought. *I don't even know his name . . .*

Buzzzzzzzzzzzzzzz! loud in her ear.

"Oh, I'm sorry." The speaker voice sounded falsely disappointed. "I'm sorry but your time is up. However, we do have some lovely parting gifts."

"No!" Lemon shouted. "Wait!"

Please, I need more time.

The floor began to shake and Lemon lost her balance. Cupboard doors flapped open and closed, making a racket.

Panes of glass exploded. The mirror shattered. Lemon covered her face and pulled most of herself inside a small cupboard. She wrapped her arms around her body as tightly as she could and folded into her knees. I'm getting closer, she thought. Closer to the centre of the universe. The inexplicable place where time and space collide and rupture memory. Backward. I'm going to remember what Ma forgot. I'm going back to get it. I have to go back for myself.

Flakes of eggshell paint crumbled off the ceiling. Plaster walls folded in like a cardboard box and, stripped of the outer layers, tall supporting beams revealed the skeleton of the room. Wind whipped through the broken windows, covering Lemon in plaster dust. It caked in her mouth and activated her gag reflex as she tried to breathe. She covered her ears to protect against the loud, piercing sound of cement crashing all around her. The game-show host disappeared and each white door flew open violently, one after the other revealing its contents: A Honda Shadow 500 with fringed leather grips. A treadmill and set of free weights for home use. A five-piece matching set of luggage with a ticket for two to Vancouver. A red-haired man in a dark green uniform. Lemon's heart was in her stomach.

Father?

She opened her eyes suddenly back in the guidance office. Claudia was clutching her throat. Lemon rubbed her temples.

"What happened?"

"You were telling me about your dream. You were only gone about a minute."

"That's never happened before."

Claudia's eye began to twitch.

"You must have been ready for it."

179

"Yeah, ready," Lemon doubled, trying to ignore Claudia's reaction and wondering what exactly she was ready for. She stood and stretched in front of the window.

"Do you believe in destiny?"

It was a troublesome question for an aspiring agent of change.

"Destiny suggests you're powerless," Claudia said. "So, no, I suppose not."

"Lucky you. *I've* always been followed around by a strong sense of impending destiny. Like I am a grenade and somewhere out there in the wide expanse of universe, time holds the pin. Father Time. Ticking and ticking, while I wait to find out what will eventually become of me."

"Your father again?"

Lemon turned to face Claudia but ignored her question.

"I guess destiny does sound sort of passive. I wouldn't say I have *no* control though. I mean, I'm not psycho yet. Right?"

"Psychic," Claudia corrected.

"Sure, whatever." Lemon moved to take her seat again.

"Are you saying you're afraid you *might* become psychic? Because there *are* different theories. We've talked about them, remember? Some people think clairvoyance is just heightened intuition. Learned, I suppose. And other people think you're born with it like a gift or . . ." She couldn't find the exact words.

"A mental illness. Some people say Ma's crazy."

"Okay," Claudia conceded. "Maybe they do, but what's important is what *you* believe."

Lemon chewed her lip.

"Claudia, do you think in the future there'll be groups for people like me?"

"What? You mean like a twelve-step program?"

180

"Yeah," Lemon smirked. "Clairvoyants Anonymous, or Adult Children of Intelligent Life Forms who Claim to see the Future. ACIF for short. I mean, a lot of people don't realize their full potential. We could all pack into auditoriums. You know? Legal assistants who were expected to become lawyers. Dental hygienists instead of licensed dentists. I could wear a name tag that says "Telemarketer," because I'll never live up to Ma's ambition that I become the next Lola Diamond, psychic to the stars. Wait. Psychic to the stars! I almost like that." Lemon raised her pointer finger to her chin curiously. "I don't know, maybe I could predict atmospheric changes. Become a cosmic weather girl, and eventually midway through my career, I could even write a column for *The Globe and Mail*. Loopy Lemon's Weekly Guestimations."

Claudia was dumbfounded.

"I . . . I really don't know what to say."

"Well I do. Ma wasn't preordained to be clairvoyant. And neither am I! She loves her job. Free will must count for something."

"It counts for a lot, Lemon. If you're asking me."

"Okay so she was sensitive from day one, susceptible to moods. Big deal. Maybe that had something to do with her level of intuition, but there has to be more. *Something* caused her insight to become activated. At least I hope so because why even bother looking forward to my future if in the end, nothing I try makes any difference? What's the point in choosing if I end up a big fat weirdo anyway?"

"So you *don't* think you were born with it?" Claudia said, trying to keep up.

"Well, maybe *Ma* was; I'll give her that. And maybe it's in me too like an allergy I'll develop when I'm older. But I say it's nothing more than the potential to learn a new language and won't happen unless I practise."

"Then we do agree?" Claudia asked. "About choice?"

Lemon sat silently for a moment, reflecting. She hadn't been doing such a great job of dealing with the less troublesome aspects of her life so what made her think she had this one figured out? She was always so busy looking for herself in an ever-shrinking reflection, looking for her father in her mother's version of events that so far she'd come up with no clear answers. But even as she heard herself think, Lemon knew she wasn't being completely honest. What *really* bothered her about having a psychic for a mother was the way that people looked at her. Like she was crazy too.

"What if, you know, Ma has made me *susceptible*? What if she's taught me to intuit?"

"Mothers do that," Claudia teased. "Pass their values and culture on to their children."

"Don't make fun of me!" Lemon said, feeling injured. "It's not funny. We're talking about foreign culture here. Subculture — no, subconscious culture!" She shook her head. "I just don't know what to think any more. I've spent hours breathing in Ma's abilities, holding her hand while the sky thunders because storms overstimulate her senses. I've waited my whole life for her to find this one kid who might not even exist! All I know is it's not a nine-to-five job being a psychic and if I wasn't born for it, I might as well have been."

"No choice again?"

Lemon looked at the floor.

"It's just . . . what if . . . what if Ma's right about me?"

Claudia twirled her pen between her fingers as if it were a cigarette.

"Would that really be so bad, Lemon?"

"Yuck. Yes. Totally."

Claudia lowered her voice to speak.

"I'd like to shift the focus of the conversation for a minute. I've noticed you've lost a lot of weight since we've been seeing each other."

"Have I?" Lemon was flattered.

"Yes. Are you okay? Have you been ill?"

"About my dreams," Lemon said, changing the subject and exaggerating her hand gestures. "Wait until you hear this one. Ma was walking around our apartment carrying my head tucked underneath her arm, chanting, 'Babygirl sometimes I think you'd lose it if it wasn't screwed on so tight!'" Lemon feigned a laugh. "Sledgehammer symbolism in that one, huh?" Claudia opened her mouth to speak but Lemon continued, "And the night before — "

"Wow," Claudia interrupted. "These are quite busy nights you have." Then, "Lemon why don't you tell me what's really going on?"

Lemon took a deep breath and sucked in her stomach.

"Ma's embarrassing."

"Embarrassing, why?"

"Because . . . because . . . she's . . . *different*."

"Do we all need to act and think the same?"

"And look the same," Lemon added.

"Right. And look the same."

"Oh come on, Claudia, give me a break!" The entire universe is governed by rules. There are laws and codes for behaviour. Just take a look around. Read the papers. Nobody acts or sounds like my mother. Nobody. So don't try and change my mind! One day I swear, when it becomes tenable to sustain life on the moon — I'm there in a second. Anything would be better. I'll do whatever. Live in an oxygenated city. Swallow pills for food."

"Feel weightless?"

"Yeah," Lemon said, dreamily.

"I think you sound frightened."

Pause.

"She just doesn't care what anybody thinks . . . or what I think or . . ."

"What do you want her to care about?"

Lemon's eyes teared up.

"My father."

Claudia leaned forward in her chair, excited as she so often was when they stumbled upon something of therapeutic significance.

"Have you told her how you feel, Lemon? Mother's aren't mind readers, you know." Lemon cocked her head to one side as Claudia rephrased. "I mean, it's best to be direct."

"I've asked. But she's sticking to her story."

"The immaculate conception?"

"That's the one."

Lemon couldn't even begin to understand for herself; how could she expect that a near stranger, using her as a test case, would know what it's like to see-saw mentally while the space before your eyes goes entirely black. And sometimes blue. No, Claudia was nice enough, and she meant well, but even she wouldn't understand a psychic bruise. And how would she react to learning that her client's belly dared her not to eat? "Just listen to your gut," Claudia had been advising. "Trust your inner voice." Yeah, well, look where that's got me! Lemon's face contorted. Cramps shot across her belly, back and forth like laser beams at the planetarium.

Claudia reached out to steady Lemon, who was by then on the edge of her chair.

"Here, take my hand."

Lemon rose slowly, pale and disoriented.

"I'm fine. No worries, Claudia. You don't miss what you've never had."

Claudia caught Lemon and helped her back to her chair just as she passed out.

"But Lemon, what if you do?"

Lemon regained consciousness after about a minute and Claudia immediately moved to her filing cabinet to retrieve Lemon's home phone number. "I'm going to call your mother." But Lemon reached out for Claudia's skirt as she swished past. "Please," she begged, gripping the material tightly so that Claudia couldn't pull away. "Please don't call Ma. She'll freak." Lemon offered Jan's phone number at university instead.

"Okay," Claudia agreed. "We'll call her first." She walked over to the phone, chewed her fingernails and fought the urge to light a cigarette while she dialled.

When Jan appeared in the guidance office doorway twenty minutes later, she was flushed from rushing. Claudia turned and stretched out her trembling hand for Jan to shake.

"Thank you for coming," Claudia said. "I'm glad you were there to pick up the phone because as I mentioned, I'm uncomfortable with Lemon leaving school property on her own, and she insists I don't contact her mother."

The girls exchanged knowing glances. Claudia stepped out of the way and Jan moved to embrace Lemon.

"I came as fast as I could, Lem. What happened? Are you okay?" Jan pulled back to investigate. "Oh my God, you're so pale! Maybe we *should* call Lilith."

"No!" Lemon said, feverishly. "Not her." Lemon lowered her voice. "You know how she is?" Lemon couldn't bare the thought of sharing this with her mother. What would she say? 'Look, Ma. I have this funny little problem — a behavioural tic you could call it — and well . . . I've been stuffing my face and then puking my guts out!'

"Really, Jan," she said. "I'm just tired."

"And hungry," Claudia added, fishing in the wide pockets of her pants and pulling out a package of cigarettes and a book of matches. "It's okay," she added, with a cigarette between her lips. "Lots of girls do it; it's going to be okay." Claudia struck the match and inhaled with desperation. When she spoke again it was too quickly. "It's an addiction or compulsion. I mean obsession . . . *Anyway* you can change."

"Let's not make a big deal out of this," Lemon said. "So I had one brush with unconsciousness. Things could be worse." She feigned a laugh. "I've just now had a breakthrough thanks to this small intervention. All better now. See?" She looked around the room for her school bag and stood up more energetically that she felt. "And by the way, there's a no-smoking rule at school."

Jan noticed Claudia's expression.

"Cut it out, Lem."

Claudia stubbed her cigarette on the inside of the garbage pail, dropped the butt and waved her hands about to disperse the smoke.

"Lemon, if your health's in danger I have an obligation to deal with it. I could get in a lot of trouble if something happened to you." She fidgeted with the pendant on her necklace. "Okay . . . ideally I'd wanted to bring this up at a better time but . . . well the thing is, I've already talked it over with my supervisor and I think you'd benefit from an in-patient program at Toronto General."

"A what! You did what?"

"It's especially for eating disorders."

"You have an eating disorder?" Jan stepped forward.

"No!" Lemon waved her back. "No. I'm just . . . just . . . I'm trying to get my life under control!"

"I really think . . . In my professional opinion," Claudia addressed Jan, "Lemon is using food to meet unconscious emotional needs."

"Don't you mean *sub*conscious?" Lemon spat. "I haven't fallen asleep in one of your sessions yet!" She reached for Jan's hand. "I don't know what's with all this touchy-feely crap, Claudia, but we're out of here."

"I can't let you do that," Claudia said, stepping in front of the door. "Not until we come to some agreement."

"Since when can you tell me what to — "

Jan interrupted.

"Excuse me . . . um . . . Claudia? I know *I'm* no expert, but what if for now *I* took Lemon home. You know, made sure she gets to a doctor tomorrow for a checkup and that she comes back to see you first thing next week. Tomorrow she'll have slept," Jan continued. "And be in better shape to talk. I'll even stay with her for the night to make sure."

"I don't know," Claudia said, looking at the girls, her watch, and back at the girls once more. Claudia had called ahead to her next school and postponed all her afternoon appointments but she was still going to be very late.

Lemon's eyes pleaded.

"I swear I'll eat something as soon as I get home."

"Oh, all right. Okay, for now I'm trusting you, but I want you to call me first thing in the morning, Lemon. No excuses. Here's my home number." Claudia tore a piece of paper from her notepad, scribbled her number on the back and turned to Jan. "And I'm counting on you to keep your word."

Jan nodded, taking the paper, folding it and slipping it into her pants pocket.

That night, after Jan had fallen asleep and Lilith was snoring loudly from the living room, Lemon crept into the bathroom with her diary and a pen. She sat on the toilet, uncapped the pen and set the diary on her lap. *What'll I do now?* she thought, full of anger and frustration and fear. And then every feeling she'd been stuffing down poured out into a letter, the pen thundering back and forth across her pages, as though she was pounding on the chest of her worst nightmare. When she was done, Lemon had filled ten pages and her hand hurt from clasping the pen so tightly. She was drained of all emotion and the urge to purge had also passed, for the time being. Lemon reread what she'd written and realized these words sounded just like every other letter she'd written to her father since she was nine: addressed to an unnamed person. Recounting the daily events of her life and then ending with a drawn-out, maudlin wish for future closeness. She stood, tore out all her pages into tiny pieces and threw them in the toilet. Not another word until I know who I'm writing to, Lemon thought. She poked her stomach. And not another word from you.

189

When James is on the diving board about to jump, or even training for competition, the routine is always the same. He follows a formula for success. He leaps and falls with total control, or he slips in to the waist, clenching his teeth because water is coldest dancing about his bare midriff, and then dunks under quickly and shoots down the centre of the lane. Gravity seems to have minimal impact there. He breathes out, expelling oxygen into chlorinated water. He lifts his hand overhead and hears his coach's advice from the deck of the pool. Neck to the right. Inhale! Hand over head, neck to the left. Exhale. Good! Again. And this time do it faster! Kick from the hip. Keep your knees locked. How many times do I have to tell you? James cuts water like a sword sliding into its sheath. He thinks of himself as a weapon and moves through the pool in perfect aerodynamic position. No splashing. Streamlined motions. Gliding like a whale, imposing and gentle at once.

He's used to this daily ritual, a little too used to it, he sometimes thinks. He's grown as addicted to weightlessness as a junkie is addicted to his next fix. More than one or two days without training and James starts to feel agitated. He becomes restless and irritable. By now his body expects the adrenalin rush, the charge to his muscular, skeletal and nervous systems. And when he occasionally turns up late for practice, he can't sleep well the following few nights. It's not just my legs and arms needing to move, James tells himself. It's my conscience that won't let me rest. When he's just sitting around or studying, he thinks about *her*. His birth mother. How she died for him.

James continues to arrive at the pool at 5:30 each morning. He can't let his coach down now, or the rest of the team. And his father wouldn't understand. Jonathan has told him on many occasions: Real men don't quit. So James returns to the pool where levity leaks out through his every pore and with it goes other preoccupations. In the pool he leaves himself behind. Always trying to improve is exhausting but he can't stop or even pause to consider other options. The idea of James without his bathing suit and cap is as unimaginable to him as it would be to his parents or the guys on his team. Instead he trains harder. Concentrates on nothing but water. Even when he's sitting in a lecture, his mind drifts towards chlorine dreams, where the meat of cheeks and thighs shakes firmly with each forward lurch. Where his arms reach and pull him towards a distant wall. There, he tucks his knees to his chest as he's supposed to and rolls away. Rolls student away. Rolls son away. When his feet meet the wall he pushes as hard as he can, pushing but going nowhere fast. James breaks into open water with the same body that he thinks was used to break through his mother's birth canal. He must win. Apparently it's his destiny.

James might be the fastest. The strongest. Immune to pain. But he's also become somewhat anti-social, like fish. Water is his only real friend. The only one he trusts. It's like a sea sponge soaking up his heaviness before that heaviness consumes and depresses him. Squeeze it out, he thinks while he swims. Let it stream between my toes. After so many years, months, hours in a straight lane in the same direction, it's easy for him to talk himself into listening only to the pounding, pounding of his heart. With each stroke, James grunts determination. He forgets gravity and everything invisible. He forgets his grade-point average, and the fact that he reminds Aggie, his stepmother, of her secondary status. James even forgets the constant twitch of his man's desire and his father's lofty expectations. Instead he sees *her* there. At the end of a lane. He sees his birth mother's impatient expression suggesting that she's waiting, waiting, waiting for him to catch up. James swims hardest in these moments and when he touches the wall, he doesn't look at the clock to verify his time; he looks for forgiveness instead. But her image has always gone by that time, gone before he can say, "I'm sorry."

And so there's water again. The pool alive. Yes, and everything above it, James has come to realize, looms larger than it should. In the pool only the present tense splashes in his face, and only the present sneaks under his goggles and stings his eyes. Because the present, James has discovered, is a neutral, guiltless place. Stay submerged in these holy waters, he thinks. Avoid thinking about the crimes time has committed. Be free. Be happy. Be safe in the water, where burdens sink to the bottom like stones.

Ironically, as unaware as James is about his own motivations, he always swims with his eyes wide open. You never know. You never know when someone else will run right into you. So from the corner of his eye, he watches his competitors. If they gain on him during a race, he turns on the extra burst of energy and makes sure he pulls ahead in time to win. If they swim too slowly in the fast lane he passes them without warning. He's beaten his own best times now, broken important records, won trophies and impressed beautiful girls. James knows all of that and still his lack of enthusiasm is beginning to show. His coach has tried cutting precious seconds off of his time trials in order to create a greater challenge. He's added dozens of the most taxing strokes to James's training regimen. But so what? James speeds across the pool in his orange bathing suit and blue U of T cap, with his coach or father or even adoring young women watching from the sidelines, and he feels invisible. Misunderstood. He feels like a monarch butterfly with wings lifting him just above the surface. A monarch, James thinks. Stuck with one identity but longing for another.

Yes, he's slowly been coming to realize that in the water, face down, he is faced with himself. Faced with following the pale blue line that is as much a part of him as surface veins and sadness. Blue like a breech birth. And when he's sure that his wings are too weary to continue and that his lungs cannot be pushed further without catching fire, James listens for his coach's voice egging him on. Go! Go! Then his father too. Win, son! Win it for me! And finally his own warbled words escaping. Mother? Mother? Working hard, it's James's voice that filters to him strongest through gallons, like a fetus through placenta. Sweating in the water is like crying in the rain.

James asked Jan out to dinner for the first date. On their second date, they'd gone to a movie and later for a walk, talking late into the night. Since then they had been out several times together and had enough fun that Jan would have been disappointed if more than a day had passed without a call from James. His interest in her was evident though, and he either phoned or swung by her dorm room for a visit regularly. Jan felt excited by the attention, and also felt a nebulous wish to try and reciprocate. "Sure," she'd said, when he asked. "We can be more than friends." After all, she relished spending time with him, they had classes in common and many women in the dormitory found James attractive. He made good enough grades — not as good as hers, Jan thought, but he was sweet, and attentive. She had to admit, he was a good catch. He was also the first guy who'd shown any genuine romantic interest in her.

James's sex appeal wasn't the thing Jan most admired in him. In fact, his sexuality, in her opinion, seemed tempered by his social status. His was a clean-cut and controlled interest in the opposite sex. Not the dirty, unbridled desire Jan sometimes found herself fantasizing about. Was he really who she was looking for? He'd gone to camp every summer in Collingwood while Jan had worked various part-time retail jobs. He'd had private French lessons, while Jan had learned French grammar from an audio tape Lemon once found at the library. She and James were different in so many ways. And although he commanded Jan's attention whenever he stood at the end of a diving board or raised his hand in lectures, his larger-than-life presence wasn't as much of a turn-on exactly as it was something she wanted to acquire for herself.

She was very drawn to Professor Walker too, but of course that was different. That relationship was based on professional respect. She'd felt similarly before about other people, though. Pat Fuller, her ninth-grade gym teacher, for one, and Neeta Chandra from her high-school newspaper. They were both friendly, knowledgeable and funny, and their enthusiasm for life was contagious. Jan couldn't help it if she was easily impressed. Surely other people felt the same. Well, not Lemon. She never seemed to feel a drastic pull in any direction unless it was towards her father. Finding her father had been Lemon's passion for years, long before Jan began to have those funny, tingling feelings she was having more often these days. Or the intrusive thoughts.

First came an image of a pretty face or a memory of a previous experience such as wanting to reach across the bed and touch one of Lemon's breasts during a sleepover. Just to see what

195

it felt like of course, just to compare the softness and the round-
ness to her own flat form. It was an innocent impulse that went
away soon after. And there was also the time in public school
when Jan and Sally Martin had played "Mommy and Daddy"
out back behind the portable classroom. Sally said Jan was supposed to push her onto the ground, climb on top of her and
wiggle around, so she did. Then Sally said Jan was supposed to
kiss her on the lips and touch tongues. So Jan did that too. Then
Sally said they were married and Jan jumped up right away. She
wasn't ever getting married! Married meant being miserable like
her mother. She was going to stay single. Find something valu-
able to do with her life: a calling of sorts. But she still occasionally remembered the feeling of heat between her legs as she
straddled Sally's body, and Sally's mouth inviting. It bothers her
now to think that Sally so easily forgot their game as the years
went by. She never had. Well, none of that matters, Jan thinks.
That was all just child's play and now I'm grown and why does
everybody have to be in a couple anyway? It's rather pathetic.

A few years earlier Jan's mother had even become distressed
over her lack of interest in dating. First, Jan remembered, Vivian
had questioned her about her feelings, then insisted she see a
counsellor, and finally she'd gone so far as to march Jan down
the hall to Lilith's apartment.

"Lilith, I'm sorry to be a bother, but I don't know where
else to turn. You're the only one she listens to."

Lilith and Jan exchanged glances.

"What's the matter?"

"She's been hiding out in her room for weeks on end, and
when she does grace us with her presence she's always wearing
that darned headset, blaring music and acting sullen. The way
she's been moping about, you'd think she was born under a

storm cloud." Jan looked down the hall to her own apartment just as her father was reaching into the fridge for a can of beer. "Anyway," Vivian continued. "Yesterday a nice boy from school called to invite her out and she told him she couldn't go! She'd rather get lost in a book. Lilith, I hate to impose but . . . well, to be frank I thought you'd know what to say because you understand what it's like. You're alone. Tell her how hard it is."

"Oh I'm never alone, Viv. I've got Lemon."

Jan gave a little laugh.

"Yes, well, without a husband, I mean. What could be wrong with her?"

"I don't know," Lilith said. "I guess she hasn't met the right person yet."

"Well, I don't want her waiting too long. She just might miss the boat." Then Vivian's tone softened and she turned to face her daughter, placing her hands on either of Jan's shoulders. "Sweetie, I want you to have a good long chat with Miss Boot and then come home when you're ready. I'll keep dinner warm." Vivian turned back towards Lilith. "I can't thank you enough."

Jan had entered Lilith's apartment, walked through the kitchen to the dining room and plopped herself down at the table. Lilith pulled out a chair next to her.

"Don't want a boyfriend, eh?"

"No."

"Don't want a husband, either?

Jan shook her head.

"Not all men are like your Dad, you know?"

"I know," Jan said.

Pause.

"Okay, then. I could use a hand with supper."

Now, as she lay in bed in the dormitory, Jan was touching herself and imagining that she was touching someone else. She squeezed the pillow between her knees. Plunged two, three, four wet fingers inside and it wasn't enough to fill her need. What's wrong with me? she cried as she brought herself to orgasm. And now that it was James's face she placed with her in some back alley, in a dark room, always a lover obscured, she only felt his hands and not the rest of him. With James in mind, Jan was the one being driven into, when all she really wanted to do was drive.

She wasn't bothered by the thought of James in bed with another girl either. But then why, she was desperate to know, when Professor Walker smiled at her husband Zack outside her office, did jealousy mount inside her like a fire-breathing dragon? Am I in love with Zack? Most of the time Jan didn't even notice him perched there reading on a bench, until he made a show of smiling. In fact, Jan barely noticed most men, especially if there were women present. If she walked into one of the reading rooms at Hart House, her eye would invariably skip over certain figures and focus upon others. It was just the girls' clothing and long hair, and musky-smelling perfumes, she reasoned. After all, women are decorated and men have less variety in the way of clothes and accessories. Less to grab your attention. That's why you had to work so hard to become attracted to them. That's why.

But Jan didn't wear bright colours or designs, and she hated makeup because it made her feel as though she were suffocating under a coat of shellac, glossing over her true nature. The only makeup she'd ever applied was used to hide bruises. She preferred to keep her hair short for working out, so she never wore it wound up on top of her head or used sparkly barrettes or bobby pins to hold it in place. And she wouldn't know how to apply a neat coat of nail polish if her life depended upon it, although her mother had tried to show her many times.

Since meeting James, Jan had all kinds of reasons — rationalizations — for why she was still not very interested in getting serious about anyone. Dating boys basically meant sex with them, and she was too busy filling her mind to be bothered with mere bodily hungers. Of course at night on her stomach — with her hand between her legs — or on her back, or on her side, she was terribly bothered.

And she knew that there were young men at school who snickered behind girls' backs joking that they were only at university to find a husband, to get their M.R.S. degrees. Silly girls! Stupid, frivolous girls who pretended not to know things when really they had the answers, made straight A's in math, science and languages but couldn't walk through doors unless some boy opened it first. It made Jan all the more determined to avoid distractions. Not me, she told herself. You could be either smart or desirable and as far as Jan was concerned, she'd chosen the only self-respecting option. Problem now was, James desired her.

Well even so, Jan wouldn't try to impress just for the privilege of hanging off his arm. *She'd* be opening the doors and pulling out chairs for herself, thank you very much! James might as well understand right away. Besides, anyone with half a brain knew real love is ethereal, cerebral at times, always romantic and unfulfilling and very often, impossible. Like Healthcliff and Catherine. Look what happened to Anna Karenina because of desire, Jan thought. Or Tess. Jan knew better.

Perhaps she'd only been thinking so much about her feelings now because she and James were helping each other write term papers on the representation of romance in classic literature. Jan was busy comparing two of Akhmatova's poems and James chose to focus on *Romeo and Juliet* which Jan thought was a predictable and overblown choice. They were just kids. What did they know about love?

"They knew what they wanted," James said, when she'd asked him.

Jan shook her head.

"No, they wanted what was forbidden."

James was everything she *should* want, Jan told herself. Intelligent, warm, and more extroverted than she. He was an athlete with a noble physique and well-knit bones, and he was honest. Then why did she still feel like it would be settling for less to be with him? Selling herself short somehow. But how? After he'd taken her to dinner and a movie the last time, she'd surprised them both by kissing him. Why had she done it? Curiosity? A stubborn resolve to be like everyone else, after all? Well it had been easier than standing in front of her door at the end of the evening, facing that awkward moment of silence again. She'd just leaned in and pulled him closer, closer, then the next thing she knew her keys were in the lock, they were on the bed, and she was running her fingers through his hair, feeling its smooth black sheen. But then he was leaning down and kissing her back harder, more urgently. His face was faintly stubbly and the scent of his cologne wafted over her. She wanted to pull back but James had wrapped his arms around her waist so instead she pressed up against his hard, flat chest and felt a sad longing she did not fully understand. Something was definitely missing. James had probed her mouth with his tongue and she'd tried hard to concentrate on the swampy sensation of tongues gliding over and around one another, darting, pushing. Together they could be water nymphs for the night, she thought. Naiads worshipping each other in wet, wonderful ways. *I am dying for it,* Jan told herself. And James ground his pelvis into hers. She felt his erection and stiffened. So hard. So obvious.

"Maybe we could have some music," Jan said, pulling back an inch and quickly moving to her ghetto blaster and the stack of CDs on top. She selected *Synchronicity* by the Police, and held it up for James to see.

"How's this?"

"Good. Anything."

Jan pressed play and returned to kissing James. His hands moved over her slowly at first. Over her strong back, her bony shoulders, cupping her cheeks, but then after a few minutes he began to grab more furtively, kneading her breasts, tweaking her nipples. It was all happening as it was meant to, James was doing exactly what he should. It was she who needed to relax. So she focused on his hands until only fingers and nipples and tongues remained. Just as it was in her nighttime fantasies, the experience soon became compartmentalized and distant. She was going through the motions more in her head than in her body. Wet, but with an estranged desire. She remembered the Walt Whitman poem she'd studied in class the day before, "Song of Myself," and just then she was one of the men described within it, floating on his back. No. She was the lonely woman in the window watching. Oh, who was she?

Jan concentrated as James's tongue probed her mouth more furtively. She could do it; she wanted to now. If everyone else could do this so could she! Jan wondered how much longer before James would reach between her legs, and how soon after that he'd want to slide himself inside. *Every breath you take . . .* the song crooned, and Jan was urged on by the music. Lust was supposed to be bestowed upon her, not be hers from the very start. Desire must be coaxed from her body. Isn't that a woman? She had to make herself more of an object, that's all. But how? And how to control it?

Jan found herself sitting up and undressing, speaking in a way she'd never before spoken to anyone in real life. "Swimmers have the best bodies," she teased, admiring James's torso, then slowly lifting her V-neck over her head. She observed James staring at her emerging breasts as they suddenly fell loose. Her aureoles were large and brown, and her nipples erect. Was it fear or desire? She wasn't sure. She slipped one long leg, followed by the other, out of black slacks and plain cotton underwear.

"You're so beautiful," James said, sounding as though he'd never fully realized just how beautiful before. Am I? Jan thought. Really? Is it me he wants? And suddenly Jan could see herself through his eyes, rather than her own. For those few minutes she became a new person, a person who no longer believed one drunken word her father had spouted over the years, a person without inhibition, a person who wanted to be loved and finally could be. James hummed along to the music *Oh can't you see? You belong to me* . . . and reached between Jan's legs, spreading them gently. So this is receptivity, she thought. Being passive. She moaned when James began rubbing with added pressure, and shuddered briefly. But just when Jan thought she might be able to fully let go of herself, she tensed. Lying with James in this way still felt wrong. She was following and it bothered her.

"Are you okay?" James asked. "Am I going too fast? Do you want me to stop?"

"No." She said. "I'm fine. I'm just . . . um . . ." Jan moved James's hand away from her body, and pushed him back on the mattress and climbed on top. "There. That's better," she said, her breasts hanging in James's face. He groaned.

"Oh, that's good." And took one nipple into his mouth. Jan stayed like that for a few minutes before pulling away. Then she placed one hand on the pillow beside James's head, the other on his narrow hips, and gently pressed her own into his. She pushed his T-shirt up with her fingers and ran her palm over his smooth chest, stopping at his erect nipples and tugging softly. She felt James's temperature rise and knew his entire body was becoming a single flaming tremor. Her own ached for touch, for friction. Connection. This must be right, Jan told herself finally. It's natural, scientific — a body is seventy-percent water and if you heat water it eventually boils.

She began to unbuckle James's belt and then with determination, ran her tongue all the way from his Adam's apple down to his chest, abdomen, and finally, his pubic region. She resumed unbuckling and unzipping until he lay in full salute, his Fruit of the Looms halfway down his thighs, his jeans strangling his ankles. James pleaded with his cryptic eyes and Jan wondered what more she was supposed to be feeling. She thought she wanted him, but was this wanting truly desire? She slid her face down James's torso. She liked him well enough, trusted him. And admired everything he was, everything he had access to. What's the difference between wanting to be with someone, and simply wanting to *be* them. Powerful. Free. Entitled?

Jan took James into her mouth, relieving her brain, and sucked and licked and pulled on his erection. He reached into her hair, sliding his soft fingers and wide palm to her cheek again, and moaned louder than before. Jan felt trenchant and indifferent to his responses. After only thirty seconds James clenched his fist, and after sixty seconds Jan felt the muscles in his legs and buttocks begin to convulse and shake. She sucked harder and faster until he released a white sea of excitement into her mouth. Jan

203

immediately closed her throat and forced the semen to stream out onto the sheets without actually swallowing. It was his smell that bothered her most. Then just as dispassionately as she'd initiated, she slipped her lips off the head of James's penis and wiped her face on his shirt. "Thank you," he said, and his tone of gratitude suddenly made Jan want to cry. As the song changed, James rolled over on top ready to return the favour.

When he lined up outside the Brunswick House a few days later, James spotted Jan sitting in the window of the Lickin' Chicken restaurant across the street. "Catch you later," he told his teammates, and darted off between a taxi and another car. He approached Jan from behind, covering her eyes with his hand. "Guess who?"

"James. Oh, hi. You surprised me. Um, hi." Jan moved her chair to make room. "James this is my best friend, Lemon. You remember, I've told you all about her."

"Yes, hi," James said. "Nice to meet you."

Lemon puffed on a cigarette.

"We were just catching up. We hardly see each other."

"Well, I won't keep you then. I was with some friends." He nervously pointed out the window and then turned back to Jan. "I saw you and just thought I'd come by and say hello."

"Hello," Lemon repeated.

"We're just finishing up," Jan said, shifting in her seat.

"What's wrong?" James asked, aware that Jan seemed uncomfortable.

"Nothing."

"Did I do something?"

Jan looked at Lemon but addressed James.

"Can we talk later? I'll come by your room when I get in."

"Why?"

Lemon stubbed her cigarette in the ashtray.

"I'm going to the bathroom. I'll be right back."

"What's got into you?" James asked, as soon as Lemon was gone.

Jan pulled her arms tightly around her torso and avoided making eye contact. She lowered her voice.

"I just don't feel right . . . About us."

"You felt right the other night." James squeezed her shoulder playfully. "I didn't hear you complaining then."

"Look, I'm serious." She shrugged him off.

"Oh I get it," he said, reaching for her hand. "I'm so insensitive. Sorry. Your first time is a really big deal."

"It's not that!" Jan said, pulling her hand away. "We have to have a talk. Things aren't working out."

The couple at the next table stopped speaking and looked at James, whose jaw stiffened. The possibilities for Jan's sudden change of heart were racing through his mind. Maybe he'd been a lousy lover? Maybe she wanted someone else after all?

"Who's CB?" he blurted, just as Lemon returned.

"Who?"

"What's he got that I don't?" This time James addressed Lemon. "Do you know this CB guy?"

"Oh my God," Jan said. "Listen to yourself. *Everything* is a competition with you." She pushed her chair away from the table and walked off.

"C'mon? . . . Jan don't leave . . . Jan?"

James threw his hands in the air and stormed out of the restaurant.

"*Who* was that?" Lemon asked, as soon as Jan returned to the table.

"Just a guy. He swims for the school team. No big deal."

"Yeah right that was no big deal. You're sleeping with him, aren't you? And you didn't even tell me!" Lemon was hurt. "He's very cute," she added, with a pout.

"Think so?"

"Sure, don't you?"

"I don't know, I guess. In an angular, stubbly sort of way." Jan wondered if now might be a good time to speak with Lemon about her confusion, but she couldn't find the right words. "Maybe he's not my type."

"Well, who is?" Lemon said.

Jan shrugged.

"Fine," Lemon said. "I'm not even going to bother trying to pry it out of you. Let's talk about me for a change."

"For a change?" Jan caught the waitress's attention and indicated that she'd like the cheque.

"Listen," Lemon said. "Never mind Claudia and all that food stuff from the other day. I've got bigger problems. You know how Ma *insists* that recessive genes don't run in our family?"

"Yeah."

"Then where do I get my blue eyes, I'd like to know? How

207

can she be solely responsible for me? Look at me." Lemon gestured to her own body. "I don't see the resemblance. Do you?" Jan knew better than to fall into that trap. If she told Lemon she looked like her mother in the slightest, Lemon would think she was calling her fat. Instead, Jan turned to watch out the window as James rejoined his buddies across the street. He's such a sweet guy, she thought. Why can't I be satisfied?

"Jan, are you listening?" Lemon was irritated.

"I'm listening. I'm just a little distracted."

"Well try and pay attention, will you? It's too late now. I mean, fishing trips, discussions about puberty, proud moments at school plays, they've all been washed away in a torrent of lost opportunities." She sighed wistfully.

Jan rolled her eyes.

"You've never been in a play in your entire life."

"That's totally not the point." Then suddenly, Lemon stood, whipped up her skirt and revealed a small oval birthmark on her inner thigh. "Do I get *this* from his side!"

The waitress arrived with their bill.

"Not the birthmark again," Jan said, accepting the cheque. "Lemon, you do this birthmark thing at least once a year." She looked up and whispered, "You're apparently puking your guts out but this is what you want to talk about? I've got more important things on my mind."

"Like James?" Lemon sat back down.

"No!" Jan snapped. "Like three term papers due in the next two weeks. I'm supposed to be back in my dorm right now, reading *The Edible Woman* and writing on the theme of consumption in contemporary North American society. *Consumption.* That's food. And by the way, you didn't touch yours." Jan pointed at Lemon's bowl of cold vegetable soup.

"Ha Ha," Lemon said. "What *do* you want to talk about then?"

"Well, for starters, how's Lilith doing on Benjamin's case and how's your new job?"

Lemon looked as though she might burst if she held onto her thoughts any longer.

"Forget stupid old Benjamin and forget my job! *You've* got a secret boyfriend!"

Jan read the bill and reached into her back pocket for money.

"He's not my boyfriend. He's just a friend."

"*Anyway*," Lemon said, changing the subject once more. "You've got no idea how miserable I am. You've been living down here, but I'm telling you, things at home are getting worse. Living with Ma's as annoying as sleeping with the lights on. Listening to her try to answer my questions, you'd think I was spawned in a greenhouse like a hydroponic fruit or vegetable. She acts like I'm a seedless grape."

Jan set a ten-dollar bill on the table, then made a triangle figure with her hands and held them on top of her head.

"Maybe Lilith *was* impregnated on a cone-shaped vessel."

"Very funny," Lemon said. "And I suppose my real name is L-747B."

"Yeah, and maybe you're adopted."

"I wish!"

The waitress passed by the table.

"I don't need change," Jan told her, passing the money. Then to Lemon, "You're blowing the whole paternity thing out of proportion. You've created an image no one on earth can possibly live up to. You're obsessing again."

"Obsessing?" Lemon was insulted. "Well, wouldn't you?"

"No. I don't believe in wasting energy on stuff I can't change."

"Yeah right, since when?"

Pause.

"Well, don't you have *anything* to say about my Dad?"

Jan was growing impatient with Lemon's self-absorption.

"Fine, Lem, if you really want to know. I don't like your somebody-owes-me attitude. People make choices you know? People make hard choices, and maybe you wouldn't understand them." Jan's voice began to tremble. She felt herself filled with frustration and anger and wasn't sure where it was coming from. Other patrons in the restaurant were by now whispering and pointing. "Maybe genes and all that have everything to do with who you are and maybe they don't. Maybe you're a miracle birth and maybe you're not! So what if Lilith's hiding something. So what? People hide things all the time. Do you think we tell each other everything? I'm sure Lilith has her reasons!"

"Holy Toledo!" Lemon said, looking around, embarrassed. "What's got into you? All I want is the truth."

"Oh, is that all." Jan felt a lump in her throat. "I'll tell you the truth," She said, standing. "I'll tell you . . . You're stubborn as a bull! Maybe *that's* what you got from your father's side."

"Well," Lemon said, standing herself and shouting over the top of the table. "Think whatever you like, but I've been cheated!"

"Cheated? Don't make me laugh. You can't be cheated out of something that was never yours in the first place. Don't you think you're being the *tiniest* bit selfish?"

"Me! *Me* selfish? Look who's talking. You don't let me in on the biggest moment of your life so far, and you're calling *me* selfish? I should've known you wouldn't be objective. You've always adored Ma!" Lemon observed as Jan's face burned a blotchy red rash spreading from her cheeks to her neck. She hadn't looked that upset since they were children together in the schoolyard being teased. Suddenly Lemon was back there again.

"Defective!" Jesse Cowan had yelled into her face.
"Defective, defective defective — just like your mother!" Until
then it hadn't occurred to Lemon that other people thought so.
Stupid Jesse Cowan. What did he know? Jesse's entire face was
covered in freckles which made him look like he was always
wearing a back-catcher's mask. He was the boy who'd been held
back twice and stuttered when he did his presentation on the
human skeletal system. "There are one hundred and thththhthir-
ty-ssssseven bbbones in the human ffffoot," he'd sputtered. How
could Jesse Cowan be calling anybody defective? I won't listen,
Lemon had told herself. I'll just ignore him. But the next thing
Lemon knew, Jan was standing right in front of Jesse with her
skinny legs apart, rolling up her sleeves.

"Try and say that again," she dared, swaggering back and
forth, all eighty-five pounds shifting from one foot to the other.
She looked like a toy poodle threatening a bullmastiff. A bunch
of kids from different grades gathered in a half-circle. Then Jesse
laughed and waved her off like a fruit fly.

"You think you can take me?"

"Right now!" Jan barked. "Come on you spineless creep!"
Lemon knew that Jan never let herself get angry in public. She'd
hardly spoken an angry word in her whole life, just gone stony
quiet instead. But everybody in the yard heard her panting, and
her fists were clenched in front of her face like a prizefighter. All
the times she'd ever wanted to strike out, and all the times her
Dad ever had, seemed to be gathered in her fists that day, ready
to explode. "Chickenshit!" she screamed, stepping towards Jesse,
and jabbing at his face to punctuate her thought. "Nobody talks
about Lilith that way! Nobody!" Jesse ducked and the other kids
stepped closer, closing the circle and whispering to each other.
Someone called out to Jesse that he'd better watch it or else he'd

get his ass whipped by a girl. Everybody laughed. Then someone else hollered, "Go get him, Jan!" And before long, Jesse backed away. Just an inch. But Jan knew victory when she saw it. "That's more like it," she hissed, still staring him down and scanning the crowd. "Like I said, nobody talks about Lilith that way."

Once Jesse backed off the others started to disperse too, and the school bell went off, ending lunch period. Jan was left shaking in her fighter's posture.

"Lezzie!" Jesse hollered from the stairs. "You're a dirty Lezzie!"

Lemon stuck her tongue out at Jesse as he disappeared inside, and then put her arm around Jan. Jan leaned forward, her hands on her trembling knees while she caught her breath. Lemon was curious.

"Hey Jan, what's a lezzie?"

"Jan?"

Now in the restaurant Lemon was staring at her friend with that same perplexed expression and Jan looked just as shaken.

"Oh, never mind," Lemon said. "You're not even listening."

"No, *you* never mind," Jan countered. "I've been watching you beat this father thing to death since I've known you. What's that been now, sixteen years?"

Lemon did the math.

"Seventeen. I moved into the building when I was one."

"Whatever. In that time has it ever occurred to you that Lilith did what was best?"

"That's absurd! She took away my birthright."

"Oh *brother*," Jan drawled. "Think about it. Maybe she did you a favour."

"What are you talking about? I've never even seen a photograph. I've never had the chance to decide for myself if I want to know him."

"Be careful what you wish for."

"Listen," Lemon countered. "Since when did you turn into Ann Landers. No wait, that would be Jan Landers. Ha!"

Jan's posture changed from confident to withdrawn and she marched outside. Lemon followed and they both stood with their arms folded across their chests. Lemon stared at Jan, who was facing the Brunswick House and no longer in the mood to listen to Lemon's complaints. After a few seconds, Jan's shift in demeanour caused Lemon to soften. Jan's was the face of a thousand secrets. The face she'd disinfected when bleeding and covered in concealer when bruised. And she felt ashamed of herself for yelling at her best friend. "Okay," Lemon finally said. "I get your point. There are worse things in life than not knowing who your father is."

After being served pitcher after pitcher of warm beer and listening to a local band cover every Van Morrison tune James had ever heard, he left his teammates and stumbled back onto Bloor Street, drunk. He hailed a cab to go back to the university, but as they were driving down St. George Street, he remembered that this was the weekend he'd agreed to house-sit for his parents. They were gone to Niagara on the Lake to celebrate their anniversary. Had it been seventeen years already or was it eighteen? Anyway, James instructed the cab driver to turn around and head up to Forest Hill. He sat in the back seat with his head between his legs, trying not to be sick.

As soon as he got home, James paid the driver, let himself into the house and collapsed on the first available bed: his parents'. In the morning he woke up with bed spins and had to go to the bathroom badly. And that's when the dreaded sense that he'd been rejected returned to overpower him. Running into Jan had been a disaster! Her dismissive tone. Her apprehension. He'd thought things had been going just fine between them. He was even planning to ask her home to meet his parents. Why was she all of a sudden so cold?

James lay in bed with a hangover, fondling himself casually, stiffening for a moment but then returning to his flaccid form as soon as he conjured Jan's face. There are other girls, he comforted himself. She's not the only one. Still, all these years later and here it was, that same eerie sense of being abandoned that had followed him like a lost puppy into his childhood and adolescence and now out the other side of it. He wanted to cry.

Typically, when James dated a girl he became less and less interested in her over time. Then once he'd slept with her, the challenge was completely gone. And now, in some cruel twist of irony, as soon as he'd fallen hard for someone he both desired *and* respected, Jan seemed to want to end the relationship! James's head filled with weighty commandments. Thou shalt not fall in love. Thou shalt not think of forever. She's probably screwing some other guy. Maybe you wouldn't want her if she was more interested. Forget about her altogether. Loyalty is for dogs. Your father's told you that. And James couldn't help but think of his birth mother just then, how sex had ultimately killed her too. Or maybe it was love . . .

James rose from the queen-sized bed and walked naked and barefooted through the master bedroom, past his stepmother's "her" walk-in and towards the "his" side. It was the sole location in the household that Aggie did not scour and reorganise — it was off-limits. Even Jonathan's office wasn't entirely his own, for Aggie would sometimes vacuum or dust if the agency hadn't sent a maid. Even then, the house was her domain to organize and keep track of, and Jonathan didn't put up too much of a fuss when she invaded his privacy. But his closet was a different matter altogether. A man needs a corner of the world all his own, Aggie had always agreed, and that morning James was grateful.

He opened the door, flipped the light switch and glanced around. The room was large enough to be a child's nursery and the walls were painted a sage hue. There was a one-inch dark green border where the walls met the ceiling, and black track lighting fixed over the entrance. James bent down to look under the row of charcoal and navy Harry Rosen suits hanging to his right. He riffled through the stack, smiling when he came upon the GQ stuck between a *Playboy* and a *Penthouse.* James recognized that there were several new selections to choose from since his last visit home. Among the forty or fifty magazines at his feet, half had glossy covers of women with glasses or business suits — a suggestion of intelligence that his father would undoubtedly find seductive. One such cover revealed a young woman in a graduation cap and gown, her breasts falling out as she leaned forward to kiss the camera. Another, a blonde California type in a lab coat, stood with one leg on a chair, holding a whip. "Dr. Lotta Payne" was written across her name tag. James shook his head at his father's predictable sexual preference. The thinking man's Barbie.

James randomly grabbed three magazines and stood to yawn, stretch, go back to bed and finally satisfy himself. When he opened his eyes again he was standing face to face with a brown cardboard box, the word "Confidential" written across the side. Funny, he'd never noticed it before, although he immediately recognized the penmanship as his father's. What could it be? Perhaps just extraneous trinkets that had been moved up from the basement to make more storage space? James debated with himself. It would be wrong to look. An invasion of privacy. He would be furious if either of his parents ever looked through his belongings. But then again, he was already snooping . . .

The box appeared easily to be ten or fifteen years old. The seams had been reinforced with black electrical tape. James grew more excited. Maybe it was full of porn videos? But where would his father have watched them with impunity? Perhaps the box contained sexy lingerie he'd wanted Aggie to wear in private moments? No. Not Aggie. Maybe it was just a stack of Jonathan's failed cases that he was too vain to leave accessible to his younger associates. Or perhaps it was nothing more than an anniversary gift for Aggie that Jonathan had forgotten to pack for their weekend getaway? But he would have made a list for packing, James thought. Maybe they were love letters? Maybe Jonathan had been having an affair and the mysterious box was full of correspondence from his mistress? Now I *have* to know, James thought, intrigued. He'd peek once, just this once, and put everything back as he'd found it. His parents wouldn't be home until morning; they'd never know and he wouldn't tell a soul, whatever the discovery.

James reached up for the box and gingerly slid it off the shelf with one hand under its bottom to prevent the contents from spilling out. Dust flew up into his eyes. He sneezed, set the box down on the carpet, and wiped his nose on his arm, then stared at the top as though he might avoid a guilty conscience by looking through it without actually opening it. Next, James unfolded the cardboard flaps and the smell of mothballs infused the closet. He looked inside and found that the box was filled with documents, all typed on an old typewriter. Not very romantic, he thought. Then he reached inside and retrieved the first of the papers from the top, unfolded it trepidatioulsy and recognized it as a receipt. He looked inside the box once more and realized that many of the papers were identical. All receipts. This time he read the typed columns more closely:

Lodging	$ 350.00.
Clothes	$ 150.00.
Down filled comforter	$ 75.00.

James stopped reading, stared at the box. Holy shit! I was right, he thought. A secret love. Father's been having an affair! James fell back against the closet wall, his head in his hand, shaking it slowly in disbelief. Poor Aggie, was the first thing that occurred to him. But then, poor me, when he remembered the many times in his father's presence that he'd tried to act as if passion was superfluous. As though a real man could turn to stone in the face of love, not become the pebble that James was, skipping across the water, hoping to one day be encircled.

He lifted the letter to his nose to smell for perfume but there was none, ran the paper across his lips pensively, still trying to take in this sudden revelation. Jonathan, who had always professed his disdain for lovers, had been lying about his own indiscretion. He too had fallen prey, he too had weaknesses. James was stunned to discover, at the age of twenty, that his father was not the man he'd believed him to be. James's very notions of perfection and self-control, of masculinity and relations between the sexes, began to crack. He turned the receipt over and read the back: "D. Moffat. Ministry of Social Services and Housing. July, 1986." He was confused and immediately reached into the box, all the way to the bottom and pulled out another receipt. Quickly he turned it over and read once more: "D. Moffat. Department of Social Welfare. September, 1968." What! What's been going on? Who in hell is D. Moffat?

218

I feel bad for how Randy and I talked to Mrs. Moffat back then. We couldn't believe that her husband just stopped visiting and that she wasn't going to do anything about seeing her son! Maybe she couldn't handle the guilt and thought letting his father have him was better than Benjamin visiting Bridgewater. Maybe Mrs. Moffat really couldn't fake being a regular wife and mother. Getting up every morning. Packing lunches. Arranging sitters and taking herself to a volunteer job. I think the day-to-dayness of life escaped her like dirty dishwater spiralling down the drain — round, round — until she'd spun circles for so long she disappeared. Without her tiara she sure wouldn't have done very well at her husband's business functions, wouldn't have been gracious or impressive. She held him back. Now I can see that, but back then I was blind.

"Aren't you gonna call home?" I asked, sitting in the cafeteria spooning my scrambled eggs.

"Never mind home," Randy said. "Call the police. He's your son too."

Mrs. Moffat stared at her cornflakes wilting in the bowl.

"She's right. It's not fair."

"You're deserting him," Randy said, her mouth full of bacon. "You're leaving him motherless!"

"How dare you!" Mrs. Moffat snapped.

"We care, is all," I interrupted. "We don't want to see you get hurt."

"Needles and pins. Needles and pins, when a man marries his trouble begins."

"Get with the program," Randy said. "You're not that much of a basket case."

Mrs. Moffat removed her tiara and set it on the table next to me.

"You want to have a good poke about?" she said, her voice rising. "You want to see where it hurts!" It didn't sound like the Mrs. Moffat we knew. She pursed her lips. "Think you're so clever, well not about me. What a luxury: leaving! Do you actually think I'm made of that kind of stuffing? Yes, I *do* have a boy to think about, don't I? And he's better off without me lying about the house, drapes drawn, too weak to lift my head off the pillow! I'm an embarrassment." She hung her head.

"No," I said. "No, you're not."

"Yes, Lilith. Now you hear me out; no son of mine will ever watch his mother divide from herself, divide and multiply into something alien that cannot care for him properly, div-ide, di-vi-de, d-i-v-i-d-e! The person pulled apart from the patient until the 'I' is completely gone, and the 'dead' takes over!" She was practically screaming through tears.

"Shshsh." I patted her on the shoulder. "It's okay."

"No it's not. No it's not! But if his father doesn't return then my job's been made much easier." Mrs. Moffat pointed at Randy. "Now, don't *you* understand?"

"Bullshit!" Randy shot back. "Think about your boy!"

"You can do anything you want," I said. "You're . . . you're . . . You're a queen."

Mrs. Moffat cleared her throat.

"It's only temporary. Who wants a queen when he could just as easily have a maid instead?"

Mrs. Moffat released my hands and fell forward on the table like a rag doll. The three of us sat in silence for a long time, nobody moving from her place. I was still thinking, it's your son who needs you most, but I didn't say so. Maybe Mrs. Moffat was right. Maybe sometimes the best you can do is keep your mouth shut. Then she lifted herself off the table, smoothed her long hair, brushed her shoulders free of lint, and replaced her tiara. She returned to her breakfast, chewing and tasting each spoonful like it had been prepared by the cooks especially to her liking. Randy got up and left the cafeteria without finishing her breakfast.

"She doesn't mean to be harsh," I said. "She just gets wound up." And then it hit me: There are many different kinds of freedom. At least one for each of us. And I was after a version that wouldn't make me live by another man's laws. I was angling for psychic freedom. Right there in the middle of the cafeteria I closed my eyes and remembered Benjamin's milky smell, heard his cry, his giggle, and saw his toothless smile. And most of all I felt the tight grip of his fingers around my own, how he gave me a squeeze that said, I am the original. I won't be forgotten. A blue light began to cloud my vision. A pillar of light appeared before my eyes and my heart ached. Then the sound of a car engine turning over drowned out everything.

I saw a small pastel-coloured house in a North Vancouver suburb, and a young man wrapping his sleepy baby in a powder-blue slicker and carrying him swiftly to the car. The baby was still in his pyjamas, but he settled back to sleep in his father's arm when they trotted downstairs and through the hall. The front door opened, letting in a new world. Then I saw who it was dreaming! And who it was kidnapping the baby! A hard rain punished them both and Benjamin began to cry; it was his first time out in a violent storm. The car was just a few feet away. Mr. Moffat was sopping wet by the time he secured the boy on the seat beside him, and tossed the duffel bag into the trunk with their other belongings: two large suitcases, a leather backgammon case, a hardcover book about the history of the Law Society of Upper Canada, and a green garbage bag full of diapers and toys. With the door to the driver's side closed and both of them safely inside, Mr. Moffat looked towards his neighbours' houses, and made sure no lights were on.

He removed his wire-rim glasses, pushed the dirty blond hair back off his forehead to stop rainwater from falling into his eyes, scratched where his goatee used to be, and struggled out of his coat, tossing it into the back seat. He looked in the rear-view mirror and a clean-shaven face and excited green eyes stared back. His lashes were matted. His cheeks flushed. He nodded to himself, pleased with his new appearance and with his decision to leave. He wiped his glasses dry on the cuff of his sweater sleeve and replaced them on his face.

The sky churned black and blue like a bruise under the surface of the universe just waiting to erupt. For an instant Mr.

Moffat looked like a stabbing pain was attacking his chest, maybe showing him what sin felt like. "She'll be fine," I heard him say. "I'll see to it." He ignored the small arms that were reaching up to be held. "There's no time for comfort now," he told Benjamin. "You'll thank me later." Then he peered out the foggy windshield, and gazed at the rented house full of spite.

Mr. Moffat didn't start the engine of his Chrysler Valiant. Instead he shifted it into neutral and let the car coast backwards down the driveway. With one finger over his lips he tried to quiet his son. "Shush. Shush. There, there, Daddy's got you now. I should have known better. Romance is for fairy tales." Then he rolled as far along Pinewood Avenue as he could without headlights and the baby screamed like he'd just been ripped from his mother's womb. Behind the dense wall of rain, and a trail of disbelief that was going to last a lifetime, they were nearly invisible. But not quite. I saw them. I saw Mr. Moffat coast as far as he could away from his wife, and when coasting wasn't good enough, I saw him start the ignition and assume a new identity for Benjamin!

I was dizzy and disoriented coming back from that first hospital vision. My body quivered and quaked so much I could've jumped right off the Richter scale. I had to blink three times just to regain my perspective. Poor Mrs. Moffat! Poor Benjamin! I'd seen what happens when love runs dry. Even in that drugged-out state I could see again, and suddenly I knew why I was made the way I am. If I could see Benjamin being abducted maybe I'd see where he was taken. And if there was one missing child, there must be others. *That's what I was made for*, I thought. *For the lost ones.* I finally had my purpose.

"Your husband doesn't deserve you!" I told Mrs. Moffat. "He'll be sorry one day."

But Mrs. Moffat sat limp and lifeless again, like an obedience plant after a hard rain.

"Peter, Peter pumpkin-eater, had a wife but couldn't keep her."

Maybe she *was* angry but didn't show it. Or maybe she was remembering Benjamin's long eyelashes and how she'd made a wish upon each one? I heard her do it the last time he came for a visit. She kissed his lids and gave her word. "Everything I have," she said, holding him away so his father couldn't hear. "Everything I have, including freedom from me." Then Mrs. Moffat sat on a yellow sofa with a bouquet of white daisies on her lap, watching them go. She whispered through her tears and gambled with destiny. "Forget me. Forget me not," she said, while she plucked the petals one by one, until each stem was bald. "Forget me. Forget me not." It nearly broke my heart.

"I promise to find him for you," I told her in the cafeteria. "If I ever get out of here I'll do my best to keep an eye on him. Okay?" But the next thing I knew, Mrs. Moffat was fully back to her Bridgewater self again.

"One two, buckle my shoe. Three, four, shut the door . . ." And I remembered all the trouble she'd taken to get to this point. Locking herself in the bathroom at home, refusing to come out for days. Swallowing sleeping pills and rubbing alcohol, and even trying to chew and swallow Benjamin's soother. And every time she got transplanted to Bridgewater. *How does she last?* I asked myself. *And why would she leave? Why when she's finally managed to convince everybody this was the right place for her?* Maybe it was. "Birds of a feather flock together," she said, like she was a mind reader. "And so will pigs and swine. Rats and mice will have their choice. And so will I have mine!" Then she added, in a very, very small voice, "I *am* out to lunch, you know?"

I didn't really believe her but it wasn't my place to judge.

"That's okay," I whispered, resigned to leaving by myself. "We'll always be a club."

"And I'm in charge?"

"Yes, you're in charge." I leaned over and gave her a peck on the cheek. "Now let's go find Randy and make up."

Mrs. Moffat looked at me like I was a loyal subject. Then she spoke the last words I ever heard her say that belonged to her.

"You're young, Lilith. Your future will cover your tracks, making fresh prints in the snow. Mine is frozen in time. You are more miserable feeling the squeeze of these walls, but I fit in. For the first time, anywhere, I fit in."

"Bbbbut," I stammered.

"No thank you," she answered politely. "We are needed here."

Solomon's fault wasn't that he was evil. But like so many folks, instead of becoming a better version of himself, he settled on average. I didn't know at the time but I know it now. Both Solomon and Randy eventually told me their sides. For almost the whole two years that I was in Bridgewater, Solomon had flirted with me; it relieved the mounting pressure in his brain. The explosion his body craved. He let himself dream. Fall asleep on top of me in his imagination, with his tongue running along the roof of my sweet mouth. But to touch me would have been wrong. He knew that. Touch would just lead to more touch and more and then before long he would've totally extinguished his soul. Better to be partly on fire, he thought. Better to be half a man.

Solomon had had the impulse with other girls before but thankfully some fluke of nature or twist of fate had saved him from getting to the point of inventing diversions like he did with me. Other girls' parents withdrew them from Bridgewater, taking away temptation. Other girls degenerated too fast from their conditions or treatments, putting Solomon off with their uselessness. Uselessness made him hard anyway, but I'm pretty sure it was *helplessness* that completely loosened that powder keg inside. Solomon cared about everyone in the hospital, but not as much as he cared about me. With me he'd been good. That's how much he loved me. But pacing back and forth in the nurses' station that terrible night, he had me on his mind and wouldn't let go. Just like any rapist.

Did he really wander through those halls happy, guilt-free most of the time? Was his conscience clear except for a flash when he swiped his arm across a well-set table like Ward One, sending breakables to the floor in pieces? Did he really have it in him to pull the tablecloth out from under the trust he'd gained in us, and leave only scratch marks and fragments and slivers, for love? Did he steal what didn't belong to him? That night it only took him sixty seconds to travel from the nurses' station to the end of the hall where I was sound asleep, for answers. Once that ugly stroke of his arm was in motion, it was practically impossible for Solomon to return to himself without completing the swing. In one direction or another. Me or Randy. But still a swing.

So Solomon heard his own boot heels *clomp-clomp* along the smooth, hard floor. Felt his thighs rub together. His pulse was like thunder followed at five . . . three . . . two . . . one-second intervals of white lightning and he saw my young form streak across his consciousness. Round and plump and rosy. He came to our room cautious at first, like by moving slow enough he might still morph into a better being by the time he arrived. His chest was tight. His head was about to explode. *Clomp-clomp* . . . He was sure he heard my voice then, and it should have been enough to satisfy him but it wasn't . . . *clomp-clomp*. I hardly ever spoke to him . . . *clomp-clomp*. I almost never gazed at him . . . *clomp-clomp*. He tried harder to resist at the same time as he hurried faster. But that wasn't fair either, Solomon thought. Why should he resist? Why not let it be him that I chose? *Clomp-clomp. Clomp-clomp*. It had to be someone. Someday. Did I think I was too good for him? He picked up speed and ran to my room. *Clomp-clomp, clomp-clomp* . . . Who did I think I was, for Chrissake? He'd show me!

His hand eased our door open and because he couldn't go through with it any other way, Solomon created a new version of events. "I want to" quickly shifted to "I don't mean to," slipped into "I can't help it" and twisted around in his brain until it became the only part he could live with, and the only part he thought was true, "I won't. I won't." He silently mouthed those words over and over until he believed in them. "I won't. I won't. I'll just check on Lilith. You don't hurt girls. You teach them. Gently. Love lessons." He entered our room, stood over my bed for a split second, leaned in closer. Then when he realized Randy was awake he quickly turned to face her instead. He would not let himself harm me, so my face melted into Randy's, Randy's into mine, until our features, even our voices, traded places. That was all the permission Solomon needed.

After it was done he rolled off of Randy and stood, tucking his shirt into his underwear. His breathing came back to normal and he calmed himself. "I'm under control," he thought. "Control, goddammit!" Then, feeling generous, he pulled out a package of cigarettes from his back pocket, and left two on Randy's bedside stand. "There there," he whispered. "No harm done." Standing there interrupting that full moon, Solomon was outlined by a faint glow. Not a halo after all, like we all thought once before, but some other energy that Randy knew immediately. It hovered over her husband many times when he worked himself into a rage, flickered like a dying ember after he was done being mean. She understood long before I caught on, that after climbing down from his lonely perch at the end of the hall and climbing into her bed, Solomon was released for a few seconds. Released from himself. Smouldering. Smoking . . . dying out. Yep she knew because she was the snuff. And Randy always said that Solomon belonged at Bridgewater, that he'd be a permanent fixture long after the rest of us moved on. Poor Solomon, nailed to the prison of his mind. Doomed and determined to rise from the dead like Christ, despite his mortal self. Or maybe because of it. But don't feel too sorry for him. We all make our own hell.

"You know what you are?" Randy asked, ignoring Solomon's gesture with the cigarettes.

"Zip it!" he hissed, knowing that Mrs. Moffat was a light sleeper. "Keep your big trap shut!" He finished fastening his suspenders and looked at Randy. Her face was lit by the moon spilling in through the windows, except where his trunk of a body cast a shadow. Randy's face wasn't the normal face of a woman humiliated. I have no doubt about that. Her jaw was set like it was made from a plaster mould. She was strong and Solomon's arms fell to his sides limp. Flaccid. His shoulders dropped. He seemed smaller to Randy then. She reached under the covers to the foot of the bed for her pyjama bottoms, struggled into them and sat up high on her pillow, using one arm as a prop. Her rear end was throbbing and her lip was bleeding from where she bit into it when Solomon entered her. Still, Randy was her smug old self. She wiped her mouth on a corner of one sheet. Smoothed down the sheets and the blanket on her bed, and sized Solomon up from head to toe, confirming what she'd suspected for ages. He was afraid to be himself with me. If he made real contact with me, he'd have knocked me off my pedestal. Sent me crashing to the floor with all the other no-good tramps. He *had* to avoid touching me if he wanted to go on admiring. He had to keep us women divided from each other somehow.

"You're a coward," Randy spat. "Don't have the balls to do what you really want." "You're a rapist, all right." She tapped her fingers on her temples. "Up here. Where it counts."

Suddenly, with no warning, Solomon lurched forward and grabbed Randy by the throat. Then he leaned in so close she could feel his moustache scurry across her cheek like a hairy spider. He smelt like sweat and she smelt like tobacco.

"You don't know me," he hissed. "You know Jack shit." He dug his thumbs into her esophagus and squeezed harder. "You're nuts! I'd never force myself on anyone."

Randy choked and tried to pry Solomon's fingers from her neck. She gasped for air and stared into his fish eyes — pale and watery. That's when I rolled over in my sleep, and Solomon turned his head to look at me, releasing his grip.

"Rapist!" Randy's pulse was in her eyeballs.

"Fuck you!" Solomon stood up. "Ideas don't hurt."

They don't?

After he left our room that night, Solomon went back to the nursing station, knelt on the hard floor again, and rocked. He couldn't stop the scene repeating in his mind. He swayed back and forth with his knees digging in and his head in his hands, and Randy's voice deep in memory. "Rapist." The word had a lofty air about it, he thought. Pretentious. Even romantic. She might as well have called him an artist or fascist, or even a psychiatrist instead. No, that wasn't him, Solomon told himself easily. *He* was dedicated to self-control, not self-expression. He'd set about to manage and redirect those urges, spontaneous bursts of lust. Besides he'd only touched Randy with cold fingers and once didn't qualify as . . . rape. Once could just be sex, or a mistake, or even a figment of some girl's overactive imagination! Most of all, Solomon told himself, you need a victim. A woman. And well, Randy was about as feminine as a football field.

Solomon shook his head with force.

"Ideas don't hurt."

Covered his ears with the palms of his hands.

"Shut up!"

But the memory of Randy's voice filtered between his stubby fingers and his white lies, and even through the cracks in his conscience. So, at 3:30 that morning, when he should've been filling out forms to account for the shift, he'd shut himself in the locker room instead. Wide awake and on his knees, he prayed and trembled and talked to himself out loud. "No. No. No. You didn't. Just because you thought about Lilith doesn't mean . . . doesn't mean you didn't control yourself . . ." He rocked and shook and pretended that nothing had really happened and that Randy had never said what she'd said. Not that her word was worth much. The prayers made no difference of course, and I think Solomon knew it too. That's why his voice rang desperate and pathetic. And that's why he blubbered like a sailor lost at sea. "No, I won't. Not again. I won't." It wasn't really strength from God or forgiving from me or Randy that he needed. He needed it from himself. "Stand up, you pussy!" he thought. "On your feet, soldier! Stop your snivelling!" But Solomon could hardly lift himself off the floor. It was like his body didn't belonged to him any more. "Rapist." It echoed inside his brain. Randy's voice, then mine. He saw Randy under him, breaking open. Then me. Me, face down in the pillow, then Randy. Solomon rocked on his knees and grabbed the sides of his head to pull common sense out again, hurl it against the stainless-steel countertop and watch it slink to the floor, murdered. Mute. He clasped his hands tightly around his ears and pulled at his hair, first soft then with more force, until it came out in clumps. The sound was like a garment tearing. Blood trickled down the sides of his face. He lifted his right hand and looked at the fiery patch of hair clutched in his palm. Noticed that the blood dried brown between his fingers. Words ran through him not confined by sentences or paragraphs any more. Love . . . Lilith . . . love . . . sex . . . love . . . sexlilithlovesexlilithlovesexlilithlilithlilithraperaperape. Those were his own words then, nobody else's. Strung together in free-flowing form and chasing his imagination without censorship. Randy was practically begging for it, he told himself . . . white trash cunt from the east side . . . all her fault . . . she wanted it . . . she started it . . . dirty . . . crazy . . . deserved what she got!

Finally Solomon wiped his nose along his sleeve and then pushed up onto his feet. His knees cracked when he straightened. He moved to the sink and ran cold water. Wiped his wounds with a handful of tissue. Disinfected with rubbing alcohol and contorted his face when the sting registered. He covered the wound with a bandage and was relieved to be able to feel again. He started to reorganize his thoughts. Shook his head over the sink, wiped his hands, and rinsed all the loose hair down the drain. He got Randy's baseball cap from inside her locker and covered his head, tucking the gauze up under the sides of the cap. If anyone asked, he'd say that he'd tried to give himself a haircut but shaved too close to the scalp. He splashed cold water on his face and dried it with a towel which he shoved into the bottom of the laundry bin down the hall. Then he set himself back to work at the station. He had a job to do. More work. Work harder.

Solomon promised himself that he wouldn't walk down that long pink corridor ever again. He would read our charts instead, memorize the names of all the meds and all the symptoms listed in that psychiatric bible. He would be the priest of Ward One. Keep his hands to himself. But he was a liar. That was only the first of many nights with Randy. There were no distractions in harm's way on Ward One, especially not after dark. There was really nothing to protect us and no one to break his path. The only thing any of us at Bridgewater had was a will of our own and Solomon made his choice that first night. I want Lilith, he decided. And I can do what I like. But since he couldn't *really* let himself have me, he took the next best thing. Someone I loved. Oh God, I get goosebumps just thinking about it. He was our orderly! What a terrible thing he did letting us all down like that.

It was almost morning by the time Solomon went back to writing and reading. One hour before the Monday-morning shift arrived. Already his wounds were beginning to heal, I'm sure. It didn't take long. And by then he felt like order had been restored. A match was struck again, lighting his way. The sun rose and the world was pure all over.

I was in the cafeteria all carefree and innocent the afternoon word got around about Solomon working night shifts only. I didn't know anything about Randy and Solomon yet. It was noisy with plastic forks and spoons clacking against teeth, the loudspeaker calling Nurse Ford to the front desk, and everybody yacking. Jean-Ann told Randy, and Randy slammed her tray down on our lunch table.

"Fuck!"

A carton of milk bounced off and landed on the floor. I bent down to pick it up.

"What's the matter?"

I passed her what was left of her milk.

"That son of a bitch is what. He's on permanent nights."

"Oh, that."

Mrs. Moffat continued to slurp green Jell-O through the gap in her two front teeth.

"You knew?" Randy asked, the light in her eyes somehow fading.

"Yep." I stabbed at my mashed potatoes. "I heard him make the request last week."

"Shit, Lilith, why didn't you say something?"

"I don't know. It didn't seem important."

"Well it is!"

Mrs. Moffat and I exchanged looks and Randy stared off across the rows of tables.

"Fuck!"

"What's the problem? What are you getting all worked up about?"

Randy stared at her plate like she couldn't lift her own fork.

"I ain't gonna stand around and watch him ruin you on an impulse."

"I don't understand," I said. "Ruin me how?"

Randy's shoulders hunched forward like two wilting sunflowers.

"No one ever took my side," she said. Not once. Neighbours closed doors in my face when I came knocking all bloodstained and shaky. Even my own family turned away. Said I wasn't worth the trouble. Said I was nothing *but* trouble." Randy was talking about her husband for once and her eyes met mine. "As long as I can give you what I never had, well . . . I'll have done a lot, wouldn't I? Even locked up in this shithole."

"Your Highness?" I said, hoping for answers. But she just turned her face away.

"For every evil under the sun there is a remedy or there is none."

236

I shook my head.

"I don't get it. What are you talking about?"

"All right," Randy said. "Enough with the mumbo-jumbo. I wasn't ever gonna tell you, Lilith. I swear. But now I've got no choice." She chewed her thumbnail. "It started a couple of months back. At night."

"What did?"

"Let me finish. I'm only gonna say it once."

Mrs. Moffat covered her ears with her hands and started to hum.

"One night I saw him hovering over your bed."

"Who?" I asked. Randy looked shocked when Mrs. Moffat piped up.

"Solomon Grundy, born on a Monday . . ."

"Is that true?" I said. "Solomon?"

"I thought you were *both* asleep," Randy said, looking straight at Mrs. Moffat.

I gasped and Randy chewed harder on her thumbnail.

"I didn't have time to think so I did what I did, is all." There was a pause and Randy made eye contact with me then. "When he leaned in about to cup your mouth with his free hand, I spoke up: 'I've got something a whole lot better over here.'"

"No, you didn't!" I shook my head.

"You heard me. I was practically purring like a kitten. And believe this too, Lilith. Flesh knows what's about to happen before the brain admits it. Every soft hair on my skin stood at attention. I was worried Her Majesty, here, would rise and find me on all fours so I was quiet. Guess I didn't need to worry, huh?" Mrs. Moffat dropped her hands. Nurse Ford walked by just then and Randy leaned in over the table, so other folks wouldn't hear. "You were snoring lightly," she said. "It was the sound of your soul getting older, I figure."

"But Solomon? How could you!"

"Okay, enough!" Randy said. "So it was disgusting, but it was . . ." She looked right at me again. "It was worth it."

Oh, God.

I suddenly wanted to stand under a shower and scrub myself clean.

"I knew he fancied me but . . ."

"Lilith, I don't want you feeling guilty or upset, or any which way about it." Randy leaned back on her white plastic chair and folded her arms across her chest. "No one asked me to. It was a test, that's all. So, I opened my legs and I passed. Simple as that. End of story. But now that he's coming on nights full-time . . . you've got to get yourself the hell out of this place."

"I want to know the rest," I said, my voice cracking. I'm not sure why, I just did.

Mrs. Moffat wagged a finger.

"No, we forbid it."

Randy reached for a banana on her tray.

"You heard the boss."

I grabbed her tray and yanked it out of her reach.

"Please, I have to know."

Randy could tell I wasn't letting up.

"Fine. But I warned you. Don't say I didn't warn you."

I slid her tray back and Mrs. Moffat covered her ears again. And that's when I heard Randy's side.

"You know what he's like when it comes to you," she said. "Pretty determined. So when he ordered me to roll over I did. 'I'm a back-door man,' was how he put it. But I knew what he meant. It's not sex if it's up the ass. Convenient. No sex. No rape.

Anyway, I just faced you, pretended your eyes were helping me through until nothing and nobody else registered. Next thing, the bed's creaking as he climbs on, his breathing grows harder, and soon he's grunting like a man working on the chain gang, but I can't feel a thing. I just leave myself behind. After five minutes he rolled off, pulled up his coveralls, fastened the straps, and tucked his shirt back in at the waist." She stared at her fish and chips. "I didn't get any pleasure from this interaction, Lilith. If you know what I mean. There was no passion." She sounded like she was defending herself to a jealous lover when she looked up at me again. "No passion. You got that?" I nodded, stunned by what she'd just said. "Don't be looking at me all sad and sorry-eyed either," she added. "I've opened myself to men before. For marriage *and* for money."

"What about *you?*" I wanted to ask. But I could see that as much as she could be, Randy was proud of herself. She didn't have many choices, but she had that one and I sure couldn't take it away from her.

"Why didn't you tell?" I asked instead. "Report him."

She shook her head, disappointed in me.

"He told me to keep it between us, or he'd be moving on."

I looked at my feet and Mrs. Moffat was so quiet I almost forgot she was there.

"We've got to report him!" I spat. "I don't care what happens to me."

But Randy said she wouldn't tell, and she'd deny it if I did.

"As long as he's occupied with me, he isn't climbing into your bed, Lilith."

"Oh."

And that's when I thought about killing, I really did. Not accidentally either. It was a new feeling: hate.

"Maybe I'll wait until he comes for me again," I said. "Lure him into *my* bed. Twist his testicles in my hands until they explode like frogs in a pressure cooker." I wanted to get rid of the problem altogether. Make it go away. I leaned in across the table and cupped my hand so staff wouldn't hear. "Let's get him," I mouthed.

"Aw," Randy said. "That's sweet. I appreciate the sentiment, I really do." Then she laughed. "But we've got bigger problems than what some dumb orderly carries around in his pants. Sure he's a mosquito buzzing in sleepy ears, but he's an insect, nothing else."

"What about making it look like an accident," I said, still thinking of revenge.

"And give my doctor more reason to think he's right about me? C'mon, Lilith! Be mad if you have to, but for Christ's sake, don't be nuts." I sighed. "It's no big deal," Randy added. "I been saving you is all. Every woman needs to be saved at least once in her life."

"But if he's done it once, he'll probably do it again. It could be Jean-Ann next time! Or . . . we have to stop him."

Mrs. Moffat straightened her tiara

"We can't stop anything, Lilith. Just escape." Then she stood and shuffled off, leaving her lunch behind. *Crumple-crumple* went her paper slippers. "We'll look into the matter," she called over her shoulder.

"Trust me," Randy said, taking a swig from her carton of milk. "You're better off forgetting I ever told you. I've spent my life seeing what's coming up behind like a ten-ton truck. I've seen it all, and what I didn't, I've seen in here. There's really only two kinds of people: the kind that remember and the kind that forget. And in my experience, the forgetters last longer."

I shuddered. Then I thought about the deep echo of Solomon's voice, how it was pure big band. Tuba. Disturbing and even-tempered. I hadn't seen that his smile was plastic and his intentions hidden. *Real wickedness gets disguised,* I thought. *Under uniforms and under the cover of darkness and mostly, under a weak character.* All along I should've been shaking in my boots around Solomon, but I wasn't. I watched him dazzle the nurses to get ahead at work. But that's no crime. He could charm the bees off a bee charmer, was all. I was so busy trying to ignore him, avoid him, that I missed the clues. I underestimated him. *That's* delusional: thinking someone's more or less important than they really are.

I guess I just didn't want to feel fear at a cellular level, fear you can't even name. Ancient, warrior fear. Fear of extinction. So deep it drives you to justify anything, in order to save your own kind. Nobody wants to feel that. But Randy did from the start, and I must have recognized it too, somewhere deep. I'd always steered clear of him. And there in the cafeteria, when I had no choice but to see the situation for what it really was, it felt worse than when Mother was angry with me, worse than when Daddy signed me into Bridgewater, because what Solomon had wanted to do to me, and what he'd done with Randy, was just the clearest example I'd ever seen of what crazy really looks like.

It still stings when I imagine how it must have been for Randy to know Solomon in full bloom without having us to talk to about it. I thought about Solomon's visits to my bed — almost two months' worth, Randy said. And I knew why she didn't tell me earlier: She wanted to be sure I was steadfast enough to hold onto that self I'd been cultivating. The real me. She knew what it was like to be with someone who you can't trust — like her husband. And Solomon's seams were flawless. Every time he indulged himself it was an invisible act. Truth was, nobody who counted was looking. If Randy hadn't interfered I bet I would've gone on blaming myself for every bad thing that happened to me. Maybe, if Solomon ever did come after me, I'd think I'd led him on. Driven him to it. Worse still, I might have fallen for him after feeling so low, and I might have offered myself to him the way a fish offers itself to a hook. Thank God for Randy. So what if she was declared a danger to herself and to others? Or needed rehabilitation? Her doctor said she'd have to say she was sorry for what she'd done to her husband if she ever wanted to be moved back to the prison but Randy said she didn't have regrets. All she had to do was look anywhere on her body for scars and reminders of why not. So reporting Solomon would stir more trouble and she didn't need that. She said she knew from experience he would be excused.

That afternoon, Randy finished her lunch as Mrs. Moffat came back to the table, sat down and continued eating — no eye contact with the two of us.

"We shall take it to the College of Fishes and Sturgeons," she proclaimed.

"Good idea," I said, right away. "We'll go together. I'll say I saw the whole thing, then the doctor will examine Randy and fire Solomon and . . ."

Randy's mouth hung open.

"You're joking, right?"

I shifted in my seat.

"We don't want him to hurt you again."

"Oh, well, in that case let me put your mind at ease. It just felt like a backwards shit. Barely hurt. Hell, it was worse with my ol' man." Randy spun her paper plate on the lunch table. That vein appeared across her forehead. "I'm so fuckin' sick of you two wearing blinkers! People are always measuring pain in here like it's something they can count instead of the experience it really is. I'm sick of being looked at from the left, then right, on top and below like these doctors can hold up my brain for close inspection, sit it on a scale and know everything about me!" *Thump.* She thumped her chest. "The best part of me is here. Best part of anyone."

"That's true," I agreed.

"Don't you get it yet? We're added to and subtracted from with names of diseases we can't even pronounce, but nothing will *ever* spell normal!"

Mrs. Moffat turned her head away.

"Treason," she muttered.

"Oh yeah? Well, any idea how I fall asleep in this place?" Randy asked. "I'll tell you how. I count every kind of sadness they have for us like I'm countin' sheep, or naming off the seven dwarfs. Let's see, we've got one, two, three, four . . . *geriatric* for the old folks, *adolescent* for the young ones, the *baby blues* for mothers like you, *manic* for the ones who aren't down in the dumps all the time, *dopey*, *grumpy*, baaaaaaah . . . You get the picture."

"Sure," I said. And by then I did.

"Don't you understand?" Randy shouted at Mrs. Moffat. "Don't you see what's really going on?"

"Little Bo Peep has lost her sheep?"

"No!" The purple vein swelled across Randy's forehead. "Patients never get to multiply or grow, that's what! Thick skins are for potatoes, not people around here. Look what happens if we're tough, if we stick up for ourselves. Things only get worse. If we rage, rant, or break furniture, we get punished like little brats. I'm sick of it. Sick of everything. Being insane is nothing but a big fancy word for shut up. Be good. Do what you're told or you'll regret it. Being insane is so all around — in the halls, in our clothes, in the food we eat." Randy flicked her banana peel with her finger. "Fuckin' insanity is so all around me it's meaningless. Now," she said, pulling herself together, "we all got something to whine about, but if you want to be safe in here, if you *really* want to be untouchable, take it from me, you gotta have nothing left to lose." Then she looked right through me. "I'm telling you for once and for all, we're not saying a word." She pointed sharply at Mrs. Moffat. "And I don't want to hear another whisper out of you. Got that?" Randy's tone softened when Mrs. Moffat started to cry, her nose dripping down her chin. "Aw shit," Randy said. "C'mon? Don't do that." She passed a napkin as a peace offering. "Here, Your Majesty. Make yourself presentable."

I pushed my tray away and held my stomach. Sometimes I think that's the day I became a *real* clairvoyant because that was when I woke up and stopped being afraid to see things the way they were. I stopped worrying so much about what other people expected too, or being so easily seduced by mirror images. *You have to see for yourself*, I thought. *You have to stay on your toes.* Ever since then I've looked harder for the truth no matter where I might find it — no matter how ugly or how familiar, I try, even looking inside where things can be ugliest of all.

You know, I started out feeling flawed at Bridgewater. Like a bottle was broken somewhere in me, floating around pricking my insides until they bled dry. During the first months almost two years before, I went to the bathroom and cowered behind the partition, lifting my dress to find the widest opening to my body. When I found it, it was like separating petals to gently insert a finger. I poked around feeling for glass, sure I was hemorrhaging and full of scar tissue. I thought there had to be evidence of my madness somewhere inside, where my doctor told me it originated. Inside where the visions lived. When my time of the month came I was afraid I'd bleed to death. Not because I didn't understand a woman's body, but I wondered if maybe the lining of my soul was so thin by then — so see-through — that I'd never be able to stop the flow. It was after Randy came clean about Solomon that I really changed my mind — or my mind changed me. I decided that even if there was a broken bottle inside, it must be floating around for a reason. It must contain a secret, encoded message. Only mine to decipher.

Mrs. Moffat lifted her water glass, finally deciding to join in.

"A toast!" she said. "A toast to the Out to Lunch Club."

Randy touched her milk carton to Mrs. Moffat's cup, and laughed.

"To the Out to Lunch Club. All three founding members."

Both of them stared at my orange juice, waiting.

I lifted it but I wasn't really in the mood.

"Cheers," I said, as we each drank from our respective containers. But I was already busy imagining what our lives would be like if we all went forward in time. Outlasted the actions that led us to the hospital in the first place. Maybe time could somehow jolt our systems and catapult us into different circumstances. Madness is, after all, just a state of mind. "Okay," I conceded. "Okay, but let's not argue any more."

By evening, Randy and Mrs. Moffat had made up and the three of us were playing crazy eights on a wobbly table in the library. Outside it was overcast and drizzly, a perfect day for cards. Twos meant your opponent picked up two, fours meant pick up four and queens meant seven. Randy put her last offering down on the table.

"I'm out," she said. "I win."

"Phooey!" Mrs. Moffat countered. She was hoarding queens like she always did, waiting to catch us both by surprise.

"Didn't hear you call it," I teased.

"Very funny, Lilith."

"We demand a re-deal!"

"Re-deal. We're not playing poker here." Randy held her hands up at shoulder height and wiggled her fingers. "I'm out. That's all."

"Oh, come on," I said. "It's no biggie."

"What a couple of sore losers."

"Well, it's true you didn't call it."

I rapped my fingers on the table.

"Fine." Randy grabbed her card and went through the motions of setting it back down again. "Last card," she said. "*Now* I win."

Mrs. Moffat and I tossed our hands into the centre of the table. There was no beating Randy. She folded her arms across her chest and leaned back in her chair, as usual, until she was balancing on only two wooden legs.

"Let's play best two out of three."

"We'd rather play bingo," Mrs. Moffat said.

"Well, there's no bingo until Wednesday, so what do you say? Best two out of three?" Randy gathered all the cards into a messy pile in front of her, scooped them up and began to shuffle. "As long as you think you've got the balls."

Mrs. Moffat scrunched up her face.

"Watch your language," I said, leaning in closer to Randy. "Remember who you're talking to."

Mrs. Moffat beamed. Then she wiggled her mouth from side to side like Charlie Chaplin, deciding whether to accept the dare, I guess.

"C'mon," I encouraged. "We'll get her this time."

But without any warning, Mrs. Moffat started to bellow at the top of her lungs.

"Houseboy! Houseboy!"

"Oh Christ!" Randy said, losing her balance and tumbling backwards off her chair. *Crash!*

"What did you do that for?" She scrambled to get back on her feet.

Mrs. Moffat kept right on screaming but she covered her ears with her hands.

"Houseboy!"

"Your Majesty," I said, tapping her shoulder. "You win. It's okay." I helped Randy up. "She wins, doesn't she?" I winked.

"Yeah, sure, you win. Now pipe down." Randy wiped off her rear end.

Solomon heard the crash, dropped his tools and ran as fast as he could down the hall, around the corner, through two doors on hinges and, last, into the visiting room. He arrived out of breath, and found the three of us sitting around the table, Randy pretending to practise her hand-to-hand shuffle, me acting like she was giving pointers, Mrs. Moffat silent the minute he skidded to a stop.

"Woah. What's the problem?"

"That's what *I'm* waiting to find out," Randy said.

Mrs. Moffat cleared her throat and at the same time touched it with her fingertips. Her posture was stiff and delicate like any one of the Royal Doulton figurines Mother keeps in her china cabinet. She reached into her mop of hair, retrieved a penny and handed it to Solomon.

"So good of you to come." She sputtered a weak cough. "Now, would you be a dear and bring us some water?"

Randy's eyes were big, and my mouth hung open. Solomon was flabbergasted too. He accepted the tip before he totally realized what was going on.

"What? You made all that racket for nothing?" He looked at the floor. "Why can't you get it yourself? From where I'm standing, there's nothin' wrong with *your* feet." He stepped aside, clearing Mrs. Moffat a path out of the room. "Be my guest. After you."

Mrs. Moffat sat up straighter in her chair and dropped her shoulders.

"Water please."

Solomon folded his arms across his chest.

"Get it yourself."

"Water!"

"What a snob!" Solomon said.

"Hey!" Randy snapped. "You must mean S.N.O.B. as in son of a bitch, right?" It was one thing for Randy to pick on Mrs. Moffat, but staff were different.

"Do I look like I'm talking to you?" Solomon asked.

My eyes narrowed and I felt my blood boil. Solomon noticed the shift in my expression and posture.

"Beg your pardon, Lilith," he said, embarrassed about raising his voice in my presence. "But why should I play her games?"

I needed a few seconds to gather my thoughts because what I felt like doing was leaping from my chair and slapping him across the face, over and over. I wanted to grab a bedpan — or a frying pan — and slam it upside his head. *Clang!* Let him go out ringing and dizzy, spinning into the next world. Destroy the sound of humiliation so nobody ever has to hear it again. But relief can come in many forms, you know? Not always a tall cool glass of lemonade. Not only a back scratch at the end of a long day. Relief can come from biding your time, and I sensed then that there was one more thing Solomon was good for. So I controlled myself and focused instead on the moment at hand.

Randy touched my elbow.

"Easy now," she said, without moving her lips.

Solomon approached me.

"Why should I treat her special, Lilith?"

"Because she's special too," I said, through gritted teeth.

Solomon twirled his moustache while he thought about it.

"All right. Just this once. And only because *you* asked."

Solomon came back a minute later, balancing three small paper cups full of water. "Here you go," he said, handing Mrs. Moffat hers first. "Anything else?" Mrs. Moffat shook her head. I shook mine. "I'll be going back to work then. If it's okay with you, Your Highness." Solomon winked at me, and with that, he swish-swished right out of the room.

"Keep the change!" Randy hollered after him, and we all pealed into laughter "You win," She told Mrs. Moffat. "Ha, ha, ha. Your Highness! You really win."

"We've got balls," Mrs. Moffat said, pushing the pile of cards towards Randy. "Now, re-deal."

That night when we were all climbing into bed as quiet as a garden in winter, Mrs. Moffat pointed at Randy like she did when she was accusing one of us of doing something wrong.

"We will all stay awake tonight," she said. "But we have questions."

"Oh yeah," Randy said. "What kind of questions?"

Mrs. Mofffat slipped her feet out of her slippers and swung her legs under the covers of her bed.

"Why don't we know?"

"Know what?"

"Why don't we know why *you're* here?"

"So what?" Randy said. "I've got to spill my guts before I get any respect around here? That's how it is? I told you about Solomon, now you want me to let it all hang out?" Mrs. Moffat and I nodded with just our heads sticking out from under the sheets. "Fine then," Randy said, all matter-of-fact. "I killed him. The rumours are true." She was in her bed by then too. "Years ago," she continued. "Before Queen Moffat here ever had a son, and before you, Lilith, knew how to garden, I wandered into my own goddamned kitchen in the middle of the night, figuring why not? Why wait until the next time my darling husband flew into a rage and did me in first?"

Randy didn't give all the details so I've had to fill them in for myself, and in my mind, the walls were mauve. Randy contemplated murder in a mauve kitchen where grease splatters made the wall dark over the stove. Ten years' worth of fried foods. "Murder In Mauve" the headlines could've read the following day. Beside the sink and under the cupboards four rectangles made of milk glass with red apples painted on their lids sat on the counter in shrinking order. One for flour, then white sugar, salt and tea. Randy opened the fridge door and the smell of stale baking soda wafted over her, filling her nostrils. Every food left too long in the fridge leaked its scent in the square box of Arm & Hammer. The plastic seal around the door was yellow. Stuck remnants of a cracked boysenberry jar glued an egg carton to the top shelf. Randy reached in for a beer. The last one. She pulled herself up a chair, her weight slowly pressing the air out of the plastic cushion.

When she finished her beer, Randy washed the dinner dishes, scraped dried spaghetti sauce off the Corningware plates and took the garbage out. The night was chilly and the usual sick air of Hastings Street was offset by the smell of heroin mixing with water, salt, and maybe fish. Randy breathed in deep, held it, closed her eyes, and remembered that not long ago she would've heard her own name being screamed in the sirens of the police wagons. Tasted poverty and desperation in the lining of her cheeks. Looked for her own image in dirty storefront windows at the edges of Gastown. Randy opened her eyes again. Yep, it definitely smelt like fish. Then her cat began to curl around her ankles by the trash bin. She bent down to stroke his smooth coat and he ran across the street, darting and hesitating between cars. Randy turned back. She didn't lock the door behind herself. By then she knew she wasn't any safer inside the house.

I tried to imagine Randy in years past, before all the meds. After Cathy. Her hair would've still been short and arrow straight, and the same light brown stringy texture. *Can't help having bad hair,* I thought, glad for my own thick mop. Randy was twenty-five pounds lighter then. Street-drug emaciated. But that night her cheeks had colour. Round circles of pink underscoring her eyes, like a child drew them in with a Spirograph. She wasn't drunk or stoned either. Randy was more sober than she'd been in a long while.

Even with my eyes squeezed tightly shut and knowing Randy's temper as I did, I still had a hard time visualizing her in a baseball T-shirt and fake deerskin slippers, as a cold-blooded killer. The image didn't fit on at least two counts. *Fit what?* I know it was Randy who had smoked a cigarette, taking long, deep drags until she'd practically swallowed the filter. It was Randy, not hardly trembling, who had soggied the butt under the cold-water tap. And Randy who had bent down in front of the stove and pulled the drawer out, screeching it along its rusty track.

One by one, she took out a pot or pan and examined it for its deadly potential. She was really just having fun with herself, I think. Teasing herself. Any woman knows what the best weapon in the kitchen is. Finally, Randy said, she pulled out her grandmother's cast-iron frying pan. And its black surface gleamed with yellow light. She rinsed it with hot water, and heated it dry on the stove. Watched as the oil from pancakes or bacon bubbled up against the water and evaporated. Randy turned the front gas burner on high. Flames shot three inches up and she placed the frying pan on top to be heated like a branding iron. *The last supper,* I thought.

Then Randy climbed the staircase, skipping over the third and fifth stairs because they creaked loudest. She climbed sideways with the smoking frying pan at shoulder height, in her oven-mitted hands. The wallpaper had to be twenty years old, beige with gold vines, I imagine, running from the stucco ceiling to the olive green carpet. Randy made sure, as she climbed, not to distribute her weight unevenly. I suppose she was used to walking on a time bomb in her own home. Why would that night be any different? From the top of the stairs to the bedroom was only two feet, she said. The door was open wide enough for her to enter without noise. Her husband liked to call down for a glass of water from time to time. Or if he was feeling lustful and wanted the comfort of his wife's flesh. That night, he'd just come off a double shift at the dock and Randy said she didn't expect him to be calling out for much.

She stood over the bed, waiting for her eyes to adjust. Everything was cast into hues of grey, blue and black. The moon cut across the floor in slivers, through wooden shutters, and striped the bedspread. My pulse jump-starts whenever I imagine the beams forming an astronomical alarm system, and how crossing the wrong one could've meant waking the whole neighbourhood. She said she stood motionless, her breathing off and on. She tried her best to steady it, inhaling first through her nose then slowly out through her mouth. Only when she raised the frying pan, both hands firmly around the handle, felt the heat of that still-hot metal penetrate her palms, did she know for sure she was making the right decision. The moonlight caught the greasy residue of the pan, lighting it up like a silver coin at the bottom of a well. Randy held her breath, thought of her previous gentle life with Cathy, made a wish, and pulled the heavy pan down as hard as she could — landing it smack on her husband's head. When she'd lifted and pulled seven times, when the smashing sound of cracking skull was nothing but a hollow noise, and brain matter flew up into her own face, Randy stopped to see the damage. The body, with its liquid contents, was convulsing. Her T-shirt was soaking red in spots, and the sharp odour of fresh blood filled the bedroom.

Randy told this story so many times — to police, under oath for lawyers, at her competency hearing — that by the time Mrs. Moffat and I heard it when we settled in for the night, there wasn't much feeling behind those words. Just like reciting "The Lord's Prayer." But Randy's telling was close to what we'd heard from other patients or even what we'd overheard from staff, plus a few important details. She said she'd taken her time, had wanted to make the moment last.

I couldn't help feeling queasy sitting there with my chilly toes sticking out the bottom of the sheets, and knowing that Solomon was lurking right around the corner. I scrunched my face in disgust.

"What?" Randy said. "You think murder is *pretty?*"

"No!" I said. But you know what? Up until then, I think I did.

"I wanted to take a few minutes," Randy said. "Savour the thought. Good thing too, I guess. Turned out to be the last time I had any control over my life."

"What did you wish for?" I asked.

"What?"

"Your wish. Before you . . . you know? Before you did it."

"Oh." The ward lights went out. "I wished for someone to love again."

We were quiet after that. And I lay there in the dark thinking about how I'd never met anybody like Randy before. For one thing, she was older, and didn't care much what other people thought. Even though we both grew up in the east end where uptown folks dump their refuse and peer from car windows or the number six Davie bus as they pass through to a fancier community, we were as different as plants and animals. My folks didn't have much money either, and Daddy never made it past Grade 8, but at least he owned the Tick Tock.

Randy worked the streets to make ends meet, back when she was practically just a baby. She told us about the men and the heroin and the money. About how when you run away from your true self like she did, you end up running straight into the arms of big trouble. Or the gutter, she said. But she didn't mention any names. After that she tried to clean up her life and do the right thing. But by then Cathy's parents had a husband all picked out for her — a nice life with a big house and maybe grandkids one day. So, they took Cathy clear across the country, to Ontario, and all Randy had left was a forwarding address in another province, and five dollars to her name. She said she was alone in a lonely way, as opposed to just being by herself, and I know what that's like. After that she figured she had nothing left to live for. She met her husband in a diner and for a while he gave her something to hold onto again. She was married within a year. I thought about all of that and everything she'd done for me since I'd come to

Bridgewater, before mentioning her husband again. Then I conjured her leathery and pockmarked face.

"Was it worth it?" I asked.

"Damn straight," was all she said.

And we never talked about it after that. I knew Randy couldn't swallow the idea that her husband didn't get what he deserved any more than she accepted that Mrs. Moffat's wiring was screwy or that my mind was jumbled. Mrs. Moffat, she reasoned, was simply making the best out of a bad hand, and my brain was special. She told me she thought so. The way she put it was almost poetic. Randy said my mind was a vast enterprise, a unique cavern that just hadn't been explored yet. Nobody had ever talked about me that way before and it made me feel like she was tickling me all over with a feather.

She didn't stop there, though. Randy said I could help people one day. *Really* help them. She said if I could read the writing on the wall, she'd be glad to help make it happen. She told me people like me got paid good money to see the future, and that I could be self-employed one day if I played my cards right. She said it wasn't my fault the doctors hadn't wandered in the darkness of a cave; they just weren't brave enough to admit their limitations. It wasn't anybody's fault that a tall spike sticking up out of nowhere like me could form from simple water droplets. *Drip, drip, drip,* I thought. *Maybe she's right.* Everything important in life didn't have to come from complicated, cloudy sources.

I searched Randy's face in my mind while I lay there, wishing I'd met her sooner. Walking up Quebec Street maybe, or riding next to me on the bus. I was sure I'd have been just as healed anywhere, anytime, by her smile. It was a hollyhock smile. A tall spike I could grab onto, climb and swing off on bended knee, look over the fence to an upside-down world waiting for me. If the smile I'd been relying on at Bridgewater wilted, I was sure to plunge to the hard earth below. Without Randy's practical jokes, even her cynical cactus laughter, I didn't know how I'd lose the weight that had spread across my brain like a lead blanket — the vast void nothingness holding my visions down. Once they were vibrant, flashes of blue delphinium. As pretty as Virginia bluebells, or as alarming as cobalt flax. But always they were mine.

Other times when Randy smiled, it was meant as a distraction: Run for your life, it said. Save yourself if you can. I didn't understand at first, but I'd changed. Everything that was unique about me was muted and dried out after so long in the hospital. I couldn't see or smell or feel beauty any more without using up all my energy. My insight was uprooted over and over, every day. Trampled. But through it all there was one voice that kept me going. One raspy, almost rabid laugh, infecting me. I didn't care any more what others said behind Randy's back. That she was dangerous. Bad. Randy knew the secret to living in a vacuum-sealed container where nothing leaks. Not air. Not water. Not differences. And she let me in on it. "Laugh," she'd say from time to time. "Laugh till you're blue in the face." Wide open and furious, like she did. A wild orchid glassed in. I know Randy must've seen hundreds of women and men living as we were then, trapped by the wrong circumstances, and she'd known herself what it was like to get halfway out of your mind and still be able to turn back. She'd never lied to me. I trusted her.

Sure Randy created turmoil inside of Ward One, but she showed me what real chaos looked like. Close to two thousand wilted wanderers, lingering without their senses like pod-people sprung up with no souls any more, all waiting for a better time and place. For a purpose. Waiting like there was no tomorrow. But not her. She was my marker, my touchstone. Nothing could damage my opinion of her by then, because Randy was for me what no one before had ever tried to be. She was loyal. *Maybe it's true what goes on inside me isn't a disease,* I thought. *Maybe I'm a hybrid instead, cross-pollinated between past and future. I am worth more than a dismissive tick on a medical chart! More than Mother's pursed lips and Daddy's disappointed shrugs.* (You can't judge on appearances alone.) Randy made me wonder who I really was. And that's when I finally understood. She was no random particle, laughing spontaneous combustion. And neither was Mrs. Moffat. And neither was I. Not even Mother. Women don't blow up without warning. They are exploded.

That day when we found out first-hand what Randy was capable of, and she found out that Solomon was on night shifts for good, each of us wondered the same thing: How much longer could she hold out protecting me? How long could Mrs. Moffat stay awake? How long before Solomon got what he wanted? But nobody said a word. Mrs. Moffat wasn't even whispering, and in my mind, Randy's eyes were as sad as lamb's ears in an English garden. For all our sakes, I knew I had to leave Bridgewater. The best I could do was to be free for the three of us. I also knew, any way out would be legitimate.

I finally saw my future clearly a few weeks later in the greenhouse nursery, when I was getting ready to plant a mixed bed of dahlia and tulip bulbs. A few patients were being supervised in the room next door, but the nursery was completely enclosed — lots of windows — all sealed tight, and I was kneeling on the mat. I had my favourite trowel all picked out, and was wearing cloth gloves when my ears began to tingle. I was set to dig a trench and put aside the topsoil on a plastic sheet when, without planning to, I stuck out a finger and wrote the word "baby" in the dirt. It came from somewhere beyond me, a time and place that hadn't arrived.

"Baby."

My permission slip, my permanent day pass. Insight bubbled and percolated up again. Above the doctor's advice. Over my

self-image. It advanced at a cellular level, like my body was the
trunk of an ancient tree with bigger and bigger rings marking
every year. Each layer of my developing folds showing another
dimension in time. *Arboreal reincarnation*, I thought. I wasn't
fighting it or letting go any more, so I grabbed at that second
vision like I was clinging to a redwood during a flash flood. I'd
been waiting for another ever since Benjamin. I clung on for
dear life, and don't you know, it was blue with the beauty of a
cosmos flower: aggressive, perennial and self-fertilizing. It moved
through me with the force of a newborn. Then insight hit again,
a deadening wallop like a plank to the side of my head. It was
the first hard evidence I had that Lemon was on her way.

The conception took place after I retrieved the bulbs from
a dark dry storage area, when I was all set to plant. First I felt
slow pressure — like something was bumping up against my
insides. Then a rhythm built as if I was on a see-saw, I thought,
because of the butterflies in my stomach. My mind seemed to
stretch in ways it never had before and there was pressure on
my bladder. I abandoned the task for the washroom twice, and
both times after returning the pressure came and went, waves
building momentum for high tide. The next thing I knew
there was a sudden, sharp pain, like someone was ripping into
my most private thoughts with a sword. After that my head
throbbed and my temples pulsed, and I felt each new wave
crashing into a virgin region of my body. My feet swelled,
retaining water. My belly bloated and my breasts became full
with milk. The flood was within. By the time I found myself
writing in the fertile earth, there was no place on my body flat
or free of sensation. Eyelashes vibrated. Lips were on fire. I was
grateful there was no staff around when I fell forward onto all
fours, my hands landing smack dab in the middle of the trench.

Prickly pins travelled up and down my thighs. I think it was a cosmic tattoo marking me permanently.

"Baby."

I grabbed my abdomen and pulled as much flesh as I could into handfuls. I wanted to stop the stinging, the cramping, by holding onto it somehow. But it was no use. The more I gathered the more pain I felt. I suppose I'd been suppressing my intuition for so long that a dam had finally burst. And that's when I thought, *psychic not psychotic. Maybe it's what happens when you push past all the voices, through to the other side of life? Maybe you turn yourself inside out. Insightful beyond return.* That time I had no way to control what I saw, but I wasn't afraid. There was violet-coloured sky pilot and homestead purple verbena. And there was baby's breath all around, so, I just knew. There would be a child and the child would be my answer. And it was done before the sunlight poured like honey over my convulsing body. Before tears streamed down my face and I realized I was meant for freedom after all.

I released one deep, soul-quenching holler as life forced the last of itself into my consciousness. Then, there were ten good seconds of silence. No voices. No more ringing in my ears. No doubt. Insight had fully arrived: desperate and blue like it was an infant cut away from its own umbilical cord. I thought about my long-ago twin, and Mother and Daddy, and Mrs. Moffat without her boy. I thought about Randy with nobody at all, and how now I'd been especially chosen to be exactly what I always wanted but never had myself: a safe home. I had a choice that day and I cut it loose. I looked at my belly and more peacefulness that I'd ever felt settled into my bones. Then I started to cry and the staff gardener rushed over from the next room to see what was the matter. "I slipped," I told her, wiping my nose on my sleeve and rising from the floor. She smiled skeptically, helped me up and dusted off the back of my dress. "Guess I lost my balance," I added, still clutching a handful of baby's breath.

Maybe my daughter really was conceived in that unusual moment on a Bridgewater floor, in the nursery of the greenhouse. I think so. Maybe miracles — like tragedies — happen in mundane, everyday places. Grocery stores. Laundromats. And maybe even in a psychiatric hospital. Maybe miracles occur where they're most needed.

Later that evening, after dinner was served, I slipped away to the library to be by myself and think. A vision of Lemon had made it clearly to the surface of my mind and out. Like Benjamin. And I was better for it. I walked beside the dusty bookshelves, ran my fingers along the spines, and stopped when I came to the *Concise Oxford Dictionary* shoved to the back of one shelf. When I lifted it out, a spider scurried across my hand so I shook my hand and dropped the dictionary. It fell open on the floor. I bent down to pick it up and couldn't believe what it said. It didn't tell me that insight was a disease or a curse. Not even that insight was the product of an overactive imagination. No, none of that. All it said was "penetration." That's right, it said insight is penetration. I lifted the dictionary closer to my face and there it was again for anyone to see:

"Insight (-īt), n. Penetration (*into* character, circumstance, etc.) with the understanding. (IN adv. + SIGHT)"

Solomon entered the room just then.

"What are you up to?" he asked.

I just shrugged while he pried the book away from me, slipped it back onto the shelf, and guided me out of the library by the elbow. But he was too late. The writing was stitched into my skin over and over, like a patchwork quilt. "Penetration and insight." I looked at him differently that day. I had a plan. My body was already multiplying just as a mind had divided in two, split cleanly across the middle. Seeds had scattered with the promise of coming life. My breasts began to leak.

I was becoming myself again.

The very next day I was leaning against a pink wall just outside the long, noisy, visitors' area where there was a bustling commotion inside Ward One. I'd been standing, pacing, stretching, for twenty minutes, impatiently waiting for Solomon to wander down at the start of his shift. *Every flower needs to be pollinated*, I thought. After fifteen minutes I poked my head around the doorway again and found him wearing his usual army green coveralls, a white long-sleeved shirt and black boots. He was preparing himself to be ignored again. "Walk with me?" I asked, smiling sweetly.

I'd selected visiting day because it was the busiest time at Bridgewater. Solomon's absence wouldn't be noticed right away because there were more nurses in the ward with the doctors not working weekends. Patients were usually distracted and excited by the door opening so often. The possibility of an exit generated a frantic energy for some folks that I can't really describe. All I can say is I planned to get it over with during the day so nobody would know.

I hadn't told the others what I was up to. Randy wouldn't have allowed it. And it was impossible to predict Mrs. Moffat's reaction. Maybe she'd keep it to herself, just whisper under her breath, but maybe she'd blab it to a nurse in a fit, worried I was taking matters into my own hands. Not that I didn't want to explain — 'course I did. I wanted to tell Randy I no longer needed a protector. But I couldn't imagine a single reason, other than my own needs, to discuss it out loud. Not ever. The details of what was about to happen were just proof of a necessity, a pinprick. *Stamen inserted, seed sown.* As far as I was concerned, I'd spread myself wide enough to populate the planet if that's what it took. I just wanted to get it over with and forget it'd ever happened.

I had the benefit of knowing Randy's experience with Solomon in detail, so I didn't want to be too obvious or too controlling. I was careful not to flirt heavily, or overcompensate for my lack of interest and experience. That could frighten him off. *He'd have to be chased until he caught me,* I thought, feeling like any wildflower waiting on an insect. I knew that any minute Solomon might feel threatened and deny me what I needed. I needed him with the steady, sure certainty of an evergreen trying to save itself from tree rot, but I only needed him once. I waved my hand in the direction of the visitors' room.

"Is there somewhere to go? Away from all this noise."

"With me, Lilith?"

"Sure," I said, looking at my nails, appraising them fingers outstretched and then curled over, the way I'd seen Nurse Ford do when she was bored. I pushed my breasts out the front of my dress like they were twin torpedoes and I was preparing for battle. I held my fatter, bottom lip between my teeth for a few seconds. Then, before letting it go, I raised my eyes to see if Solomon's interest was piqued. I couldn't help but stare at the key chain dangling from his pant loop. *Foreplay,* I thought. *Freedom jangling there.* "'Course," I repeated, with a shy smile. "My folks aren't coming for a while. I could use some company?"

Solomon stopped in his tracks and examined me from head to toe, just to be sure he hadn't misunderstood. I shifted all my weight onto one round hip and touched my collarbone with plump fingertips like I was after something I couldn't name, which was true. There were lines in his forehead I'd never seen before. His eyes were full of fading restraint. Lucky me, they said. Lucky me. And any doubts he had about my intentions, or any promises he might have made to himself during those two years must have evaporated. He'd found ways to avoid touching me without my permission, but not a single way to defend against my willingness. When I finally offered myself to him as a tree sacrifices itself to fire, he couldn't resist the temptation to fell me. "Follow me," he said, probably growing stiff under his uniform.

I glanced up at Solomon's pale face once more, hoping to find some gentleness there to grab onto. Maybe he was telling himself I wanted him? I hoped so. Maybe he even thought about love? He led me down the hall, away from the commotion, and was probably already forming an alibi in case he was questioned by other staff: I had spontaneously burst into tears, he might say, and he was escorting me away from the visitors to regain my composure.

My heart pumped hard in my chest, and fear settled over my skin like a giant cat about to sink teeth into live flesh. My lips quivered, registering panic, but I steadied myself, remembering the vision — the baby — and continued without obvious hesitation, to move one paper slipper in front of the other. Then I thought about Randy for strength, and remembered the plastic bouquet she'd made for me in the factory after her most recent night with Solomon. "Stole this for ya," she'd said, throwing the arrangement in my direction. "Seems like now we're practically hitched." Following Solomon down that endless corridor, I knew some of the petals were inside the pocket of my dress. I brushed my hips with the fingers of my right hand and felt them bunching under the material.

"Biggest day here after Christmas," Solomon said, his gait bouncier that usual. He was right too. Mother's Day brought almost as many visitors to Bridgewater as major religious holidays. For the week leading up to it, occupational therapy was dominated by us making cards from coloured paper and gold glitter, heart-shaped cellophane with the words "I love you" and "No. 1 Mum" cut out of red tissue paper. Some patients stole scraps of material from the clothes they made in the factory, and used them later to make more elaborate gifts. I hadn't even made a card, hadn't learned how to honour Mother or wish her well from the sickest place on earth. But I'd found out how to give myself something wonderful.

As Solomon and I turned the corner and walked down another empty hall, I felt an overwhelming sadness for Mrs. Moffat, whose son was growing without knowing her, and I vowed right then and there that I'd never be apart from my child, never let anybody come between us. No matter what. Solomon stopped in front of a steel door with the word "storage" plated at eye level. My face reddened and a rash flushed across my neck and chest. I could feel the heat burning under my skin, but I didn't run from it. I knew the act I had decided on required the opposite of instinct. My freedom demanded the willing suspension of disbelief. Belief in a strong will, I mean, in the idea that something beautiful can come from something hideous.

Storage.

"It's quiet in here," Solomon said, sliding a key into the giant keyhole. I tried my brightest smile. The door wouldn't open so he removed and reinserted the key — this time with force. He noticed me blushing which I'm sure aroused him more. He'd wanted my young body in his hands for so long; I knew he was aching to pluck me at the root. I bet the head of his penis was already leaking.

I tried to prevent my legs from trembling by flexing the muscles. Again, I wiped away a thin layer of sweat that was sitting on my upper lip. Solomon jiggled the key in the lock impatiently and glanced down the hall. Mrs. Moffat shuffled out of view. Nobody, he must have thought, 'cause he pushed even harder. The door finally opened, releasing the nauseating odour of cleaning fluids and rubbing alcohol into the hall. *The first time is supposed to hurt*, I thought. Then I unclenched my fists and stepped inside.

When I slipped out of the supply closet and came back down the hall, the best part of Solomon was trickling down my legs. I tried to hurry. Randy was sitting in the visiting area, playing cards with Jean-Ann. She didn't speak as I passed the open door without even waving hello. Mrs. Moffat was nowhere to be found, probably hiding from the crowds. Since Jonathan and Benjamin had stopped coming by, she pretended there was no such thing as visiting day any more, declared it a statutory holiday. She slippered around the ward ordering everyone's relatives to go home. I don't know what Solomon did when I left him. Maybe waited there a short while and snuck out when I was long gone. When I had my hand on the doorknob ready to go, he'd started to speak, telling me this long sob story and even confessing about Randy. But I'd heard it all

before. He was slumped into a ball in the corner of the closet
when I pulled myself together and left.

I waited for Daddy back in my room. My body was sore —
especially between the legs. I changed my dress because of the
blood, and tore the other one into pieces, strips, and finally
shreds. Then I threw it all in the garbage pail. I doused myself in
talcum powder and felt almost new again. Next, I laid on my
bed with both my feet up in the air for a good fifteen minutes.
I wanted to make sure. When I sat up it really hurt, so I walked
over to Mrs. Moffat's bedside stand and opened it, something I
never normally did, and was surprised to discover that inside
there were other patient's belongings, things that had gone missing over the years: a couple of paperbacks, a book of comics,
someone's wristwatch, a pile of miscellaneous trinkets, and her
stack of paper angels, all cut from material used in the flower
factory. There were so many angels in fact, that I had trouble
closing the drawer when I was done. Each with the letter *B*
written across the front in messy, crayon letters. It must have
taken her hours to put that collection together, and I thought
about taking one for myself but I didn't. I shook my head and
crossed my fingers for good luck instead. *It was going to be a close
call, this plan of mine. It could backfire at any stage.* Daddy might not
react the way I hoped, stand up to Mother. But I knew he'd been
finding our weekly visits more promising and, well, I knew how
he felt about babies . . . *He signed me in,* I thought. *He got me into
this mess, even though it was mostly Mother's idea. He'd done it with
his own hand. And he could sign me out too!*

Daddy wouldn't hear of any doctor's suggestion to end my
pregnancy like some parents might. That kind of thing went
against his beliefs. I heard him say, on more than one occasion,
it was wrong to interfere with Mother Nature. Besides, just to

be sure, I was going to say I was further along than I really was. Giving my baby up for adoption wasn't possible; I'd heard him clearly the day we discovered that Angela Massero had come home thin and gaunt and marriageable once more. "No child should be given away," Daddy said, while he lit his pipe. "Imagine what that would feel like."

Yeah, imagine.

For Mother it was like I was born to be at Bridgewater, a bad seed. No different than most folks' way of thinking, really. And in her opinion motherhood was a moral obligation, not a choice. So I wasn't telling her a thing just to be on the safe side. My doctor couldn't prove I'd pass any illness on to the baby; that's what I'd tell Daddy. The father's gene pool might temper my negative influence. But "Who is the father? Who did this to you?" Daddy would demand to know. The thing is, and I *was* banking on it — he would be red-faced embarrassed to have his only daughter "with child." And while under professional care too! He would want to cause a ruckus, get to the bottom of it — make the father responsible — but Mother would want to keep everything hush-hush. And that's the way they'd always operated: What Daddy wanted got left behind in favour of Mother's wishes. I had an answer ready if he pressed me for it. Nobody did anything to me, I'd tell him. I did this to myself. I cross-pollinated. I am a self-fertilizing entity and I'm perennial. Every woman is, if only she realized.

I thought about the twinflowers who'd just died out for the season and how Daddy took it real hard when Mother lost her other baby — my brother. Everybody said so. He didn't go into the shop for a week, according to Olivia Appleby, just stayed out back in his shed, banging things around. Then the drinking started for the first time. I thought about the jack-in-the-pulpit I tended in the greenhouse and hoped Daddy wouldn't judge me too harshly. I hoped against hope that he had it in him to understand. We shouldn't tell anyone about the baby coming right away. We should just get me out of Bridgewater first. One thing at a time.

That afternoon, I felt wild like columbine, and as nasty as hooker's evening primrose. What a relief! And I knew it didn't matter if Daddy changed his mind and wanted me back in the hospital later, or if Mother was furious about the baby, because I would be turning eighteen before I delivered. Once I was out, as long as I seemed harmless, nobody could ever send me where I didn't want to go. Nope. I was leaving. Getting far away from locked doors and family problems, from the mountains that had started to feel like giant bars on all sides of me, and the unstable, unpredictable ocean flowing underneath. I was sure I'd never get my bearings there. I would move to Toronto, I decided. Where it was flat but reliable. Where Randy said Cathy was supposed to live happily ever after, and where nobody knew me. As soon as my baby was old enough to travel. And I'd use those measly monthly government baby bonus cheques Mrs. Moffat said she collected for Benjamin, and I'd find a job where my skills were appreciated. I was going to grow round and fat and soon be twice my usual size! Randy said people don't pick on those who are larger than them. She said size changes everything. I patted my belly, making a circular motion.

While I waited for Daddy to visit that day, I leaned against Mrs. Moffat's bed and thought about my first few months at Bridgewater. I practically heard her voice whispering in my ear. "Seven, seven go to heaven . . . What's your lucky number, Miss Boot?" I didn't have patience for superstition and desperation back then, didn't have an answer, didn't understand much about fate. Like how it could be mapped if I only knew what to look for. That every one of us has a colour or a number or a friend that's our saviour and that, with that saviour in mind, people are improved.

From that day on I'd keep my lip buttoned about Solomon. If I told anyone, the hospital administration would take action. 'Course Solomon would lie, and Alice Woodward would stand behind him all the way. Maybe then security at Ward One would be increased, patients — my friends — monitored even more closely. Without a doubt, they'd never have let me leave. They'd have let me carry to term, then they would have given my baby to Mother, or maybe Solomon if he'd wanted that. Any woman who allowed herself to be taken advantage of like me, and then went on to deny it, was still in no good frame of mind. I knew how they worked. I saw what happened to Mrs. Moffat. Everyone would encourage me to deliver but then sure as sunshine, someone would kidnap my baby!

A few minutes before Daddy finally showed up, I walked across the room and opened Randy's dresser drawer. Inside I found a yellow piece of lined paper with an address on it: "401 Davisville Avenue. Toronto, Ontario." I figured it belonged to Cathy. I pulled out the photograph I'd inspected so many times, and lifted it to my face. How smooth the glossy page was on my cheek. I could still smell heavy developing chemicals. I admit I felt a twinge of jealousy that time when I turned it over and read what had been written by someone else. "To Randy, with all my love, C."

Again, I thought about what Randy had done for me, how she'd bought me time, gallantly laid down a path to lead me away on miles of baby-soft velvet — lavender cushioning my fall. She was a forest all her own, my friend, a wild tangled garden where anything can take root if you believe. And I saw her in every flower that ever weathered a storm. By then, I even saw her in me. I searched for a pencil in the drawer but couldn't find one so I opened the bedside stand and found a stash of cigarettes, a box of matches, an empty jar of Vaseline petroleum jelly and a fountain pen. I took up the instrument and added my own words to Randy's photograph, hesitating at first; it wasn't my picture after all. It wasn't a memento of my time with her, or our experience together eating and laughing and holding one another freely. But somehow, I tell you, it was. Somehow that picture screamed everything I'd ever wanted to say to Randy but didn't have words for. Like "thank you." I signed it, "For Randy, my best friend too. L."

Two full days after my hard labour had started in mother's kitchen, the nurses in the maternity ward of Vancouver General *finally* let me hold Lemon. First thing I did was draw the curtain around my hospital bed, lay her on the mattress, unwrap her from the blanket and count all her fingers and toes. I knew all along that it was going to be a girl, but the rest I didn't know for sure. I counted each precious digit, examining them for the sliver-thin nails that were already formed and the resemblance to my own. I kissed each tip, gently rolled the knuckles one by one, between my thumb and pointer finger, measuring her strength. It was in the hands, I knew. The hands and the eyes, but the eyes took a few weeks longer. Children aren't totally finished when they arrive.

After I'd inspected my Babygirl's hands I turned her over and examined from behind. I inhaled her damp, sleepy smell.

Her head was perfectly shaped with hardly any hair. I lost consciousness during labour — after nine centimetres dilated, when her head crowned — so I didn't even know for sure if forceps had been used, or if Lemon's wormy blue body had heaved through my birth canal right there on Quebec Street. As I inspected her head I could see there were no bruises or indents. The back of her neck was solid, her spine was strong. I ran my thumb over each vertebra, pressing in slightly to gauge resistance. Her skin was fused with colour — proof that blood was flowing like sweet wine under the surface. On her inner right thigh I discovered a small oval-shaped birthmark. It was the only blemish. *My baby is okay*, I thought. *It's hard to believe but she's really okay.* And when I turned her over again we were both silent. All I could hear was the sound of our respiration. *Baby's breath,* I thought. *Used in wedding bouquets.* I sighed a big one.

In the maternity ward, I knelt on a hard cement floor, my arms on either side of my newborn, my right palm delicately stroking, barely moving over her unripe head. She curled her limbs into her torso like she wanted me to know she was there, but hadn't decided if she was happy about it. It was just like Lemon already. She stared back at me with wide, cloudy eyes, already faint specks of green beyond fish-eye blue. Not roaming but focusing, landing on my face with purpose. I felt naked. Pane of glass. Tarot card. What did this child already know? And what would she uncover?

It was there: I could see it clotting in her bloodstream, knotting itself around fresh organs. It was germinating for now, but one day it was going to resurface and take control. A human is nothing but a vessel and it waits for the proper time. Timing is everything. There would be warning signs, leaking. There would be moments of clarity, flashes of white static. Black holes and dreams of the past. Dreams she'd never fully wake from. I could tell then as I was having a closer look: the future was lying dormant, woven throughout her tissue, multiplying and dividing like an undiscovered gene. Like pure potential. Yes, I knew. And it was the only part I feared. I pressed my mouth to her cheek and whispered so the other women in the room wouldn't hear, "You're going to be just fine. We're going to be fine." Then I curled my fingers into a fist, digging the nails as far into my palms as I could stand — trading one feeling for another. But I didn't need to break skin; I could see what was coming and because I could visualize it, I knew it was real. People would recognize me in our soon-to-be new neighbourhood, the woman next door would hear my TV left on after I fell asleep — my daughter would be allowed to become herself.

Later that night with the sound of new life crying down the hall, I sat higher on my feather pillow, propped first on one elbow and then on the other, wondering which voice belonged to me. I strained to stay awake until I was sure I knew, and after, I rolled onto my side and stared at the colourful wallpaper. Flowers again: honeysuckle. Adam's needle. *I might be stitched and sewn together from the painful delivery*, I thought. *I might be in a hospital again, but I'm no longer a mental patient!* I sobbed and wailed like a war widow. Soon, sleep took over. When I woke up the next morning, Daddy was there to take us home for the second time in a year.

August 12, 1986.

Dear Mr. _____,

I'm going to run away. I feel like Jonah swimming in the belly of Ma's instincts, scrambling my way towards a beast without a name, swallowed by the whale-like force of it. Okay, maybe that's a bit dramatic. I just don't want to be left in the dark not knowing you. Not knowing if we like the same foods or watch the same movies, and even whether you'd make time for nonsense like intuition, dream interpretation or even for daughters like me. Maybe you don't care if time bleeds into itself. That would be cool. I mean, for once I'd like not to care too. I'd like to not feel surrounded by a thick emptiness I can't escape because time and gravity keep me rooted. Here I am though, like spilt mercury dancing down a table leg, sliding through each new day no clue where I'm going. I curdle and separate and curdle again, winding and snaking around the city like it holds the truth, grabbing at it, clinging to the nearest particle. Who are you? Where are you? Why won't Ma tell me! My life is fringed by a tie to her past, like a leathery umbilical cord I can't completely sever. Sure I see the relativity of truth. Who doesn't? But is it wrong to crave only one version for a change? I don't want to be a lonely participle dangling on the precipice of my own event horizon forever. I want answers!

Freddy would understand. Oh, Freddy's my boss and he's as serious about outer space as I am, but knows a lot more. Every Saturday from 9 a.m. to 5 p.m., Freddy's been blowing my mind with facts about constellations, asteroids and quantum possibilities. It's what's giving me the courage to finally up and leave home to find you. (All things in the universe are connected. Time can be travelled.) I'm really going to miss my job at the planetarium, with all those twinkling, endless possibilities.

Anyway, at work I take tickets and guide people to their seats in the theatre, and sometimes Freddy lets me give the introductory speech before the film. But most of the time his overbite and coke bottle glasses get him laughed at, so I try and keep the kids well back behind the velvet rope, away from Freddy. Once they're seated, they become their parents' problem again, not his. I've actually managed to save two hundred dollars (minus my plane ticket). And I don't even mind the really troublesome brats because after the projector gets rolling they settle down and Freddy and I sit in the back where it's quiet, arguing about whether there are such things as extraterrestrials or life on Mars.

Jan hardly ever comes home from university even though it's only a half-hour walk from our building, and I can't eat without wanting to, you know? Repeat. I don't sleep much and if I do, I end up having weird dreams. My secrets aren't my own any more — the blue light, the rescue dreams, the voice in my stomach. I even went to see a counsellor and now everything seems too real. I think Claudia, she's my counsellor, can tell there's something wrong just by looking at me. Like my every thought is jiggling on my flabby thighs as certain as there are molecules jiggling in my neuron cell walls. As if all my worst fears are swinging on my hips for the whole world to know. I'm pretty sure that I could throw up until I'm empty, but I'll never be empty of you. Of the past. Maybe it's not mine to discard. That's why I'm going back to face it.

I can just hear Ma trying to talk me out of it. "I don't get it, Lemon," she'd say. "Why do you have to ditch out on me?" Or, "If I've told you once, I've told you a million times, fathers are people we *all* wish we'd known better." Oh brother! Pretty soon she'll be driving me crazy from an entirely different province.

In my dreams I fly over skyscrapers, dodge jagged buildings. I'm forever one step ahead of Ma's pursuers. You're never one of them but there are visions of sterile rooms, sterilized implements, lab coats and lonely, crowded corridors. It feels like you might be lurking there behind a door, if I only knew which one to open. I dream about Grandma Connie and Granddad Jack, too. And Ma with long braids down to her waist, so tight they pull at her scalp and bruise for days after. She has blistered feet that are too narrow for her black oxfords. I see her wide eyes pleading for approval the way Jan used to look when she showed up at our place after one of her Dad's mood swings. And then I smell blue vervain and see fields filled with chicory and wild lupine. That's the point in my dream when I sit up startled, my heart palpitating like a caffeine blood rush. Ma's afraid, I can tell. It doesn't seem possible, but I can see that she is. And all of a sudden I really know what it's like to be different in a world that doesn't want you. In a world that doesn't understand. I don't even understand. If I do manage to sleep, I see Ma's life as clearly as if I'm looking at it through *her* eyes, and it makes me nauseous. These aren't dreams. I am remembering back! What if I am my mother's daughter after all? And what if time and space have an estranged relationship just like us, and Freddy's right that the farther a star moves away from the galaxy, the faster it keeps going?

Do you think that just because you got a head start, I'll never catch up?

Lemon

At work down at the precinct, or inside the Allan Gardens, Lilith always hears a dull, distant noise warning of information about to bubble and burst before a vision. Sometimes it's the sound of radio static or the sound of a flooded car engine turning over: relentless, soothing — hopeful. Usually the sound grows, floating from the back of her mind up through her inner ear and finally settling behind her eyes. After the noise, seeing is easy. Child's play: I spy with my little eye, something that is . . . missing. Then louder for hot, softer for cold. But around the time that Lemon was planning to run away, all of Lilith's signals became confused.

Mother and daughter sat in a restaurant waiting on service. There were long, cinnamon velvet curtains, a row of red leather booths and a few tables and chairs — mostly vacant. Behind the long counter was a blackboard, with a recipe for a dozen types of juice written in white chalk. Lemon ordered for them both at the counter and then carried the drinks to their table. The whole place smelt like a newly mowed lawn to Lilith, who wriggled her nose, leaned in, and whispered as though speaking about someone at the next table: "Babygirl, there's no colour any more."

Lemon unzipped her coat.

"No colour? What do you mean?" There'd always been colour; she knew that. A giant wave smearing aquamarine, sapphire, indigo, azure. A tide of melancholy colouring space and time. "Does Sergeant Grant know?"

Lilith leaned back, satisfied she'd made herself understood.

"I haven't told him. These days all I can think about is Benjamin."

"Maybe that's the problem. Try someone else for a change."

Lilith closed her eyes and concentrated on the pillars of light, but no blue haze, and nothing of Benjamin or any other child arrived.

Lemon peered over her mother's shoulder to see who might be watching.

"Ma, I didn't mean right this minute!" She caught the waitress's attention and waved. "Could we please see menus?"

Lilith opened her eyes and found Lemon staring at her double chin. She took a swig of papaya juice.

"This tastes like tree bark," she said, spitting it back into the cup.

"It's full of Vitamin C. It's supposed to prevent cancer." Then, realizing she'd just used the C-word, Lemon bit her lip. Neither of them had spoken about Grandpa Jack since Constance's call a few days earlier. Jack was unwell, she'd said. He was having respiratory problems. The cancer had spread.

"Are you sure you want to come to Vancouver, Babygirl. You've got to keep your grades up."

"Of course I'm coming! I want to see Grandpa Jack too."

"Okay. Okay, I'll look into tickets for next month."

Lilith had always wanted to take Lemon on a grand vacation to an island with a white sand beach, somewhere she could see the ocean, but not the Pacific. Not a body of water that began at the edges of a city that once tried to drown her like an unwanted kitten. Whenever Lilith imagined the two of them travelling, it was always in the opposite direction. But where exactly is the opposite of home?

"Don't you think that's too far off . . . considering?"

"Two weeks?"

Lemon nodded.

"Ma, I know you're afraid to fly but you can sleep the whole way. And I wouldn't worry about your visions either. It's probably just a menopause thing." Then she smirked. "Maybe you're turning into a regular person."

"I *am* a regular person!" Lilith snapped. "Anyway," she swatted at the air and adjusted her tone of voice, "how come they've got men in there?"

"Where?" Lemon nodded to the waitress, agreeing to a refill.

"In the *men*opause," Lilith said. "What's *it* got to do with men? *Men*struation, *men*opause . . . *men*tal illness . . . How come if you look close enough, all the shittiest things got men in 'em?"

The waitress laughed.

"Isn't that the truth." She dropped two menus in the centre of the table and moved on to her next customers. "Now, here's something else for you ladies to complain about."

Lilith was famished so she opened hers immediately: "Bar-

B-Que Tofu Steaks." "Hummus." "Alfalfa and wheatgrass." And on and on. She turned the menu over and looked at the other side.

"How am I supposed to eat here. There's no *real* food — just ingredients."

"Ma, I told you. It's health food."

"But I don't want healthy," Lilith said, closing her menu. "I want a cheeseburger with fries and gravy."

The waitress returned, ready to take their orders.

"What'll it be today, ladies? Our house specials are: a garden salad with raspberry and sesame dressing, dairy-free tomato soup with cornbread — unbleached flour, no sugar — and vegetarian meatloaf. Oh, and hibiscus tea is new on the menu."

Lilith wrinkled her forehead.

"Flowers aren't meant to be drunk!"

"Ma, c'mon, hurry up." Lemon was impatient.

Lilith bit the inside lining of her cheek.

"I can't decide," she said.

"In that case," the waitress intervened, "let me suggest a bowl of soup?"

Lilith nodded.

"And I'll have the brown rice bowl with tahini and tamari," Lemon said. There was a good long silence before she spoke again. "So . . . about your work, Ma?"

"It's like writer's block," Lilith continued. "It's like staring at a blank canvas or looking up into the sky and not seeing the moon where it's supposed to be!"

A few minutes later, when the waitress arrived with their food, Lilith proceeded to smell hers first, before tasting.

"Don't mind her," Lemon said, mortified. "She's an actress."

"I am not!"

"Well, whoever you are," the waitress said, shooting Lemon one of those you-ought-to-be-more-respectful looks, "enjoy your lunch."

That night Lemon gathered her belonging and emptied the stash of money Lilith kept in the freezer for emergencies. "Can't trust the banks, Babygirl." She'd already packed, told Freddy she needed a temporary leave of absence, and used her savings to buy her own ticket to Vancouver, which was sitting in her desk drawer at home. She'd also been to visit Jan at the university.

"I might be going away for a while," Lemon told her. "To find my father."

"Lilith will worry," Jan said. "Besides, what difference does it make who he is. *You* will never be something you're not."

But Lemon was bound and determined.

"I have to try," she said. "Or else I'll always wonder."

"Fine, Lem," Jan relented. "Fine. Leave home if you have to. But I guarantee home won't leave you."

When I woke up to find my Babygirl gone, my heart sank into my chest like a heavy anchor hitting the ocean floor. *I've been cast out of the human race,* I thought. *Disowned. Have I done something so terrible? Am I being punished for another lif time, maybe? An eye for an eye.* I held on tight to my shadowy sense of intuition by trying to jump-start the comforting sounds that had always been a part of me. I listened to see where my daughter had gone to, but nothing came.

After that I really understood what it was like not knowing where your baby is. All the worst fears grab hold of you and won't let go. "Where is my daughter?" I asked, every minute of every hour, of those few days. Even though the question never stopped tormenting me, there were no fast answers. *Where are you, Lemon? Balled up in the corner of a rooming house? Curled naked*

around some stranger's torso like a snake coiled into the trunk of a rot-
ting tree? Are you hibernating, waiting for the season to pass, waiting for
your mother to change? Like other parents in similar situations, I
was mixed up with emotion.

Sometimes I wanted to clutch her to me. Rock her like I did
when she was first born. Other times I was so mad at her for running off that I wanted to holler. She needed to know: We each
only get one mother in this world, and like it or not, she got
stuck with me! But there's no one to yell at when your only
child's gone missing. So you wait and think and wait and disappear too. Further into yourself than you ever knew was possible.
And if you can stand to, you work a little harder to try and take
your mind off your personal life.

I still had to earn a living so I did go into the office — sat
in my chair behind my desk and tried to find her myself. I wandered to the Allan Gardens and paced in the conservatory for a
clue. I tried to draw up a contract but my hand wouldn't stop
shaking long enough to write her name, so I ran through alleys
in my mind looking for her. Climbed into playground cylinders
and out the other side, but she was too fast for me. Sometimes,
if I was lucky, I grabbed the back of her dress when she lunged
forward, and tore a coloured piece of material, gripping it tightly in my fist. I climbed fences, catching myself in the barbed
wire. So I felt pain for a moment? What's physical pain to me
without my Babygirl? I left bits of flesh on the fence, hoping,
like sharded bread crumbs, they'd help her find her way back to
me. I guess I did what all parents do when their children disappear: I opened the hundred heavy oak drawers of my mind, a
cabinet with images of my child stored safely inside.

At least that way I could see her again. At six months old,
rolling from side to side on a flannel sheet in the middle of

the living-room floor, her smile was toothless and proud. At two years old, screaming "Mumma bad!" whenever I got my coat to leave for work. At ten, informing me that her best friend, forever and ever, was Jan from next door. At fourteen, embarrassed to the bone when I meet her at the fence after her first day of high school. So many images, each hanging on a wobbly nail, ready to fall from the plaster the second the drawer is closed. And I stepped over and into each one, making sure they were empty, the way you check by habit for runaway socks in the dryer. Every time a drawer was slammed, I forgot where I'd already looked and started all over again. But I couldn't make it real.

Back at the apartment, I touched Lemon's belongings and stared at her empty bed. I called her work, her school, everyone I could think of. I washed the floors and cleaned up so it would be ready for her when she returned to me. I decorated her bedroom walls. Replaced the press-on galaxies she'd taken off with, and regretted every time I ever came home late from work or laughed at her interest in stars and planets. Or her need to know her father. You want it all back once it's gone. You want that chance to do it over differently. And treasures like a stuffed black cat with orange whiskers or a yellow blanket with satin ribbons start to be as priceless to us parents as they were for our kids.

Ever notice that in English there are widows and widowers, and there are even orphans, but there's no word for a mother who loses a child? I'll tell you why. It's because you feel like you never want to speak again. I understood Mother better during those days than ever before. Her grace under pressure. Her handling the worst of life pretty much on her own. She needed to be unflinching. Unbreakable. Even frozen. And

I'm not ashamed to admit it, even though it's all really just a cover, I wished for the same strength: to turn myself so cold that nothing except a tornado would ever make me shiver again. My baby was gone! That's a pain with no mercy.

Sergeant Grant called early the morning after Lilith reported that Lemon was missing. He needed help on a new case, so she showered in a hurry, walked past her daughter's bedroom without opening the door (she hadn't slept all night), and reread Lemon's note: "Gone to find father. See you soon. Don't worry. Love, Lem." Lilith threw on her clothes, stuffed the note into her brassiere, and hurried one block over to Ossington, wondering how she was going to focus on any other child. She wasn't even sure her senses would kick in.

When Lilith entered the station and tried to pass through the turnstile, she ignored the yellow and black police tape cordoning off the area, and tried in her own cumbersome manner to duck under. The transit attendant hollered at her, knocking on the window of his booth to get her attention.

"Hey, wait a minute! You can't go down there."

"I'm with the police," Lilith said, but he was too busy looking her over to listen.

He started with her rubber boots, and worked his way up to her windblown hair. He noticed that her legs were bare under her long winter coat, and that her mittens didn't match. Lilith pointed to the escalator. "I'm supposed to be at work."

"Sure, and I'm supposed to be a millionaire," he said, waving her back. "Listen lady, you'll just have to walk over to Christie station like everybody else."

Lilith burst through the yellow tape.

"Call down, if you like." *I don't know how many times I've told Sergeant Grant I need some sort of security pass,* she thought, in no mood to argue.

The attendant bellowed into an intercom to his co-worker below on the platform. Lilith heard him as she was carried underground.

"Joe, there's a bag lady on her way down. Tried to warn her, but she wouldn't listen. Just have your guys — "

Pause.

"Yeah, big. Yeah, grey hair . . . With the police?"

Pause.

"That's what she said . . . oh, okay . . . sorry."

"Told you!" Lilith hollered up. Then she stepped off the escalator and was met by Sergeant Grant.

"Thanks for coming, Boot," he said, right away. I want you to know the boys are keeping their eyes peeled for Lemon; we're working around the clock. I guarantee we'll find her."

"I know," Lilith said, even thought she wasn't confident. Sergeant Grant handed her a cigarette and she squinted at him like he'd just offered a line of cocaine. She walked a few feet along the platform, right to the edge. He followed on her heels, then held one cigarette between his fingers while he lit a second, which he tossed into the ditch, puffing nervously on the original. Lilith watched the thin beige stick fly through the air, rotate from end to end and land on the middle rail.

"It's not fair," Sergeant Grant said, taking the last long drag off his Players, dropping it to the cement platform and crushing it with his heel. Lilith didn't know if he meant about Lemon leaving her, or about the man who'd jumped holding one of his children. *No one said life was fair,* she thought. *Just bearable.* After all, there she was at eight o'clock in the morning, watching two fellows from the fire department clean the track while Lemon was busy gallivanting around town.

"This one's no unsolved mystery," Sergeant Grant said. "It's just you can form a picture of the victim's motivation faster than anyone. Are you sure you're up to it? I can always call the profiler."

"It's worse hanging around the apartment doing nothing," Lilith said. She covered her ears to avoid the distraction of the cleaning crew. Their machinery made an ugly sound, and she felt a vague and distant resentment rising in her solar plexus.

"Must have been some nutbar," Sergeant Grant said, reaching into his back pocket for a small notebook and pencil. "Simple case of the crazies."

"Naah," Lilith said, dropping her hands, removing her mittens and stuffing them into her coat pockets and closing her eyes. *Crazy's never simple.*

Sergeant Grant waved to a junior officer who hurried over. Then he handed him a piece of paper with a name.

"Brown, run a check on this guy, will you? See about a psych history."

Lilith opened her eyes.

"A psychiatric history?"

What did the past matter now?

"Paperwork," her boss explained. "I need a full report."

Lilith tried her best to concentrate on the remote sense of life that was quickly fading from the subway tunnel. Workers hoisted industrial cleaning equipment into the ditch, and louder machines scraped the track below. The noise filled her eardrums and closed in slowly, climbing into her brain, hurdling synapses as if decibels could jump fences. *Lemon, Lemon, Lemon,* she thought. Within seconds a high-pitched squeal flooded all her thoughts: It was a tsunami state of mind. Lilith tried harder to concentrate but she was getting angry. *Where the hell is my daughter! Why did she ditch out on me — And this guy, jumping with one kid, and leaving behind a wife and daughter! What's wrong with everybody?* If there's one thing Lilith Boot can't tolerate, it's people who overlook their intuition. She covered her ears with her hands once more and focused on the work, visualized. Her temperature shot up and she didn't hear her boss address her. The noise all around was rhythmic: ebbing and flowing ancient music. Song of the dead. Unbiblical chords.

"Got something?" Sergeant Grant asked. Lilith let go of her ears long enough to unbutton her wool coat, and rustle out of it. Sergeant Grant tried to pick it up and dust it off but she was still standing on part of it, so he let go. Lilith clasped her hands to her ears again. "Boot, you okay?" Her face started to itch as if she were walking through a cobweb or rolling around in a field of Queen Anne's lace. Her head was pounding so hard, she felt she might be developing stigmata. She was turning into some kind of holy psychic, sent from another century to remind folks of the timeless way children are sacrificed. *Lemon, Lemon. Benjamin.* Her hands curled into claws, and she tucked her head into hunched shoulders and imagined a canvas with herself inside a tall blue pillar, but the image crumbled just as soon as the high squeal reached a deafening pitch. Her eyes turned around in her head. The past and the future collided. She moaned like a wounded animal.

A man's hand struck a woman's face. Terrified, she cowered in the corner between the stove and the wall. The open wound burned her cheek like hot coal. A tea kettle was unattended on the burner, steam evaporating quickly into the kitchen air. The hand continued to strike. Backslap. Closed-fist thud. The woman was silent with fear. A child cried out in the distance. The kettle screamed for help . . .

Sergeant Grant was loud.

"Boot! You there?" He thumped Lilith on the back. Two members of the cleaning crew looked up from below as she eased one hand away from the side of her head, testing the waters. The noise was slowly fading. Sergeant Grant removed a cotton hand-kerchief from the breast pocket of his coat and held it out.

"Thanks." Lilith accepted it, wiped her face and passed it back damp. "Sorry."

"Never mind that. What've you got for me?"

"Talk to his wife about the marriage."

Sergeant Grant wrote in his notebook.

"Domestic perp?"

"Not the kind to get caught," Lilith said, feeling her breath return. "Probably never been charged."

But Sergeant Grant needed terminology for his report.

"Sociopathic?"

"Socio*pathetic*," Lilith answered, regaining her focus. "Jumped to punish his wife. Or . . . maybe . . . out of love." Her voice trailed off.

Sergeant Grant jerked his neck back.

"That's not love!"

It was almost unthinkable, Lilith knew, but she suddenly understood both things could be true at the same time: *You could treat a child like a pawn in this game of troubled family life, and you could be doing everybody a favour by disappearing too. Benjamin,* she thought again, for no reason. Then, *Lemon.* Lilith swooned and Sergeant Grant reached out to steady her.

"Love is what you make it," Lilith said, looking down and realizing that she was still standing on her coat. *How far would I go to keep Lemon with me?* she thought. *What would I do to get what I needed?* Sergeant Grant didn't argue. Instead he waved and called out to a group of officers. Another young man, this one wearing a turban, quickly joined them. Lilith slipped one arm into her sleeve as her teeth began to chatter. All along the platform were details she usually overlooked: The walls were the orangey plastic colour of Lemon's favourite doll from childhood and the floor a dapple grey. Lilith noticed the wall-sized posters advertising Saviour House — a shelter for runaway teens — and the digital clock which was running behind.

"Check on local women's shelters," Sergeant Grant instructed his officer. "See if the wife made any recent visits. Oh, and bring her in. We'll need her to identify the bodies."

Lilith slipped her other arm into her coat and hugged her thick waist. Her blood-sugar levels had dropped faster than usual and left her with a splitting headache. Sergeant Grant could tell the work was taking its toll. "Now Boot, it's bound to get to you." He said. "Happens to the best of us." He faced Lilith. "You're long overdue for time off."

"I had two weeks' vacation last year."

"No, I mean some real R and R. Away from all this."

She shook her head.

"Not now, Bill. I need to feel useful. Keep my mind occupied."

"Clean up around the house then."

Lilith took a deep breath.

"You asking or telling?"

"Just for a short while," he said. "To recoup. I can see you're not clear-headed. Once Lemon's home safe and sound you'll be back to your old self in no time. There's no shame in it Lilith," he used her given name for the first time in all the years they'd worked together. "And Boot, we couldn't do without you." Then he walked off to join the other officers and the fire marshal, leaving Lilith alone to wrestle with the future.

"I'll be at home," Lilith shouted, "if you have news."

"I'll call as soon as I hear!"

Lilith reached into her pocket and pulled out a block of sponge toffee. *Stressed spelled backwards,* she thought with some degree of comfort, *is desserts.* Then a black vortex spread beside her eyes and threatened to swallow her entire field of vision. "Benjamin," she repeated, stepping back from the edge of the platform, pulling apart the plastic wrapping on the toffee and sinking her teeth into the hard, crunchy candy. *Benjamin. Lemon. Why can't I find you?* Lilith devoured the sugar within seconds and the trembling in her hands stopped: aftershocks. Almost immediately the sweets banished the disorienting force waiting there in the recess of her mind, just waiting to drag her backwards. *What's the difference between the jumper and me?* she thought, trying to distance herself from the menacing questions with thoughts of separation. *He's tall, I'm not. He's young, I'm older. He's married . . .* The technique wasn't working because all that came were similarities. *He's a parent. So am I.*

He was desperate . . . Lilith gasped, short of breath. *Maybe it is time for a break from work.* She reached into her coat pocket once more, and turned towards the escalator. Or maybe it was finally time to find Benjamin.

The following weekend James held his drink at eye level and peered impatiently through the ice cubes, across the dance floor. He checked his wristwatch. Jan had demanded they meet. He'd managed to avoid her since that whole Bloor Street fiasco, but he couldn't very well ignore a handwritten note shoved under his door. "James, I wanted to apologize for the other evening with Lemon," it said. "I owe you an explanation but I haven't seen you around and you didn't show up for classes. Meet me Saturday? 10 p.m.? I'll be at Cherry Bomb on Alexander Street after I finish my essay. Hope to see you then." James looked around and noticed that practically everyone in the club wore black and sported short hair, body piercings, tattoos, and combat boots. Women were dressed in suits and men wore skirts fashioned from recycled rubber and chain-link. I don't fit in here, James told himself, embarrassed by the white of his Converse running shoes that was now glowing purple under the ultraviolet light.

James craned his neck and sifted through the maze of dancers. He peered over mountains of flesh pouring from merry widows and flinched at the sight of a dog collar tightened round a slim neck, attached to nipples and connected to someone else's hand. He blinked, reoriented himself, put his drink down on the ledge and rubbed his temples. The Scotch helped, liquefying flailing and gyrating bodies so they blended and merged into one single golden mass that he could drink down confidently while waiting.

The bass from the music thrashed and pounded and James felt his chest cavity vibrate. This was a style of music he would not normally listen to, with unintelligible words that conjured a sinister mood. He felt uneasy, and associated this style of music with headbangers, as Aggie called them, or raging anarchists, or Goths, or mall rats from the suburbs who were already bored out of their skulls. Not for the sheltered rich kids he hung out with. Other athletes — swimmers and occasionally runners who trained in the pool during off-season. Maybe on week-ends they drank copious amounts of beer or did tequila poppers, but they weren't exactly hard-core partying types. Occasionally the guys dragged James out to scout women at dormitory parties or at the RPM — excursions that were painfully awkward and rarely successful in his opinion. He would ask girls to dance, sometimes making out with one of them behind the building afterwards, but most of his time was spent standing on the sidelines while his buddies honed in on those with tight tops or slim-fitting jeans, and a vulnerability that screamed like lambs in the slaughterhouse.

Strategies of any sort felt unnatural to James because he felt watched. All his life he'd identified more with the prey than the predator in himself. And he preferred to meet women casually, at the library studying or in line at the cafeteria. There he'd be comfortable turning on the charm — complimenting an outfit, acting impressed by a high grade-point average. Besides, he'd never met a woman at a bar who he could envision introducing to his father. "Wait for a good woman," Jonathan said. "Like Aggie." But the women James always found himself involved with were more forward. More opinionated. Less refined than his stepmother. Maybe it was because he was easygoing, James thought. Or maybe he enjoyed being pursued. Well, it doesn't matter what Father thinks any more, James told himself. Maybe I'll ask someone here to dance. Since discovering the box in Jonathan's closet, James hated to admit, he'd lost some respect for his father. And it was mutual respect that had always been the strongest sentiment between them.

There in the crowded, smoky bar James looked ahead of himself through the darkness and dry ice and still did not find Jan. Overdressed and uncomfortable, he began to perspire. Heat seemed to rise off bodies all around him, and people pushed into one another, rubbing nakedness into strangers without permission. He struggled out of his leather jacket and decided to move to one of the bar stools along the side wall. He'd sit in the corner until Jan arrived. Where the hell was she, anyway? Perhaps he should call her at the residence. James scanned the lineup at the bar . . . the crowded staircase leading to the second level . . . the ramp on the opposing wall, but saw no pay phone anywhere. So many men out tonight, he lamented. Nothing like numerous competitors to worsen my odds.

James's eyes then fell upon a beautiful figure with auburn shoulder-length hair. Her dress was the colour of cranberry glass, and cut above the knee, her black boots heeled and laced all the way to mid-thigh. He watched her dance to a slow song; she trusted her lead implicitly, swaying to and fro off her partner's hip with her eyes closed. The other of the pair was wearing a black leather vest, fastened up the front with silver snaps, and black leather pants. The couple gyrated and ground their hips together, lifting their legs, alternating in a four-part arrangement. From a distance, they had become one figure. James enjoyed their languid movements, as if a wave had captured them and they were being tossed from side to side with abandon. He was envious; he too wanted to be trusted so thoroughly. Then the pair kissed, squeezed their thighs closer together, and kissed once more — this time without pause. The long-haired beauty was still held tightly around the waist, one of her arms behind her partner's neck, the second slack at her side. The song changed, the couple spoke to one other and turned towards James, to exit the dance floor. Two women!

James choked on his drink, recovered, and glanced around to see if anyone had noticed his reaction. He scanned other faces for details. They didn't avert their eyes, preventing themselves from being devoured, but instead held gazes defiantly, confidently, as if they were about to reel in a fishing wire swallowed by a shark. His head was spinning. Perhaps he'd heard the name of the meeting place incorrectly? Maybe right this minute Jan was sitting elsewhere, angry with him for standing her up? Quickly he withdrew the paper from his jeans pocket and reread the message. No, it said Cherry Bomb. James looked over the top of the bar where the name of the club were painted. Yes, this was the right location. And then it hit him. This was "CB's"!

James felt an acute sense of betrayal mounting. It was as if he were an orphan from whom bedtime stories and fairy tales had been deliberately kept. Looking down, the floor seemed to opened up at his feet with the impact of yet another secret sinking in. First his father and now Jan withholding. In one swig James finished his drink and immediately moved to the bar to order another. Why hadn't Jan told him she was . . . she was . . . ? Is this why she'd been so distant? Why the hell did his father keep a mistress? James stepped forward into the dry ice and felt as though he was swimming through a cloud, unnoticed, invisible, shut out once more. Irrelevant to all that is love.

James was indifferent to the storm drenching him as he meandered back to campus reeking of alcohol. He stood outside the dorm under Jan's window, hollering and slurring his words.

"Jan! Jaaaaan!"

She cracked her window an inch.

"Go around to the front. I'll let you in."

"I'm not coming in there. Next thing I know you'll shoot me in the ass with a BB gun or tell me you've got a terminal illness and watch how my expression changes. I'm not up for any more humiliation thanks." The storm soaked Jan's windowsill. "Why didn't you tell me!" James was furious. A light beside Jan's room came on.

"James, you're waking the whole dorm," she hissed. "Just come inside. I'll make us coffee. You're going to catch cold."

"What do you care? You don't give a damn about me. You . . ." He trailed off, pointing at Jan through the glass. "You . . . you . . . I love you, Janet Hines," he bellowed. "I love you, and I wanted you to marry me!"

"Marry him already!" Jan's neighbour yelled. "Maybe then we can all get some sleep!" Jan slammed her window shut and marched downstairs and outside to where James was still hollering. She grabbed him firmly by the arm and led him away from the windows, beneath the shelter of a nearby tree.

"This is exactly why I didn't tell you," she hissed. "See how you're reacting? It's embarrassing."

"*This* is embarrassing?" James said, incredulously. "Try being the only guy ever stood up at a dyke bar!" Jan took a deep breath.

"Oh my God, oh shit! I was supposed to meet you at Cherry Bomb!"

"Where the hell were you?"

"When I didn't hear from you, I just assumed . . ."

"You said show up," James interrupted. "You said to meet you there."

"James, I'm really sorry but I guess I got it confused. I waited for your call and when I didn't hear, I figured you were still not speaking to me so I decided to keep working on Professor Walker's term paper."

"Great."

"We've been through this before, anyway."

"We have not!" James hollered. "We've never been over *this*." Jan turned her back to the dormitory windows and lowered her voice.

"I tried to tell you I don't want a serious commitment."

"Everybody says that," James muttered. "But they don't really mean it." There was silence.

"I'm sorry for sending you to the club by yourself," Jan said. "You just can't keep on about us. I've been wanting to speak with you, but I didn't know how . . . I didn't realize until we . . ."

"Fucked?" James said, sarcastically. "It's called fucking, just so you know."

"I'm going inside," Jan snapped. "Call me when you're not an asshole any more." She turned to go and James reached for her arm.

"Wait, I didn't meant it."

Pause.

"So, what then?" he asked.

"Just friends."

"Just friends? Fuck that! We made love. Doesn't that mean anything to you?"

"Of course it does," Jan said. "It does, but let's not blow it out of proportion."

"Well, fuck being 'just friends!' If I'm not your boyfriend, who am I? Just a harmless pet? A study companion? Oh, wait, I know: the brother you never had?"

"That's not fair."

"Let's be honest," James continued, pushing his soggy bangs back off his face. "What has any of this meant to you, really? Nothing, right?" Jan was silent. "Well, you can just forget I mentioned it," James fumed. "Forget it happened. In fact, forget I ever cared."

"Fine!" Jan said.

"Fine!"

Pause.

"James, you're being ridiculous, you know it wasn't like that. Besides we hardly know each other. How can you say you're in love?"

"I don't know anything," he said. "You must be right. Apparently I'm the guy who's not supposed to know anything."

"Look," Jan said. "Do I have to spell it out? I do care about you. You're my closest friend at university. You're a great guy, and I *do* care; just not the way you expect." James began to sober up.

"How could you do this to me? How could you lead me on and make me think we had something special. How can you leave me? I thought I knew you. I thought I could trust you."

"Excuse me, but you're the one who won't take no for an answer!"

There was silence. For once James felt just like his father.

"James?" Jan's voice was barely audible.

"What?"

"Most people around here don't know."

"Don't worry," he said. "Your secret's safe with me." Then he kicked the base of the tree. "Is there someone else?"

Jan bit her lip.

"There *is*?"

"Cut it out," she said. "It's none of your business."

"Yeah, I know." James sighed. "Everything's none of my business."

The cold, damp weather penetrated his bones and his teeth began to chatter.

"You could still come upstairs for a coffee if you want."

"What for?"

"Come on," Jan tugged on the soggy sleeve of his jacket. She might not want to be romantic with James, but she knew there was a good reason they had become friends. "Maybe you have a secret too?" she offered.

James immediately recalled his father's mysterious box with all those receipts.

"There is one," he said tentatively.

"What?"

"I don't know, it's pretty personal."

"Oh, come on," Jan coaxed. "It's only fair. Tell me. It can't be as big as mine."

The counter help was busy scooping fresh curried buns into wax paper bags for customers at the Yung Sing Pastry shop on Baldwin Street. Outside, where Lemon sat on a picnic bench, she could smell fried pork fat, coconut, and sugar-coated buns. Her mother used to bring her down in the summer for tempura sweet potato, her favourite treat. They would sit on the bench in front of the store, trade bites, and compare each other's selection. Lilith usually ordered the gooey stuff — red-bean pastries and bean-curd sesame balls. "Cheapest eats in town," she used to say.

Lemon was struck by how her mother still occupied her thoughts. I've become expert at recalling her face, the speckled and reddish cheeks with tiny blood vessels bursting below the surface, her soft, wrinkled upper lip, the fine pale fuzz that

formed a faint halo of a moustache. Lemon would still sometimes steal glances at her mother's face when she didn't think
Lilith would notice. As if in memorizing the details and remark-
ing on changes, she might stumble upon the meaning of life. As
if her father was in fact lurking in Lilith's sparkling eyes or
creeping along her jawline. When had she become so angry with
her mother? How could she leave? Lemon wiped the grease
from her mouth with a paper napkin and the napkin turned yellow. She sat her knapsack and her lunch on top of the bench. I
wonder where Ma's looking today? Lemon felt a wave of nauseous guilt as she took a bite of her sweet potato, and told herself to never mind, and with all the walking she'd done — back
and forth — across the city she'd walked off at least as many
calories as there were in her lunch. She was determined not to
vomit any more. She was free to enjoy. Free. Her stomach had
shrunk so much that it was forced to whisper. Lemon was
pleased with the silent concave indent of her abdomen.

Last night she'd rolled a sleeping bag into the smallest version of itself and tied it to one strap of her knapsack. Before
Lilith got home from work, she'd cleaned the cupboards of
peanut butter, tuna fish and brown beans. Packed a fork, knife
and can opener along with her toothbrush, a tube of Colgate
and some deodorant, into a pencil case. She pulled her favourite
stars from her walls and brought the galaxy along with her. Since
then, she'd wandered Toronto, and even lingered brazenly in the
hollow of the Henry Moore statue outside the art gallery. The
last place the police would expect to find me is right next door
to the station, she thought. Lemon had stopped outside Jan's
dorm room a couple of times yesterday, listened to her radio filter through the window, and watched the yellow glow of Jan's
bedside lamp through dark green curtains.

Lemon's three-ring binder was open to a blank page. Her arms stretched around the binder, making certain that no one could read what was to be written. She began a letter, this one addressed to Lilith. "Dear Ma, I'm miserable without you." No, scribble that out. What's the point? She started over one last time. "Dear Ma. I want you to know I'm okay. Nothing terrible has happened." Lemon imagined the response that line would provoke. "Nothing terrible? Nothing terrible!" Lilith would repeat, waving her arms up in the air. "What could be worse than losing my Babygirl?" Lemon continued: "I'm in good health. I'm not lost." But then she set her pen down. Am I? To be lost you must first know where you are. Who you are. She made the change. "I know what I'm doing. I'll see you at Grandma Connie's." Lemon removed the chain from around her neck and tucked it into the envelope. She took a long look at the pendant before giving it back. It was a silver piece from a cardboard puzzle of a map of Canada. As a child she'd tried to complete the puzzle but could not find the last segment to seal off Vancouver. That year for her birthday, Lilith had given her the pendant — the missing component plated in white gold. Lemon believed her mother had found the piece and saved it, but today she wondered if Lilith hadn't hidden it to begin with. On her birthday card Lilith had written: "You won't always have all the pieces so just do the best with what you've got." Lemon added one final message to her letter: "Doing the best I can. Love Lem." Then she licked the envelope shut and sealed it tightly. She packed up her belongings and started to walk along Baldwin, east to McCaul Street, where she would purchase a stamp and then call the airport to verify her departure time for tomorrow.

In the early hours of the morning Lemon awoke startled, cold and frightened. She'd been crying in her sleep and the pillow was damp. The odour of expensive cologne and cheap perfume closed in on her from all sides, filtering under her door and in through the ventilation system. Beds from the floor above creaked with poorly oiled springs; water ran in the washroom next door, rinsing blow jobs down the drain. A door frequently slammed somewhere down the hall throughout the night. The words "Motel Heaven" swung above the only window, creaking and complaining like an old woman with gout. Lemon found the noise distracting, aggravating, as if nature itself had conspired to keep her from sleep. *I give up*, she thought, pushing herself up, but as soon as she did so the dream came back full force, knocking her down onto the pillow once more. She felt heavier than ever. What's going on?

Dreams. The space between imagination and objective reality. The place where Lemon lay stripped naked of her defences, reminded that looking for truth during consciousness is like trying to guess weight from the image in a funhouse mirror. Dreams: subconscious peeling back onion-brain one transparent layer at a time, telling Lemon what she already knows. She'd tried to wash it out with salty tears. Erase awareness. Run away. Wind through back alleys and north to the Mount Pleasant Cemetery to avoid being seen. Sleep on graves, never feeling alone. Collect quarters not properly digested by pay phones and spend the night on Yonge Street playing pinball and arcade games. Rent a room. Stare at the ceiling looming overhead and realize her ceiling is someone else's floor, her beginning another's end. Don't eat. Eat. It's all futile; nothing stops the night from repeating. Lemon listens in slumber to whispers too profound for waking life. Sees what she needs: wet dreams. Nocturnal emotions.

Lemon's night was as disturbing as ever: her mother in some dangerous predicament with herself in the role of saviour. She

woke with her teeth chattering, certain that until she solved her
nightly puzzles, she'd never solve the rest of her life. She grew
anxious and fearful, and so pretended she wasn't alone, that Jan
was sitting on the edge of the bed comforting her. Or that
somehow Claudia was presiding over the whole experience,
waiting, waiting, for Lemon to snap out of it. Lemon spoke the
dream out loud to her pretend audience:

"First I hear a splinter, Spitfire ragweed, fast-burning flames
— like a match has ignited wicker furniture. Then in an instant
everything is dry, singed. Crackle crackle, I hear wood burning
in the wind, spreading like wild bamboo, flames shooting high,
blue with heat. Then the comforting sound of my bare feet stepping on twigs. This is the forest of my mother's mind. I see
weeping willow reaching so far above, there seems to be no end.
And with every step, a different wildflower appears at my feet.
Bunchberry lowest to the ground. Twisted stalk and smartweed
thriving as ground cover. Lives I've never paid much attention
to. I smell their fragrances and become dizzy. Walk on cool
earth, grateful for temporary relief from flames. Snap. Pop. Prick.
Minuscule slivers slide into my calluses, splinters so tiny they
aren't noticeable except by touch. Blood pin-dots the dirt, and
sharded skin — like scales — trail behind. I stop, look back and
am surprised by a smouldering wake. Everything green is suddenly brown, then beige, then white. The flowers lose their fragrances, trees disappear. There is no oxygen left so I grab my
throat and dry heave. I subsist on sandpaper air and liquid: my
own saliva and my mother's tears . . ."

Lemon opened her eyes, inhaled — one, two, three times —
exhaled, and recounted the rest as if in a trance: "I watch as
flames flicker and flash; fire feels like it's slapping me, punishing,
burning my retina. I see my room at home without the press-on

galaxies. I see Ma in our apartment, and the violets on the windowsill withering. I see her office at the precinct with unopened file folders, and her rubber tree leafless and bent. Something is wrong. It's too hot to continue much longer so I call out, 'Ma where are you?' Fog and ash mix with natural precipitation. I never knew there could be so many colours of grey. Dust from overhead falls like snow and settles in my hair, on my shoulders. And a sweet chalky residue coats my tongue. I smell stale plastic containers full of colourful pills. And cafeteria food, and semen. I think it's semen. The earth is about to boil and rupture, and that's when I know: I'll have to sacrifice myself. Fall forward to save her. Be baptized in fire. It's unbearably bright when sunlight filters through indigo smoke so I squint and follow Ma's voice. Always an echo. Always an echo.

"'Babygirl!'

"I hear the need that cannot be filled unless I return. The endless, aching need.

"'Babygirl!'

"I look up towards a rolling, hysterical sea of flame moving overhead like storm clouds. Hear laughter everywhere. I stretch my arms out, wanting to be held. Time is running out. Fire tumbles ahead like a red carpet. I step forward but look back, see that on the other side of hell there is water. Oceans, lakes, rivers of time. Sweat and tears. Blood. Yes, there is blood connected to my past. 'Father? Ma?' I reach up through thick fire with bare arms and watch as the baby-fine hair is instantly and mercilessly evaporated, singeing my skin. Take another step forward. Feel about with red and orange fingertips, flames shooting out the ends like the weapons of a twenty-first-century superhero. I make a promise: 'I will find you. I will. I am coming for you both, I'm coming to take us home.'"

Lemon slapped her hands on the mattress and was finally able to push herself up into a sitting position. The heavy curtains were partially drawn and shadows gyrated and swayed across the walls like a belly dancer. She choked on the smell of fumigation chemicals still lingering in the mouldy carpet. Her eyes adjusted to the night, and urine, coffee and bloodstains on the mattress beneath her came clearer into focus. The stains did not belong to her. She hadn't marked this territory. This motel at Dundas and Sherbourne is not where she is meant to be. Vancouver really is the place now.

Lemon scrambled for the phone, dialled in the dark, fingers finding their way along the keypad by memory. Memory is waiting. Memory is always waiting. She cleared her throat, placed the receiver in her right hand and rolled onto one side. Ma will understand.

Ring . . . Ring . . .

"Hello?"

Pause.

"Are you there?"

Then a groggy voice, immediately alert.

"Lemon, where the hell are you?"

She fumbled for cigarettes in the drawer beside the bed. Strained sideways, cradling the receiver between her chin and the side of her head. She dusted the surface of the end table with fingertips, found the book of matches, sat up higher and placed a pillow behind her back.

"I'm still here, Ma."

Stomach grumbled.

So am I.

"It's goddamned four o'clock in the morning," Lilith said. "I've looked everywhere. Where's here?"

Lemon struck the match, lit her cigarette, inhaled with determination and waved the flame out. Stand your ground, she thought, making an airy "pah" sound as her lips clung to the cigarette paper.

"That's a *disgusting* habit!"

Lemon smiled in the dark, comforted. It felt right to have called.

"Hey, you there or you just call for kicks?"

"I'm here, I told you." Lemon scratched her forehead, exhaled and took another drag. "I had a bad dream."

"Been flying around again?"

"No . . . Yes . . ." Try to explain but immediately forget. Yawn. "You were there."

Lilith's voice peaks.

"Me?"

"You're in all my dreams."

"Why, you mad at me or something? You scared the bejesus out of me, Lemon Boot!"

"No."

"Then it's chocolate! The life section of the paper said caffeine in choc —"

"I *know* Ma." Impatience. Irritability. Try again. "I know chocolate's full of caffeine."

"And gives you worse period cramps too."

Periods. Marks to punctuate the end of childhood. A sea of woman-time passing at regular bloodstained intervals, and remember how she missed your first because of work, because of some other child. Let's see if you can guess what's happened to me? you'd thought, but it wasn't until days later, when Lilith asked where all the Kotex had disappeared to, that you enlightened her. "Okay, so I had my period. Guess you don't know everything!"

313

Pucker your lips to practise smoke rings.

"The point, Ma, is I can't sleep."

"So?" Lilith said. "Join the club."

Lemon sighed.

"This is not why I called."

Silence.

"Hey, you coming home?"

Stomach turned.

Tell her. Tell her where you're going.

Lemon's voice disintegrated like tree skin in a bushfire. Confidence turned to ash.

"I just . . . I just wanted to make sure you were . . . there."

"I'm right where you left me," Lilith said. "Waiting. Where else would I be?"

Yeah, where else would she be?

Lemon's voice quivered.

"Lost . . . and blind."

"Lemon, you don't sound so good. You all right?"

"Uh-huh." Nod but no one's there to see. Reach for the reading lamp. Fumble for the switch. With the room now lit, butt the cigarette in an ashtray the shape of a maple leaf. Turn onto your other side, knees to chest. Ignore the fact that there's probably a missing person's report. A file in her office with your full name and date of birth, smudged in black ink because of the tears that fell as she wrote it. You've finally managed to become one of your mother's unsolved cases; the guilt is overwhelming. You don't know how to say you're sorry for leaving. Maybe you're not.

Lilith is desperate.

"Meet you in a few minutes?"

"No Ma, I — "

"Meet you for breakfast then?"

Pause.

Last chance to fess up.

Tongue's heavy with unanswered questions.

"Okay."

Liar!

"One hour? Futures Bakery?"

"Um." Then make the correction. "There's no *S*, Ma."

"What?"

"There's no *S* on Future — it's not plural." Practically hear Lilith's head swivel from side to side with renewed sense of purpose.

"Still need your ol' Ma, don't you? Haven't learned yet, Babygirl; where there's one future, there's sure to be another." Lilith gets ready to hang up, begins to cry. "See you?"

"Okay, soon."

Lilith set the receiver down first.

Click.

Hear the buzz that reveals a disconnection. It drones steadily until you also hang up. What a relief; it can be survived. Disconnection can be survived.

Lilith hadn't fallen back asleep after speaking with Lemon, she'd been too agitated. Finally, she was about to have her daughter back safe in her arms, protected. She'd immediately taken herself to the meeting place, paced out front before the doors were unlocked, and remained in the doorway, anxiously awaiting their reunion while men and women gulped coffee and nibbled on muffins. When after two hours it was evident that Lemon had no intention of turning up, Lilith tapped her foot on the sticky floor and muttered under her breath, "Lemon Boot, how could you do this to me?" Lemon was, in fact, fastening her seat belt and lifting off for Vancouver while her mother drifted back to 52 Division, crestfallen.

After having a good, long cry at her desk, Lilith headed home to wait. There was no sign of Lemon, but Constance called to say that Jack had just died. "Come right away," Constance said, a slight tremor in her voice. "There's much to be done."

When I travelled back to Vancouver without Lemon it was almost eighteen years after the first time we left. Strange, but everything looked and smelt pretty much the same. The Japanese plum trees lining our street were damp, tearing up to see me, I thought. Their cotton-candy blossoms gave off a powdery scent. The sidewalk under my rubber boots was clean and wet and crawling with earthworms. I was surprised by how shiny everything was compared to where I lived in Toronto. I'd forgotten how the windows in Mother's house glistened from the street. And it'd been ages since I'd seen folks with clear, rosy skin, wrapped in so much rubber and plastic and nylon, sauntering along the sidewalk like everyday was a day for rain. In Toronto I was always rushing to get somewhere, pushing my way onto public transit, and acting like a little water would melt me.

I'd forgotten about the way the Rocky Mountains gather clouds over the city, and rainwater falls into eavestroughs, gutters, into the brims of hats and pocket linings — down the back of necks. I'd even forgotten about jumping in rainbow-coloured puddles, and breathing in the smell of rich BC earth as it quenched its thirst. Funny how some things leave you even when you're sure they won't. Until I was standing there getting the courage up to approach the porch, I'd forgotten all about Daddy's summer barbecues and the stink of his pipe, and of mother's Chanel No. 5 and hairspray. I'd lost the habit of waking up each morning knowing that the salty Pacific was running through my bones. But when I looked closer, everything in my old neighbourhood was sort of faded too. Turned from vibrant to vague, from electric to eclipsed. In many ways, home looked like it had washed away in a thirty-year, overnight process. The bushes at the side of the house were limp. The blossoms of the dogwood in the backyard had blanched from their original little-girl pink to practically white. And the camellia bush was thinning. Then I remembered how the damp winds used to chill my younger self.

The stoop in front of Mother's house was still five up to the door, and made of wooden planks that were avocado green. Only difference was they were peeled and sunburnt, and gave off a faint, rotting smell. The mailbox at the southwest corner still wore its original coat of rusty paint. The sign was flapping in the breeze outside Appleby's storefront like before too. It still read "rocery," like it had ever since that afternoon in 1953 when a telegram came about Lumpy's son, Greg, being killed in the Korean War. After reading the letter out loud Olivia broke into tears and ran back into the house, but Lumpy climbed thirty feet on a decrepit ladder and insisted on repainting the badly faded sign. The wind picked up, he rushed but gave up when the rain came down like darts. The letter G was all he got through that day, and that storm smeared it away, leaving the rest of the faint old word just sitting there incomplete. I always sort of thought it was like G stood for Greg who was never coming back. Maybe that's why Lumpy never bothered to fix it. We all have our own way to mourn.

The houses looked pretty much the same to me too: three- or four-bedroom wood-panelled structures, all with a front or side porch. All painted white or pale green or even pink. Mother's house was still the colour of sour milk. All the yards were well manicured. A yard is everybody's business you know? Front yard especially. When the grass or the weeds at our house grew too high, somebody down the road always talked behind Daddy's back, said he must be hitting the bottle again. Yep, yards were public property, but gardens . . . gardens were like whole other worlds where you could practically get away with murder. I stopped to glance around the side of the house, and stared at what used to be my garden with Daddy. The soil was flattened and the fresh grass overgrown. You'd never know you were look- ing at a graveyard. I felt like crying then.

I wasn't surprised to notice our neighbours staring out their bay window like papier mâché dolls. I waved at Olivia and she dropped back behind the curtain. Lumpy saluted me. Imagine? All that time later and I was still a local curiosity! I guess on Quebec Street I'll always be crazy. Anyway, I climbed the stoop, knocked firmly on Mother's screen door and was wringing my hands when Lemon's face peered out from behind the living- room curtain. I jumped back and clutched my chest. "Babygirl," I mouthed silently. Then, "You're in so much trouble!"

I could tell the minute Mother let me in that she was lost without Daddy. His galoshes were still on the floor mat and his trusty Canadian Tire raincoat was hanging on the hall tree. There was dust on top of the buffet and around all the picture frames in the dining room, and when I put my bags down just outside the kitchen, I could smell that the garbage hadn't been taken out for days. I even noticed unwashed dishes in the sink! I was suddenly glad I'd been able to exchange my ticket for an earlier one at the last minute. Still, Mother didn't want to talk.

"How are you doing?" I asked, after we'd all said our hellos.

"Fine." She squeezed Lemon. "We're getting on famously. Lemon's told me all about her good grades and her part-time job. I couldn't be prouder."

"Is there anything I can do?" I asked, ignoring my daughter for the time being.

"No, Lilith," Mother said. "Lemon here arrived just in time to make herself useful."

"Yep," I said, turning to face my runaway daughter. "I've always said she has good instincts."

Not two days later we were getting ready for Daddy's funeral. Lemon was drying her hair in the guest room, my old bedroom, Lumpy had taken the old station wagon to the car wash, and I was dressed and waiting for him to return. I went upstairs to give Mother a hand, stood in the hall outside her bedroom and watched her staring at the floor of her closet, dripping water onto the wall-to-wall. She didn't even notice me there when she reached up to the plank shelf, all the way to the back as far as she could and pulled out an old shoebox. "These ones," I heard her say, like Daddy was still around. "Don't you think the oxfords would be best?" I think Mother chose those shoes for their thick and steady appearance. Maybe she'd have some sure-footed strength to get through the visitation and funeral and the burial, avoid falling forward into the emptiness of a life she hadn't asked for. She knew she'd be looking down, and the shoes could be there supporting her, reminding her who she was all of a sudden: a woman without her past. In a way, I knew just how she felt.

On our way to the burial Mother was distant and silent. There had been over a hundred people pass through Downing's funeral parlour that morning and most of them stayed for Daddy's service. Mother greeted each visitor, even people she'd never met before, introducing herself and welcoming them all. The sight of Daddy's bleached-out, embalmed face in the open casket didn't seem to affect her the way it affected me or Lemon, who cried as soon as she saw him and ran into the hall. No, Mother acted tough as nails until we arrived at the cemetery and were standing around the empty grave. Then, with my twin brother's tombstone on one side of her, and Daddy about to be laid out on the other, she wrung her hands and for the first time ever, I saw my mother cry.

As the crowd gathered, Mother distracted herself by telling Lemon about my pregnancy. She spoke like I was the first woman on the planet to have been impregnated without sex, as if Mary-Mother-of-God herself hadn't set the example.

"Your grandfather was so humiliated by the whole unfortunate incident," she said. "No offence intended, dear." Lemon chewed on her nails and listened with greed, even though she was being referred to as some kind of mistake. I was standing between them and Mother spoke with the authority of a one-room schoolteacher. I hate to admit it, but I still had a hard time drawing sympathy for her, couldn't imagine her ever being an innocent, a new bud. *Mother was formed deep inside the earth's crust,* I told myself. But I was wrong too, short-sighted.

Daddy always understood. Mother was just like the Queen Elizabeth roses he planted in our garden, the most common flower at the top of its class, with rigid stems, narrow buds, and very elegant petals. But also sharp protection keeping people from getting too close. (Roses think they're better than all the others, even if they don't smell pretty for very long.) Too perfect to be real, I always thought. Too busy trying to impress. And to tell you the truth, even though I do respect them, admire them, even love them like I love the rest, I never really liked them much. Still, they were the only flowers I ever saw Mother cut from my garden to bring into the house. "The red ones are a symbol of Christ's blood," she told me once, arranging them in a tall vase. "Mrs. Massero says so." The white ones, I wanted her to know, stood for the immaculate conception. But I didn't say a word.

From the front of the cemetery, half a mile down the dirt road, we could see a dark, steady vein of cars snaking through the gate. Mother stood with her shoulders down and her head up. *She's still as stubborn as stone,* I thought. Then I took a good hard look at her clenched jaw and bewildered eyes and saw my mistake. *No. She's just petrified wood.* Even if she'd never say so, Mother was thankful that Lemon and I stayed at the house during those few weeks after Daddy died. A family of women is more efficient in times of stress, she always said. Men just get underfoot. *Underfoot!* I glanced across the graveyard to the bulldozer in the corner by the fence.

Up until then, there had been no time for grief, just hasty planning. Caskets were unusually important it turned out, and the one thing Mother and I agreed on was that Daddy would've been just as pleased with a plain pine box as with anything fancy. But Mother couldn't have people thinking he was unloved, and it seemed to her that a coffin was the vehicle delivering Daddy to his final outpost, so she chose the most expensive model. Secretly, I think she wondered if he was travelling north or south.

Phone calls and directions to out-of-town visitors were made during the two days leading up to the funeral. Relatives I'd never met drove all the way from the Okanagan Valley and Williams Lake. Minute details took on a magnified importance. Lemon wrote the newspaper announcement. I cleaned and cooked, and contacted Daddy's long-time customers who wouldn't have known. And then there was the question of what to wear. For me it was easy. I bought a new dress covered in daisies, because for some reason I find it impossible to cry around daises. Lemon wore a skirt and blouse with a twighlight pattern that she borrowed from her grandmother's closet. But for Mother the decision was complicated. Any outfit would reveal a great deal to visitors too polite to ask, "How are you?" Too bright a pattern on a scarf or blouse suggested overcompensation, she said. People might be led to speak of her in cars on the way home from the visitation. "I think Constance is still in shock," they'd whisper. On the other hand, Mother explained, a demure navy or forest-green pantsuit hinted at quiet resignation, even defeat. "Constance looks for-lorn," Olivia and Lumpy might agree, shaking their heads, click-ing their tongues against their teeth. "Just like she's given up." Mother could feel empty — robbed blind — but admitting it in public was for other people. So in the end, she wore nothing but black from her shoes to her jet earrings: the traditional shade of mourning. She looked dramatic and understated at the same time. She felt it was a dignified response to anyone passing. Mother's always been a firm believer in people needing clues.

At the cemetery, as the last of the cars pulled up, she con-tinued on about me.

"Your mother has quite the imagination," she told Lemon.

"Jeez." I smiled a big, phony grin. "Tell some people you're clairvoyant and before you know it, you're pigeon-holed!"

"For crying out loud," Mother said under her breath. "Psychics are for travelling road shows, not for the Boots." She turned her attention back to Lemon. "Fathers are important, dear. Fathers are the backbone of any family."

I looked at Daddy's coffin. Breathed in the scent of freshly dug earth. Maybe if Lemon understood what it was like for me? How this stunning place I was born in had only ever felt unsettling to me. How the mountains and water and fresh air was a paradise for so many, but for me, nothing compared to breathing free and roaming as my oddball self back in Toronto. Or how Daddy and Mother were a different breed of parents than they turned out to be as grandparents. Maybe I could help her understand why I never wanted to bring her to Vancouver. For a split second I wished Lemon could know Mother and the rest as I had, then just as fast I changed my mind. I'd loved my baby from the moment she sprung to mind. She was everything to me and me to her, before we even met. Mother couldn't really interfere with that, could she? No one could, right? And Daddy was an honourable man — at least he tried. But really it was fate — not fatherhood — that had changed my life for good. How could I have ever explained *that* to Lemon when I'd all but forgotten it myself?

I guess the way Mother turned me into a snit just with the curl of her lip, or by folding her napkin into smaller and smaller squares, was impressive for Lemon. Mother's face was pretty smooth for sixty-four years. She sure knew how to last. Her outfits never wrinkled or showed lint. I never saw her once with loose hair falling down the back of *her* blouses, gathering on her shoulders like the ugly weight of the world, but I could only stay quiet for so long when she interfered. She did it every chance she got, like by getting Lemon on side, she'd finally proven I was wrong. Mother looked so smug, knowing my daughter had run away to *her*.

She was still Mother. Not "Ma" or "Mommy" or even "Mom." Simply Mother with ramrod-straight posture and no time for telling jokes or even laughing things off. In some ways she was still the Rock of Ages; you couldn't convince her of anything she didn't already believe. "A leopard never changes his spots," she used to say about Daddy's drinking and my being confused, but she was wrong. Anything can change with enough trying. It was only Mother's opinions that were fixed. So, even though Lemon saw the tightness of Mother's forehead, heard her ordering the pallbearers and the minister around like a shepherd herding sheep, and acting as if the slightest turn of events would ruin the entire experience for her (How can Daddy's funeral be ruined, I asked myself? What's the worse that can happen?), Mother was also fragile and lonely and my Babygirl could see that too. She looped her arm through Mother's and I turned away, washing my face in the wind.

"From the beginning of our courtship I encouraged your grandfather to start his own business," Mother explained to Lemon. "Believed in him. Then after our wedding, I agreed we'd work as hard as it took to make a new life. It was me who put the past behind us so we could have some semblance of a life together, me who said the dead baby was a blessing. Said we couldn't have afforded twins anyhow. I did what a good wife should do, and where did it get me? Nowhere, that's where. Your grandfather's drinking spun out of control again when your mother started with those fantasies. As vain as any floor mirror, she was, sharing every thought that popped into her head. She's always been too good to follow rules like the rest of us."

Just then, the minister stepped out of his car and walked towards us. Lumpy and Olivia stood under a cluster of birch trees with their arms around each other. Every few minutes,

Lumpy shifted his weight from his club foot to the other one. Eventually, all of us mourners formed a semi-circle around the dug hole. The minister squeezed Mother's hand, and then moved to stand at the opposite end of the plot, by Daddy's head. West, where the sun also rises. We waited for stragglers. It was quiet except for the trees. Mother's charcoal eyes steeled themselves. Then she took two solid steps forward, bent, and placed a handful of freshly cut daffodils on Daddy's casket. (It was my job to order flowers and 'course I picked his favourite.)

When our small flower bed at home lit up with jonquils, Daddy said it was the high point of the season. I liked daffodils too, because almost more than any other flower science has tinkered with — dreadful black tulips, blue roses, and not to mention all those poor lilting peonies who can't get through life without a sturdy crutch now — daffodils have survived centuries without losing their true identity. I ordered four dozen for the funeral, and asked that they be arranged with grape hyacinths because they smell so sweet. Mother thought the colour combination was loud and obnoxious, and that my big-city ways had made me even more boorish, but I thought it was proper for Daddy to leave this world making a bold statement.

Finally.

I ordered seeds too, which I intended to plant around his tombstone. Perennials, to come back year after year, even if I couldn't. Next, the minister opened his Bible and Mother stared into the rectangle below like she was staring into a total eclipse of the sun. Lemon said nothing when I took her hand, just sort of let it go limp. I lowered my head without lowering my eyes. It was hard to believe Daddy was under there, motionless. Part of me — the little girl part — still expected him to push open the coffin and storm his way onto both feet, waving his hands and calling out the way he did so many times during my early years. "Where's my sack-o'-potatoes!" But Daddy had been really sick for months, hadn't visited Toronto in a year, and in the end, his lungs went black and shut down.

Suddenly I regretted not pushing myself on him, expecting more of him — maybe it would have brought us closer in the end like we were in the beginning. I felt exhausted by the weight of so many unopened possibilities pressing down on me. Why hadn't I hurried west the minute Mother called with the news of his failing health? Why hadn't I arrived one day sooner, when I could have held his hand and said "goodbye," or at least "see you later." I didn't know if the red fishing hat he was being buried in was really his favourite after all, or how he felt about his cousin Thomas, who'd perished in a bushfire. What hopes did Daddy think were worth clinging to for a lifetime? I heard the minister's voice trying to get our attention and I felt an ache in my heart. *I didn't really know my father,* I thought. *And Lemon doesn't know hers either.* Then, despite my daisy dress and it being too early for fall, I started to weep as the silver birch leaves fell all around like paper tears.

I doubt Mother heard the minister's speech, even though she was standing perfectly still, her feet in those black oxfords like she was rooted into lead blocks. She scanned the crowd — a lifetime in each face — then ground her teeth. If she heard the same ferocious scream inside her head as me, she didn't make a sound; Mother didn't share grief. She never admitted she could hurt. Not herself, and not anyone else. At a late age she was having to learn she'd always needed a reflection to recognize herself, and I knew by then, Daddy had been that mirror. He was there so she could hurl all the rage and disappointment growing inside of her over time at someone else, see it from a safe distance. In his eyes.

327

Or sometimes in mine. Maybe she had to forget things too. And make hard choices. And suffer the consequences. I don't know. But without Daddy there to blame, I knew one thing for sure: Mother was going to have to face herself.

I remembered that even when Daddy's drinking got out of hand, she didn't involve outsiders, didn't even complain to Olivia, or talk to the women at church. Just got quieter and took it out on me. And finally one night she threw Daddy's clothes and furniture, and fishing magazines, along with every bottle in the house, onto the backyard. I peeked out from behind my bedroom curtain. "It's either that," Mother pointed at the messy heap of broken glass, "or it's me!" Then she walked back inside, leaving him alone in the yard to choose.

I crept downstairs and outside where he was sitting against the house, sobering up. I took his hand in mine and spoke without raising my eyes.

"Daddy?"

"Yeah, Lil?"

"Please don't leave me."

The burial was over sooner than expected. After the minister's closing remarks there were murmurs and shuffling towards cars, but the three of us stayed back, forming a string of generations linked through loss and time. My vision was blurry from so much crying, but Mother's heavy shoes were perfect: They'd given her the strength to stand where she'd probably rather have folded into the fresh earth below.

Since I'd arrived in the city, she'd seemed weightless. Barely eating and sort of floating along from one task to the next. She meandered through the house without noticing Lemon's questions or the telephone ringing. Only in the shower that night — her first since discovering Daddy in the den — did Mother remember her own flesh-and-bone body. I waited to brush my teeth. Steam snuck out from under the bathroom door, smelling like a zesty soap. The hot, scalding water of the shower was pelting Mother's body for a long time. I guess she was going through the motions of a normal routine: maybe she lathered up, washed behind her ears, maybe cradled her breasts in her palms, lifting to make the stretch marks disappear the way I do. *Not bad for an old lady*, she might have thought, and then realized where she was, what day it was. How long she'd been standing there. After forty-five minutes under a teeming faucet, her flesh must have been tender and raw, her nipples wrinkled and blistered like the meat of a ruby-red grapefruit. And just when I was getting worried enough to knock, Mother finally emerged to start that endless night. Another twenty-four-hour period turning over, a period in which I think she finally learned how short a time endlessness can be.

Lemon approached the large brick complex trepidatiously, a scrap of lined white paper in her hand, her heart in her throat. She'd been clutching the address since that morning when she spoke with her grandmother and Constance had pressed it into her palm. The name Isadora Moffat was scribbled there.

"I've always thought you have a right to know."

Lemon held up the paper.

"Is this where my father lives?"

"No," Constance said. "But if anybody knows where he is, it would be her."

The banister leading up to the front veranda was larger than regulation size, with a wide cement staircase. The rest of the building was chunky, indestructible as though made for children. Lemon ascended on wobbly knees, gooseflesh covering her

body. I want to know and soon I will, she thought, remembering years of conversations with Jan and all that she'd discussed
with Claudia. But was she prepared to live with the consequences? Was she feeling strong enough? It's my only chance,
Lemon thought. Who knows when I'll be back again? She stood
for a couple of seconds squinting through the blinds in the door,
composing herself, before pushing on the big silver button.

Ding-dong.

Ding-dong.

An emaciated young woman in overalls and a short-sleeved
yellow shirt opened the blinds and peered outside. Her sunken
cheekbones and the thin skin stretched across her face made her
eyes appear to be jumping out of their sockets like two bulging
malnourished abdomens, blue with hunger. Lemon smiled, waved
nervously and noticed her own stomach grumbling. A lumbering
six-foot man in his fifties also appeared, and beamed at her with
thick white teeth, a bulky chin and a bulbous nose. His hazel eyes
were wide with excitement, his clumsy hands curling long fingers
into his chest, as though he were fanning himself, or waving.

"Visitor!" Lemon heard him announce in a unexpectedly
high voice. "Visitor!"

The young woman spoke cautiously through the closed
door, while ordering the man to settle down and go back to the
living room.

"Can I help you?" she asked, trying to ignore him.

"Visitor! Visitor!" The man continued to yell.

"I hope so. Um, I mean yes." Lemon's uncertainty made the
worker impatient. "I'm looking for a woman named Isadora
Moffat." She glanced at the paper clue in her trembling hand
and pressed the name up to the glass, offering proof. "I was told
she lives here." The woman stared blankly, and as though an

apparition had mysteriously appeared or a condemned draw-bridge had suddenly been raised, she arched her eyebrows and her mouth fell open. The man still tugging at her sleeve became even more excited, jumping up and down and drooling.

"She's got a visitor!" he screeched loudly, and ran back into the house with the pronouncement. "Got a visitor! Got a visitor! Got a visitor!"

"Is she available?" Lemon asked, now certain this was the right place.

"Yeah . . . Sure . . . Come on in." The young woman turned the bolt on the door without taking her eyes off Lemon. She wasn't much older. "It's just that I didn't think Dori — I mean, Mrs. Moffat — had family." Lemon wasn't certain whether the young woman meant she didn't know if Mrs. Moffat had ever *received* a visitation or whether she wasn't permitted one.

"Oh, I'm not f— " Lemon stopped herself. Not family? She didn't know that for certain. Family could be a cluster of stars sharing approximately the same distance from earth, scattered loosely in a recognizable pattern. Family was often a world away. Lemon thought of her father, closer now than ever before. "I'm not planning to stay long," she said. "I just need a few minutes. My name is Lemon Boot." The young woman looked over her shoulder to make certain the man wasn't rearing to bolt, and then opened the door.

"Albert likes it outside," the young woman said, partially explaining her hesitancy in allowing Lemon to enter. She contin-ued inspecting Lemon, glanced sideways first, checking Lemon's profile. Was there a resemblance? Next, she examined Lemon's rubber boots, her jeans, her cable-knit wool sweater, and her freckled face, as though she might join the dots, solve a mystery, and collect a substantial reward. Lemon recognized the deep state of wonderment, the penetrating questions that had waited too long for answers. She figured Mrs. Moffat's history was up for grabs too. The young woman stopped herself from staring. "Come in quick," she said, hurrying Lemon into the foyer. Once inside, she became more formal. "Hello." She extended her hand. "My name is Mary Jane. I'm one of the staff here." She pushed the door shut, until it clicked. "Locks on its own," She reassured Lemon. Immediately inside there was a brass plaque with etched words. Lemon read it in passing:

"Ministry of Social Services and Housing
offers this award of excellence in recognition
of outstanding community service provided by
staff at the Turtle Group Home."

Mary Jane's fascination with Lemon was temporarily replaced by a professional demeanour of absolute confidence. Lemon could now see that the laminated tag she wore on a string around her neck said "Shift Supervisor." Mary Jane caught Lemon reading.

"I know I look young," she said, leading Lemon past a long, rubber shoe mat and a sliding closet door, without breaking stride. "But I've been doing this kind of work for a very long time." Lemon was unsure of exactly what type of work Mary Jane did. But she tried to sound grateful as she was led around the corner into a small office.

"That's wonderful," she said. One wall was made of glass and Lemon quickly realized a few people had gathered on the other side to appraise her. "I hope I haven't upset the . . . the . . . patients," She said, beginning to make sense of her surroundings.

"No. They're just curious." Mary Jane tapped a pen on the desk in front of her. "We call them residents now — not patients." She was stern on the point. "This is a home, not a hospital." Lemon nodded, acutely aware of the understimulated faces staring at her. A home as in "to a good home" for a neglected pet, she thought. Or "the home for the aged." She looked over her shoulder at the residents on the other side of the glass partition. But not home where the heart is. Not home sweet home.

"Right," Lemon said in a deferential tone. "*Residents.*"

Albert was waving so Lemon waved back.

"You shouldn't encourage him," Mary Jane instructed. "He's on a behaviour mod program. It's a chronic problem." The program or the waving, Lemon wanted to ask, but didn't. She was here for one reason only and she didn't think it included anything involving waves. Waves of seismic proportions, she knew, could be dangerous. Even deadly.

"Sorry," Lemon said, dropping her arm to her side. "Do you live here too?" Mary Jane's lips thinned into two sharp lines, and her voice deepened, sounding resolutely authoritative. Parental.

"No. I live in Kits," she explained. "We rotate shifts." Mary Jane pulled a stack of papers out from one of the filing-cabinet drawers next to the desk. "I'm sorry, what did you say your name was?"

"Lemon Boot."

Mary Jane clucked her tongue to the inside of her cheek.

"Isn't *that* unusual. Don't think I've ever heard that one before. Is it foreign?"

Lemon decided she didn't like Mary Jane at all.

"Yes, it's French," she said without flinching. "There's an accent over the *e*." Lemon watched as Mary Jane added her name — a small accent aigu above the first vowel — to a form labelled Visitor Requisition.

"How beautiful!" Mary Jane exclaimed, admiring her own handwriting. "Now, would you please sign in." She pointed a skinny finger to indicate the dotted line. Her knuckle protruded like an arthritic inheritance. Lemon wished she didn't think thin was so admirable. "Normally we don't allow drop-ins," Mary Jane continued as Lemon finished signing and set the pen down. "But I'm going to make an exception in your case."

Lemon exhaled for what felt like the first time in her life.

"I'll need to see some identification, though. Driver's licence or a birth certificate," Lemon didn't drive and she'd left her birth certificate and her health card inside her suitcase.

"Let me have a look," she said, fumbling in her knapsack, trying not to appear frantic. She pulled out the receipt from her aeroplane ticket. "It's all I brought." She said sheepishly. "But it has my name on it, see?"

Mary Jane accepted the carbon copy and shrugged.

"From Ontario?"

"Uh-huh." Lemon looked around the office.

"I didn't know there were French in Ontario."

Mary Jane said "French" like she was referring to salad dressing.

Lemon ignored her. Beneath the glass wall there was a loveseat covered in green and pink cushions, and to the right of it, on the floor, stood a miniature refrigerator. Mary Jane noticed Lemon's intense curiosity. "For their meds," she said. "*Your* first visit, I see." Lemon felt guilty, as though she'd neglected a long-standing family obligation and ought to be deeply ashamed of herself. Perhaps Mary Jane would think she didn't deserve to speak with Mrs. Moffat after all?

"My parents wouldn't let me — before now," she lied.

Mary Jane softened her manner. She tilted her head an inch and sighed sympathetically.

Lemon hung hers, avoiding eye contact.

"Well, you're here now," Mary Jane said. "Better late than never."

Lemon wanted to scream.

Albert began to bang on the glass window with a baseball glove. A younger man with buck-teeth and thick glasses stood bug-eyed and motionless wearing a crash helmet. A short, portly woman with a shaved head and a tight purple sweatsuit was beside him steadily swaying forward and back, back and forward — like a rocking horse — simultaneously rubbing her hand furiously across her lips. Everybody's got something they're afraid to say. Everybody's got at least one good secret, Lemon thought, not sorry for fibbing.

"That one," Mary Jane said, gesturing with her chin. "She used to be Mrs. Moffat's roommate after she was transferred from Bridgewater, and before we built the extension. That was way ahead of my time. But I've heard they didn't get along. And that one — he's a real sweetheart. Mostly deaf now; likes to bang his head." Bangs until he sees stars, Lemon thought. A headbanger. Bang. Big bang! Mary Jane placed the requisition in the bottom of a three-tiered shelf on the filing cabinet. Albert knocked louder to divert her attention. "He goes to his parents in Surrey, on weekends. Visitors get him all wound up." Albert pounded on the glass once more and Mary Jane tried not to look as she addressed her guest. "You can leave your belongings here and come right this way . . ." Lemon threw her knapsack onto the loveseat, slipped off her sweater, and silently followed Mary Jane upstairs. "I'm working alone this afternoon," Mary Jane continued, as they mounted. "The other Friday staff have taken some of them to the mall. You have good timing. Mrs. Moffat insisted she wasn't going out today."

The carpeting on the second floor was also the same pale green and pink as the walls. From the landing Lemon could see three open bedrooms along the right side of the house, each with a turtle-shaped nameplate on the door, then a room marked "Washroom" at the end.

"There's a Jacuzzi in the basement," Mary Jane offered. "It's great for physio." Mary Jane turned to the left, walked down another corridor that looked identical to the first one, and stopped in front of a closed door at the end of the hall. The plastic turtle said "Dori."

"Now, if she doesn't want to see you," Mary Jane whispered, "I'm afraid I'll have to ask you to leave." Lemon nodded in the affirmative. "We like to encourage them to make their own choices."

"Good," Lemon said, hoping against hope that her cover wouldn't be blown.

Country music played quietly as Mary Jane knocked on the door. A squeaky voice sang along

"You got to da-da-da-da."

"Mrs. Moffat? — Dori — you have a visitor . . ."

"Don't do-do-do-do."

"Maybe she didn't hear?" Lemon suggested in a panic.

Mary Jane knocked louder.

"La-la-la-la."

"Someone's come a long way just to see you," Mary Jane said in a chirpy tone. Then leaned in closer to Lemon. "Very difficult to communicate with. Don't say I didn't warn you." Lemon could barely stand still, she wanted to kick the door down, demand answers, she wanted to know why she was here in the first place. She stepped in front of Mary Jane and yelled directly into the door:

"My name is Lemon Boot!"

The music and the singing stopped with a loud vinyl scratch and Mary Jane winked at Lemon.

"I'll be downstairs if you need me," she said. "Otherwise, you've got forty-five minutes before we serve lunch." Before Lemon had a chance to respond, the door cracked opened. A dark brown, almost black eye peeked out at her. Lemon waved her fingers feebly. Then the door swung wide open and Lemon stepped across Queen Moffat's threshold, set her feet firmly on the plush wall-to-wall, laid just that summer, and left a soft, cushioned imprint inside of yet another universe.

"We have been waiting," the squeaky voice whispered.

Mrs. Moffat's room was brightly lit, with sunshine spilling through open blinds. Light reflected off an opposing closet door — a wall of mirrors — and Lemon was temporarily blinded as she stepped directly into its brightest point. She raised her hand to shield her eyes. Mrs. Moffat sank her wiry frame into the teal easy chair, pulled the side lever and stretched her legs onto the footstool that emerged. A mahogany cane leaned up against the chair like a sepulchre. Her hair was a salt-and-pepper planet shooting off in spiralling directions. Mrs. Moffat sat comfortably, one arm along each armrest, her head held proudly high, crowned with a glittering, shimmering, two-inch-high rhinestone tiara. Lemon blinked slowly to be certain her eyes had adjusted properly. Mrs. Moffat also wore a flannelette Peter Rabbit pyjama top and matching bottoms, with rose-coloured slippers. Her fingernails were painted a deeper hue, but the lines extended guiltily over onto the skin of her fingers, looking more like she'd dipped her hands in blood and hung them to drip dry. *Drip, drip, drip.*

Lemon looked back at Mrs. Moffat's wrinkled face for confirmation. Dark half moons slept beneath her eyes, as if she'd been awake for sixty or seventy years. Her forehead had a deep trenching groove. From a distance it appeared to Lemon that her host had been wounded and left with a permanent battle scar, eternal worry marks. But Mrs. Moffat's lips were full and pink, informing Lemon that the appearance of advanced aging was little more than a convincing exaggeration. Mrs. Moffat's pupils were so dark that they were indistinguishable from her iris. Her lashes, like spider's legs, were long and thick and when she closed and reopened them, which she did periodically to punctuate a thought, Lemon believed they might cast netted shadows at her feet. Why am I here, she wanted to know. What was Grandma Connie thinking sending me here?

Lemon stepped through the light and stood in full view of Mrs. Moffat. She felt as though she was expected to kneel, bow or curtsy. Above her, hanging on the wall, were two rows of paper angels, identical figures each made of plastic. To the left was a bedside stand with a framed photograph of an infant wrapped in a blue blanket with the letter *B* embroidered on it. *B* for boy, Lemon thought. And she felt a stabbing pain in her chest, and for the first time since arriving in Vancouver, felt a formidable pull back to Toronto. A yellow, windup alarm clock with big arms and numbers sat behind the picture. Lemon turned counter-clockwise towards a single box spring and mattress with a white goose-down comforter. Someone had sewn hundreds of silver, red, and gold sequins along the edges for decoration. Two handmade pillows were on top of the bed — one in the shape of a crescent moon and the other of the sun. In the middle of the bed, with a plastic cord running to an electrical wall socket, was a red and white Mickey Mouse record player. I had one just like it, Lemon thought. A cardboard box of forty-fives peeked halfway out from under the bed. Lemon felt as though she'd stepped into a time warp and scooted a decade into the past. She cleared her throat of cobwebs and faced her host.

"Like I said, I am Lemon Boot!" She spoke slowly and loudly, as if she was a native English speaker and Mrs. Moffat was practising foreign language skills. "I would like to ask you some questions, if that is okay?" Mrs. Moffat didn't look directly at Lemon. She fidgeted with her hands, wringing and squeezing them for what seemed like a long while. Lemon paused and tried to assess Mrs. Moffat's level of comprehension. The alarm clock kept track of each loud second. Then, out of the blue, Mrs. Moffat began to sing.

"Root toot toot. Got a lovely daughter to boot."

Lemon stopped herself from rolling her eyes.

"No. I don't have kids. Actually, I am looking for my father."

Mrs. Moffat raised her voice. Each word was forced through clenched teeth as though she were reluctantly holding on to a bad taste.

"Mary had a little lamb. It's fleece was white as snow." She pulled the footstool lever, closed it and leaned forward, looking deeply into Lemon's eyes. "Everywhere that Mary went, that lamb was sure to go."

Lemon gazed up at the ceiling for strength.

"I was told to speak with you. Can you help?"

Mrs. Moffat leaned in closer.

"Georgy porgy, pudding and pie, kissed the girls and made them cry."

Totally discouraged, Lemon thought about retrieving Mary Jane to act as an interpreter. But then she plugged on fearing that in a few days Lilith would want her heading back to Toronto where she'd be stuck with her sleepless nights and her stupid flying rescue dreams for the rest of her pitiful life. A father was . . . a question that cannot be answered . . . elusive even as a definition . . .

Mrs. Moffat continued before Lemon could excuse herself.

"Solomon Grundy born on a Monday."

A familiar cloud of insignificance moved overhead and Lemon turned to go.

"Sorry to have bothered you," she said.

"Simple Simon went a fishing, for to catch a whale. But all the water he did find was in *your* mother's pail!"

"My mother?" Lemon asked. "You know Lilith?" Mrs. Moffat waved in a wide, controlled manner, like the queen after a coronation. "Tell me," Lemon pleaded. "*Please*. Is my father's name George? Is it Simon? Solomon?"

Mrs. Moffat snapped her fingers to a quick beat.

"Hey diddle, diddle," she said, snap snap snapping. "The cow jumped over the moon." Lemon felt defeated once more. Her throat was dry but she wanted to run to the washroom, flip up the toilet seat and hurl unknown worlds into the bowl.

"You forgot a line," she said, looking at her feet. "You forgot about the cat and the fiddle." Then, as she turned to go, she caught her own disappointed image in the mirror. Mrs. Moffat scoffed and waved her off with a dismissive gesture.

"We forget nothing," she said.

"If you know anything, anything at all," Lemon added one last time, "please tell me. You're my only hope."

Mrs. Moffat slapped the side of her chair and boomed each subsequent word.

"Fee! fie! foe! fum! I smell the blood of a selfish man."

"An Englishman," Lemon corrected.

341

"Just a man," Mrs. Moffat said, nodding and sticking out her tongue. She scrunched up her face, and held her nose between pinched fingers. "There was a crooked man, and he walked a crooked mile."

Lemon was exasperated.

"What are you saying?"

Mrs. Moffat dropped her head, changed her expression dramatically and raised both hands, finger to finger, at clavicle height in a solemn prayer pose.

"Forgive me, Father, for I have sinned." She looked up at Lemon through a veil of hair. "It's been seven days since my last confession."

"Seven," Lemon doubled for no apparent reason.

"Room seven-forty-seven," Mrs. Moffat quipped. "Seven-forty-seven." Then she spread her arms widely at her sides and leaned to the right and then to the left, demonstrating flight. "Ladybug, ladybug, fly away home." Lemon jumped in, "Your house is on fire . . ." They continued in unison, "And your children all gone!" Lemon sighed. She'd finally made a connection. "Whose children?" She asked. "Me?"

Mrs. Moffat held out her arm inviting Lemon to sit and Lemon carefully moved the record player to the floor and sat on the edge of the bed. As she rested her weight, the sunlight caught some of the flickering sequins and projected brilliant stars onto the end table. Mrs. Moffat also noticed, and she watched Lemon bouncing up and down on the mattress, continuing the miracle. Mrs. Moffat stuck out her bottom lip and hunched her shoulders in resignation.

"Twinkle twinkle, little star." Lemon listened for the next predictable line, "How I wonder where you are." Then she looked at the framed photograph on the end table, and watched her host gaze up at her ceiling like she was staring into a familiar galaxy, but one that only she could see. Lemon thought of her own bedroom back in Toronto as she watched this strange woman so apparently lost in space. Mrs. Moffat turned once more to stare at the photograph on her end table. Lemon took stock of her surroundings. This was a group home, for people like Mrs. Moffat who didn't communicate in the regular ways. The doors were locked, the residents supervised. Just then Lemon realized she and this odd stranger both sought the freedom of other worlds. Perhaps, she thought, we have both been prevented from being with someone we love. Mrs. Moffat sat motionless, perfectly still, hanging her head dramatically and examining the carpet just as intensely as she'd examined the ceiling. Then, without lifting her eyes, she spoke once more.

"Are you like the sound of a tap dripping?" she asked. "Or are you like a dam that burst?" Lemon stared blankly, fearing the connection she'd established was gone. "We are still waiting?" Mrs. Moffat said impatiently. "Lemon, Lemon, how does your garden grow?"

Lemon glanced at the clock and saw she'd been in this room for fifteen minutes, with already one third of her opportunity to find her father behind her. Tears welled in her eyes. She bit her thumbnail.

"I suppose ... I'm ... th ... th ... the dam." Drowning in my own fluids, she thought. Swallowed by an insatiable need to know.

Mrs. Moffat propelled herself out of the lazy chair with the use of her cane, and moved to join Lemon on the bed.

"We knew your father," she said, gingerly.

"Can you tell me his name?"

"There was a little girl who had a little curl, right in the middle of her forehead ..."

343

"Excuse me? Mrs. Moffat?"

"When she was good, she was very good. And when she was bad she was horrid."

"Please!"

Mrs. Moffat's tone was suddenly flat. She adjusted her tiara.

"Randy. A loyal subject."

"Randy?" Lemon repeated, and her eyes began to tear once more.

Mrs. Moffat nodded and then offered comfort in the best way she knew.

"Row, row, row your boat. Gently down the stream." Lemon wiped her eyes and permitted Mrs. Moffat — a stranger — to hold and rock her as if she'd been storing her comfort for years. Lemon sobbed as she'd never done before, and Mrs. Moffat somehow seemed to understand her better than anyone. Together they sang in an ever-sinking tone.

"Merrily.

    Merrily.

        Merrily.

            Merrily.

                Life is but a dream."

Lemon fell asleep almost as soon as she returned to Grandma Connie's house from the Turtle Group Home. She was confused and excited, but did not yet want to confront Lilith with news that she'd met her old companion, or report back to Constance, who was eagerly awaiting a name. All Lemon wanted was to finally sleep. So she spoke politely to both women when she entered the kitchen. "Hi, I'm beat. Think I'll take a nap." And ignored the delicious smell of Mrs. Appleby's homemade pea soup warming on the stove. Lemon climbed the stairs, flopped herself across the guest bed, and was out like a light within minutes.

In her dream she stood on a bridge staring at the fast-moving currents below. I can jump, she thought. I can jump and probably wake before I ever get wet. I can jump and finally find my father down there. She looked around. The bridge was fashioned from thick steel beams shooting fifty or more feet into the air. The structure stretched one hundred metres on either side of her and joined the highway to the main road leading up around a small hill to a large structure. Lemon looked over the top of the hill. A hospital, she understood instinctively. Then she observed her bare feet, knees, abdomen, breasts, and realized with great distress that she was entirely naked and her body was expanding at an accelerated rate. Quickly her breasts became pendulous, with aureoles pointing south; her hips expanded; her chin multiplied. As cellulite emerged beneath her skin, dimpling like cottage cheese, Lemon jumped back repulsed, but she was unable to escape herself. "No!" she screamed, poking at her stomach, trying to reverse the process and push the roles of developing fat inwards once more. Then, when she didn't think she could expand further without exploding, a figure approached from a distance, slowly advancing in the sunlight, and Lemon made out the familiar silver hair flashing like grey fire. "Ma?" The nearer Lilith came, the bigger Lemon grew. "Stop!" she demanded. "Stay right where you are. Don't come any closer!" But Lilith continued to advance, herself shrinking with each forward step. She stood barely four feet ahead, looking through Lemon as if she were not there. "Ma?" Lemon spoke softly, unnerved. "It's me. Don't you recognize me?" She waved her swollen hand before Lilith's sunken and expressionless face. "Ma?" Lilith walked past, without any sign of acknowledgment, and stood peering over the bridge, staring out at the water. "Ma, can't you see me? I'm huge — look what's happened."

Suddenly Lilith turned her head and Lemon was horrified to find that her mother's eye sockets were empty. Oh my God, what's happened? What's been done? Next, Lilith leaned as far over the side of the bridge as possible, searching for her missing eyes below, floating in the river. Just as Lemon ran to her mother's side and reached for her shoulders to pull her back down onto her feet, Lilith's head detached from her body and tumbled down, down, in slow motion, round and round, with the two circles of darkness rotating towards Lemon every few seconds. As the head fell the mouth screamed, "Randy! Randy! Randy . . ." until it hit the surface of water with a heavy splash, some of which sprayed up into Lemon's face. Lilith's figure, still held in her daughter's hands, crumbled into a pillar of blue dust at Lemon's feet. Lemon screamed and her stomach felt as though it were full of exploding grenades.

Without forethought, she climbed awkwardly onto the ledge of the bridge and spread her arms out for balance. She would jump. She too would plunge to the river, retrieve Lilith and her father, or drown on her way out to ocean, but surely she must somehow cleanse herself of what had just happened — erase, obliterate, forget, forget, forget the fact that she'd ever witnessed her own mother's disintegration. This is no dream, she thought. And just as Lemon was about to rise onto her tiptoes and leap, she felt someone at her back, and turned to find a second figure — older — with a leathery face, a baseball cap and fake deerskin slippers. The figure gently attached wings to Lemon's shoulderblades. "Psychiatric wings," the figure said. "Just for you. Because you want them so damned bad." When Lemon turned to face the river once more the figure had disappeared and she found herself looking out through the Ward One visiting-room windows. She was momentarily relieved to find herself thin once more. Everything as it should be. Everything back to normal. *And* she could fly now, Lemon thought. She could fly, and find what she needed, find the truth.

Unfortunately, there was nowhere left to go.

A lmost a week after Daddy was buried, Lemon was still not speaking to me. I got dressed for bed and lounged on the maroon pullout in the den waiting for sleep to take over. I put my glass of water down on Mother's small pine sewing table, and thought about work. I missed the office, the telephone ringing, Sergeant Grant barging in with a new case — finding the lost ones . . . The vertical blinds covering the small window in the den were closed and only a tall brass floor lamp gave off any light. Lemon was curled at the other end of the couch, her legs folded under her body like a grasshopper, her arms across her chest. Mother had just climbed the staircase and was brushing her teeth when I turned on the TV, smudged the bottom of the plastic popcorn bowl, and gathered the remaining butter and salt onto my fingertips. I licked them one by one. Lemon was staring at the idiot box. "How're you doing, Babygirl?"

"Christ Ma!" she burst. "I'm almost eighteen. I'm no baby! How many times do I have to tell you!" She lifted the remote control and pressed the channel changer. The television screen went black, and all that was left was a pinpointed white star in the centre until the electricity cut out. Lemon sat in a silent, hostile stupor, maybe wanting to ask about Mrs. Moffat, maybe wanting to share her dream, but how was I supposed to know? No one told me she'd been to the group home. She sat forward, unfolded her legs and stretched them out in front, cracking her toes inside her socked feet. Then she gathered her nerve, because next thing I knew she was speaking in a low, solid voice. "Ma, I want to know the truth."

I looked out through the open doorway, along the runner to the grandfather clock in the hallway. It had rung Westminster chimes at half-hour intervals since Daddy bought it the year *before . . . before . . . before what?* I suddenly visualized sprawling residential grounds like the image had always been sitting there just inside the hallway of my brain, waiting to be cleared out. *Before . . . before . . . before I'd gone away for a while?* I figured I was in some kind of mixed-up mental space because Daddy had died. I was reeling from the shock. And I found myself wondering the strangest things. *Just how many heartbeats had it been since Bridgewater?* Then I choked on the very idea of that hospital, coughed, reached for my glass of water and swallowed time down again.

Time's as unreliable as Gallileo's pulse, you know? (I read that somewhere.) It advances by a different measure, depending on how you count it. Minutes, hours, days in chronological, ascending order. Or snowdrifts of memory and puddles of self-reflection leaking backwards, down, counter-clockwise. Was time a slave clock imprisoning me in 1968, the year I gave birth? Or was it a galley clock with a spring mechanism that could free me from the past and jump to the present on demand? I still don't know for sure. Sometimes now I think time's not to be followed like an arrow at all, or a page turning year after year. Maybe it's just an invisible spiral staircase leading us like a question mark round, round, round forever while we climb closer to ourselves. Maybe if you're really brave, you have the courage to look down over the banister and see how far you've come without falling.

I replaced the glass of water on the table, and was lost in thought again. The grandfather clock chimed, calling me against my better judgment, to remember . . . *People get locked up*, I heard myself think. *People like me.* I ran my fingers along the smooth insides of the popcorn bowl and tried my very best not to see a strong-jawed woman in a hospital gown face down on an unmade bed, but I saw her anyway, and I reached out for that face I could no longer identify. *Randy?* My hand slapped helplessly against the greasy residue of the popcorn bowl in my lap. Lemon repeated herself. "I said, I want to know the truth."

"What truth?" I asked that time. "What are you talking about?" Truth had always been a shock of sound waves that ripped into my skull. Big brass sounds, hammering out an endless echo, or steel drums pounding harried, chaotic madness. *Hadn't it? Wasn't it?* Didn't truth spill like bottles of cheap wine, staining everything? All I know is that it always seemed to belong to everyone but me. Mother had her version. My old doctor had his. Truth was behind me back then and I wanted to rise, stretch my arms to the ceiling and become tall enough to grab the past and pull it from the pedestal Lemon always stood it on. But that noise was still there; I didn't dare move. Water, blood and saliva stirred in my body; my temperature vaulted.

Since I'd arrived in Vancouver, I'd had nothing but pressure from Lemon. *Why is Grandma Connie so angry with you? Why can't you change?* Too much pressure after Daddy's death and my failing vision. Too much! I felt ambushed. Lemon had been asking hard questions for a long time, and I'd put her off as best I could, hoping — without even realizing — that a twenty-year-old nightmare could not boomerang.

"I have a right to know!" she yelled.

"And I have a right to my privacy!"

But the truth? Lemon still wanted an answer.

She raised her finger for a good chomp.

"I'm old enough to hear it from you," she said. "Whatever it is."

"There's no such thing as old enough. No such thing." Then the crowded, overwhelming noise in my ears slipped away.

Lemon shifted her position on the couch, cracked her knuckles, and chewed her fingernails loudly. I continued crunching semi-popped kernels and spat the indigestible ones into the palm of one hand. *She'll outgrow it*, I told myself, as if a desire for the truth was like a hand-knit sweater that could actually be outgrown. 'Course even without dwelling on the point, I knew truth could be stretched through excessive use, handed down from one generation to the next. I knew truth was relative.

There is no father. There is no father.

Memories don't improve with time. They just grow less fruitful, less clear. Maybe sometimes it's better to forget. For other people if not for yourself. For the sake of your children. Besides, a woman who breaks a promise could lose her home, her health — even her mind. Yes, a woman only has one thing in this life that's sure not to be undone and that's her word.

Without it I'd be worthless, crazy — nobody all over again. I'd have lost all self-respect. So without understanding why yet and without realizing I'd made two different promises that cancelled each other out, I closed my mouth determined as a taproot. Even a mother has her limits.

"Don't get to choose your family," I said, ignoring Lemon's angry expression and her impatient fidgeting.

"I *know* that. Ma. Believe me, I know." She hesitated. "But what about my father? He's my family too."

Family, I thought. *Relatives. Genetically linked kin, sometimes people you only have blood in common with.*

"No. I'm your family!" I shouted. "Relativity's not just some theory you read about in a library book. It doesn't *really* explain why matter rises and falls. "Relativity could be a fallen woman, or a fall from grace. Or just a regular, predictable season in time. *We* are a family," I barked. "A family of two!" I grabbed up the TV remote control, clicked the "on" button, zipping through the channels, one after the other.

Lemon jumped up off the couch and threw her hands to her hips.

"Grandma Connie says she's going to make some calls. She's going to see if she can locate anyone from the past to help me. Grandma Connie says *you* were in a mental hospital!"

My finger continued to press down on the channel changer until it reached the end. I stared into static. The past was everywhere all of a sudden, in the walls, in the sofa propping me up. In the woolly face of the TV screen. I felt like the floor was turning to quicksand and about to swallow me whole. Lemon could know what I forgot? Then that terrible noise started up again . . . the sound of china cups rattling on shelves, the sound of smashing bottles, and finally, noisy electricity tingling in my eardrum. A high-voltage image was on its way, but Lemon leaned over and screamed in my face.

"Fine, Ma! Keep your eyes closed, and your ears covered and bury your head in the sand, but you won't stop me for seeing for myself!" She dropped her arms at her sides and waited for a reaction.

"You're just upset because of Grandpa Jack," I said, rubbing my temples as another migraine came on. "You'll be back to your old self tomorrow."

Lemon shook her head.

"No. With or without your help, I'm getting to the bottom of this."

The bottom, I thought. *Bottom of the barrel. A bottomless pit. A bottom feeder.* Then for no good reason, I remembered the one flower I'd never planted — false Solomon's seal. I heard heavy breathing, heavy, heavy breathing. *Oh no, not again,* I thought. *Please, not again.*

My ass was bare and cold on the stainless-steel shelf. My good red visiting dress was hiked up, my panties on the floor. Solomon was between my legs — pump — his right arm wrapped around my waist — pump — his left arm holding us both in position. He fed on my flesh and I tore every time he pushed farther inside. Pump. I gasped the first time which he seemed to enjoy, so I continued quietly gasping and moaning like I heard women in the blue movies did. I dug my short fingernails into the back of his neck. He bit my shoulder and I pretended I was unbreakable. The storage closet was cramped, my legs were under his arms, a shelf of toilet paper and cleaning fluids was beside my head. I closed my eyes to find comfort in darkness, and thought about the baby. *Come to me,* I thought. *Come.*

Solomon moved into me faster, harder. *It wasn't so bad*, I told myself. Pump. *It was almost over.* Pump. His sweaty face pressed closer into my neck and I arched backwards. He spread his legs farther apart, pulled my torso into him, and continued thrusting. The pain was almost unbearable. I thought I might pass out, but the bottle inside that I once believed was broken had disintegrated into tiny particles of dust that I imagined were flowing out through every opening. I was about to be cured. I smelt urine and fermenting vomit from the dirty floor mop standing in the corner and tried not to gag. Solomon's key chain hit the stainless-steel counter every time he thrust. *Clang. Clang.* It made a vacant, starved sound. I followed its rhythm. *Clang. Clang.* His breathing quickened, he grunted through clenched teeth, clutched me a little too tightly — *clang clang clang clang* — and finally exploded. With each note, I came closer to freedom.

When I returned to the argument in the den Lemon was gone. I was shivering. My thick thighs were pulsing and turning purple like bruised fruit, especially where they joined at my centre. I tasted blood and quickly realized I'd bitten my tongue. *What happened?* I wondered. *Ward One? Bridgewater?* Then memory began to fade back to the store pile where other unwanted visions sat. I shook, confused. Pulled the elastic band on my housedress away from my belly for relief, wiggled my toes to stop the pins and needles. Maybe it's happened to you too, where something suddenly hits you years later, and you wonder how could I have forgotten that? Was it there all long but I just chose to ignore it? How can parts of my life be clear and crisp when others are invisible? Well that's what happened to me. And as I started to remember in the days after Daddy's funeral, the future and the past seemed like they were working against each other. I couldn't make my Babygirl happy and I still hadn't found Benjamin.

I heard Lemon above, the floorboards creaking as she climbed into bed. I was still too agitated to sleep. Daddy was dead. My daughter was drifting even further away. The past had climbed on top of me and pinned me down. And there was nothing I could do about any of it. I rocked back and forth. *Why didn't I see it coming? Why can't I see?* A few minutes later I opened my hand and wiped the sticky kernels from my palm into the bowl. Then before I knew what hit me, I was being flooded all over again. I remembered being fifteen and washing dishes just like it was yesterday. Daddy came home late for the third time that week.

"You drunken fool!" Mother exploded as soon as he stepped through our back door. "It's almost eleven o'clock, Jack. If you honestly think I intend to wait forever, you've got another thing coming!" Mother walked over to the stove, bent down to pull out the bottom drawer, and tossed in a saucepan as loud as she could. "You bloody idiot!"

I didn't bother to turn around, just scrubbed the last of the pots and pans with liquid dish detergent and steel wool.

"Oh Christ," Daddy muttered. "Don't start. Why are you such a goddamned nag? What's the big deal?"

"The big deal is that Lilith here," Mother pointed at me, "should have been in bed hours ago. It's a school night. But we waited dinner on you again!"

Daddy fished in his breast pocket for his pipe and his Zippo.

"I lost track of time. I was over at the pub."

"No kidding, Jack." Mother hooked one hand onto her hip bone. "Were you *really*? And here I thought that odour of gin and tonic was some fancy new aftershave."

Daddy scoffed.

"Who busts his ass at the shop all day? Who spends all his free time with her?"

"You play and leave the real raising to me," Mother snapped. "And I've tried in every way I know to change her attitude — Lord knows I have — but with you always out gallivanting around town, leaving me to deal with her on my own, it's no wonder she's so bizarre."

I scrubbed harder wondering what exactly bizarre looks like, sounds like. Maybe a high-pitched squeal or a short-wave radio between channels? Or flowers breathing? Or maybe a dozen voices whispering inside your head all at the same time? I plunged my hands into the sudsy water. *I better be more careful.* Then I watched my parents through a reflection in the window.

"I've been working like a dog," Daddy said. "For you, Constance."

He fumbled with the lighter, unable to flip the lid, then placed the pipe between his lips and sucked even though it wasn't lit. Mother kicked the stove drawer shut with her foot, untied her apron at the back, and threw it at him. He tried to catch it but missed. It slunk to the floor in a pathetic little heap.

"I've been trying to save the business."

"Well you wouldn't have anything to save if you weren't so busy running it into the ground! You make me sick! Your clothes stink and you can't even stand upright. You're a Neanderthal! I told you the last time Jack, I don't want alcohol in my house again and I meant it. That includes when it bumbles through the door!"

With that, Mother picked up a potted geranium from the countertop and hurled it at Daddy's head. He stepped away just seconds before it smashed to bits in the corner of the room. Mother stormed past, and Daddy spun her around by the arm.

"Hey, don't you walk out on me, woman! Don't you ever walk out on me!"

I stopped scrubbing.

Mother stared at his firm grip and then directly into his red eyes.

"Take a long hard look at yourself, Jack Boot. And then look around here. You better think twice before you lay another hand on me if you ever want to see any of this again."

I dropped the steel wool in the sink, turned around and ran towards them.

"Let go, Daddy!" I pleaded, putting one of my wet, wrinkled, soapy hands on his. "Please let go." He did, and Mother immediately left the room. Then Daddy turned and walked out into the night again, not even one word to me.

A few minutes later, I finished washing and drying the last of the dishes, put them away, wiped my hands on the tea towel, and turned out the kitchen lights on my way out back. I couldn't face the injured geranium, fractured and split into a million tiny pieces, so I just left it where it was and tried to tell myself it was no big deal. As soon as I had my hand on the knob, Daddy appeared again, opened the door and walked across the kitchen to the pantry, where he reached around behind the door for the broom and dustpan hanging there.

"Lil, what's say you and me clean this up?"

"Why is she so mean?" I whispered while he swept and I held the pan.

"Don't say those things. It's not easy living with an old fool like me."

"You're not old," I defended, and Daddy laughed.

"Your mother has a strong character. She sacrificed a lot to be with me. She was expected to stay in the Okanagan Valley and take care of everybody there, you know? Your uncles Donald and Joe. It isn't easy to go against the grain. Things didn't work out exactly as we planned, and well, sometimes . . . sometimes she gets a little upset."

"More than a little."

"She's a tough cookie," Daddy agreed. "I know that. She never so much as made a peep when you were born, never flinched or protested when the other baby . . ." His voice got really, really soft and cracked. He cleared his throat and tried to look sober. "Lilith, your mother is the model of womanly stature — even under the worst circumstances." A faraway look seemed to take him from me then. "You know what she told me after those twelve hours of labour?" I shook my head. "'It's the Lord's work. Woman's lot. And no amount of complaining will change it.' Remember that Lil. In this life, it doesn't pay to complain." There was more sweeping and more holding after that, and I dumped the broken clay pieces, dirt and loose geranium stems into the garbage.

"Think we can save it?" I asked, holding up the severed roots.

Daddy smiled meekly and spoke as if he was still thinking more about another place and time than about the houseplant.

"All we can do," he said, "is try our very best."

Funny, I always seem to remember him at his best, but really, nobody's perfect. And usually in evenings if he was home, he was sitting in the den in his black wingback chair after dinner while Mother and I cleared the table and scraped dishes. (There was a dishwasher by the time I got out of the hospital, but Mother still insisted each plate be rinsed thoroughly before placing it in the machine.) Cleanliness was next to godliness. Daddy was comfortable in the den, like a big hairy cat. Mother said he was lazy and always licking his own wounds, but I remembered him lounging just outside the centre of activity. Observant. Detached. Letting Mother have her way. For a long time, I believed Daddy was indestructible because nothing seemed to reach him. Not threats of Vancouver collapsing and sinking into the ocean after an earthquake. Not losing a child or Mother's temper. No matter what happened, he came through it all the same. Like me being pregnant.

"It's going to be a girl," I'd told him the day he signed me out of Bridgewater.

"How do you know?"

"Just do."

Daddy often held his pipe clenched between his teeth when he spoke, and the smoke filtered out one side of his face. In his right palm he squeezed the golden tobacco weeds of an Export package. It was mesmerizing. I always watched his hands. Sometimes he spun a pencil between his thumb, index and pointer fingers. Other times, he picked at his cuticles with a bone-base pocket knife. Because he was over six feet five inches, his body filled the easy chair. His pectoral muscles flexed as he squeezed the tobacco packet. The veins running up the insides of his arms. from wrist to the bend in his elbow, were thick and purple. Bluish black in the dim light of his shed, reminding me of a thousand roads shooting off Highway 99, the sea-to-sky highway. I thought his bulging veins and arteries looked like the electrical wiring inside the lamps he fixed. There was once a time when I used to think there was nothing my Daddy couldn't do, except maybe say "no" to Mother. Looking back, I was wrong about so many things.

There was beige wainscoting on the den walls when I was a girl, and an orange lampshade hanging from the centre of the ceiling. Mother decorated the walls with plates, instead of paintings. The odour of Daddy's pipe filled the house, coating the wallpaper, and the plastic-covered upholstery. *Oh, the smell!* Mother complained that no matter how hard she scrubbed, she couldn't ever get the curtains white again. I remembered the giant tear on the right arm of Daddy's chair, and the yellow stuffing with strands of ebony thread that poked out. It looked like a dead man's wound: no blood, no arteries or capillaries — only the yellow and black shades of formaldehyde on bloated, rotting flesh. Just like his lungs, from so many years of smoke. How fitting he slumped over there, rattled like death, and never inhaled again.

I curled into a fetal position after all that remembering, and cried and cried, and cried myself to sleep. When I woke up in the middle of the night the storm thundered to its natural conclusion. My knees were still tucked close to my body, and the corduroy pattern of the couch was pressed on my face. There was a wet spot on the cushion under my head from where I'd been drooling when I drifted off. I found myself with my face in my hands, focusing on Daddy's triumphs instead of his betrayals. He was the one who took me to the Tick Tock and let me mingle with customers, feeling useful. He was the one who taught me how to love a garden. He signed me out of Bridgewater. You couldn't take those things away from him, no matter what else he didn't do.

It was almost dawn by the time I wiped my nose on my sleeve, stood, and walked into the kitchen to place the popcorn bowl in the dishwasher. I looked out the window. Rain pelted the roof of Daddy's shed, adding music to my sorrow. After a few minutes standing there feeling sorry for myself, I grabbed Mother's yellow slicker from the hall tree by the side entrance. It was too small and wouldn't close around me to do up. I walked out the door towards the shed half-covered, thinking about Lemon's threat to dig up the past. *What more would she find?*

My socks were wet by the time I turned the door handle, pulled until its rusty hinge creaked. Inside it was pitch black and stank of Varsol and furniture polish just like the Tick Tock did so long ago. The only light snuck under the door. I left it open a foot until I found my way to the string with a screw hanging on the end, dangling exactly where I remembered. I tugged gently; pulling with too much force might have caused the ramshackle ceiling to collapse. A bare bulb overhead lighted my way. The centre of the room was brightest, with an electric white glow. Everywhere else, around the edges, was still dark. I stepped forward anyway.

When I was younger I never noticed how unfinished everything was in the shed. It had seemed perfect back then. Safe. Now the floor was nothing but dirt covered with thin, unconnected wooden planks. Dust from between them must have dirtied Daddy's shoes and socks, eventually making its way into Mother's clean house. There were no windows in the shed, and the rafters above were piled high with deflated rubber tires, rope and twine, and a lot of wicker furniture. Daddy's furniture was always in some stage of rotting, which filled the place with a smell like wet straw. The shed was about unfinished business. Admissions of imperfection. A confessional. I looked up and found Lemon's old bassinet attached to the ceiling with chicken wire. I remembered how Mother wasn't impressed when Daddy hauled his garbage treasures through our backyard. "You can judge a man best by what he throws away," she used to call out to Mrs. Appleby across the fence. I know better now.

You can judge a man by what he keeps too.

The only fresh air inside came from a crudely constructed vent made out of a former exhaust pipe. The pipe was pushed through a hole in the wall and fastened with duct tape. Cotton batting had been used to secure it. As I stood around inhaling, it felt like invading foreign territory all over again. I blinked. Five rows of Gerber's baby food jars were mounted on the wall directly in front of me, their lids nailed into an overhanging cupboard so the jars looked suspended in mid-air. Each contained something different. Some held screws with square heads, others flat. Some were filled with nuts and washers of varying widths. And others displayed nails and small hinges. His unfinished pine work table stood underneath the hanging jars. His sander sat on the floor to the right, propped up against the leg of the table, and beside it there was a small pile of wood shavings. I smelt balsam. To the left of the table under a large photograph — the only one in the shed — was Daddy's wooden trunk with its lid open, leaning against a supporting wall. I took a step towards it, feeling like a girl again.

I could hear a gentle *tap tap tap* on the roof as if God was rapping his fingers to show he was bored or impatient. But I wasn't rushing. Soon enough Daddy's Canucks T-shirt, his ancient corncob pipe, all his belongings, would be packed away for good, given out to friends and trucked off to the Sally Ann downtown. Besides, I hadn't found what I was looking for yet. I searched for the gardening shears he kept in his trunk. If only I could find them I could leave with more than just regrets. I found cloth gloves, and a small spade, but no shears. And then the worst thought hit me: *What if I lose my Babygirl too?*

I dropped to my knees and scrambled around on the floor frantically, swiping under tables and shelves looking for the missing shears. After a few minutes my knees hurt so I stood up again, and wiped off my legs. *Gone,* I thought, and glanced at the bassinet one more time. I was touched that Daddy had saved it all those years. Then I also noticed the picture again, hanging just inches away in its old wooden frame. In the photo Mother was holding a baby swaddled in a cotton blanket. *That must have been me,* I realized, stepping closer. She looked tired and overworked, but her colourised cheeks disguised her true state. She was holding me close to her bosom, maybe grieving in private, but for the camera she was pretending to be grateful that one of her babies had been born alive. My tiny features were clouded by the blanket and the grainy quality of the photograph, but my arm stuck out waving, gloriously unaware then of what the future would bring. Daddy stood tall in the photo, one arm squeezing Mother, proud of his new family, the other reaching for my exposed hand. We connected freely. I was stuck on the image. It was from before the business took off, and both my parents looked like a hearty and practical team, the way farm people do in unpredictable seasons. Even though they left the way of life they grew up with to take a stab at city living, I could see it was still in their blood to need each other but not dwell on that fact. Daddy stared directly into the camera lens, his walnut eyes wide with expectation.

I pulled a chair over from the farthest corner of the shed, climbed it and lifted down the photograph. The place on the wall where his picture had hung was naked and exposed, except for the buff rectangle. It was the only surface clean and free from time. I choked on dust and swiped at a cobweb tickling my face. I could see Daddy's engraved words on the bottom of the frame: "Boot family." And the year, "1950." The *F* in "Family" loomed large and flared at the tails. *I wasn't perfect,* I thought then. *I wasn't the son Mother missed out on, or the daughter anyone expected, but I was happy and healthy.* I stared at the photograph and saw pride and respect in Daddy's work. Maybe there wasn't a lot of tenderness in Mother's grip, or understanding, but in her guarded face there was some hope — even a sliver of love escaping. I thought about bitterroot, how ugly it gets over time, and pearly everlasting which grows all over Western Canada pretty much unnoticed. I didn't

363

want to be angry any more. *We all do what we must to get by,* I thought. *Go where we have to.* Into ourselves, into cold, dead reserves where nothing hurts any more. Into detached, make-believe worlds where everything looks rosy through bloodshot eyes. *Yep. Lemon will just have to trust me,* I realized. *A person's best might not be good enough, but sometimes it's all you get.* I hoisted the large frame under my arm, pulled the cord to turn off the light and for the last time, walked out of Daddy's shed and into the dying storm with love tucked away protectively.

For the first time in years Constance found herself behind the wheel of an automobile, and cowering behind it, felt shrunken and uncharacteristically unsure of herself. Lemon was sitting beside her on a brown bucket seat that squeaked from rusty springs. The dash before them was wide with an old cigarette lighter built in, an AM radio, and no air conditioning. Constance glanced across at her granddaughter, who was deep in thought. As they drove beyond Vancouver's city limits, Constance could hardly fathom how the view to New Westminster had changed. Of course now that she was doing the driving, not Jack, she was missing much of it. But she saw enough to recognize that time had enabled the city to spread, erecting condominiums and retail outlets in a steady infectious stream, practically all the way from Quebec Street to the hospital. The past was somehow creeping nearer, Constance thought, creeping and crawling and now her time had finally come. She felt vindicated. She was a messenger, left to see to it that common sense prevailed. I am the way and the truth and the light, Constance told herself. And those who come to the Father, come through me.

Constance recalled the early years, when Lilith hung on Jack's every word, clung to his coat sleeves as he prepared to leave for work. She'd cried agonizing tears in the front window whenever her father had disappeared up the walk. Such a fuss still pinched (and insulted) if Constance thought about it hard enough. She didn't object to the division of the world into male and female spheres — certainly not! But she deeply resented that hers was somehow less desirable. Jack was decadent, always hugging and kissing on them, but someone had to be reasonable. Someone had to think about birthday cards, new shoes for school, and paying the bills. "And with his drinking," Constance told herself, "it certainly wasn't Jack." No, hers had had to be a practical kind of love.

Constance had lived through each agonizing Bridgewater moment, back and forth in the car, and did not once speak of what it meant or of how it pained her. Just as well, for Jack would have been no help. He was the only man she'd shared a bed with, Constance thought. The only man she'd ever loved. But most of the time he understood just what could be gleaned from the inside of a bottle of Southern Comfort! And no one knew how it felt to be the mother of a child so damaged, Constance thought. To wait month after month for the phone to ring and hear that a cure had been found or progress made, or some plausible explanation given. What did any of them know about that? Or the embarrassment. And guilt. A mother's guilt was paralyzing. It could prevent tenderness lest a person splinter into tiny slivers of a human being. If she'd only made her presence felt by inflicting it, well, what alternative had Jack provided? Constance clenched her fingers tightly around the steering wheel. Jack was unavailable again. And despite the twisted tangled ache of missing him, it seemed that death was her late husband's best attempt at skipping out.

The Boots, like most couples, had divided their worlds into mutual exclusivities — into skills, interests and silent agreements — as though two people who joined bodies could not also share an admiration for the glow of a waning moon or the thrill of a fishing expedition. Indeed, marriage had afforded little room in which to be entirely oneself so they had each selected parts for emphasis, magnification and sole ownership. Constance did the books while Jack made sure the furnace was in order. She did the groceries while Jack spent time with Lilith. She had the house and her church groups while Jack had the Tick Tock and the pub. He took care of lawn mowing. Car repairs. He drove. And before either of them knew it, patterns had been firmly entrenched.

Constance checked the rear-view mirror, clicked on the left-hand turn signal, and changed lanes.

"What was Olivia going on about at the funeral parlour?"

"Stories about Grandpa Jack," Lemon said. "She told me he was a natural-born entertainer."

Constance chuckled.

"Olivia always did have a way of understating the obvious."

"What do you mean?"

"Your grandfather could be the life of the party, dear. Any party."

"Really?" Lemon stretched her feet out onto the dash. Grandma Connie was full of insinuations but Lemon wanted more direct communication. "Was Ma really ... *sick*? I mean, sick like Mrs. Moffat?"

"Worse," Constance said, pointing sharply at Lemon's feet.

"What could be worse?"

"Believing there's nothing the matter is worse."

"Oh."

Lemon dropped her feet and sat up straight once more.

"Grandma? Don't you remember *anything* about my father?"

Constance pushed her foot to the brake pedal slowly, stuttering the car to a stop at a traffic light. Better to be safe than sorry. Lemon could wait. She'd waited this long, a few minutes more wasn't going to kill her.

"Well," she said. "I wish I could say that I did, but you'll just have to ask around when we get to the hospital."

Lemon returned to her definition, universalizing it, making it a better measure. Her divining rod. A father is someone who participates in the conception of the child, she thought. No wait, what about adopted kids? What about friends at school who'd been raised by their stepfathers? She wanted to be more accurate: A father assumes responsibility for a child. But what kind of responsibility? Financial? Emotional? Jan's father paid her way but what good was that? No, a father puts his child's need ahead of his own. Good. She liked that. But wait, so does a mother . . .

"What was Grandpa Jack like as a father?" Lemon asked.

Constance sucked her teeth before responding.

"As good as could be expected, dear."

Constance knew that Jack had always adored Lilith. In the privacy of their bedroom he'd often defended her. "Connie, go easy," he'd say. "She's a sensitive child." He eventually came around when he saw I meant business, Constance thought. He never admitted it, but he knew I was right. The child needed outside help. Then as the light changed, the notion that Jack had once deceived her came back full force, just as if it were that same alarming afternoon all over again, and Constance was learning that he'd signed Lilith out of Bridgewater without her approval. Constance hadn't asked for much from this life, only that she come first in someone's heart. Yet even that seemed to have been too much. And she'd never intended to play second fiddle — not to the bottle, and certainly not to a daughter. Constance stepped down hard on the gas pedal. The car lunged forward.

Father, Lemon thought. *Someone respectful. Solid. Loyal. Yes loyal!* A father must be that above all else, because a mother can never successfully escape it, the world will hold her to it. But for someone else to offer devotion freely? Maybe that's the unique gift of fatherhood. As Lemon and Constance turned right onto McBride Boulevard and then right again through the Bridgewater gates, Lemon was so nervous that her chest felt as if it were laced into a Victorian corset. She knew who to ask for when she arrived, although she hadn't yet had the nerve to share his name with anyone.

Not five minutes later in the parking lot, Constance turned the key in the ignition and silenced her vehicle. "Here we are, dear." Lemon smiled at her grandmother and stepped out of the station wagon, ducked under the guardrail and hurried along the newly paved road. She was so eager she practically flew. But not quite. She had chosen this path of searching and that meant caution. Perhaps she sensed there was no sparing herself the truth now, no sparing or avoiding or protecting against the hardship of moving consciously by foot. Perhaps, Lemon was learning, there are some places you simply cannot get to without baby steps.

It was an unusually warm summer afternoon and grass tickled her toes through the straps of her sandals. She stopped first at a small security building and knocked on the locked door. No answer. Then she carried on towards the sprawling grounds while weeping willows bowed at her feet and oak trees stretched out their sturdy branches like welcoming arms. There was a steep staircase in front of a concrete building and the word "Factory" carved into the front. Both its heavy front doors were boarded up. Lemon walked on farther until she came to the first in a row of small white buildings labelled "Ward Four," "Three," "Two," and finally "One." She approached the last of them and stood on her tiptoes peering in through the windows.

Inside it was spacious with high ceilings. Three beds occupied the room, and their uniform down-filled mattresses were spotted with dark stains. No sheets or blankets or pillows were visible. Lemon stepped back and continued a few feet farther along before peeking again, this time down a long pink corridor. The lights were off inside and it seemed deserted. Lemon turned to face the Fraser River, which shone like a sea of liquid topaz. Why had her grandmother brought her to this beautiful, deserted location? Lemon's head began to spin.

Off at the far end of the grounds, Lemon glimpsed a rectangular building with a wall of dewy windows sparkling in the sun. Maybe someone there could help find her father? She set one foot in front of the other and thought, how many light years away is he now? The air was moist and thick and Lemon felt as though she was walking alone on the surface of the moon with only the sound of her own controlled respiration for company. She cut across the lawn, passing a fire hall and an abandoned stable, and a medium-sized building marked "clinic," before reaching the front doors of the greenhouse. She pressed her face up against the bevelled glass.

The greenhouse was full of bushy shrubs and mixed flower beds, and there were petals scattered on the stone floor. Lemon called out hoping someone was tucked discreetly in the back, out of view. "Hello? Anybody here?" She knocked loudly and waited, but when no response came she pulled open the unlocked screen door and stepped inside. Immediately the scent of eucalyptus wafted over and reminded her of the many times she'd snuck home from school in the middle of the day. Lemon practically expected her mother to emerge from behind the bougainvillea waving a thick finger and hollering, "Babygirl, what the hell do you think you're doing here?" Farther inside she found a bed of frilly red begonia, and from the ceiling hung fuchsia, in large round planters. At her feet sat a groundsheet and several trays, one half-full of seedlings. Lemon bent down to touch the rich black earth and found herself tracing her name in the dirt. Suddenly, the screen door swung open and she heard a bottomless voice: "You shouldn't be in here."

Lemon immediately stood and faced the man. He was sturdy with a full head of hair, grey and a colour not unlike her own. His skin was similarly pale. He wore overalls rolled up to his bony knee and a clean white short-sleeved cotton shirt. Lemon noticed a key chain sticking out of his pocket. All of a sudden her stomach turned violently and she grew faint. "Sorry," Lemon said, swooning. "I was just looking for someone. Do you work here?"

"Used to be an orderly before I retired." The man approached and reached out to steady her. "Stayed on to work security at the gate." He guided Lemon to a nearby beam for balance. "Here, rest for a minute."

"It's really a mental institution?" Lemon whispered.

The man nodded.

"Where you from?" His cool blue eyes made Lemon feel translucent.

371

"Ontario," she answered. "Toronto." The nausea was now supplemented by a throbbing in her temples. Lemon pointed over her shoulder and out the window, in the direction of the central building. "Maybe I should just speak to an administrator there. Sorry to bother you." She turned to go.

"Hardly any staff around on Sundays," the man said. "Bet I can point you in the right direction. What name you after?" Lemon took a deep breath before answering.

"Randy," she said, in almost the exact tone of confidence Mrs. Moffat had used. "Do you know him?"

The stranger scratched his chin pensively, dug his hands into the pockets of his overalls.

"Hmmm. Randy what?"

Lemon shrugged.

"That's all I know. He lived there I think." She pointed at Ward One.

"Can't be, Miss. That one's always been a women's ward."

But Lemon had already lost her precarious balance, and fallen to the floor, her face ashen now. She'd not heard what the stranger had told her. This was the right place; she was certain. Her father had walked these grounds, swung open these very doors. Yes. She could *feel* it

The man helped Lemon stand and guided her out of the greenhouse.

"I think we better get you some fresh air."

"Randy?" Lemon repeated once when they were outside. "Are you sure you don't know him?"

The man twirled his moustache.

"Oh . . . wait. There *was* a Randy all right. Yeah, a real wild one. Always stirring trouble. Came here in, now let me see — sixty-six I believe it was. From the penitentiary. And roomed with two others — one scatterbrain, what was her name? . . . And the other, the special one. Lilith." The stranger spoke her mother's name in a way that sent a shiver up Lemon's spine.

"But . . . but . . . Mrs. Moffat said . . ."

"That's it!" The man blurted. "Moffat: the scatterbrain. Thought she was some kind of royalty, that one. Got moved to one of those expensive new homes a few years back when the prime minister released patients onto the streets. Put up quite a fuss she did, said she didn't want to be on her own. They sent her to a provincial facility while most of the rest were trucked off to rooming houses and the like. Only patients here now come to detox . . ." His voice trailed off. "The other one though . . . the other one she just up and left without so much as a goodbye . . ."

"Can you take me to Randy?" Lemon insisted.

"I don't know. You don't look so good."

"I'm fine!" Lemon clutched her abdomen. "Just take me."

The man led her back up the path, behind Ward One, into dense foliage. Alone in the secluded area with this stranger, Lemon became conscious of the fact that perhaps she wasn't safe and just as she'd decided to turn back, they came upon a smaller clearing with rows of tall thin cedars, each standing four feet apart. The man stopped and pointed.

"There," he said, indicating a small grave marker. "Is that the Randy you're looking for?"

Lemon's heart stopped. All remaining colour fled her face. Dead. Was it true? Had she waited too long, too long, and now there was really no one left to find? Then sadness turned to rage. This was all her mother's fault! Why didn't she tell me? It's unfair, terribly unfair. A father is . . . My father is . . . but it was no use. Reason and logic and science itself couldn't temper the finality of death. For once Lemon used her imagination in more than just theoretical terms, and she was desolate. She'd bargain with the universe, she thought. Never look on stars again, never think about space. I'll give up the whole galaxy, Lemon told herself. If . . . if my father isn't really . . . She was unable to finish the thought. The planet seemed to have stopped rotating. She'd finally fallen into empty space. Or tumbled, like Alice, through the looking glass. Lemon plunked herself down at the head of the tombstone and reached out with numb fingertips to read the engraved plaque.

"Miranda Smith (a.k.a. Randy) 1921–1980."

"Miranda?" Lemon was baffled.

"Heart gave out," the man said. "Plain stopped ticking in the middle of the night. A nurse found her stiff as a board in bed one morning. And get this? The word 'no' was carved into her arm with a pen."

"But that's a lady's name?"

Now the stranger appeared to be confused.

"Well she wasn't a man but she wasn't a lady either, that's for sure."

Lemon wiped her eyes. If Randy wasn't her father then who . . . ?

The man bent down to swipe leaves off the grave marker and Lemon caught sight of the side of his head. His hair parted to the left with curls dancing menacingly over the eyes as did hers. His legs were short and his hands thick and bulbous like her own. Then she noted a small, reddish, lemon-shaped birthmark on the man's inner thigh and she gasped.

My namesake!

She looked up at the stranger with wide, stunned eyes.

A father is . . .

"You okay, Miss?"

Lemon dropped her head and covered her ears with her hands because she heard the whimpering of trees and it sounded as though the entire forest had been slaughtered. Reduced to a paper shadow of itself like Mrs. Moffat, and her mother once a patient in this barren place. And maybe like the mysterious Randy who had died alone in the dark, resisting. Then she heard another whisper but realized that it was her own voice this time, praying out loud. "Blessed be the daisies. Bless the dandelion weeds bending in the wind . . ."

What?

Lemon lurched forward, falling onto her hands and knees, and tried her best not to vomit across the plaque. She heard the man's voice calling to her like an ancient song in the distance. "I'm sorry, Miss, didn't mean to upset you. You knew her well?" His voice entered Lemon's eardrum an octave lower each time he repeated himself, and it moved through her thick and electric with pain. She opened her eyes and saw flashes of blue delphinium, then bloodstained sheets. She saw Randy's defiant posture, and heard her maniacal laugh. She saw a woman on her knees, her face contorted: It was herself over a toilet! She blinked and witnessed her own mother on all fours too, her belly round with life. Lemon screamed as a cord was severed.

Time had finally caught up to her as it eventually catches up to everyone, and she wasn't quite prepared. Every act and indiscretion this stranger had perpetrated rolled off his tongue without his awareness, filling Lemon's eardrum. Each syllable felt like attempted murder. Each vowel, a stake through Lemon's heart. Suddenly she knew this stranger inside out — from *inside* memory. That cerulean curtain closed in around her and the past continued to invade. "There, there, there," the man said, patting her head and trying to calm the obviously distressed girl. "Solomon will make it better."

Solomon. So-lo-mon. Solo man. Solo.

Sitting on the ground, the contents of her stomach churning, Lemon stared at the stranger's boots, his knees, his thighs, torso, his neck and finally at his face. And in the span of time it took her to travel through that black hole and come out the other end, she retrieved what had long ago been erased. She saw as she was meant to. Lemon remembered who her father was.

But it couldn't be.

She forced herself to lift her head and right there behind Ward One for anyone willing to see, stood the difference between lust and love, between paternity and parenting and the pathetic distinction between a man who impregnates a woman and someone who deserves to be called "father." *No!* Lemon thought, trying to catch her breath over the top of Randy's grave. *This can't be. A real father sacrifices for life. A real father protects . . . My father . . .*

"Are you okay?" the man asked, alarmed by his inability to console. But Lemon heard only the steady endurance of patient trees, and the jangling of keys and air pressed from rubber soles. And as she climbed through the thawing tundra of her intuition, the past — that icy vision of Solomon and Lilith, Solomon and Randy, of her father — rose up so sickeningly that she too was forced to make an impossible choice. Lemon looked down at her hands spread out and solid upon the earth, counted to ten, and in those seconds of silence decided for herself what was true after all. *My father is dead,* she thought. *Dead to the world.* Then she backed away slowly . . . faster . . . faster . . . shaking her head and finally turning and running from the smell of ammonia and Ajax and vomit. From the questions she'd been asking all her life. She ran from the past as her mother once had, with her instincts guiding her home.

"Hold up!" Solomon called out with a vague, incomprehensible tone of loss as distance grew between them. "I'll come with you."

"No!"

Lemon charged full force along the path and out onto the lawn.

Oh God, no.

A woman crossed in front of Lemon with hair that was pulled severely back into a bun, and a shoulder that raised up in a pronounced manner. Lemon sped past without a word. And from Randy's grave, Solomon called out once more. "Sorry about the shock, Miss! Sorry!" he repeated himself until Lemon was fully out of sight, his voice reverberating behind her eyes. But all she heard was rape. *Rape. Rape. Rape.* And it never sounds worse than it does ringing in your own ears.

Lemon ran until she reached the car breathless and parched, and found her grandmother sitting in the driver's seat. She looked at her hands and feet certain she would find them black and rotting from frostbite, but they were pink. She touched the car door certain it too was a mirage, but felt solid metal. Her stomach was silent. Her bossy stomach always so full of advice. She placed her hand upon her concave belly. So now she knew; after everything is said and done, there's only compassion to fall back upon.

"Are you all right, dear?" Constance asked, when Lemon slid onto the car beside her. "You look like you've seen a —" Lemon raised her hand as if to say "stop, don't interfere." She neither looked at her bewildered grandmother nor back from where she'd come. She simply focused out the window directly ahead.

Finally, finally on the future.

"Let's go," Lemon said, with a voice much older than ever. "I want to see my mother now."

"Ma!" Lemon called out, pushing past her grandmother as soon as the key was in the front door. "Where are you?" She bolted in ahead, scanned the hall, the living room, poked her head across to the den and stood at the foot of the staircase. She jumped the stairs two at a time, knocked furiously on the spare bedroom door — Lilith's room from childhood — and marched down the hall to the master bedroom. Still no sign of her mother. Then she heard water running in the bathroom.

"Ma? You in there?" The door was cracked open an inch and Lemon's feet pressed into soggy broadloom as she peeked inside and found Lilith sitting on the bath mat, the tub overflowing all around, and two inches of water covering the floor. She immediately turned off the faucets. The old claw-foot tub was overflowing, more water spilling when Lemon reached in past her elbow to unplug it. Lilith was naked beside the radiator, rocking with open eyes and her head turned away from her daughter.

"Ma, what happened?"

Lemon covered Lilith's shivering body in the towel.

"I can't see at all," Lilith said, rocking harder. "I've gone blind."

Lemon moved closer and waved her hand in front of Lilith's face. No response.

"What do you mean?"

"I got up this morning feeling . . . well . . . the same as I have since the funeral," Lilith said. "I got up, ate some cereal and drank two mugs of coffee. I used the decaffeinated kind, so I know it wasn't that and — "

"Ma?" Lemon interrupted.

Lilith rocked back and forth, forward and back.

"You weren't here, Babygirl, so I figured you'd gone shopping or down to English Bay for a walk. I waited a couple more hours — listening to the radio, spraying Daddy's houseplants, reading the paper — until all the words spun on the pages like lettuce in the crisper. I shook my head and looked away but the whole room just kept right on spinning. Round and round. Then it hit me: where you were. You'd gone back."

Lemon hung her head.

"That's what I wanted to — "

"You'd gone back and she'd gone with you. I didn't know what to do with myself so I paced and even lost my appetite. All these people I used to love were talking to me like they'd been waiting for years to get the chance. I heard Mrs. Moffat whispering. Lilith lowered her voice to demonstrate. "There blind mice, three blind mice. See how they run." She sat up taller on the floor, gooseflesh appearing over rolls of fat. "I heard Randy too. Good ol' Randy, laughing herself silly. And I heard other sounds, not so funny, not so kind. That's when I thought about taking the bus, trying to talk some sense into you, but I knew it was too late. By the time I got to Bridgewater you'd have decided you knew everything there was to know about me." Lilith stopped rocking and forced herself to turn and face Lemon. "It's my life you've been picking at like it was a sliver under your own skin. My life!"

"Ma, if you'd only let me fin — "

"No you listen. When I thought you'd gone there without me Lemon, well I couldn't open my eyes without seeing what you'd see. It was like I had no vision of my own. None at all. Everything belonged to you all of a sudden. And the more I remembered the whiter the space in front of me, the room, everything, until there was just a blank. White pills, white walls, white coats. White lies . . . I never wanted to go back, you know? But what if you got stuck there? What if you couldn't get out!"

"Ma, I feel like such a thief."

"I closed 'em tight. Shut my useless eyes until they hurt inside my head. But then there it was anyway."

"What?"

"The past. Like this damned house, like it hadn't changed one bit. There it was with all its brute force. It all came rolling, Babygirl. In black and white. And instead of being gone when I blinked, it just kept on before me, like there were pictures on a projector in back of my forehead. Silent pictures with me moving in jerks and starts from one reel to the next. Me in the kitchen pantry all by myself. Me flooding the garden. Me working in the factory at the hospital. It was awful! Without sound and colour my life had no soul. I wasn't me. It wasn't the *real* me, Lemon. It wasn't!" Lilith began to sob. "Are you happy? Are you finally happy Lemon? Did you get what you wanted?"

"It's not you're fault. It's okay. I understand."

"I stood to walk out of the kitchen. Maybe get some fresh air, pick some sweetpeas, bring them into the house for the table, but every direction I tried to move felt like down, down, down. By then the one good eye I had left was gone too and I never felt so heavy in all my life. I felt like I could fall right through the centre of the earth and be buried next to your granddad, planted deep down underground. I always wanted to be myself that's all, an entire field of swamp candles lighting up a mountainside for you, Lemon. But I'm not a field or a garden, or even a flower. Oh, God! I'm just a human being!"

"You're fine the way you are, Ma. Just the way you are!"

"Oh, Lemon, I felt my way up here along the banister, not thinking very clearly I guess. If I was in the water I might save myself, be weightless and maybe . . . I don't know . . . maybe everything would be different . . . and time could go back the way you always wanted and I could be younger and younger and finally, just a seedling floating in Mother's belly, one half of her stillborn future erased, one half of Daddy's sorrow gone, with no need for my eyes at all. If I could go back . . . Well . . . Benjamin wouldn't have been taken . . ." Lilith reached her arms up to Lemon. "Do you forgive me?"

Lemon moved to assist her mother, but before she had a chance, Constance was in the doorway unbuttoning her jacket.

"My good God! What in heaven's name is going on?"

"Don't worry, Grandma," Lemon said, dropping Lilith's arm. "I'll clean up."

"Clean it up? Just look at this? My floor's been ruined. Ruined! Lilith, your mess is leaking all the way through to the foundation — it's coming across my kitchen ceiling! How did this happen?" She turned towards Lemon. "Has she gone off again . . . Should I call the doctor?" Lemon pulled the towel more tightly around her mother's shoulders. Constance spoke as if time had passed her by as well, as if the name of Lilith's old psychiatrist and his phone number were still stuck by magnet to the refrigerator door. "You finally going to face the truth, Lilith Boot?" Constance flattened her open jacket, removing the creases. She stood straight as an arrow. "No matter," she added, looking directly at Lemon. "I think she already knows. Don't you?"

Lemon nodded and Lilith resumed rocking, that time more violently.

She knows. She knows. She knows, Lilith thought, feeling like a failure.

"Ma, don't do that."

"What's his name!" Constance shouted. "What *is* his name?"

Lemon squeezed Lilith reassuringly, but it was no use. Water was everywhere, spilling from her mother's face onto the floor, seeping into the carpet. There was nothing big enough to plug a hole like that one. *Was there?* Lemon caught her own reflection in the puddle and saw cheeks that were wide like Lilith's. A nose that was small, and eyes . . . *My eyes,* she thought, lifting one of Lilith's hands and touching her fingers to her own lids. *My eyes are just like yours.* She leaned closer and brushed Lilith's cheek with her eyelashes as they used to do when she was young. Butterfly kisses. Or flutterby strokes, as they'd called them. Then, without sounding mean or angry, Lemon addressed her grandmother.

"I have no father," she said. "There is no father."

Constance stepped back suddenly, like she'd been kicked in the stomach.

Lilith stopped breathing. *Did I hear right?* she thought. *Did Lemon say what I think she said?* The truth. *Mine? Ours?*

"What a spectacle," Constance said. "What a disgrace!"

She turned and clicked the bathroom door shut behind her. For the first time in her life, Constance knew when she didn't belong.

Lilith began to warm, and her forehead tingled and burned as if a sleeping limb was waking. The bathtub in front of her came clearer into focus. Then the basin, the toilet. She glanced around the room and found the magazine rack, the wastebasket. She heard a slow, rhythmic drip. *Drip, drip, drip.* And Lemon heard it too. Faster and harder and then there was a leak. But this time it was Lemon who saw the splash as if somebody had dived into a swimming pool, and she instinctively grabbed on with her strongest muscle — her mind — as though hanging on the dorsal fin of a blue whale. She followed it under and all of a sudden the room was filled with a dark blue-grey colour.

Lemon saw a baby wrapped in blankets. She smelt the sweet, mouth-watering scent of butter icing. Then she saw a boy at a birthday party and a table full of children all wearing party hats or blowing kazoos. The boy's hat was tilted and the elastic string around his ears irritated his skin. The cake was made from scratch and sitting at one end of the table in front of the child — chocolate with strawberry filling. Lemon heard a man's voice: "Make a wish, son." Then, she heard a woman, "Happy birthday to you, happy birthday . . . dear Ben-ja-min . . ." And it was etched on her brain as though drawn on in charcoal. *Benjamin. Ben.* It was a strong name. A name that connoted belonging. *Ben. Son of.* It had always hung off her mother like a wet T-shirt clinging to every roll of flesh. And now Ben was clinging to her. Lemon saw him in the photograph on Mrs. Moffat's end table. It hit her hard: He belonged to Mrs. Moffat! Lemon reached out, grabbed her mother tightly by the shoulders and looked her directly in the eyes.

"Ma? I see him too!"

"Who?"

"Benjamin. I can see him now. Here." She pointed to her forehead.

Lilith hugged Lemon, tried to rock them both and squeezed her own eyes shut.

"Oh no! No, you were right before! You can't see anything! Don't be like me; bad things will happen. If you see ahead I might . . . I might . . . see all the way back. No. I can't. I won't remember! No!"

"Ma," Lemon said gently. "There's no one left to forget for."

Now I remember everything. The morning I left Bridgewater for good it was early November of 1967 and I wasn't eighteen years old yet. I looked pretty much the same as today — give or take a hundred pounds. My hair was just starting to turn grey at the roots like it does with all the Boot women, and my ankles were beginning to swell. I wasn't showing yet. When I finally told Randy I was leaving, when she scooped me and the baby up and twirled us around the room, she didn't seem to notice anything out of the ordinary, nothing, that is, except I was finally escaping. "I knew you'd do it, Lilith!" she said. "I knew you'd find a way out." And then she put me down and became stiff like candy in a taffy pull. She turned away before speaking again.

"Promise to forget me."

I looked at Mrs. Moffat, who stopped bouncing on her bed. She shrugged to show she didn't get it either.

"Oh, I could never do that," I told Randy, approaching her again.

But she insisted, her voice cracking.

"You will."

Then I reached for her arm.

"But — "

She pulled away without turning.

"Do it!" she yelled. "Promise!"

At first, I shook my head, no. I could go home and from there I could visit, make phone calls. Sure I'd have the baby but even if we moved to Toronto as planned, I could still write them both letters. Send my own photographs for Randy's drawer.

"No. I can't," I repeated, and that made her even more mad.

Randy's demands shot out of her like gunfire, one after the other. Deadly.

"Say you won't set foot on these grounds again! Say you'll pretend you never laid eyes on us or never tasted the cafeteria food or never wore any god-damned uniforms!" Her shoulders began to bob up and down. A whimper came from her direction. "I hate you, Lilith Boot," she told me. "You're nothing to me, nothing but another chump who landed in my room. I had no choice but to tolerate your stupid ideas and listen to you whine about your family. Go away. Don't come back. I never even liked you. I was just entertaining myself!"

My heart sank deeper into my chest than you can ever know.

"Just say it!" she screamed. "After what I did for you, say it!"

Oh God, I thought. What she'd done.

389

Mrs. Moffat took off her tiara like she was removing her hat at a funeral. Then she rocked back and forth on the edge of her bed whispering under her breath like always.

"Rain, rain, go away. Come again another day."

Randy still wouldn't turn around.

"Promise?" she repeated, finally in a desperate tone. And I realized the time had come to repay my debt. I owed it to my friends to move forward, be happy, and I had my baby to think of too.

"I promise," I said, so soft you could have missed it. "I promise to forget."

So on that last day I visited the greenhouse, walked beside the foxglove with their dramatic spikes and legend of healing properties. For two years I'd tended all of them with devotion. I'd planted sweet scabious, or pincushion flower, and thought about how their deep purple, almost black petals looked like mourning brides. Loss seemed inevitable. Love just disappeared and sometimes it could be gone for ages before anyone realized.

Under lock and key, I'd studied the birds of paradise, noticing that each stem was enclosed by a boat-shaped leaf. *A boat's an ark that sails on water,* I told myself so many times, and then finally there I was — the lucky one — about to sail off in a new direction. The three sepals of each flower held one small petal that sprang out and formed a blue tongue. The ends of the sexual structures were inside a groove. Organs and genitalia. For floral reproduction. Just about everything I needed to know about making a life, I learned right there in the greenhouse.

Many places I only dreamed of visiting came to me while I was gardening. In every flower bed I found reminders of foreign destinations. Japanese cherry blossoms. Turkish tulips, Mexican campion, Peruvian marigolds, all cheering for me. Every bloom was a promise of hope, so on that last morning I wandered from room to room filled with respect for all of them, no matter how unusual. I followed the window boxes, the humble ivy trailing low and, farther along, reaching skyward. I was also reaching then, reaching and lifting up, up, and out of that dry bed. Arid place of lifelessness.

In Bridgewater it seemed, the majority of flowers were labelled with personalities they didn't really have. The tall calla lily was a member of another, shorter family. The African violet was not even a true violet, and the blackberry lily, loved for being rare, was just the offspring of a popular iris. Nothing was what it appeared. I guess it's true, many of us are members of families who don't really recognize us.

That last day I leaned against a long pine work table, ran my fingers over dense green leaves where the blackberry bent like an archer's bow, and let the vines tickle my face, neck and shoulders. We were saying goodbye. I would've spoken, called each flower or shrub or weed by its given name, but Nurse Ford was within earshot and I couldn't risk being overheard and then have my doctor suddenly inform Daddy I'd had a relapse and wouldn't be going home after all. By then I'd learned to keep what I knew to myself when I was in the company of adults — especially professionals. Instead, I smiled into the face of each bloom and reached out to them, my silent companions. Clematis, the star-of-Bethlehem, and morning glory still scrambling to get over the wall. Hanging ominously overhead was the Japanese wisteria. I felt tears well in my eyes. Wisteria always seemed to make me weep. It sounded strange and familiar, brittle — like the pattern on so many of Mother's china teacups. Whenever I saw it I felt as if someone had planted a sad reminder to us patients of our predicament, our diagnoses. Maybe as a curse.

It was the zinnias I first told about my migraines and my joy that I was pregnant. I trusted them because they were special too. Each flower had an inner disc and an outer, petal-like ray. Zinnias were actually two flowers in one — like a mother-to-be. On my last day as a patient, I stood with my plump fingers in a bed of zinnias and felt a sense of belonging I hoped to hold onto after I left. But most of all, I saw beauty in the witches' brooms, the pine growths everyone said were genetic mistakes. Nature's error. They become thick, tight, round masses and staff wanted me to cut them down. *They're fat and plain and don't do what's expected,* I thought. *Like me.* Instead of destroying them, I'd planted them together in a corner in the hopes that they'd expand, cling to each other, and find comfort among their own kind.

Walking along I came to a row of grey spiny stems with scarlet bracts: the crown of thorns. I bowed my head. I understood humiliation. Then I saw pink flowers with small white tears falling from bleeding hearts. My lip began to tremble. You see, in the greenhouse I could complain about our treatments, or fume at Mother for her severity or at Daddy for his weakness. I could plan for my release and whisper my true feelings about the visions, never being doubted. *But who would listen to me once I left?*

At eye level out the window, beyond the dying carpet of lobelia, I saw the sturdy hoopsii and weeping spruce just outside of Ward One, my ward, and as usual, they were showing me how to be stable. *I will make new roots,* I thought. *I will be proud. For the baby.* I turned around to face the small pond at the back of the greenhouse. I'd often told the Victoria waterlilies there what it was like to be so afraid of sinking, and with turned up margins and small white florets, they'd patiently, gently, shown me how to tread water. Then I stopped in front of the Centaurea and noticed their clever disguise, how they managed to have fuzzy round heads, but at the same time have spindles sharp enough to cut flesh. I forced a needle into my thumb and became a blood sister just like that.

Along the far end, I came to a fiery patch of poppies, brazenly contorting their skinny little bodies. *No shame whatsoever,* I thought. *Good for you.* Then I leaned over a patch of gladioli, looked out a west-facing window, and searched in the parking lot for my parents' station wagon. I spotted the beige vehicle and closed my eyes immediately. Beige was a feeble watery colour. For blending. For fitting in. *Beige is the colour of nobody special,* I thought. Not like the crimson or vermilion or magenta found in any garden. Not like a rainbow or a prism, or even a human being. A few feet away, to my left, were the chrysanthemums standing firm in their multicoloured convictions. *Not everybody has to be the same,* they seemed to say. *Normal's just a figment of group imagination. Normal's what happens when you stop thinking for yourself.* I licked my lips and tasted sweetness and bitterness all at the same time. Finally I was being discharged. Daddy was coming to take me back to our house; I'd agreed to be released back into his care.

Walking through the greenhouse for the last time I remembered that it was Daddy who once explained "gladioli" — like most plant names — comes from Latin and means "little sword" because of the sharp leaves that can easily penetrate your skin. 'Course I remembered Solomon then, and kept right on walking.

I had no regrets.

I was starting to get my life back, and Solomon had almost nothing to do with it. He was like the wind, a natural resource scattering seeds across a field like a farmhand. Every garden has a thug like him, you know. An invasive colonizer taking up larger and larger patches of the perennial border. *Gooseneck loosestrife,* comes to mind, with its arching white flower and boastful four-foot stalk. The key to dealing with it, I knew first-hand, was to contain it. Besides, there was more than one creature to watch out for in a greenhouse, as many as there are versions of the truth. There was the teddy bear cactus which can't be touched without injury, and skunk cabbage which thrives under the worst conditions, and of course there was false Solomon's seal. So I decided right then and there not to sign a second name on my baby's birth certificate, just leave it blank where it said "father."

Nurse Ford was waiting closer to the exit beside the small patch of quivering, blue forget-me-nots. I started to tremble too. *So many friends I've made*, I thought. *What will I do without you?* And then my mind turned back to my roommates, Randy and Mrs. Moffat. *How could I leave them behind?* I walked through the greenhouse drawing strength from the flowers for my new life as a mother, and I prepared to let it all go. Let Bridgewater and my friends fall away from me like old seasons in time. It was the only thing Randy ever asked me for. It was the price I paid for happiness.

And I knew when it came to my doctor or Alice Woodward, to keep my lip buttoned as tight as the petals of any snapdragon. I wasn't suitable according to most people; I was unfit. Mother would have never agreed to my pregnancy and that would have been the end of me. Back then it was basically against the law to give birth without being married, and as far as I know, it's still against the law to be crazy. No, I wasn't listening to outsiders any more. Just turned an ear inward to my baby's heartbeat, to my own desire. Besides, a woman's worth nothing if she's not worth her word.

"It's time to go, Lilith," Nurse Ford said before long.

"Okay," I told her. "I'm coming."

Then, with her watching from the doorway, I had one more good look around the greenhouse. It had taken me hours, days, months to cultivate those gardens. I put every bit of confusion and self-doubt, every bit of terror and anger from childhood, and every bit of forgiveness I had for my parents, into the soil. Worked it with my fingers until they were sore and swollen, and blistered, dug, dug, planted and pruned so there could eventually be growth. Change. And, without knowing it at the time, I was going to bury my past there too. For a split second I thought about taking some seeds as a souvenir, but I didn't. What I really wanted was to take my friends with me, keep a visible link in that chain of events I was going to drag behind from then on. I wanted that, and my memories. But no. You can't have everything in this life, and I'd been given at chance at the future instead.

James stood before a wall of mirrors in his dormitory washroom wearing only brown leather slippers and a towel wrapped around his waist. He shook a can of shaving cream, sprayed some of it out into his palm like a cloud, applied it and scraped the razor up his neck and over his chin. The faint scent of mint tingled his nostrils. James rinsed the razor under the running faucet and scraped his face again and again until his skin was soft and smooth. There would be two new additions to the diving team, his coach had told him. Two younger, stronger, favoured stars in the fall. Big deal! James was surprised by his own indifference.

He'd started slacking off last month and just hadn't been able to regain his momentum. His lap times were slower at each practice, the efficiency if his dives replaced by a disorganized lack of poise and all enthusiasm for sports gone for now at least, gone as though sucked down the pool drain. "Where's your champion spirit?" his coach had yelled across the deck. "Better work on your attitude, son!" Having his coach and teammates recognize that he was losing his competitive edge somehow led James into a downward spiral of caring even less. And less. And then less. Lately, just the thought of climbing into lukewarm water before six in the morning made him yawn. He was tired, he'd realized. Tired of the sound of his alarm clock jolting him into reality, tired of trudging across the soccer field barely conscious and immersing himself in a monotonous routine. Most of all, he was exhausted from feeling as though he must keep moving, do better, pull himself forward. Now it simply felt as though he was being chased. James no longer cared to perform, and that's what diving had become. A way to impress. Besides, a world divided into winners and losers was his father's version, not his.

Oh, I have nothing to whine about, James thought while he shaved. By most people's standards I lead a charmed life. There's always been enough money to entertain any whim I've had. When he'd wanted to go to Disney World, his parents had taken him for his birthday. When he'd wanted to learn to play the piano, his parents had indulged him with private lessons until he'd grown bored. When he'd wanted to swim competitively they'd built an in-ground pool behind their house. Who could ask for more? His mother, well his stepmother really, had always been there to manage the home. Aggie supported James's father through the first, long days and nights of his developing law practice, and later — a year ago — when James trudged off to university, she'd begun caring for a dozen or so "delinquents" — in her husband's words — whom she invited into their large Forest Hill home for Sunday brunch. For every birthday, Easter, Christmas and Thanksgiving, James could count on Aggie to be standing in the doorway of the family room in anticipation of his approval. How he hated letting her down, of not smiling widely enough, or not hiding his disappointment. He was so ungrateful! She was angling for a place in his heart that neither one of them realized had already been spoken for.

Aggie's devotion did not go totally unappreciated. James knew it was she who'd dabbed calamine lotion on his chicken pox, she who'd driven him to early morning sports practices, she who'd tucked him in at night — but Aggie wasn't the original. She was a gentle, caring, carbon-based copy. James knew the single most flattering compliment he could offer his stepmother was to say that she'd always *been there*. Ironic, he thought, rinsing his razor under the tap, that an absence like that of his birth mother could loom so much larger than a presence. Perhaps he'd retained a shadowy sense of her from swimming through her birth canal, or maybe another influence altogether had placed limits and conditions upon his feelings.

Aggie hadn't altered any aspect of her appearance in nearly two decades, James thought. Her hair still swept up off her face in a honey blonde wave that sat motionless in the wind. Her clothes remained in a style more than a decade old, now including wide leg pants; long scarves; neon, geometric patterns; and pastel colours. If it was *his* wife so behind the times James would've been embarrassed, but this, he knew, was precisely what pleased his father. Aggie was timeless. "I never wanted any part in that women's libbers nonsense," she'd told James once. "I'm not a career woman. I'm not interested in looking at my genitals in a hand mirror. I wanted nothing more than to be a wife and a mother to you: in that order." She sighed after those words, dropped her head, and then raised it stoically once more. "Unfortunately, I was unable to bear children of my own. Your father knew before our wedding and that only proved all the more how much he loved me." Aggie blew her husband a kiss across the room. "Why else marry me when he — wealthy and good-looking — could have any woman he wanted?" Aggie walked over to her husband's chair, climbed on his lap, and pushed aside the book he was reading. "I know you love me," she said. "Even if you still can't say it."

Jonathan had looked into his wife's hopeful eyes that evening, the eyes of a deer caught in the headlights of oncoming tragedy.

"Yes I do . . ." he said. "I knew you'd never change."

Aggie appeared flabbergasted by the comment.

"People change, Jonathan. All of us, eventually."

"Yes." Resignation fogged his voice. "But it's a question of degree."

Not change? James stared at his face in the bathroom mirror. It made no sense. Sure he'd railed against change too, as most people do. He'd avoided new experiences. Moved on to university and tried in vain to stick with his old friends from high school instead, hang out at the old haunts. But everyone had moved on. He'd grown taller and sprouted facial hair, and his voice had deepened. Change was inevitable, and James suspected what he would never give voice to. He suspected that his father had been so deeply wounded when his birth mother died that he had not actually wanted additional children. He suspected that Aggie's inability to carry to term was possibly the most attractive feature she could have possessed. It didn't make his father a bad man, just selfish and insecure, perhaps. Maybe he refused love because love was unpredictable. Or maybe he simply couldn't bear to part with another wife. Perhaps father long ago closed himself to fate, James thought. And since then, he'd assumed the godlike burden of making all decisions, large and small.

This year James had finally discovered that he no longer wanted-ed to feel burdened by his accomplishments, kill himself for another string of A's. There was more to living than public achievement. He actually enjoyed doing nothing remarkable, standing still. Waiting until everyone else was out of the pool and gone from the changerooms, so that he might float on his back uninterrupted, and stare weightlessly at the rafters. Motionless. It wasn't only pounds that disappeared in the water. It really was time. Seconds, minutes, hours, days and years. All running into each other and floating still, like a reflection. He never would have been able to guess, if someone had asked him even six months ago, that he preferred life when he wasn't going anywhere in particular. James inspected himself closely in the mirror for places he might have missed. Who am I? he thought. Who am I without my arms helicoptering over my shoulders, working hard to travel nowhere fast? He dragged the razor up one cheek and shook the last of the white foam from the blade with a sharp flick of his wrist.

It was hard to imagine not training or even being in the water every day. Even as a boy he'd loved taking baths, and he'd been mesmerized by Lake Ontario and by storms. At four years he'd deliberately slipped into a neighbour's backyard pool, nearly giving Aggie and his overprotective father a heart attack. James was submerged with his eyes wide open, secure someone was watching over him. He never for a moment considered drowning, not even when Mr. Warner, the neighbour, his collie and James's father all jumped into the pool simultaneously, causing a flurry of underwater activity. Mrs. Warner dashed into the house sopping wet to call for an ambulance, and returned moments later. Aggie, who couldn't swim, was teetering and flailing on the edge, crossing herself and screaming, "James! Oh, Mother-Mary-of-Jesus, James!" The dog barked and paddled round in circles, snapping at waves. The pool was a blur of colourful clothes and white froth. Mr. Warner climbed out and helped Jonathan lift

James onto the grass. He hadn't been under even for one minute. He was conscious and breathing. Still, his father panicked. "My son almost drowned, Agatha! Why weren't you watching him!"

"*Our* son," Aggie said, practically in a whisper.

And years after that, James remembers he was holding his breath in his own pool upside down, leaning backwards, knees bent, torso immersed. With his back against the wall his exposed legs were uncrossed at the knee, and his heels dug into the concrete deck for balance. Seven . . . eight . . . nine . . . he'd made twenty-nine seconds the previous week when Aggie was counting. James remembers opening his eyes and seeing neighbourhood kids upside down, their skinny legs barely rooting them to the pool floor, most of them standing on tippytoes, bobbing from one foot to the other. His eyes were as wide as his cheeks were full. He was the man from Atlantis, a half-mammal, half-human superhero from a secret underwater planet. He could breathe like a fish, swim upstream, and rescue girls in trouble. Well, that day at least, he was concentrating on bettering his time. Fourteen . . . Fifteen . . .

James's eyes had bulged, trying to take in his surroundings for distraction. In one corner of the pool he saw pink polka dots pretending to have a tea party with a yellow and white striped bikini; somebody poured while somebody else sipped from invisible china cups. Stupid girls! he'd thought. Nearby was a navy blue Speedo practising handstands in the middle of the shallow end, and Peter McGillvary in his underwear again, peeing a yellow cloud into the water. Peter, Peter, pumpkin eater. Peter Piper picked a peck of pickled peppers . . . eighteen . . . nineteen . . . twenty . . . Helen Sourtzis wasn't in the pool that day. James couldn't locate her fluorescent green swimsuit anywhere through the maze of splashing and waves. And that weirdo Jack Thomas — one eyed-jack — the kid with one ball, was climbing on and off an inner tube. Twenty-three . . . twenty-four . . . twenty-five . . . Almost there. Twenty-six . . . twenty-seven . . . James's body levitated despite his flexing and straining to stay flat against the wall. Twenty-nine . . . thirty! He exploded away from the ledge and kicked himself frantically to the surface for air. His face emerged purple and his mouth wide open. Catching his breath, he felt invincible. Free. If Dad could only see me now, he'd thought. Yes, it was all so exhilarating back then. But today, the idea of water presses down upon James like God's punishing hand and makes him feel that he's been assigned to a life he never really chose. Expectation guides most of what I do, he thinks. From now on I will please myself first.

He and Jan were planning brunch off-campus today, and a talk about their final term papers for Professor Walker's class. Jan was almost done hers, but James hadn't even started. He'd chosen to write on Atwood's *Surfacing*. Something about the summons to search for a parent, the feeling of being watched, the unanswered questions spoke to him directly. It was his favourite novel at the moment and it hadn't even been on the required reading list. Jan had recommended it. "It's about identity," she'd said. "Finding yourself. I loved it." But more than anything else, it was a line from the final chapter that had gripped James. Something about a lie, he thought. That a lie was always more disastrous than the truth. He'd felt a lump in his throat when he'd read to that point. Why did it mean so much to him? James set his razor down on the edge of the basin, bent over and splashed his cheeks and neck with cold water. When he looked up there were beads of water dripping down his smooth face, hanging off his eyelashes as if they were tears that had never been shed.

Half an hour later, James was sitting outside the dormitory on the yellow brick stairs facing St. George Street in his khaki shorts and Roots T-shirt. The sun was warm and the sky was clear, but there was a cool breeze. Jan approached in a black sundress, a cream-coloured sweater tied around her waist, and Birkenstock sandals. She was wearing her knapsack.

"Hi."

"Looks like a great day," James said, rising. "Where do you want to eat?"

"I don't know, let's just start walking and see what we find." They headed south towards College Street and then turned east. Jan explained about her paper. "I can't seem to write the conclusion," she complained. "I'm drawing a blank. Maybe it's because the term is almost over and I'm impatient. You know?" James was thinking about the mysterious Dori Moffat who was folded neatly on hundreds of single sheets of typing paper in his father's closet. "James?"

"Oh, sorry. I spaced out."

"What are you thinking about?"

James shivered. They were walking along the shady side of the street.

"Remember the box?"

"The one in your Dad's closet?"

"Right." James rubbed his arms for warmth. "I was thinking, long-distance relationships are pretty inconvenient."

"That crossed my mind too," Jan said. "But if your Dad's not having an affair then what?"

The word "affair" suctioned into James's eardrums as though he was wearing a bathing cap that fit him much too snugly. *Affair. Affair.* Unfair! His father had misrepresented himself. James felt betrayed, as if the family pet that he'd always been told had run away had actually been put down. Goosebumps covered his bare arms.

"I just can't believe father's been lying all this time. Poor Aggie!"

"Do you think she knows?"

James shrugged.

Jan stopped on the sidewalk, removed her knapsack, unzipped it and pulled out a canvas jacket.

"Here," she said, handing it to him. "I'm nosy, so you know what I'd do? I'd call the place on those papers. What was it? Ministry of something or other?"

"Social Services and Housing. God, I never thought of that." James slipped one arm into the jacket.

"Maybe she works there."

"But what would I say. Hello? I'd like to speak to your resident home-wrecker?"

They both laughed.

"Hey, what if you ask your Dad outright. Just say you accidentally found the box and that you have some questions?"

"Are you crazy! Father would be furious if he knew. He's very private. He doesn't talk about anything. I don't even know my birth mother's name." Just then James realized how ridiculous that sounded. How sad a fact. And not only did he not know her name, but he'd never been comfortable speaking with his father about her. He'd never seen a photograph. Never heard a story, other than the story accounting for her death. Why had he not felt he could ask?

"Really?" Jan said, incredulously. "You don't know your own mother's name?"

James shook his head. And in that moment he was suddenly desperate for answers.

Lilith is sitting on her bench inside the Allan Gardens Conservatory, preparing for work. She unlaces her sneakers, removes her socks and stuffs them inside her shoes. Her hair is pulled back loosely in an elastic band at the base of her neck. Working today will be different than ever before, she thinks. Because today is her first day searching with Bridgewater and Randy and Mrs. Moffat in mind. Lilith knows why Benjamin is missing now. And she knows that you can't find what you can't remember. Still, with so much behind her, there remains the daunting task of actually locating Benjamin. She closes her eyes and concentrates, using only the top half of her lungs to breathe, hovering over time like a butterfly hovering over an expectant flower. She faces her faint image in the whitewashed window opposite, bare feet flat on the floor, and leans her weight deeply into the wooden slats of the bench. How much more grounded she feels today, she thinks. How much more real her search.

From where she's sitting Lilith can see left, up the ramp through the princess vines or right, to the far north where the cycads gather. Behind her there is a short plant called yesterday-today-and-tomorrow, and a copper leaf masking a radiator, but not the sound of its fast-trickling water. Condensation from the slanted roof splashes down onto the bench. In the stillness of the peaceful room Lilith hears each drop clearly as it falls.

Drip.

Drip.

Drip.

She reaches into her purse and selects Benjamin's red file folder, a piece of blank paper and a purple crayon. On the sheet of paper she writes his new contract. "I hereby promise to do everything in my natural ability to find you — Benjamin — and return you to your parent." She repeats the promise out loud and adds, "Child, I'm your finder." Then she signs and dates the contract, "October, 1986. Lilith Boot; clairvoyant at large. She adds one final message before folding the paper into smaller squares and tucking it into her brassiere for safekeeping. "PS. You can trust me. I'm a friend of the family."

Finally, Lilith closes her eyes, and imagines four pillars of light, one in each corner of the greenhouse, one for each direction on a compass. A pale blue luminescence fills the rooms inside her imagination. She bows her head and in hushed whispers, prays out loud . . . "Blessed be the daisies smiling stupidly above the grass. Bless their forgotten petals plucked in good faith. Bless *all* the weeds that bend and compromise in the wind. Amen . . ." After a few seconds the sound of footsteps grows louder and louder. Lilith follows the rhythm and pace of their movement, loses herself in the even sound of shoes on a city sidewalk. Faster, faster, along College Street, past Yonge, past Church and Jarvis, closer, closer until the smell of mint leaves and chlorine fills her nostrils. She breathes it in deeply and holds him there. Then all of a sudden, the vision fades. The footsteps soften as if they've moved from sidewalk to grass, and Lilith's heart sinks. She slumps down on the bench, defeated. *Maybe I won't find him,* she admits to herself for the very first time. *Maybe this is one child lost forever.* She opens her eyes slowly.

Nothing.

Lilith sighs. Then she stands to stretch and walks off into the succulent room, her soles sticking to the damp stones underfoot. Through open doors, she admires two large golden barrel, some pinwheel and, near the exit, a giant aloe. She bends down and gathers a handful of black soil, perlite dotting it, and lifts it to her face. Lilith breathes deeply and blinks in slow motion. Then she notices through a clear spot in the bottom of one window that a familiar figure is coming across the property. *Who is it?* She stands, leans closer to the window and squints. *Oh, it's just Jan.* Lilith pushes open the exit door and stomps barefoot out behind the conservatory onto the lawn, waving.

"Janet Hines. Yoo-hoo? Over here!"

Jan doesn't see her at first, but James does and he points.

"I think that lady is trying to get your attention."

"Miss Boot!" Jan picks up her pace and when she reaches Lilith, opens her arms for a wide embrace. "I haven't seen you since you got back."

James follows and stands next to the women, smiling awkwardly while the two hug. "Oh sorry," Jan pulls back from Lilith. "I didn't mean to be rude. Miss. Boot, this is James, a friend from school. James, this is Lemon's mother."

James reaches out to shake Lilith's hand. She feels his strong fingers encircle her palm. Time stops. She stares wide-eyed. Her fingers, toes, her entire body begins to tingle. She turns red and cannot release James, as though she's just touched an electric current with a wet hand. Instead she pulls him closer with her free arm, hugs him to her chest, and begins to weep. "Benjamin! Oh Benjamin I was just looking for you!" James allows himself to be embraced but stares at Jan as if to say, what the hell is going on? Help! Lilith cries through her tears. "You probably don't know me 'cause you were so young, but I'd remember that firm grip anywhere." She musses his hair, and steps back to fish up her sleeve for a tissue and then wags a chunky finger in his face. "You were a hell of a lot of trouble, young man. But look at you? Look! Benjamin Moffat you're all grown up!" James's forehead wrinkles and he steps back from Lilith.

"Moffat?" He says, his mouth hanging open. "How do you know that name? What? Jan? What the hell is going on?" Jan is speechless for a moment. She glances from James to Lilith and back to James.

"Oh my God!" Her lips move without sound. "You're *him*." Then, not knowing what else to do, she loops one arm through James's and the other through Lilith's. "Don't worry," Jan reassures. "I can explain everything. I'm just not sure where to begin."

November 1, 1986

~~Dear Mr. ____,~~

To Whom it May Concern,

Did you know that flowers can look remarkably like space
matter? Some of them even have spacey names. Cosmos. New
dawn roses. Shooting star. I don't know why I never noticed
before. My favourite so far is witch hazel. I know it doesn't
sound intergalactic and it's just a sort of skinny aster-like life
form, but if you look close it has these long gold petals that
twist and turn like the rings around Saturn. And the totally
amazing thing about witch hazel is that the capsules burst like
an earthly star, ejecting seeds up to thirty feet into the atmosphere! Anyway, I thought I'd fill you in on all the news, like
what happened after Grandma Connie drove us to the airport
and Ma said her heart was stuck in her throat like a lump of
coal in the bottom of a Christmas stocking. She said leaving
with me that time — the second time — was harder than the
first because everything's harder when you remember to feel.

When our plane turned and headed directly into the setting sun, Ma closed her eyes but I kept mine open. From the
sky I saw a few large boats floating in the Georgia Strait and
North Vancouver sprinkled like confetti on grass miles below. I
searched for the Turtle Group Home in case I might somehow
pick it out. I vowed to write to Mrs. Moffat, send photographs
and visit again when we go back to stay with Grandma for the
holidays. Fog, pollution and mist filtered between mountain
peaks and the thousands of trees softened the ground below. I
wanted to run my fingers through the planet's scalp, touching
palms to fur, catching pine needles under my nails. I never

knew there could be so much sensation just from seeing. Nothing I've ever read about in a book compares to ripping through time at 950 miles per hour!

The captain assured us that visibility was good, but I knew better. There's always some chance of turbulence. Or as Ma would say, women are lost to turbulence every day. My stomach grumbled then, so I reached into her sweater pocket and pulled out a chocolate bar. It felt really good to eat. You'd be so proud of me! I'm gaining willpower, I really am. The power to accept what I most fear in life. Myself I guess. Anyway, Ma fell asleep until I woke her five hours later with the 401 and the business sector winking up at me like electronic galaxies. Toronto had tumbled and landed upside down. I gazed at constellations made of subdivisions and then closer to the city centre, a supernova of lights as they rolled across the downtown core like tossed dice. Going back is always a gamble. And it's not for everyone, I know. Gravity sucked the plane down, my ears popped, wheels touched pavement. Outside a blue light guided us along the runway. Blue, like strong thunder rolling backwards off time. Like a prediction. Blue for old bruises that have begun to heal.

There's so much I still don't understand but I know a few things for certain. I know people come into your life for a reason. I know time can't be easily pointed to with a crooked finger, traced with a thick Magic Marker or pinned to the wall for the neighbours to see — like a diagnosis of mental illness, a murder indictment, a missing child, or a scar from the day you were raped. Rape. I know this too: It depends what part of the world you're standing on and how fast you're rotating around the sun — even rape changes for the sake of convenience. And sanity.

Ma went back to work right away; there's no stopping her. She says she's in line for a big fat raise. And Freddy not only took me back, he granted me a promotion. I'm the head weekend tour guide at the planetarium now, complete with a new uniform and my very own presentation on time and creation. I figure I'm the right person for the job. I'll be graduating high school in a few more months and may apply to the university for a scholarship, and live with Jan. Jan finally told her Mom to stop asking when she's getting married because, as she put it, "it's never gonna happen." And James, I mean Benjamin (that's what he wants to be called now), isn't as annoying when you get to know him.

As for my future, well now that I've conquered my stomach I plan to quit smoking. And I'd like to study astronomy, I think. Or physics. Maybe become an astronaut. Also, I'll be meeting with Claudia one more time to tell her my news. What makes a father? Who are you? These questions don't nag at me any more. I don't need a grand unified theory to explain about you and Ma. Parents are like any rulers, I think. In the end they only retain titles their sons and daughters are willing to grant them. Labels like "mother" or "father" must be earned. Any other way simply makes for an undeserving relative. Not a monster, not a monarch — and sometimes not even an ordinary man. I'm as sure as anyone can be. There's really no need to divide life into past, present, and future conditions if you have even one person who believes in you. Love is the only unconditional tense.

Yours very truly,

Lemon Boot.

Acknowledgments

I would like to thank Timothy Findley, most especially for Lilah Kemp — the spark who ignited my Lilith, and both he and William Whitehead for attention given to cultivating another emerging writer. I must also thank the Canada Council for the Arts for granting support. Joe Kertes and the Humber School for Writers, and my skillful agent Margaret Hart. I thank Barry Jowett for his clear and dedicated editorial vision, my publisher Kirk Howard, and the entire Dundurn team. Many thanks to Cheryl Cohen for a painstaking copy-edit. And Susanne Tabur at the Gerstein Science Information Centre. I am indebted to friends who read the manuscript in the early stages: Anna Camilleri, Roewan Crowe, Camilla Gibb, Margarita Miniovich, and Kathleen Olmstead. I must also thank Collette Baron-Reid for her interview, the writers of "EasteEnders" for encouragement, and Aunt B for wearing tiaras to supper. Thanks to Anjula Gogia and the Toronto Women's Bookstore, and the men and women who maintain the Allan Gardens Conservatory in Toronto. Heartfelt appreciation goes out to L.D. Pettigrew and to others who have supported me over the years: The Phelps Clan. David Goutor. Jan T. Elizabeth Willett. And not the least, my grandparents, Mona and Milton Pettigrew. Finally, I have Shannon Olliffe to thank for patience, unshakable faith, and for listening to each word out loud.